Love is Lovelier

by

Donna Simonetta

Rivers Bend Trilogy, Book 2

Love is Lovelier

COPYRIGHT © 2018 by Donna Stevens Simonetta

Cover Art by *Debbie Taylor*

The Wild Rose Press, Inc.
PO Box 708
Adams Basin, NY 14410-0708
Visit us at www.thewildrosepress.com

Publishing History
First Champagne Rose Edition, 2018
Print ISBN 978-1-5092-1911-7
Digital ISBN 978-1-5092-1912-4

Rivers Bend Trilogy, Book 2
Published in the United States of America

"Stick close. I'll get you out of here."

He used his broad shoulders as a wedge to propel himself though the crowd. Heather scurried to keep up with him so she could take advantage of the gap he created, not wanting to be so close she could feel the warmth of his body through his elegant suit, but because she needed somehow to beat this crush of people to the Retreat to make sure everything was in place for the post-christening party she'd planned for Bethanne. Only perfection would do for her BFF.

She watched Mick's back as she stuck close to him; he looked so strong and fit. It was hard to imagine him from ten years ago when he'd suffered his NFL career-ending injury, but the same business acumen that kept him with the Portland Pintos organization back then was the reason Jeff and Cisco hired him at the Retreat.

He'd be good for business. She'd just have to keep chanting those words in her head like a mantra, or else she'd do one of two things she'd regret—kill Mick or kiss him. She'd gone the kissing route with him before, and it did not end well. As tempting as the killing option was at the moment, it probably wouldn't end any better.

Dedications

To Leo, for your unfailing support of me
and my wacky mid-life career change!

~*~

And to my mother, Mary,
thank you for sharing your love of books and reading
with my sisters and me.

~*~

Speaking of my sisters,
thanks also to Mary and Judy
for all of your help spreading the word
about my books.
No author could ask for better publicists!

~*~

Thanks to Max,
for patiently answering all of my
out-of-left-field questions
when I waylaid you at your mom's house.
It was a huge help to me in planning the final scene.

"Love is lovelier the second time around..."
                                              ~Sammy Cahn

Chapter 1

Damn D.C. traffic!

Michael ground his molars together and conceded it might not have been the most appropriate thought given he was standing in the doorway of a church where his friends were currently christening their baby. But double damn, now he was late and the only open seat was next to Heather Braden—the one person he'd hoped to avoid as much as humanly possible here in Rivers Bend.

He walked as unobtrusively as possible, which wasn't very, given he was six-foot-three and the church was roughly the size of a postage stamp. As all eyes turned to him, he felt grateful he'd traveled in his favorite custom-tailored charcoal gray suit. At least he looked appropriate for the occasion.

He slid into the pew next to Heather whose eyes reminded him of stormy seas. Mostly it was because of the glare she bestowed upon him, but their steel gray color, with hints of blue sparking at him were reminiscent of the Atlantic during a hurricane.

"Nice of you to show up on time, Mick," she whispered.

"Traffic from the airport was a bitch. I got here as fast as I could," he whispered back out of the corner of his mouth. His gaze was trained forward to the altar where two couples stood at the baptismal font with a

1

baby wrapped in a fluffy, white blanket.

The older lady behind them clicked her tongue in disapproval, and Heather glanced back through her stylish, choppy bangs. "Sorry, Mrs. Warren, we'll be quiet."

She looked at him and narrowed her eyes in warning, before turning to face forward.

In spite of the situation, he felt a smile playing at the corner of his lips. Heather always managed to entertain him. Actually, she alternated between infuriating him and driving him crazy with lust, and once again, his thoughts took a distinctly non-church-appropriate turn. Given their current situation, he had to squash all those emotions where Heather was concerned. He was here to start a new job as the CEO of the Corporate Retreat at Rivers Bend, owned by the two men at the altar, both old friends of his, and one of whom was Heather's big brother. Her very protective big brother.

Francisco Cardoso and his wife Bethanne were the proud parents of the baby, who was held by his godmother, a tiny blonde with a head full of crazy curls. Jeff Braden was the godfather, and he stood behind the cute blonde with his hands resting possessively on her shoulders. Interesting—she must be Jeff's new squeeze. She wasn't Michael's type, but he could see her appeal, and Jeff certainly looked smitten.

"Don't let Jeff catch you eyeballing Magda like she's the last slice of pizza in the box, Mick."

"Michael," he corrected through gritted teeth.

Heather rolled her eyes and made some sort of symbol with her hands.

"What the hell does that mean?"

The old biddy behind them huffed her disapproval

Heather shot her a furtive glance, before whispering in response, "It's a 'W' for 'whatever,' *Mick.*"

"I don't go by Mick anymore."

This time the old lady actually smacked him on the shoulder with her rolled up program. "Young man, some of us are here to listen to the service; *not* to pick up young women. Would you please be quiet?"

"Sorry, ma'am."

Heather's smothered giggle at his mumbled response did nothing for his already bad mood.

He'd never imagined Jeff's sister still lived in Rivers Bend, Virginia. And in his wildest dreams he wouldn't have thought they'd meet up in a church on the first day in town.

****

Heather fidgeted in the pew to try to move her leg from where Mick's muscular thigh pressed into hers. The man took up way more than his fair share of space.

Did he have to be just as devastatingly handsome as he used to be? Mick—she couldn't think of him as Michael—was very bad for her peace of mind.

Darn her brother for dragging this man out of her past and into her present. And he threatened to be as big a pain in her ass in the present as he'd been in the past.

She scooted over a little to her right until her younger brother, Jason, used his shoulder to shove her back into Mick's big, solid, warm body.

"A little personal space here, sis? Hey, Mick."

She frowned at Jason but pulled her arms into her sides and pressed her legs together as tightly as possible. She took a deep breath and tried to concentrate on the service, which felt interminable since Mick had arrived. Probably because she had herself twisted up like a pretzel on the already uncomfortable wooden pew. She heaved a sigh of relief as the service finally wrapped up, and she could flee from Mick's close presence. Heather jumped to her feet, which caused her small clutch bag to fall to the floor with a thump.

"Jeez, Heath, where's the fire?" Jason laughed.

She bent at the knees to retrieve her bag, which put her eyes right at crotch-level with Mick as he stood. Her heart pounded, and in spite of their ugly history, her palms itched to touch him through the fine wool of his trousers.

She straightened as fast as she could, but based on the knowing smirk and raised brow on Mick's face she hadn't been quick enough, and he'd seen just where she'd been looking.

Oh, if they weren't in church, she would knock the annoying grin right off his face, and she hated the blush she could tell was spreading across her cheeks. Mick had managed to make her feel like an awkward seventeen-year-old girl again in under half an hour.

She tried to keep her voice calm and detached, even though her heart pounded in her chest. "I've got to get back to the Retreat before the other guests. I need to make sure everything is set for the party."

Mick cocked his head, and he reminded her of her mother's old hound dog when he was confused by his humans. He couldn't possibly be baffled by her lack of warmth. Did he *really* think she'd welcome him to Rivers Bend with open arms?

"I guess I was too subtle there for you, Mick. You

are blocking my way out of the pew and I need to get to the party before everyone else. Please move."

He frowned, but he did step out of the pew to join the crush of people in the aisle.

"Stick close. I'll get you out of here."

He used his broad shoulders as a wedge to propel himself though the crowd. Heather scurried to keep up with him so she could take advantage of the gap he created, not wanting to be so close she could feel the warmth of his body through his elegant suit, but because she needed somehow to beat this crush of people to the Retreat to make sure everything was in place for the post-christening party she'd planned for Bethanne. Only perfection would do for her BFF.

She watched Mick's back as she stuck close to him; he looked so strong and fit. It was hard to imagine him from ten years ago, when he'd suffered his NFL career-ending injury, but the same business acumen that kept him with the Portland Pintos organization back then was the reason Jeff and Cisco hired him at the Retreat.

He'd be good for business. She'd just have to keep chanting those words in her head like a mantra, or else she'd do one of two things she'd regret—kill Mick, or kiss him. She'd gone the kissing route with him before, and it did not end well. As tempting as the killing option was at the moment, it probably wouldn't end any better.

****

He didn't know whether to be relieved or disappointed when he cleared the church door and Heather scooted around him and high-tailed it to the parking lot.

"What have you done to send my baby sister running for her car, Mick? Not even in Rivers Bend for one hour and I *already* have to kick your ass."

His old friend's amused southern drawl belied the harshness of his words. At least here was someone who was happy to see him in Virginia.

He turned with an easy smile on his face. "Hey, Jeff! Heather said she needed to get to your house before everyone else to set up the party or something, so I used my NFL blocking experience to get her out of the church."

They did that awkward one-armed hug men do and Mick added, "But I go by Michael now. I left 'Mick' behind after my playing days."

Jeff smiled. "You'll always be Mick to me, get used to it."

The little blonde from the church stepped up beside Jeff and looped her arm through his. Her smile was warm but shy. "Sorry to interrupt, but they need us for pictures."

"A godparent's work is never done," Jeff joked. "Maggie, this is Mick Evans, but he's gone all high-falutin' on me and wants us to call him Michael. Mick, this is my girlfriend Magda Horvath, aka Maggie."

"Nice to meet you, Magda."

"You too, Mick—I mean, Michael. Sorry, Jeff always refers to you as Mick. I'll try to remember to switch to Michael."

Jeff was a great guy, but he hadn't been serious with anyone since his late wife, and Mick had been none too fond of her. Magda was cute as a bug and seemed friendly and down-to-earth. He heaved an internal sigh of relief Jeff seemed to have picked a woman worthy of him this time around.

He smiled down at the little bit of a woman. "No worries, you can call me whatever you like."

"Hey man, we've got to go do the picture thing, but I'll see you back at the Retreat. We're having the post-christening reception there, if you're not too beat from traveling. If you're up to it, it's a good chance to get to meet some folks from town, and then afterward I can show you to your cabin."

"I'm not too tired—sounds good. I'll see you at the reception."

Jeff grinned and looped his arm around Magda's shoulders, before he turned to say one last thing to Mick. "Oh, hey…I just wanted to say I was happy to see you sitting with Heather in the church. I know you two don't get along, but I appreciate the effort."

Sitting with Heather hadn't been a choice so much as a necessity, and given their history, and her chilly attitude toward him this morning, Mick was fairly certain they'd never be as close as they used to be, but Jeff didn't need to know any of his problems. He'd grown up in a small town and knew he'd have to run into Heather at social events. He could certainly suck it up and be a grown-up around her when the need arose. It probably wouldn't happen too often.

"She's your sister; of course I'll try to get along with her."

Jeff smiled with bemusement. "Yeah, she's my sister, but the reason I want you two to play nice is because she's the Director of Guest Relations at the Retreat. You're going to be her boss."

Chapter 2

Mick followed the directions to the Retreat the GPS in his rental car gave him without any thought or attention. All he could think about was Jeff's parting words.

Heather's boss?

He was going to be Heather's boss?

How could that be? Rock, hello—meet hard place.

His feelings for Heather were just as much of a confused jumble as they were when he last saw her so many years ago.

As the GPS system's too-cheery voice told him to turn left, and then announced 'he had arrived,' he made a conscious effort to relax his jaw, as he followed the long driveway through the woods.

His teeth were sore from clenching them together; he really had to get this train wreck of his emotions under control. He hadn't gotten to where he was in life by giving in to his base emotions and popping off like the hillbilly redneck his former college teammates had taunted him about being. He had hated being the butt of their jokes, so he'd polished the coal miner's son until he'd shone like a diamond.

By the time he arrived in Portland, he'd left the raw boy behind and become a smooth pro athlete. And when he blew out his knee, his first year on the team, his intelligence and sophistication helped him transition to the front office.

His molars ground together again, but he wouldn't let his veneer slip. Not many things stirred him enough to make him fear letting urbane Michael slip up and release his inner West Virginia mountain boy, but Heather always got under his skin, and it didn't seem like much had changed with time.

He needed to rein in his emotions before he got to the reception. He took a deep, calming breath and looked out at the beautiful scenery along the winding entrance to the Retreat.

It was a sunny, early spring day in Virginia, and the leaves on the trees were that gorgeous light green you only see when they first burst to life. The branches of the tall trees met over the road, and he felt like he was driving through a green tunnel.

Here and there he saw a dirt road leading to the guest cabins scattered across the Retreat grounds. One of them would be his new home, until he found his own place and got settled here in Rivers Bend.

And settle here he would.

He was excited about his work at the Retreat. Jeff and Cisco were looking to him to build and manage the business with the opportunity for him to buy in as a third partner on the table if he did a good job.

Heather working for him did throw a monkey wrench in his plans, but he could make it work; he *would* make it work.

He pulled out of the woods and got his first look at the Retreat at Rivers Bend. The Potomac River was to his left and the sprawling two-story plantation style house was to his right. He followed the circular drive around the neatly groomed lawn to the steps, which led up to the front porch that ran the length of the house.

A young man in a white shirt, black slacks, and a matching black vest opened the car door for him.

"Park your car, sir?"

Mick swung his long legs out of the car and smiled. "Sure, thanks. Where's the party?"

The boy gestured with his head. "Through the front door and to the left—in the Retreat's dining room."

Mick slipped the boy a large tip. "Thanks."

He climbed the stairs and took a moment to notice the rocking chairs lining the left side of the porch, and the swing and cushioned outdoor on the right. Jeff lived on one side of the Retreat with his eleven-year-old daughter, and Mick guessed it was the side with the swing.

Opening the door, he entered the lobby, noting the tasteful combination of antiques and new items. It managed to be cozy and welcoming, but still elegant.

He heard the happy yip of a small dog, and Heather's throaty laugh. Drawn like a magnet, and very much against his will, he followed the sound to the Retreat's dining room, decorated in white and baby blue for the christening party. The tables were all set with white linens, and bouquets of blue hydrangeas at their centers.

The room was devoid of people, except Heather and the young man behind the bar. The guy was dressed in the same uniform as the parking attendant, but he somehow managed to make it look stylish. His dark hair flopped over one eye, but was shorter in the back. He remembered the hairdo as being favored by the Lacrosse players back in high school. Lax dude smiled flirtatiously at Heather as he handed her a flute of champagne.

Heather was in the same outfit she'd worn in the church—a yellow sundress and a small, white cardigan. As she smiled back at the bartender, she looked as springy and fresh as the day outside. Around her feet danced what appeared to be a tiny one-eyed dog of some sort. He'd always figured Heather to be a big-dog person—like a retriever or a hound—not a little frou-frou dog like this one.

He felt a sharp pang in his gut as Heather threw back her head and laughed at something the bartender said to her. *Huh. Jealousy?* What the hell was up with that? It had been years since Heather and he had been together. He'd moved on with his life, and there had been no shortage of women. He was sure a woman as amazing as Heather had no problem attracting men. So why did he want to stride across the dining room and punch Lax dude in the face?

The dog spotted him and yipped, which drew the attention of Heather and her admirer, who both turned to look at him.

"Nice place here. We conducted our interviews via Skype, so this is the first time I've seen it in person. Jeff and Cisco did a great job outfitting it."

He watched the smile fade from her face at his remark, and her eyes shuttered as clearly as if she'd drawn shades against them. He'd meant to pay a compliment, so why did she look like she wanted to deck him as much as he wanted to deck the bartender.

"As a matter of fact, *I* decorated the Retreat. I oversaw the entire renovation while the boys were still in Portland playing their last season for the Pintos."

Her tone was so chilly ski resorts could hire her to

make snow. Why did it bother him to be on the receiving end of her frosty tone of voice, while the bartender got her warmth and humor?

Maybe she was insulted he'd ignored her contribution to the Retreat? Hell, he hadn't known; when had she gotten so prickly? He remembered Heather being a lot more laid-back when she was younger.

Reminding himself they needed to be able to work together, he said in a conciliatory manner, "I didn't know. You did a great job. I'm lucky to have you working on my team."

Her jaw set, and he wondered if she had the same issue with teeth grinding he did. If he wasn't mistaken, Heather didn't look any happier about working together then he was.

"*Your* team?" She saluted smartly. "Well, Cap'n, I'm off the clock right now, so if you'll excuse me, I need to get back to what I was doing."

His gaze darted from the bartender, who looked between them with undisguised interest, as though he were at a championship table tennis tournament.

Heather put her hands on her hips, and he wouldn't be surprised to see steam coming out of her ears. Clearly he was mishandling this whole situation. Lax dude now had an irritating smirk on his pretty-boy face as he observed a thoroughly cheesed-off Heather, and his own complete lack of an idea of what to do next.

"May I speak to you in private for a moment? Before the other guests arrive." Mick wasn't sure what he was going to say, but he obviously had to do something to clear the air between the two of them.

"Sure." Heather waggled her fingers at the

bartender. "Thanks for all your help setting up, Kyle. If we don't get the chance to talk again, I'll see you tomorrow night."

"Looking forward to it." The kid had the nerve to waggle his eyebrows at her lasciviously, before exiting through the swinging door to the kitchen.

"Tomorrow night?" Damn it all to hell! He really needed to cool it with the green-eyed monster, but he couldn't stop himself from asking, "Isn't Kyle a little young for you?"

Heather's eyes flashed, which perversely he liked more than the cool indifference he'd seen in them before. At least now he knew she felt some of the heat he always felt when he was with her.

"Not that it's any of your business, but Kyle and I go to school together. We're both majoring in Management, so we have a lot of classes together. And, yes, he is a little younger than me, but if I choose to date him, it's between the two of us—not you—so keep your damn opinion about it to yourself. You're going to be my boss, not my father. What I do on my own time is my own business."

"Really? You decided to go to college? That's great."

"Seriously?" She huffed and took a hearty swig of her previously untouched champagne. "*That's* your take-away message from everything I just said?"

Her exasperation made him smile inside; not many people stood up to him the way Heather just did, but he was speaking to her in a professional capacity right now, so when he spoke his tone of voice was stiff and formal. "Sorry. I heard everything you said, but the boss part is what I wanted to speak with you about.

Obviously, we have a history between us, but we need to find a way to put it behind us, and work together in a professional manner."

She wrinkled her nose as she surveyed him from top to bottom. "Did they have to surgically implant that stick up your ass? And when precisely did it happen? I don't remember you being such a stiff."

He threw back his head and roared with laughter. "I still enjoy your company way too much for my piece of mind, Heather Braden."

She gasped and her eyes opened wide, but before she could respond, a cluster of partygoers entered the room, and she smoothly segued into hostess mode, but she did send him one last glance over her shoulder as she walked away, and confusion clouded her eyes.

Join the club sweetheart. I'm just as out of my element about my reactions to you as you are about yours to me.

Chapter 3

Mick watched Heather slip out of the party with a tray of desserts and champagne glasses. He scowled as he realized he hadn't seen that bartender in a while. Was Heather sneaking off to meet him? And why did the idea feel like a punch to the solar plexus? What—or who—Heather did wasn't his business. Not anymore, and it hadn't been for a long time.

"You're looking tired and cranky, man. I'm sorry I can't get away quite yet to get you settled."

He started at the sound of Jeff's voice. He'd been so lost in his thoughts about Heather he hadn't heard his friend come up behind him.

He turned and laughed as he saw his brawny friend holding the little fluffy, one-eyed dog in his arms.

Jeff grinned. "This is Petunia. She's Maggie's dog."

Mick scratched behind her ears, which made her tail thump against Jeff's side. "Cute. I saw her earlier with Heather and thought she was her dog."

"She's officially Maggie's, but she spends most days at the Retreat while Maggie's at the library. She job shares the librarian gig here in town with Bethanne. So, Petunia is the unofficial mascot of the Retreat. Hope you're cool with dogs."

"I am. I love dogs."

"Good. At least you'll get along with Petunia—if

not Heather. I'm sorry, man; I don't know what her deal is with you."

Mick knew all too well, but he was not about to share that nugget of information with Heather's older brother. They'd never told Jeff about their relationship back in the day, and he saw no reason to dredge up ancient history now, as long as their history stayed in the past. "I know it's a small office, and dissension can be really disruptive to the organization. I'll do my best to smooth things over with her. We're both grown-ups, I'm sure everything will be fine."

"Good, good. Glad to hear it. Heather does a great job here, and I know you're going to be terrific for the Retreat. Cisco and I don't want to lose either one of you."

"Jeff! Can we get a picture of you with Cisco and the baby?" one of the partygoers yelled from across the room.

"Sure thing," Jeff replied. "I'll be right there. Excuse me, Mick; the party seems to be breaking up, so I should be able to take you to your cabin in a little bit."

"No worries. I'm enjoying getting to know everyone here in Rivers Bend."

And he wanted to stick around long enough to see if Heather was with that bartender when she got back. Not that it mattered to him, or anything. Right.

****

"Hello, ladies, I thought you could use a little refreshment during your nursing break," Heather called out as she entered the living room in Jeff's private living quarters.

She had decorated the room for Jeff when he bought the Retreat, and she chose a comfy, homey theme with turquoise and brown as the predominant colors. Family photos were in frames everywhere, including a large professional photograph over the fireplace of Heather with her mother, sister, and two brothers on the family horse farm. They were all in jeans with white shirts; their mother was seated on a hay bale and the rest of them were standing or seated around her.

Bethanne sat in a chair in front of the fireplace, nursing baby Francisco, and Magda was sprawled on the sectional sofa with her high heels kicked off and on the floor next to her.

"Bless you, Heather!" Magda exclaimed.

Heather handed her a glass of champagne from the tray she carried. "Champagne for you and me, sparkling cider for Bethanne, and desserts for all of us!"

She set the tray on the coffee table, after putting Bethanne's cider on the table next to her chair, and sat down next to Magda, who closed her eyes in bliss as she took a sip.

"Long day, huh?" Heather asked with sympathy. "I think the party is starting to wind down now."

"The guest of honor and I better get back out there now that he's had his dinner," Bethanne said, as she burped the baby.

She rose and picked up her non-alcoholic cider with her free hand. "Thanks, Heather, for dessert and for everything you did to make this party special. You two are the best friends a girl could have! Once more into the fray for me, but y'all can chill in here for a little longer."

Magda wriggled her toes as she leaned forward to select a mini-cheesecake from the tray. "Thanks. My feet are killing me. If I weren't such a midget, I wouldn't have to wear such high heels. And of course, I had to fall for your brother, who's a virtual giant."

Bethanne laughed before leaving Heather and Magda alone.

Magda looked at Heather with speculation in her steady gaze. "You and the new guy seemed to be having an intense conversation when I got to the party, and he's been watching you like a panther watches his prey all afternoon. What's the story with you two?"

Heather hesitated; Maggie had become one of her best friends since she'd moved to Rivers Bend, but she was also Jeff's girlfriend, and Jeff never knew what went down between Mick and her, way back when. And Jeff wasn't just her big brother, he owned the company she worked for and there was no way she could share with the boss's girlfriend how hurt she was Jeff and Cisco were considering taking Mick on as a third partner in the Retreat, when they never offered her the same opportunity. She was hurt. And angry. She worked her tush off for this place, and felt seriously under-appreciated.

Maggie was thoughtful and intuitive, so it was no surprise she sensed the reason behind Heather's hesitation.

"I know I'm involved with your brother, but I'm *your* friend, too, and I can keep a secret."

Heather popped a chocolate covered strawberry in her mouth and savored the combination of the tart fruit and the sweet chocolate, as she thought about Maggie's words. She couldn't talk about the work stuff with Maggie, but maybe she could get her friend's input on the personal situation with Mick.

"I need to talk to someone, and I really value your opinion, but it would have to stay between us."

Magda crossed her heart. "I promise."

Heather took a deep breath. "Mick and I knew each other back in Portland, when I moved there to help Jeff take care of Sam after her mom died."

It was a dark time in her brother's life, so she never regretted the sacrifices she made to care for her brother and her niece, but it did lead to her first heartbreak. And her last, because she made sure to guard her heart more carefully from that point forward.

"Why do I feel as though there's *so* much more to the story than you 'knew each back in Portland'?" Magda asked as she nestled into the chair and took a sip of champagne. "Tell Auntie Magda all about it."

Heather smiled at the woman whom she was fairly certain would be her sister-in-law one day soon. She was so happy Jeff brought this smart, funny, and kind woman into all of their lives, but she didn't want to put Maggie in a bad position with Jeff. "I would like to talk about it with you. I could really use some advice, but it's about stuff Jeff doesn't know happened, and with Mick working here now, it's probably best if Jeff never finds out about it."

"If you want to tell me something in confidence, I can keep it quiet. I don't especially *like* keeping things from your brother, but you've been a good friend to me, and if you need an ear now, then I've got one." She winked. "Not to mention two feet that are in no hurry to squeeze back into those heels."

Heather laughed. "Well, if it's to spare your tortured toes, then I have no choice but to tell you."

Magda leaned forward to grab a lemon bar from

the tray. "My feet thank you, and your secrets are safe with me."

"Mick and I hung out in Portland and I never told Jeff about it. He was seriously over-protective of me when I lived with him."

Magda nodded her understanding. "Contrary to his laid back image, Jeff takes his responsibilities very seriously, and he felt responsible for you, since you'd moved across the whole country to be there for him when he needed you." She paused and arched her eyebrows. "Was Mick as GQ handsome back in the day as he is now?"

Heather exhaled as she thought. "I'm sorry to say I think he is even more attractive now. He was young then, so he was probably more cute than handsome." She thought about the sharp planes of his cheekbones over his sculpted lips, and remembered his softer appearance ten years before; she shivered. "Yeah. Definitely more handsome now."

"And was he as serious then as he is now?"

"Yes and no. Around the guys he was all business, but when we were alone, he'd let down his guard and we had a lot of fun. He even let his West Virginia accent slip when he'd really forget himself. It made me feel like I was going out with a boy from home."

Magda's blue eyes opened wide. "Mick had an accent? Wow. There's no trace of it now."

"No. He really worked to lose it in college, I guess, but sometimes he'd let it slip, and I loved it! All smooth, like honey and home."

"Jeff didn't know you were hanging out?"

Heather shook her head. "At first we did just hang out—"

Magda reached across the empty seat on the sofa between them to rest her hand on Heather's, when she spoke her voice was gentle. "Was Mick your first?"

Heather shook her head vehemently. "No. At first, we were just friends, but then one day, we kissed. There was some serious chemistry between us, and if we'd stayed together I'm pretty sure he would've been my first."

"What happened?"

Heather frowned and furrowed her brow. "I don't know. To this day, I don't know! Everything was great between us. We were even getting ready to brave the wrath of Jeff and tell him we were dating. Mick hated keeping it from him. The guy code is firm on not dating sisters, but evidently once you do, you need to come clean about it."

"And with two alpha males like Mick and Jeff, I'm sure fisticuffs would ensue."

Heather raised her eyebrows. "Fisticuffs?"

Magda shrugged and grinned. "I read a lot of historical romance, and I've always wanted to work the word 'fisticuffs' into a conversation."

"You are one odd woman, but I like it."

Magda waved her free hand, as she took a sip of champagne. She swallowed and said, "Thank you. Carry on. You two were about to tell Jeff…"

"Right. So, one day I brought Sam to the stadium to watch Jeff practice. Mick was on the sidelines with a bunch of other players. I know he saw us. He watched me like a hawk, but he didn't come over to say 'hi'. It seemed like the other guys were teasing him. If it were happening now, I might have handled things differently, but I was so young then, I just went up to him and said hello. The other guys hooted, a couple made crude remarks they didn't think I could hear, like I was deaf, I was standing right there. I don't know why they thought they were in the cone of silence. I knew they were teasing Mick more than me, but it was really uncomfortable."

"What did Mick do?"

Heather felt the burn of tears and blinked them away, refusing to allow the memory to have the power to hurt her after all this time. "Nothing. He did nothing. He just set his jaw and walked away leaving me standing there with my niece in her stroller, and a bunch of dumb jocks laughing at me. I didn't even know what the hell was going on—I still don't—but I know I felt like I was about this tall." She held her thumb and forefinger a fraction of an inch apart.

"And the next time you talked?" Magda prompted. "What did he have to say for himself?"

Heather scrunched up her eyes and rubbed her temples. "He never talked to me alone about anything."

"Ever?"

"Nope. He avoided being alone with me, and he wouldn't return my calls. Then he got injured at the end of that season."

Magda nodded. "Jeff told me about it, he said Mick really did a number on his knee."

"It was a career-ending injury. The Jurgenson family, who owned the Pintos, loved him though, so they put him to work in the front office. I had no excuse to run into him then, so we practically never saw each other. And slowly, the sweet boy from West Virginia morphed into the iceman you see today."

"What do you think happened?"

Heather shrugged in an attempt to feign indifference, even if she was far from feeling it. "I guess he was just playing with the stupid farm girl."

Magda shook her head. "I don't think Jeff and Cisco would've stayed friends with a man who would do that to a girl. There has to have been something more."

"Whatever." Heather plunked her empty glass on the table. "It was a long time ago; I don't really care what his deal was back then. I just don't want it to impact our working relationship now."

Magda smiled in sympathy. "Are you sure?"

Heather took a deep breath and stared straight ahead. "I'm positive. I could care less about Mick Evans."

She pasted on a smile and turned to face Magda, but something she saw through the tall bank of windows overlooking the front yard caught her attention. Her smile turned into a scowl as she asked, "Is Mick outside with Gloria Peterson, of all God-forsaken people? It didn't take them long to find each other! What do you suppose they're talking about?"

Magda grinned. "It's good to see how you could care less about Mick."

****

The woman was beautiful, no doubt about it, but she did nothing for Mick, even though she was sending out signals as strong as a broadcast tower.

Jeff turned his back to the tiny raven-haired looker and rolled his eyes at Mick. "Gloria, this is Mick Evans, the new CEO of the Retreat. Mick, this is Gloria Peterson, her daughter is my daughter's best friend."

Gloria advanced on Mick like a slinky predator.

He'd met her type plenty, and sometimes he even took them up on their blatant invitations, he was no saint, but right now all he could think about this woman was she didn't hold a candle to Heather. And that kind of thinking needed to be squashed. Pronto.

He extended his hand. "Nice to meet you, Gloria."

Her fingers slid up to caress the inside of his wrist. Her long fingernails scratched him, and he thought of Heather's sensible short nails, neat and buffed, but not done up like Gloria's talons. Heather was like the Anti-Gloria, with her willowy, athletic body and her face like sunshine. He felt a nail prick the sensitive spot at the base of his palm and realized Gloria was talking.

"Welcome to Rivers Bend, Mick. I'm sure you'll find us to be *very* welcoming. If you need a tour guide…"

"Tour guide?" Jeff interrupted with a burst of laughter. "We have *one* stoplight in town, Mick. I think you'll manage to navigate Main Street without a tour guide."

Gloria released Mick's hand to swat at Jeff's arm coquettishly. "Oh, you!"

Mick received Jeff's message loud and clear— *don't be taken in, because this woman is a she-wolf.* The problem was, since he'd hit Rivers Bend today, all he'd been able to think about was Heather, and that wouldn't do at all. Maybe Gloria could be a distraction for him. She was the type of woman who knew the score, so he wasn't worried about leading her on and hurting her. She knew how to play the game. Hell, she probably invented the game.

""I don't know, Jeff." He winked at Gloria. "I think I could use a little help finding my way around town."

Gloria smiled like a cat just finding a mouse hole. "Then I'm your woman. I have to find my daughter now, but I'll be in touch soon."

Jeff waited until she'd wriggled her behind up the stairs to the house and then frowned. "Maybe you're not as smart as I always thought you were, but your personal time is your own, and Gloria certainly knows her way around. Just be careful of her; she's on the prowl for husband number five."

"*Five*?"

Okay. Using this man-eater as a distraction from Heather might not have been his best plan, but Mick needed to do *something*. Heather was his friend's little sister, not to mention said friend was now his boss, and Heather was now his employee. Plus, his behavior toward Heather in the past was something that always deeply shamed him.

Nope, he had to fight his attraction to Heather. If not with Gloria, then he'd bury himself in his new work here at the Retreat.

Chapter 4

Mick put his plan into action early the next morning. He strode into the Retreat offices, located off the lobby. He noticed a light on in one of them and heard the furious clicking of fingers flying across a keyboard. He peeked through the door and froze, so much for his good intentions to put the woman out of his mind through hard work.

"Morning, Heather. What are you doing here so early?"

Heather jumped and her chair rolled backward with a squeak. She put a hand to her heart, which had the unfortunate reaction of drawing his attention to her breasts. He never would've guessed a navy blue polo shirt with the corporate logo of a winding river, surrounded by trees, embroidered in white on the upper left breast, could hold such erotic appeal.

"Mick! You scared me. I didn't expect anyone else to be here so early. It's only six-thirty!"

"I could say the same to you—well, not that you scared me, because you didn't—but, I did think I'd be the first one in the office. You used to like to sleep in, said it came from being raised on a horse farm, where you always had to be up before the sun."

Her eyes narrowed. "Old habits die hard, and I went back to waking up early. Besides what time I choose to get out of bed isn't any of your affair."

Why did she have to talk about them and bed, and use the word 'affair'? It pushed his thoughts farther down the path they'd started on this morning. Back to business. Going down the other path led to badness.

"You're right, but your work *is* my business. What are you working on?"

She turned to look at the computer screen. "Organization and paperwork are not Jeff or Cisco's thing, so I like to get here before them on Monday morning and get the week's schedule in a spreadsheet for them."

He leaned over her shoulder to look at the data. "You have all the groups we've got coming in this week, their activities, what rooms and facilities will be utilized—good work." He tried hard to ignore the citrusy smell of her glossy, sun-kissed brown hair. "May I have a copy?"

She twisted her neck to look up at him, pleasure and surprise shone in her eyes. "Thanks. Of course you can have a copy. I usually print it out for Jeff and Cisco, but I also email it to them, so they can access it from their smart phones when they're leading activities on the grounds."

"Like hiking?"

She nodded. "Right. We also offer training on the Alpine tower and horseback riding. The guys lead all of those activities, so they're not in the office a lot during the day."

He leaned in closer to see today's activities, and felt her silky hair brush against his cheek. His whole body reacted to the feathery sensation. He clenched his jaw and jerked away. He recited football stats in his head to will away his semi-erection, which started with

27

no more than the touch of her hair. What the hell was his problem? Business—get back to business and his comfort zone. "What's happening this morning?"

****

Excellent question.

What the hell was happening this morning?

Mick certainly was consistent in his mixed signals. She was picking up a vibe from him that he wasn't thrilled to be working with her, but he went on to praise her work. Then to round it out, he went back to the jaw-clenching thing he did that gave a girl the definite impression he'd rather be anywhere but in her company.

To be fair, her reactions to him were just as confused. It pissed her off this man was waltzing in here to be her boss, and could get a partnership in the business *she* helped build. Not to mention having a constant reminder of her first heart-breaking rejection by a man. She really, really wanted to hate him, but when he praised her for her organizational abilities, and leaned into her to look at the computer she felt his hard, warm body; smelled his minty breath, and she wanted to pull him on top of her and kiss him senseless.

He waved his hand in front of her face. "Heather, I asked you what's happening this morning?"

She straightened her spine. Right. Mick was her boss. Leave the wildly inappropriate thoughts at the office door. Better yet—leave them ten years in the past where they belonged.

"We have the Sales department from a manufacturing company checking in for team-building exercises. They have lunch scheduled in the dining room, and then Jeff will take them on an afternoon hike along our trails."

"You'll oversee their check-in?"

"I always do. I've checked their flight, and it's on schedule for arrival. The minibus we use to pick them up is en route to Dulles as we speak."

He looked impressed, and she hated the way it made her heart flutter.

"You keep everything here organized. I'm impressed."

Great. Now the flutter was an out-and-out pound, and the heat she felt in her cheeks told her she was blushing. Lots of men had praised her for things that were just good genes—her smile, her hair, her body—but to have a man praise her for her work was new and nice. She had to admit if felt really good.

Her brother's voice from the door spared her from making what she feared would be a breathless response.

****

"You should be impressed. Heather's the grease that keeps this whole machine running smoothly."

Footsteps pounded down the hallway, and Jeff's eleven-year-old daughter, Sam, burst into the room.

"Aunt Heather, I've got that history test today, can you quiz me one more time?"

"Samantha Jane—manners," Jeff reminded her in a warning tone.

The coltish child hung her head and her honey-blonde ponytail swung behind her head. "I'm sorry, Dad, I'm just really nervous about this test." She glanced up at Mick through her fringe of bangs. "Good morning, Mr. Evans."

He smiled at her. "Good morning, Sam. I always used to put a lot of pressure on myself at school, so I understand how you're feeling."

Heather stood and grabbed her empty coffee mug from the desk. "C'mon, Sam. We can do this in the kitchen while you have breakfast, and I grab a second cup of coffee."

As they walked out of the room, Mick heard Heather soothe the child. "I know you're stressing about this test, but you've got this Colony stuff down, so no worries."

Jeff smiled after them with obvious affection. "I was really happy to see Heather and you working together so well this morning. I've got to be honest with you, Mick; I don't know what I would do without her around here."

"She seems to be very good at her job."

"She is, and she always goes above and beyond her job description, even though she's the boss's sister. She decorated this place—the Retreat rooms and my personal quarters. She oversaw the renovations while Cisco and I were playing our last season with the Pintos." He paused and shook his head in wonder. "And what she's sacrificed to help me out personally— there's nothing I could ever do to repay her for all she's done."

"Do you mean when she moved to Portland after Crystal died?"

"Yeah. I don't know what I would've done without her. Sam doesn't even remember her mother. Heather's the one who's helped me to raise her."

"Which was great of her, don't get me wrong, but I think moving across the country, being surrounded by pro ball players was an adventure for her."

Jeff scowled and pounded his right fist into the

palm of his left. "But you bastards all knew enough to leave my baby sister alone."

Mick swallowed hard, and hoped Jeff couldn't see his Adam's apple bob with the action. Two things he wanted to avoid doing here in Rivers Bend—seeing Heather Braden, and discussing his past history with Heather with Jeff. So far he was zero for two.

Time for him to take evasive action, since his plan was not exactly working like a charm. "Did I hear talk of coffee somewhere?"

Jeff hoisted his cup of hot, aromatic coffee. "In the kitchen—follow me. Mrs. Wilson, my housekeeper, keeps a pot going all day."

****

She heard Mick and Jeff talking as they approached the kitchen, and Heather struggled to concentrate on the U.S. History textbook propped up on the table in front of her. Sam sat across from her and shoveled in a spoonful of cereal before hurriedly swallowing to answer Heather's question.

"Connecticut was the fifth state to join the Union."

"Right! You've got this stuff down, Sam. You're going to ace your test."

"Of course you are, Peanut." Jeff poured a cup of coffee for Mick as he spoke to his daughter.

Heather feared it would look weird if she kept reading the textbook, and reluctantly looked up at her brother and Mick. Maybe Mick wouldn't even be looking at her.

She gulped.

No such luck, his light brown eyes focused on her with such laser beam attention she could imagine sparks shooting from the gold flecks in them.

31

"Heather," her brother's voice broke the spell firing up between Mick and her. "I was just telling Mick we're more casual around here."

Her gaze took a leisurely tour from his Italian leather shoes, up to the impeccable suit personally tailored to fit his broad shoulders and narrow waist, and on to the crisp white shirt and blue silk tie.

She raised her eyebrows and looked down at her own low-slung khakis and navy Retreat polo shirt. "You do look a little over-dressed, Mick."

"Michael," he replied automatically.

Jeff leaned against the granite countertop, cupped his mug in his hands, and laughed. "I'd give up on that Michael business already; you're Mick to us. Always have been; always will be. It's a losing battle."

Sam gulped down the last of her orange juice. "Dad, can you give me a ride to school now? I don't want to be late today."

Jeff put his mug in the sink. "Sure, Peanut. Grab your stuff and I'll meet you at the truck."

"Thanks, Dad!" Sam beamed at Heather as she put her dishes in the dishwasher, and then ran over to throw her arms around her aunt's neck. "And thank you, Aunt Heather, for all your help getting ready for this test! Bye, Mr. Evans!"

"Call me Mick," he replied with a deep sigh of resignation. "Good luck on your history test."

Jeff grabbed his truck keys off a hook by the back door. "Heather, can you get Mick set up with Retreat gear in his size—polos, tees—you know what he'll need. Can't have him looking like he stepped off a fashion runway every day. It'd scare the livestock."

"Livestock?" Mick's jaw dropped. "We have

livestock?"

Heather laughed, but it stuck in her throat at her brother's next words.

"Oh, and take him on the grand tour this morning." He tossed a set of keys at her, which Heather caught one-handed. "Take a golf cart and make sure he's sees everything."

No.

Hell to the no.

Heather did not want to spend her morning pressed up against Mick in a tiny golf cart.

Okay, maybe she did want to, but it scared the bejeezus out of her.

"Sorry, Jeff, but I have a group checking in this morning. I need to oversee the process; make sure it all runs smoothly."

Jeff flashed her a charming grin that would probably have worked on any woman who wasn't one of his sisters. "Don't worry about it, it's a small group. I'll call Cisco and have him handle the check-in."

She opened her mouth to argue, but Jeff was gone like a flash before she could say a word. He'd been out of the NFL for years, but when he wanted to avoid something her brother could still move like lightning.

She dragged her gaze to Mick, who seemed torn between amusement at her obvious discomfort, and his own annoyance at being thrust together this morning.

"Looks like you're stuck with me," he said with a rueful grin.

"Looks that way." She threw the back door open and said with resignation, "Let's get this tour on the road. The sooner we start, the sooner we finish."

****

33

Mick grinned as he stepped outside. "I don't think I've ever had such a gracious invitation before."

Heather screwed up her mouth. "I'm sorry. My mom would have my head on a platter for being so rude. Even to you."

"Impressive. You almost got your apology out without another insult."

She led the way to the golf cart, and he remembered the crazy way she used to drive. She might have improved in the past eleven years, but he wasn't ready to take the chance she hadn't. "How about I drive?"

"But you won't know where to go."

"You can tell me where to go."

"Oh, I'd like to tell you where to go, all right," she muttered.

Mick pretended not to hear, in order to try to keep both the peace and his promise to Jeff that Heather and he would get along with each other. "I'll learn my way around better if I'm the one driving."

She tossed the keys at him, and he wasn't kidding himself, she threw them *at* him, not *to* him.

She sat in the passenger seat with her arms crossed against her chest. "Fine. You do the driving. You can drive a golf cart, can't you?"

He got behind the wheel, and his arm pressed against hers in the close confines of the cart. "Sure. A lot of business gets done on the golf course, so I had to learn the game. Plus the Pintos sponsored a charity golf tournament every year, and part of my job was to organize it."

He felt her pull her body away from his, and he missed her warmth. She held onto the cart with one hand, and leaned out to the side to avoid contact. He frowned. Was she still so mad at him she would rather hang out of a moving vehicle than to have any incidental contact with him? For the first time, Mick worried he wouldn't be able to keep his promise to Jeff. Heather and he seemed incapable of getting past their history together, in order to get along in the present.

He'd really been counting on Heather's forgiveness for his past douchebaggery, although he wasn't sure he deserved it. She turned her head to look at him with a frown. "I think the first stop better be the supply room. Your suit looks seriously out of place on a golf cart. Let's get you changed and into some Retreat gear. Do you have khakis or something more casual to wear back at your cabin?"

"Of course I do—do you think I only own suits?"

"Well…yeah."

"Nope. They're not comfortable for sleeping. And don't get me started on the beach, all that sand getting in the cuffs…" He winked at her. "How do we get to the supply room?"

She gestured with the hand not gripping the frame of the cart. "Follow this path—there's a cabin down here where we keep the hotel linens and Retreat gear."

He squinted in the bright sunlight, and took one hand off the wheel to pull a pair of sunglasses out of the interior jacket pocket. "I forgot how bright the world is outside of Portland."

Heather chuckled. "Welcome back to sunshine. The weather could be a little gloomy, but I really enjoyed living in Portland. Are you missing it?"

"A little bit. I miss my house. The cabin is great, don't get me wrong, and I really appreciate Jeff letting me stay there, but I'd like to get settled in my own place soon."

The ghost of a smile played around Heather's lips, and he would *not* look at her lips anymore. He gripped the wheel, and focused his attention on the winding path ahead of them.

"You always were a homebody," she said.

"I like to chill; there's nothing wrong with that."

She turned her head to look at him and raised her eyebrows. "Take it down a notch, Defensive Man, I didn't say there was."

"Sorry." And he was, but he'd always felt a little dull compared to Heather's lively personality, so her statement struck a nerve. "Is that where we're headed?"

Heather looked where he gestured, and nodded. "Yep. Pull up in front, and we'll get you all fixed up with the full complement of Retreat clothing. Then we'll head over to your cabin, and you can change your clothes."

****

Heather sat on the overstuffed red sofa in the tiny living room of Mick's cabin, while he changed into more casual clothes before they continued their tour of the Retreat.

The thought of him in the next room stripping out of his suit, left her feeling a little warm. She fanned her face with one hand, and shook her head in irritation. This was *Mick Evans* she was having hot and steamy thoughts about. She really needed to get a grip. He was the only man she'd ever really trusted with her heart, and he'd taken it and stomped on it. Just because he was still so handsome he was almost beautiful was no reason to start softening toward him.

She squirmed in the seat. Every once in a while, she caught a glimpse of the young man she'd fallen in love with, and it made her wonder if he was still there, under all his sophisticated veneer.

The bedroom door creaked open, and she turned her head to see Mick emerge in a navy Retreat polo, a pair of khakis riding low on his lean hips, and Topsiders on his feet. He held out his arms and spun around like a model on the end of the runway. "Better, Ms. Braden?"

"Much better. You look like you belong here now, and not at some corporate office in Manhattan."

"That's good, because here is where I want to be."

She wrinkled nose. "Really? I didn't think you'd ever move this close to your home again."

He plopped down in one of the two chairs opposite her, and sighed. "I didn't think I would either, but things change."

"What changed for you?" Heather flapped her hands. "You know what? It's none of my business. Forget I asked."

"No, it's okay. You're the only person who really knows about my family crap; I don't mind you asking." He paused and took a deep breath, before continuing, "Things with my dad are still strained to the breaking point, and I'm not too popular with my brother Danny, either, but I keep in touch with my mom, sister, and my two youngest brothers."

"That's good. Isn't it?"

He bobbed his head. "Yeah, it is. I was starting to miss them, and as Billy and Dave get older, I'm afraid my father is going to try to do the same thing to them he tried to do to me. I don't think they want to work in the mine, but he's really pressuring them to do it. I thought maybe I could help them more from here than from three-thousand miles away. Susan is getting married soon, my baby sister. I can't believe it, and I want to be here for her, too. Once she starts having kids, I didn't want to just be a picture on the fridge to them. I want to be a real uncle when the time comes."

"What about the Pintos? You've worked for them for so long; it couldn't have been easy to leave."

He shrugged. "After the Jurgenson family sold the team, it wasn't the same."

"I heard about the sale—what happened?"

"You knew Old Man Jurgenson retired, right?" At her nod, he continued, "His son took over, but he was no spring chicken when he started, and he retired at the end of last season. And *his* son has a successful business of his own and zero interest in football, so he decided to sell the team."

"And you don't like the new owners?"

"They're okay, but it's not the same. Remember how there was always a real family feel to the organization?"

"Oh yeah, everyone was so great to me when I moved to Portland to take care of Sam. It was like having a huge, built-in extended family."

"It's not like that anymore. Now there's a much more corporate vibe."

"I would've thought you'd like a formal work environment."

He frowned. "Because I'm such a stuffy, corporate drone? Never mind. Don't answer that, I don't think my ego could take it. No, I didn't like it, so when your brother and Cisco offered me the opportunity here, I jumped at it. The chance to work with friends, and be close to family—I couldn't do anything else."

Heather could definitely feel herself weakening where Mick was concerned, and didn't like it at all. How could she keep her hate on when he was acting like a nice guy? Time to get moving and away from this kind of intimate conversation. "We better get back to our tour of the Retreat. My new boss is kind of a hard ass, and I don't want to get into trouble with him for goofing off."

"I hear he's not too bad." One side of Mick's mouth quirked up as he stood and held the door open for her.

Heather wasn't sure about that. In her opinion, he was really bad for her peace of mind, especially when he was being all down-to-earth and charming.

****

After Heather's tour of the Retreat a couple of days ago, Mick felt like he made some progress in making things better with her, but between school and her job, he'd barely seen her since then. He'd always thought of himself as a nose-to-the-grindstone kind of guy, but next to Heather, he felt like a real slacker.

The phone on his desk trilled, and he tapped the button for speaker phone, so he could keep working on his laptop while he talked.

"Mick Evans."

"Mick? Since when is that your name?"

An amused, upper-crust drawl sounded through the phone.

Damn. Everyone here had been calling him Mick, and he'd said it automatically. He glanced at the Caller ID and winced. Philip Exeter—double damn.

"Pip, good to hear your voice, old man. Thanks for returning my call."

"When I heard you were at the Retreat at Rivers Bend, I couldn't resist."

Mick frowned and his fingers paused in their keyboard tapping. "Why is that?"

"The whole town is buzzing about your new employer at the moment. Bitsy was especially interested in the possibility of visiting."

Bitsy was Pip's wife, and possibly the biggest gossip in New York society, but as far as Mick knew, she considered a trip to the Hamptons to be a safari, so the idea of her venturing to Virginia boggled the mind.

"Isn't this a little off the beaten track for Bitsy's taste?"

Pip chuckled. "Yes, but it holds a certain appeal for her."

Mick loved Rivers Bend, with it's rustic Southern beauty, but he couldn't imagine what would appeal to Bitsy Exeter here, unless she'd been hit on the head and forgotten who she was.

"The Retreat is for corporate team-building events. It's not an Inn. Is Bitsy working with you at the Exeter Investments now?"

Pip's chuckle turned into full-on laughter. "Bits—working? Oh Michael, you are such an amusing man. I'd bring my group down, and Bitsy will tag along in hopes of visiting with Elizabeth Mallory's granddaughter."

"Does she have a place here in Virginia?"

"Do you mean you haven't met her yet? I understand she's very cozy with your friend Braden."

"Do you mean Maggie?"

"What is it with that town and the ridiculous nicknames? You haven't even been there a week and you're 'Mick,' and Magda is 'Maggie'?"

It was a little tough to take the insult to 'Mick' and 'Maggie,' from a grown man called Pip, whose wife goes by Bitsy, but Mick was hoping to do business with him, so he ground his molars and said, "Her last name isn't Mallory, so I didn't make the connection."

"You miss all the good news when you choose to live in the hinterlands. She ran away to your little town, and threw over Pierce Allen for Jefferson Braden."

"I don't know anything about it, sorry." Okay, that was a big, fat lie. Mick wasn't at all sorry. He liked Maggie, and no way was he going to gossip about her with this snob, but Pip knew everyone, and could steer a lot of business the Retreat's way if his investment firm came here and had a positive experience.

"They were engaged, although no date had been set yet. Allen's a good man. We were at New Haven together."

Mick knew enough about Pip's world to know the phrase meant Allen and Pip had attended Yale together, not just gone on a day trip to Connecticut. He rolled his eyes at Pip's snobbery. "Maggie's a lovely person, so I'm sure she had her reasons. Anyway, Pip, back to your idea of coming here for a corporate retreat—I'm happy to send you some materials on the Retreat at Rivers Bend. I think we'd be the perfect spot for…"

"I can't imagine *what* reasons she could have for leaving an *Allen*, old man. It's a top-notch family. I mean, who is this Braden? I heard his people are *farmers*! Can you imagine such a thing?"

Mick's hands clenched into fists over his keyboard,

and he was glad Pip and he weren't on a video call, so he only had to control his voice, and not his expression. He was fairly sure if there had been livestock at the Retreat, the anger on his face would have them running for the hills in fear right about now. No business was worth this fucker coming into Jeff's home to insult his woman and his family!

"Jeff Braden is the best man I know, and his family has been nothing but warm and welcoming to me. I don't know anything about your friend, Allen, but Maggie couldn't ask for anyone better than Jeff."

"I'm sure he is fine, but a *farmer*? He better watch out. She might try to climb up the social ladder in your new town and run off with the plumber."

"You know, Pip, I've re-thought things, and I don't think the Retreat would be a good match for Exeter Investments after all."

"What! Why ever would you say such a thing? Bitsy will be so disappointed."

"Old Bitsy is going to have to survive without coming here to savage a perfectly lovely young woman, whose only sin is choosing a good man from outside your social circle."

"Now, now, old man, no need to be rude."

"That's rich! You're telling me not to be rude, when you were about to install your pit viper of a wife into my friend's home, merely in order to ferret out gossip about his girlfriend? I may just be a simple former football player like Jeff, but even I know rude behavior when I see it."

"Oh come now, you're nothing like him. You went to Stanford, and I hear he could only go to college based on his ability to play a game, and actually went to

Alabama! I mean, really, there's no comparison. I don't believe I've ever even *flown* over Alabama."

"You know for such a *sophisticated* man, you have a very narrow world view, *old man.*"

Even Pip was going to have a hard time pretending not to hear the disdain in his tone.

"Perhaps you're right. Rivers Bend may not be the right place for our corporate retreat," Pip's voice was stiff.

Mick hoped he hadn't burned too many bridges by alienating Pip, but he couldn't stand by and listen to him insult Jeff and Maggie. Oh well, he'd just have to try extra hard to have some of his other contacts come through with new business. "No. It most definitely is not. You can tell Bitsy, and anyone else who asks, Jefferson Braden and Magda Horvath are two of the finest people on this Earth, and are blissfully happy together. If anyone legitimately wants to come to the Retreat, because it's the best place for a corporate team-building experience, they'll be more than welcome here, but if they only want to come here for gossip and to hurt decent people, then their money is no good in Rivers Bend. Good bye, Pip."

"Good bye, old man." Pip sounded a little bewildered as Mick pressed the button to disconnect their call.

Mick dropped his head against the back of his desk chair and screwed his eyes shut. What a painful telephone call! He really was counting on this partnership thing working out, but if he couldn't bring in new business it wasn't going to happen. Maybe he shouldn't have insulted a prospective client, even if the man was a world-class jerk.

The sound of applause from his doorway made his eyes fly open. Heather stood at the entrance to his office and clapped her hands together.

"Thank you for defending my brother and Maggie from that snooty windbag! I can't believe he would book a whole meeting here just to try to get some dirt on Maggie! No wonder she couldn't wait to leave that world behind. And for the record, Pierce Allen is an insane drug addict who tried to kidnap Maggie, so he may be an *Allen*, and we *Bradens* may just be simple horse farmers, but she definitely traded up when she fell in love with my brother."

Mick's eyebrows reached for the ceiling. "Allen tried to kidnap her?"

"Long story, but yeah, he's a flipping sociopath, so thank you for not bringing his friends into Jeff's home."

"I don't know if Jeff will thank me for losing my temper and turning away business."

"You were defending his girlfriend and our family. I don't know what hoity-toity New York society thinks of it, but here in Rivers Bend it's the way things are done. Jeff will understand. I'm proud of you."

Heather's approval was extremely gratifying, but the flush of pleasure her words brought on was squelched by his fear he'd behaved like a hot-head just like his old man, and Heather deserved a lot more.

Chapter 5

Heather knew she should be working on her paper instead of sitting on a porch swing and enjoying the peaceful sounds of the spring evening at her brother's house. She cast a guilty glance at her laptop on the wicker table by the rocking chairs, but she took another sip of her tea and pushed off with her foot to swing a little more. There'd be plenty of time to work on her paper later; right now, she needed to decompress.

After the week she'd had, maybe she should be doing something to blow off steam on Saturday night, like going out dancing with her friends, but she promised Jeff she would sit with Sam so he could take Magda out for a nice dinner. She had a lot of schoolwork to do, so normally she wouldn't mind. Plus she got to hang out with her niece, which was always a bonus in her book. However, tonight she wouldn't have minded putting a little distance between herself and the Retreat.

Any hopes of going her own way at work and not having to interact too much with Mick had been squashed by her brother's constant interference. She'd tried to keep busy and dodge Mick as much as possible, and things had gone according to her plan until Wednesday when she'd overheard—okay, eavesdropped on—Mick's phone call with the jerk from New York. It stood her opinion of him on its head.

She'd softened toward him, ever so slightly, and her buttinsky brother picked up on it, and in his attempt to keep everyone at the Retreat one big happy family, he'd thrust Mick and her together at every opportunity.

She gritted her teeth and swung a little faster. Why did she have to use the word 'thrust' and Mick in the same sentence? Now all she could think about was Mick thrusting.

Into her.

Above her.

Beneath her.

Gah! Think of something else, anything else. Okay, she would count to twenty in Latin.

Unum. Duo. Tres.

The silence of the night was broken by a voice. Mick's voice. It sounded deep, velvety, and surprised. Man, she so couldn't catch a break. What was the world coming to when a woman couldn't count to twenty in Latin in peace on a Saturday night?

"Heather? Is that you?"

Illuminated as she was by the porch light, Heather thought it was pretty obvious who was here. The night beyond the warm glow of the porch was pitch black and she couldn't see Mick, so she responded in the direction from which his voice had come. "Yes, Mick, it's me. If you're here to see Jeff, he's out on a date with Maggie, so there's no need to stick around."

"Sorry to disappoint the hopeful tone in your voice, but I'm not here to see Jeff. I'm not going anywhere."

He stepped into the circle of light around the porch as he spoke, and now he climbed up the steps to the porch.

God, the man was beautiful! Why did he have to be

so handsome—with his sharp, high cheekbones, perfectly formed lips, and eyes as intoxicating as the bourbon their color resembled? It would make the fight against her attraction to him so much easier if he was a troll. She sighed. Hell, who was she kidding, certainly not herself. She'd always felt this pull to Mick, and his good looks were just a part of the reason.

The light glinted off his brown hair. He looked positively edible in an ancient, worn-out Portland Pintos sweatshirt , and worn denim jeans that lovingly caressed the parts of him Heather would most like to lovingly caress herself

He walked until he was directly across from her; then leaned his very fine backside against the porch railing, with his arms crossed. "I wanted to get some paperwork done. I keep getting interrupted during the day, and I thought I'd be the only one here tonight."

He looked pointedly from the laptop to Heather, and asked with a raised brow, "Are you working on a Saturday night too? I'd have figured you'd be dancing the night away in some club in D.C. with that bartender."

Heather furrowed her brow. "Bartender? What bartender?"

"The kid from the party last weekend."

She shook her head. "Kyle? I told you, he's just a school friend."

He jerked his head to her sweatshirt, which she'd thrown on over her T-shirt and leggings, when she'd made the now fateful decision to come and sit on the porch. "George Mason University. Is that where you're going to school?"

"Yep. I've been commuting there for years, but I'm

finally going to graduate this spring—if I can concentrate enough to finish my paper."

"The Heather I knew wouldn't have been doing a paper on Saturday night."

She felt a flash of anger at his words. "The Heather you knew was seventeen years old, for God's sake! You've changed since then, why do you seem to think it's so impossible I have too?" She ignored the little voice in her head reminding her she *had* just been wishing she were out burning up a dance floor tonight.

Heat flashed in his eyes, and it didn't have anything to do with anger. A smile curled up his beautifully formed lips. "Believe me, Heather, I have been noticing all week how you've grown up. I didn't mean it as an insult. I always liked how full of life you are." A smile played at the corner of his lips. "You might not have noticed, but I tend to be a little on the serious side, and you brought a lot of fun into my life back then."

Flummoxed by his words, and the honesty in his eyes, she was speechless—a rare occurrence for her. She took a sip of her tea and tore her searching gaze from his face.

Perhaps realizing he wasn't going to get any kind of response from her, Mick said, "Think that swing will hold up if I get on too?"

"Sure, Jeff sits on here all the time and you're about the same size as him." She wanted to smack her forehead as he eased onto the seat beside her. Why didn't she tell him no? His mighty weight would surely pull the swing down. But, no, her innate honesty did her in again, and now Mick was pressed against her in the cozy confines of a swing built with romantic trysts in mind. He felt good beside her too—all hard, masculine heat.

They rocked for a little while; the only sound was the creaking of the swing.

Mick was the first to break the silence. "Why are you studying here? You don't live here do you?"

"No. I live in an apartment over my sister Deidre's café, you know, the Nosh Pit?"

"I didn't know your sister owned it. I had lunch there this week."

"With Gloria Peterson. I know."

He frowned. "I forgot how fast news travels in a small town."

Heather wanted to warn Mick about Gloria, the woman was a gold-digging man-eater, but she didn't want to appear jealous. Instead, she answered his earlier question. "I'm babysitting Sam tonight. She's up in her room on the phone, probably talking to Gloria's kid, they're BFFs. I thought I'd come out here to work on my paper, but it was so peaceful I decided to just have a cup of tea and enjoy the quiet."

"And then I showed up."

"And then you showed up." Heather took the final sip of her tea and stopped the swing with her foot to put the mug on the porch. Before she could get up, Mick pushed off, and with the squeak of his giant sneaker on the wood porch they were swinging again.

"It's been good working with you this week, Heather. You're really great at your job. Jeff wasn't kidding when he said you're the person who keeps the Retreat rolling."

She turned her head to him and blinked in surprise. If her brother felt like her work was so crucial to the

Retreat, why was Mick the one being offered the chance to become a partner? She knew she should be angrier with her brother and Cisco—and they *did* get a fair share of the blame—but the man in front of her was the one taking what she'd earned, and she was surprised he was complimenting her. Was her playing her in some way? Her voice was equal parts shocked and cold when she said, "Thanks."

He turned too, and their faces were just a breath apart. Heather's heart stuttered in her chest.

"You don't have to sound so surprised I paid you a compliment."

She turned away to face forward and stared into the night. "I don't know what to think about you, Mick. I thought maybe you were being sarcastic."

"No. I'm serious; you're really great at your job."

She was close enough to see the muscles in his jaw working overtime.

"While I'm being serious, Heather, I wanted to apologize to you."

Ha! He knew she deserved the partnership more than he did, and felt guilty about it, if the haunted look in his eyes, and the tight lines bracketing his mouth were any guideline. Heather frowned as she realized he looked too anguished to be talking just about work. Maybe he was talking about something else.

"Apologize for what?" Heather asked.

"For what went down between us eleven years ago."

She took a deep breath. "You mean the way you shunned me like we were Amish, and you'd caught me using a light bulb?"

"Yeah, I'm sorry about that."

Huh. It wasn't about work after all. She frowned, unsure she wanted to discuss the more emotional issues of their past, rather than their current situation, of which he appeared to be as oblivious as her brother and Cisco. Men! They could be so frustrating in their cluelessness.

She peered at him through narrowed eyes. It looked like he was clenching his jaw again, which made his cheekbones look even sharper than usual. Damn the man for looking so sincere. And handsome. But it was the sincerity making her say, "Okay, thanks."

He rolled his neck, and she heard an audible crack. "I've always been really ashamed of my behavior."

"You should be. If you didn't want to see me anymore, why couldn't you have told me in person? Why the shunning?"

He paused before speaking, and when he did, his voice was rough. "I didn't trust myself to be alone with you and not keep my hands off you."

"Not generally a concern when you're dumping someone, so why were you drop-kicking me, if you still felt so attracted to me you couldn't even be alone with me long enough to break up with me?"

"It was *because* I still felt attracted to you." He gripped the arm of the swing so hard his knuckles were white and Heather feared he'd snap it off. "Jesus, Heather, why didn't you tell me you were only seventeen fucking years old?"

Her jaw dropped as she gaped at him. "You *knew* I was seventeen. I didn't feel the need to tell you."

"See, that's the thing. I didn't know."

"You knew I'd just graduated from high school. How old did you think I was?"

"Eighteen—about to turn nineteen."

She shrugged. "I was seventeen about to turn eighteen, what's the big difference?"

He laughed once, but without a trace of humor. "About twenty years."

She frowned. "What do you mean?"

"You were underage. If we had done the wild thing, I could've been arrested. Not to mention what it would've meant for my career."

She shook her head sadly. "Wow. All those years of wondering why, what I might have done wrong, and it was something so *stupid*?"

"Stupid?"

She punched his arm, and the wall of muscle she found there made it feel as if she'd hit a stone wall. "Yes, stupid. We weren't having sex. There's no law against a twenty-two year old and a seventeen year old hanging out with each other."

"You know it's where we were headed. Our attraction was like a runaway train; there was no stopping it."

"When did you realize I was seventeen?"

"I was at practice; you'd brought Sam by to see Jeff."

"I remember," she whispered. Hearing him describe the day when he'd broken her teenaged heart, tore at her guts, but she didn't stop him. She'd waited a long time to hear why he acted like such an ass, and as much as reliving one of the worst moments of her life hurt, she prompted, "What happened on that particular day? Everything was fine up until then."

"I know. I was so psyched to see you there I was staring at you like the lovestruck horn dog I was, and the guys starting busting my balls about it—saying Jeff was going to kick my ass, and the ever popular 'once a hillbilly, always a hillbilly' taunt, because I was hot for such a young girl. Then one of them said 'seventeen will get you twenty,' meaning twenty years in jail."

"But why didn't you talk to me about it? I turned eighteen less than two months later; we could have cooled things down until then if you were worried. Why the silent treatment?"

"That's the part I'm ashamed of, and what I'm apologizing for. I was young, too, and stupid. I would handle you differently now."

She turned and his face was close enough she could smell his minty breath. "Oh yeah? How would you handle me now?"

"Like this," he said, before closing the distance between them and pressing his lips to hers.

The heat that had been simmering between them all week erupted into a full-blown inferno, and at her soft moan, Mick groaned and pushed his tongue into her mouth to claim it. He pulled her onto his lap and the thin, black fabric of her leggings provided no barrier to the hardness she felt beneath her bottom. Feeling his reaction to her drove her wild with eleven years of pent-up desire for this man.

She felt said hardness jerk as it grew impossibly harder, and she twined her arms around his neck. She slid her hands up to tangle in his silky hair. And when she felt one of his big, strong hands slip under her sweatshirt to cup her breast over her lace bra, she thought she might explode in a fireball of hot, wet lust.

"Aunt Heather? Where'd you go?" Sam's voice called from inside the house.

She pulled her kiss-swollen lips away from his and

touched her fingertips to them in wonder. She cleared her throat before she answered, "I'm on the front porch, Sam."

She slid off Mick's lap and picked up her teacup with an unsteady hand.

"Okay! I'll be right down," her niece shouted.

Mick looked pointedly at the bulge in his jeans. "Mind if I borrow your laptop to hide this from your impressionable young niece?"

Heather laughed, but it even sounded shaky to her own ears. "Feel free."

He picked up her wafer-thin computer and put it on his lap, just before Sam flew out the front door. The screen door slammed shut behind her.

"Hey, Mr. Evans…um…I mean, Mick. I didn't know you were here."

"I just came by to get some work done."

"Oh, okay. Aunt Heather, I'm off the phone, so can we make popcorn and watch the movie now?"

"You bet. Why don't you go get us a couple of sodas, and I'll be right in to pop the corn."

"'Kay!" Sam ran back into the house.

Heather took a deep breath. If Sam hadn't interrupted them, Mick and she would be seriously rocking this swing right now. What was she thinking? Mick Evans was the only man she'd ever let close enough to touch her heart—to *break* her heart, and it happened without the two of them having sex. If they were ever to cross that line, she'd be way too vulnerable to the man who'd hurt her so badly in the past. Not to mention all the issues in their present—he was her *boss* for Pete's sake.

She smoothed her hair. "I've got to go in. Now that

the coast is clear, may I have my laptop?" She balanced the mug in one hand, and reached for her computer with the other.

He handed it to her reluctantly. "Heather..."

His deep voice sent tingles to places in her body she didn't want tingling any more tonight. "Good night, Mick," she interrupted with finality, before going into the house and using her hip to shut the door firmly between them.

Chapter 6

"To our first dinner guest in our new home." Francisco tilted his beer bottle at Mick before taking a drink.

"Jeff and Maggie are having Sunday dinner at his mom's, but they'll be over for dessert," Bethanne said with a warm smile.

A baby's cry sounded through the baby monitor, and she jumped to her feet. "Excuse me, gentlemen, it seems as if someone wants his dinner now."

Cisco watched her go with a loving grin, and then turned back to Mick. "I noticed you working closely with Heather this past week, and I've been wondering. How are you handling it?"

Mick took a hasty swallow of his beer to stall for time. "What do you mean 'handling it'?"

"Please, *meu amigo*," the amiable Brazilian said with a kind smile. "I know about your history with Heather."

Mick choked on his mouthful of beer and sputtered. "How do you know about my history with Heather?"

"The way you two circled each other back in Portland? C'mon, everybody knew there was something between you."

"Even Jeff?"

Cisco shook his head. "No, not Jeff. He still

thought of Heather as his baby sister and he seemed incapable of realizing she had big-girl feelings for you."

"We never…you know…"

"Made love? None of my business, *meu amigo*, but even without sex, things seemed pretty intense before it all crashed and burned. Is it awkward working together now?"

"Awkward? Yeah, you could say that; I thought I was fixing things between us last night, but I think I made things worse."

"You saw Heather last night?"

Mick nodded. "I stopped by the office to get some work done…"

"On Saturday night?" Cisco interrupted. "Jeff and I are not slave drivers; you don't have to work on Saturday night."

"I know. I just want to do the best job I can for the two of you. I really appreciate the opportunity you've given me."

Cisco smiled and shook his head. "Always the hardest worker; always trying to prove yourself. Where does that come from?"

Mick shrugged. He knew Cisco came from humble beginnings too, but he wasn't about to lie down on the sofa and spill his guts to Dr. Francisco Freud.

When the silence between them made it clear Mick didn't intend to answer, Cisco said, "Forget about all the other stuff. What did you do to mess things up with Heather last night?"

Mick leaned forward, rested his forearms on his thighs, and dropped his head. "I kissed her."

Cisco's dark eyes bugged out of his head. "What were you thinking? Jeff is going to rip you a new asshole! And you're her *boss*!"

Mick swung his head back and forth. "I know, man, I know. You're not telling me anything I don't already know."

"Are you two dating now?"

"No. I don't know what's going on between us."

"How did you leave things last night?"

"We didn't talk at all. Heather was babysitting Sam, and she had to go back in the house. She ran off the porch like her hair was on fire."

"Do you mean you two were making out on the porch like a couple of horny teenagers while Heather was babysitting?"

Mick nodded and groaned.

Cisco shook his head and said with a frown, "Remind me never to ask you two to sit for baby Cisco."

****

Heather sat in the back seat of her brother's truck and watched him drive to Cisco's house one-handed, while his other hand clasped Magda's on the center console.

She was happy Jeff finally found love, after many years of loneliness.

She really was. And Maggie was the best—the perfect woman for Jeff—but Heather couldn't deny the pang of envy she felt when she saw them in an unguarded moment, like this one. Holding hands, because they couldn't *not* touch each other, and it wasn't just passion between them. There was a deep, abiding love and respect Heather wanted to share one day with a man.

Her life was full and happy. She was crazy about

her family and friends, and they adored her in return. She was good at her job and, as an added bonus, she enjoyed it; she was about to, at long last, finish her college degree. She had really expected to be offered a partnership in the Retreat after her graduation. She worked so hard on the business from its very inception; to her at least, it seemed like the natural next step. Apparently it was not so obvious to her brother and Cisco, who offered the potential partnership to Mick, of all people. Her natural optimism strained to focus on the positive, and she thought how lucky she was to have a job, lots of her fellow graduates didn't, let alone a job she liked as much as she enjoyed her job at the Retreat at Rivers Bend.

She looked out the window at the flowering cherry trees in full bloom, which lined the driveway to Cisco and Bethanne's house, and wondered anew at the beauty of Virginia in the springtime, and felt fortunate about living here, too.

Yep. Her life was pretty darn good. It was probably selfish of her to want someone to share it with, hell, who was she kidding? She didn't want *someone* to share it with; she wanted to share it with Mick. Ever since he'd walked into church last Sunday, like a somber storm cloud, her emotions had been in turmoil.

She wished she could just hold on to her old anger at him, but working together this week had reminded her of how smart, funny, and at his core, *kind* he was. And that kiss last night? Oo la la! The fire between them was just as hot as it was eleven years ago. And while she would accept his apology for her own sake, she couldn't quite forget the pain, or feel his explanation wasn't good enough. Not to mention the

Donna Simonetta

small fact he was her frickin' boss now, and soon to have a stake in the business, which by all rights belonged to her. *Stop thinking about it.* There was no place for negativity on this sunny afternoon.

She smiled as she saw the house Cisco and Bethanne had built on the Retreat grounds. It was nestled in the woods, away from the guest cabins, with a view of the Potomac, and their architect had designed a more family-sized version of the main house.

The Retreat was lovely, but the Cardoso's house was a *home*—warm and welcoming. Her eyes widened a fraction, because it was a home with Mick's rental car parked in front of it.

Wonderful, apparently even on her day off she couldn't get a break from the man.

"Mick is here?" Heather asked.

Jeff pulled up next to Mick's sedan and stopped the truck. His eyes met hers in the rearview mirror. "Yeah, he had dinner here. Is that a problem?"

Maggie, bless her, unbuckled her seat belt and answered for Heather as she threw open the door of Jeff's behemoth of a pick-up truck. "Of course, it's not a problem! Now be a gentleman and come around to help your very short girlfriend out of your very tall monster truck."

As Jeff loped around the front of the truck, Heather murmured, "Thanks."

Maggie flashed her a smile. "What are friends for, if they can't be counted on to provide a diversionary tactic every now and then?"

****

Mick waited in the cozy family room with the baby, while Bethanne and Cisco answered the door. He made a funny face at the tiny bundle in his arms and was rewarded with a gummy smile.

As soon as Bethanne heard he was the oldest of five kids and pretty experienced in the care and minding of babies, little Cisco's proud mama passed the infant off like a quarterback handing off the football.

He looked at the wall of windows in the back of the room to the amazing view of the river below, and sighed with satisfaction. It felt good to be back in this part of the country, with his two oldest friends and their families...and with Heather.

He really didn't want to think about the ramifications of those feelings, especially since she ran from him like a deer from a hunter last night after their amazing, world-shaking kiss.

"Where's my favorite godson?"

He smiled when he heard Magda in the front hall, but the voice he heard answering her made the smile fade from his face.

"He's your *only* godson," Heather teased.

She froze in the doorway at the sight of him, and her gaze darted around like she was looking for an escape route. At least he wasn't alone in his confusion about the emotions whirling around the two of them.

Jeff gave Heather a brotherly shove into the room. "Just for future reference, the entrance is *not* the best place to stop. You make a better door than a window."

"Jeez, Jeff, what are you—ten years old?" Heather rolled her eyes.

Jeff laughed without concern as he leaned over to chuck the baby under his chin. "Hey, Mick. Hey, little man."

Magda was hot on his heels, and bent down to kiss

the baby's soft, chubby cheek. "Hi little godson. Don't let mean, ole Heather spoil it. You *are* my favorite godson." She turned her warm smile to Mick. "You're a man of hidden talents, Mick Evans. I never would've guessed you'd be this comfortable holding a baby."

"I'm the oldest of five kids. I've had some experience with rug rats."

"Wow!" Magda's eyes grew round. "That's a big family. Do they all still live in West Virginia?"

"Yep."

Mick knew his answer was clipped, but his family was not a topic he wanted to discuss, unfortunately Maggie didn't know it, and being short on family herself, she didn't seem to realize Mick might have issues with his own.

Maggie pressed on with her questions, "When are you going to visit them, now that you're back in their neck of the woods?"

Mick frowned. "I don't know."

He glanced at Heather, who knew he wanted to be part of his family again, but his father and one of his brothers wouldn't welcome him, and saw sadness and sympathy in her eyes. *Damn it all to hell!* He hated being the one to make her feel sad. Heather was sunshine: bright sparkling, witty. He didn't want his gloomy past to infect her good nature. He grew up watching his cheerful mother wilt under his father's bad temper, and he didn't want history to repeat itself in his personal life. Mick wasn't at all sure he was any better than his nasty old man—yet another reason to stay the hell away from Heather. She deserved better than a bad-tempered man in her life.

****

After an interminable dessert, spent watching happy couples, babies, and Heather, the evening was finally winding down.

"Whaddya say, Heather, ready for Maggie and me to give you a lift home?"

"I'll take her home."

Mick wasn't sure whose face looked the most surprised by his blunt offer. Probably his own, although Heather's wide eyes and dropped jaw left her running a close second. "I've got to go into town to pick up some groceries, so I'll be driving right by her place."

His explanation was accepted, and before he knew it, Heather was buckled into his rental car driving into town.

"Thanks for the ride."

He gripped the wheel and kept his eyes on the road. "I wanted the chance to talk to you about last night before our work week begins tomorrow."

Heather glanced at him, and then looked out the side window. "About what happened, I may not quite have my Management degree yet, but I know making out with your boss is frowned upon in most business situations."

Mick grinned, in spite of himself. "Most?"

She shrugged. "There have to be some situations where it's acceptable. Like a mom n' pop market, where a married couple owns it together, or a brothel."

Mick laughed. "Two good possibilities, but we don't work in either one of those businesses." One corner of his mouth quirked up. "Unless there's something about the Retreat's mission statement I've missed."

She smiled back at him. "Nope. No hidden house

o' pleasure."

He pulled the car into an available parking space on the street in front of the Nosh Pit. "Which is why I think we need to clear the air."

She fumbled with her seat belt as she pushed her door open. "I suppose we do, but this is my stop." She hopped out of the car.

Damn it, Mick didn't want to talk either, but they had to, otherwise work would be unbearable. He turned the car off and followed her to the sidewalk, where he lightly caught her by the upper arm to slow down her forward progress. "Heather, hold up."

"Evening, folks. Heather, do you need some help here?" The deep voice, with its pleasant southern drawl, was polite, but there was a clear implied warning.

Mick turned and saw a man approaching them on the sidewalk. His skin was a slightly darker shade than his tan sheriff's uniform, and his smile held a hint of warning.

Heather smiled at the newcomer. "Hey, Dan. Thanks, but I'm fine."

Not convinced the sheriff narrowed his eyes and asked, "Who's your friend?"

She followed the sheriff's eyes to Mick's hand on her arm, and they both spoke at once to clear up any misunderstanding.

"This is Mick Evans, my new boss at the Retreat."

"I'm Mick Evan, an old friend of Heather's from Portland."

The sheriff frowned; evidently their conflicting versions of their relationship did not set the sheriff's mind at ease. "Which one is it?"

Mick removed his hand from Heather's arm, which

64

caused the other man to relax his stance a smidgeon, and Mick extended his hand to the sheriff. "Both, actually. I used to play on the Pintos with Jeff and Cisco, now I work at the Retreat."

"He's our new CEO," Heather added. "Mick, this is Rivers Bend's sheriff, Dan Monroe."

Dan shook Mick's hand, and flashed bright, white teeth in a grin. "I used to play ball with Jeff too, at Rivers Bend High." He winked before continuing, "Not quite the same league."

"A teammate's a teammate, no matter where you play," Mick disagreed with a smile.

"If all is well here?" Dan paused, and at Heather's almost imperceptible nod, he continued, "Then I'll be on my way."

He tipped his broad-brimmed sheriff's hat at them. "Enjoy the rest of your evening."

"Night, Dan."

"Good night, Sheriff, it was a pleasure to meet you."

Heather rolled her eyes. "You're so stiff and formal most of the time. Loosen up! We're on the street in Rivers Bend, not at the spring cotillion."

"I'm sorry I like to present myself as a professional and a gentleman."

"Mick, you've got nothing to prove here. This is the kind of small town where people value loyalty, good friends, honesty. All of which you have in spades. No one here is going to think you're a rube or a redneck." She paused and cocked her head. "And even if they do, it's not necessarily an insult."

Mick felt his cheeks burn. Leave it to Heather to remember his youthful confidences, and cut right to the chase.

This time, she was the one to reach out to grasp his arm, and the reaction in his body was so electric, she might as well be grabbing another body part, which was beginning to stand up in interest to her touch.

"I'm sorry, Mick; I didn't mean to embarrass you. I just want you to feel at home here, and not worry about how people perceive you."

"You know a lot about me, Heather," his voice was rough. "More than anybody else."

"And your secrets are safe with me."

He reached up and laid his hand over hers on his arm. "I know, and it's one of the reasons I value your friendship so much. It's why I can't risk it, or my job, for the…well, hell. I don't even know what to call it. Whatever is going on between us."

Her mouth twisted into a wry smile. "Why don't we go with calling it 'attraction'?"

He would have gone with inferno, wildfire, or atomic blast of lust, but there was no need to scare the woman. "Attraction sounds reasonable. Can we agree for the sake of our friendship, and our work at the Retreat, we'll ignore our attraction?"

He wasn't sure he could ignore the attraction any more than he could ignore a cattle stampede, but it sounded good, and he knew they had to try something.

Heather pursed her lips, as she considered his suggestion. "We can try. I love my job, and I don't want to do anything to jeopardize it. And, God help me, Mick Evans, I value your friendship too, and I don't want to lose it again."

They shook on it, and Mick tried to ignore the wave of pleasure even such an innocent touch sent through his body.

Friends, he reminded himself. They were friends. And friends didn't get to see each other naked. No matter how much they might want to.

Chapter 7

Friends! Why had Heather ever agreed to Mick's proposal to be friends? They weren't lovers, and they were more than boss and employee, but they sure as hell weren't just friends!

But it was her stupid promise to be friends, which had her tooling down Route 15 with Mick on this lovely spring Saturday, to help him shop for a car, so he could turn in the rental they were currently driving.

She pointed ahead. "There's the dealership Jeff recommended. The one where he bought his truck."

When they parked and stepped out of the rental car, a salesman who was helping a young family called out to them. "Someone will be with you folks shortly."

Mick raised his hand in acknowledgment. "Thanks, we'll just look around while we wait."

Heather put her hands on her hips and looked around. "What were you thinking of getting?"

Mick stared at a vehicle like it was the Lombardy trophy. "An SUV or a sedan would be sensible."

Heather grinned when she saw the car his gaze was riveted on, and teased him. "Yeah, but they wouldn't be nearly as sweet a ride as that convertible."

His answering grin was rueful. "Definitely not sensible, but, oh man it's a nice ride!" He whistled between his teeth.

"It's a beauty."

"Yeah, but if I was driving it, everyone would think I was having a midlife crisis. She's a young man's car."

"She?"

"Cars are always 'she.' "

Heather laughed. "I'll have to take your word for it. What I can tell you, is no one will think you're having a midlife crisis if you were driving her. Your only crisis might be caused by your view being blocked by the panties getting thrown at you from women in passing cars."

"Why, Miss Braden, are you trying to tell me you think I'd look hot driving this car?"

"Smoking hot," Heather replied honestly, without thinking, and could've bit her tongue off as the words left her mouth.

"You folks see something you like?"

Mick's intense stare incinerated Heather, as he answered the salesman without looking away from her face. "I sure do. But for now, I'd settle for taking this convertible out for a test drive."

****

Within a couple of hours, the deal on the sports car had been made, the rental car had been returned, and they thundered down Main Street on the way back to the Nosh Pit. The convertible top was down, and Heather looked like she could care less her hair was whipping around in the wind. She tilted her head back to let the sun wash over her face, and hung her hand out of the window, as if it were surfing on a wave of air.

He grinned at her as he parked in front of her place and cut off the engine.

She smiled back. "I can't believe you wouldn't let

me drive Lola."

"Lola?"

She nodded. "I decided it's her name. Lola was a showgirl in that old song, and this vehicle is flashy enough to headline a show in Las Vegas. But you're distracting me from my original point. Let me drive Lola, *please!*"

He turned to her, and his heart pounded like a boy's about to ask a girl to his first school dance. "If you agree to do me a favor, I'll let you drive Lola next weekend."

Her eyes narrowed with suspicion. "Favor? What kind of favor?"

He cleared his throat. "You know one of the reasons I wanted to come back East was because my baby sister is getting married."

"And how does this completely unrelated piece of information lead to me driving Lola?"

"My sister's wedding is next weekend."

"That's nice, but I'm still not seeing the connection."

For a smart woman, she was being kind of dense; he shifted on his seat. "I was wondering if you'd do me a favor, as a friend, and come with me to West Virginia for the wedding. We'd leave Friday and come back on Sunday, so you wouldn't have to miss any work or school." He smiled at her and added as an enticement, "I'd let you drive Lola part of the way."

She shook her head once, and he noticed what a snarled mess her hair was; why it was such a turn-on, he didn't know, maybe because it put a man in mind of how she'd look rolling out of his bed the morning after a night of good loving.

"I don't know, Mick, a family wedding seems way more date-like than friend-like."

"But it wouldn't be a date. It will be the first time I've seen them since I've been back. Hell, Dad and Danny don't even know I've moved, as far as I know, and I could use the support of a friend, and you're the only one who I can ask."

"Now that's mighty flattering." She scowled.

He held up his hands. "That's not what I meant! There are other women I could get as a date."

"That is absolutely *not* any better. I know you and your dad aren't close, but didn't he ever teach you when you're in a hole, you stop digging? Why don't you bring Gloria Peterson?"

He thought of snooty Gloria in his parents' humble ranch in coal-mining country, and couldn't hold back the start of a smile.

Bad idea, based on Heather's narrowed eyes and frown.

"If the thought of it makes you so happy, why don't you take Glo and leave me out of it?"

"I was just smiling at the idea of Gloria in West Virginia. I can't imagine she even knows mining exists, let alone a family who makes their living working in one. Look I don't *want* to go with anyone else. You're the only woman who knows about my effed up family dynamic, so I just meant you know what you'd be walking into, and I'd like to have you at my back. There's no one else I want with me."

"Knowing about your family situation is precisely *why* I'm not sure this is a good idea. I mean, how long has it been since you've seen them?"

"My mom, Susan, Billy, and Dave have come out

to Portland at least once a year."

She raised her eyebrows and prompted, "But…"

"But I haven't seen my dad or Danny in years." He hung his head at the admission.

"And now you're suggesting going to a major family function after all this time…with me. Your family will definitely *not* think we're just friends."

Then they can join the club, because I'm not altogether convinced of it either. "Who cares? Let them think what they want. I told you already. I could really use your support—the support of a *friend*—this weekend, and no one else knows anything about my family."

"No one? Not even Jeff or Cisco?" Her eyes were wide.

"No, you're the only one, Heather.."

She faced forward and flopped back against the leather seat. "Wow. I always thought you meant I was the only *woman* you talked about them with, not the only *person*. I'd always assumed the guys knew too. Why me?"

He also turned to face forward. "I trusted you, and I still do."

She snorted, and he was surprised by her derision.

"You certainly didn't trust me enough to discuss why you were dumping me back in Portland."

"That's where you're wrong. I trusted *you*. I didn't trust myself. If I spent time with you, even to explain, I knew I would just forget my reasons and get right back together with you. Hell, I was even ready to brave telling your brother! Now that's got to mean something."

She bobbed her head. "He would have seriously

kicked your ass."

"He would've tried."

They sat in silence for a few moments. It looked peaceful, but Mick's mind was whirring. He didn't want to admit it, not to himself and most certainly not to Heather, but he was nervous about going home for Susan's wedding. He didn't want the weekend to be about his homecoming. Susie deserved the focus to be entirely on her for her big day, but he knew his father and Danny would kick up a fuss about him being there. He'd given it a lot of thought this week, and if he brought a date, they would have to dial their antagonism down a notch, and Susan could have her dream wedding without their drama. He never once considered taking another woman, not even Gloria, whom he'd been casually dating. It had to mean something to Heather, but the woman was not going to make it easy for him. For Susie's sake, he had to give it one more shot, and this time he would speak from his heart.

"Please, Heather, please come with me to my sister's wedding. I don't want to face it alone, and I swear you're the only woman I want by my side."

Her face brightened and she squinted in the sun that bathed her features in light and made the highlights in her brown hair glisten like gold floss. "I love it when you let your accent slip. It used to make me feel like I was back home when we lived in Portland."

Sure, *she* loved his accent, but if he ever let it slip in front of anyone else, they'd assume he was one step away from donning overalls with no shirt, and playing an empty moonshine jug as a musical instrument.

She searched his eyes, and took a deep breath

before saying, "Okay. I'll go with you."

The woman never ceased to surprise him. "What? You will? What changed your mind?"

"Your accent just now—it reminded me of the boy I fell in l—" She stopped short with a snap of her jaw, then took a breath and continued. "The boy I loved to spend time with, back in the day."

Interesting. He'd fallen for her hard back then, but he thought he was just a fun diversion for a homesick Heather. He was so serious, and she was so fun loving. He'd never dreamed she returned his feelings.

She grinned and waggled her eyebrows. "Plus, I'll get to take Lola out on the highway to see what she can do. I couldn't resist."

****

"Yum. This is delicious. What do you call it again?" Magda smacked her lips after taking another sip of the frozen concoction in her cocktail glass.

Heather sat in the other tiny, folding chair on the small deck/fire escape off the back of her apartment over the Nosh Pit. The alley between the red brick buildings might not be the most scenic view in town, but she treasured her little bit of outdoor space.

"It's a frozen mint julep; I'm trying to perfect the recipe for my mom's Derby party. Y'all are my guinea pigs—glad you like it!"

The fire escape rattled as someone climbed up the metal steps. Her sister Deidre's voice preceded her. "If I had a liquor license at the Nosh Pit, I would hire Heather as my master mixologist." She stepped onto the deck. "Can I have one of those?"

"Hi, Dee, sure." Heather stood and opened the screen door in need of a new spring. The door slammed shut behind her as she entered her tiny kitchen and poured another drink from the blender, before returning to hand it to her older sister, who leaned her backside against the metal railing.

Deidre shut her eyes as she took her first sip. "Manna from heaven after the day I've had. The Nosh Pit was a zoo today."

Magda nodded. "The library was crazy busy too."

Deidre opened her eyes wide and blinked at Heather with feigned innocence. "I don't know about the library, Maggie, but there was only one topic of conversation at the Pit today—our girl Heather stealing Mick Evans away from Gloria Peterson, and going home with him to West Virginia this weekend to meet his family."

Heather choked on the sip she'd been taking while her sister spoke. She felt her face heat up as she coughed and sputtered, "That's crazy talk! Mick and I are friends."

"So, you're not going away with him? Because I heard the same thing at the library," Magda asked. "If it's not true, I'll be happy to set people straight about it."

Heather felt her cheeks heat up and cursed her fair complexion, with its tendency to blush. "Well…yes…I *am* going with him to his sister's wedding this weekend, but just as *friends*. It's not a *date*."

"You're right. I wouldn't call a weekend away to attend a family wedding a *date*. It's more like a sign of serious commitment," her sister observed.

Magda nodded and swallowed her drink. "Mrs. Warren agrees. She wanted to know if I was going to be one of your bridesmaids, and asked if Mick and you were going to beat me to the altar since Jeff is dragging his heels about 'making an honest woman' out of me. Mrs. W.'s words, not mine."

Heather scowled. "Sometimes living in a small town is too much! Everyone is always in your business."

Magda shrugged. "It's because they care. Trust me, I've lived in a big city, and it's not all it's cracked up to be. I like the way everyone looks out for everyone else here in Rivers Bend."

"You two really aren't an item?" Deidre made a moue of disappointment. "That's too bad. I like Mick, and he deserves better than Gloria. I've seen them in the Pit a couple of times for lunch; he doesn't look very interested in her, but you can tell she's ready to book the church and hire the caterer for their wedding. Still, if he needs a date, why isn't he taking her?"

"Mick has a"—Heather paused to search for the right word, one that wouldn't betray Mick's confidences—"*complicated* relationship with his family. I know a little bit about it, so he thought I'd be a good support system for him."

"He's right." Deidre beamed at her. "There's no one you can count on more than my baby sister."

Magda still looked skeptical. "I know Heather is a rock, but it still seems like a pretty relationshippy thing to do to me. Are you *sure* there's nothing romantic going on between you two?"

Heather held up her right hand, as if she were swearing an oath in court. "I swear to you, we are not involved romantically. There are some feelings between us, but we've decided to be friends, just friends. And this trip is just as friends, there is no hanky-panky happening. Mick told me he's getting two motel rooms for us."

****

Mick held his breath as he hit the last digit on his cell phone and waited for the ring. He'd carefully timed his call so his father and Danny would still be at work in the mine. He wanted to face them in person first, not over the phone.

"Hello?"

His mother's voice came through the phone. He loved his gentle mom, and hated the way her spirit was squashed over the years by his father's cold, domineering ways.

"Hi, Mom, it's me."

"Mickey! Oh my stars! It's wonderful to hear your voice! How are you? Have you moved yet? Where are you? Did you know Susan's wedding is this weekend? Are you going to be there?"

He laughed at her stream of questions and answered them in order, "I'm fine. I have moved, and I'm settling in here in Rivers Bend. Yes, I know about the wedding; it's why I'm calling."

His mom giggled. "Oh, you! My, it's good to hear your laugh. I'm so happy to have you in Virginia. It's not as good as home, but it's so much closer than Oregon. Do you like it there?"

"I like it very much. Rivers Bend is a nice little town, and everyone's been real welcoming. So, about Susie's wedding…"

"Don't worry; I'll break it to her gentle."

He frowned at the resigned disappointment in his mother's voice. "Break what to her? I'm just calling to see if it's all right if I bring someone with me to the wedding?"

"Oh thank heavens! I thought you were calling to say you couldn't make it. Of course you can bring someone."

"Thanks, Ma, I appreciate it; I know it's short notice."

"Who are you bringing?"

His mother's hopeful tone made him think maybe Heather was right about his family drawing the wrong conclusion about their status. He better set his mom straight right now. "I'm bringing a *friend*—Heather Braden."

"A girlfriend? This cannot get any better!"

"Not a girlfriend, Ma, just a friend. I wanted to check with you to see if the Dew Drop Inn was still open. I need to book us a couple of rooms for the weekend."

"At the Dew Drop? It's still open, but don't you even think about staying there! You and your girl will stay here at the house. We've got plenty of room; I won't hear of you staying at a motel. Folks would talk."

They had plenty of room? His family lived in a tiny house—his parents, three brothers, and his sister, who'd be getting ready for her wedding. They most certainly did *not* have room for Heather and him, but he recognized that tone in his mother's voice and knew she wouldn't be budged.

And, hoo boy, would his father would be several steps below thrilled about Mick staying there.

But he swallowed hard and lied like a rug, "Sounds good, Ma. We'll be there Friday in plenty of time for the rehearsal dinner."

Chapter 8

They flew along the highway with the convertible top down and the music cranking. Heather's ponytail danced in the air behind her. She laughed, and it sounded like pure joy to Mick. Unfortunately, he wasn't feeling quite so joyful.

She glanced over at him, and took one hand off the wheel to point at his feet. "Will you please stop working the invisible brake pedal? I'm an excellent driver; I've never been in an accident. Well, not a *serious* one."

"I feel so much better. Now, please put both hands on the wheel, preferably in the ten and two position," he shouted over the wind.

"Don't be such a stick-in-the-mud! It's a beautiful day; we're in a shiny new car. Just relax and let yourself enjoy it."

"I'm enjoying this high-speed trip to my gallows very much. What makes you think I'm not?"

"I can tell. The white knuckles are a dead giveaway, and would you try to grind your teeth a little more quietly? I can't hear the radio over the noise."

"Cute, but I find that hard to believe. I think they can hear our radio in Montana," he hollered over the blasting rock music pounding out of the speakers.

The perky, mechanical voice on the GPS notified them of an upcoming exit, and Heather checked the rearview mirror and moved from the left lane to the right. "Is this the exit to our motel?"

Mick fidgeted in his seat. "No, it's the exit to my family's house."

"Oh, okay. Are we stopping by there first, before we check in to our rooms?"

"Um…yeah…about the motel—we're not going to stay there after all."

"We're not? Where are we staying?"

She took the exit ramp and stopped at the sign at the bottom of it. Mick loosened his grip on the door and stretched his stiff fingers out, while he avoided her eyes and said, "We're going to crash with my family."

Luckily there were no cars behind them, as Heather didn't turn onto the street, but kept the car at a dead stop and turned in her seat to gape at him. "We're staying with *your family*?"

"Yep."

"In the same house with the father and brother you haven't seen in years? With the father you parted from under such angry conditions? We're staying at your family's house the weekend of your sister's wedding, which is bound to make for an already emotionally charged atmosphere?"

"One thing I've learned about you since we've been working together that I didn't know before—you have an amazing ability to take a complex problem and sum it up concisely."

A horn tooted behind them, and Heather jumped. She waved her apology to the driver waiting for them to move, and took a left turn onto a country road.

"You could've warned me."

He turned down the radio, since it was much

quieter without the wind caused by Heather's speeding on the highway. "I know, and I'm sorry. I've just been trying to keep my concerns about it in the back of my mind, or I wouldn't have been able to do my job this week."

She reached over and patted his thigh, a sensation that immediately shot a couple of inches higher and to the right. What was wrong with him? She was his friend first, and his employee second. There was no room for this inappropriate physical reaction to her.

She shot him a cheeky grin. "Everything will be fine. I'm good with parents."

He wished he shared her confidence, but no one was good with his father—least of all him.

****

Heather turned in at a mailbox painted like a cow and pulled the car up the driveway to a tidy, but humble, brick rancher. A rusty old muscle car sat on blocks in the front yard.

"This is it, Casa Evans," Mick tried to joke, but Heather heard the tightness in his voice, and the muscles in his jaw were working overtime, which she'd learned was a sure sign he was tense.

Trying to lighten the mood, she beeped the horn cheerfully.

"What are you doing?" Mick looked appalled.

"We always beep when we pull up to my family's farm."

"That's because your family is normal and are always happy to see you. This is a different situation."

The front door flew open and a petite woman in a T-shirt and jeans, with an apron tied around her waist ran out of the house. The lines etched on her face made her look older than Heather suspected she was, but her beaming smile lit her up from within.

"Looks like one person here is happy to see you. Is that your mom?"

A sappy grin softened Mick's harsh features. "Yep. That's my Ma."

The woman trotted toward the car, and Mick got out and ran to meet her. He picked her up in his arms and swung her around.

Heather surreptitiously wiped a tear from her eye as she got out and stretched her long legs. Mick so rarely let his emotions show, and his joy at the sight of his mother touched Heather deeply.

A tall, thin, pretty girl in a tank top and jeans appeared in the open front door. She held her hands over her mouth and then squealed. Loud.

Mick hugged his mother to his right side and held open his left arm, and the girl ran to the spot and hugged him around the waist.

"Look at you, Susie Q, all grown up and getting married."

A trio of large, young men, who all reminded Heather a lot of Mick when she first met him, came around the corner of the house from the backyard.

"What's all the ruckus?" the youngest looking one asked.

"Mickey's home!" their mother cried out. "Your brother Mickey's come home for Susan's wedding!"

"And in a sweet ride," one brother observed.

"And with an even sweeter traveling companion," the oldest one observed with a feral grin.

Heather glanced out of the corner of her eyes at Mick, who did not look pleased at the observation, but he kept his voice under control as always when he spoke. "Where are my manners? I forgot to introduce Heather to y'all. Mom, this is Heather Braden. Heather, this is my mom, Carol Evans, my sister, Susan, and my three brothers," he pointed to the oldest one first, "Danny, Billy, and Dave."

"Surprised you remembered our names," sniped Danny.

"Daniel," their mother warned. "You will not spoil your sister's wedding weekend with old grudges."

Billy touched Lola reverently and gaped at Mick. "Is this *your* car?"

Mick nodded. "Just bought her last weekend."

"I decided to call her Lola." Heather grinned.

Mrs. Evans laughed and clapped her hands together. "Like the showgirl in the song?"

Heather nodded, happy to find a kindred spirit, who got the joke. "Exactly!"

"Oh, I like her, Mick. She's fun!" His mother beamed.

"Lola or Heather?" Mick deadpanned.

"I bet Heather's plenty fun," Danny said sotto voce.

"You'll never know," Mick replied in a low rumble.

"Now boys," his mom implored, but she was interrupted by a man's voice from behind the three brothers.

"Well, well, well, look what the cat dragged in."

Heather looked around them to see a sour-looking older man. His face was weathered and scowling, but she could tell he must have been as handsome as his sons when he was a young man. Now, he just looked pissed.

Heather watched, as Mrs. Evans seemed to shrink before her eyes. Susan, Billy, and Dave also wilted under their father's glare. Only Danny puffed out his chest and drawled, "That's right, Dad, the prodigal son's returned."

The old man snorted. "Let's hope he's not looking for a fatted calf, 'cause he ain't gonna find one here."

Heather could see Mick winding up to retort, and she decided to diffuse the situation before he said something to totally ignite this tinder keg. She did it for two reasons: 1) she hated a bully, and Mr. Evans was most definitely one. And 2) Mick would regret it later, and she didn't want him to have to suffer any more regrets where his family was concerned. If there were a way to reconcile him with his father and Danny, she would try to help it along.

With that goal in mind, she pasted a bright smile on her face, and walked to the old grump with her hand extended. "Your boys all look just like you, so I know you must be Mr. Evans. I'm Mick's friend, Heather Braden, glad to meet you."

Her innate honesty cringed at the social lie. She couldn't bring herself to say she was *happy* to meet him, but she was *glad* to have the opportunity to see the man who so thoroughly drove his son away, and who played such a strong, albeit negative, role in forming the man Mick had become.

Mr. Evans frowned at her hand for a moment, and Heather feared Mick was right and she'd finally met the one parent she couldn't charm, when she realized confusion reined in Mr. Evan's eyes. He clearly didn't know what to make of her sunny greeting, in light of his calculatedly unpleasant entrance.

He finally extended his own hand, which Heather grasped and shook briskly.

"I'm Phil Evans."

"Y'all must be so excited about Susan's wedding tomorrow!"

"Exhausted is more like it," Dave griped with a good-natured grin. "We've spent the whole morning getting ready for the rehearsal dinner tonight. Martin's folks have retired and moved away, so Ma offered to have it out back."

"Can I help?" Mick offered.

His father and Danny snickered, before Danny answered with derision, "In *those* clothes, I don't think so."

"Always did want to be more than he was—with his fancy clothes and car." His father sneered.

Boy-oh-boy, no wonder Mick had run from this house and didn't stop until he got to the west coast and ran out of land in Oregon. Heather thought if she was in the same situation, she might have hopped in a boat and kept paddling until she hit Japan on the other side of the ocean.

Mick was dressed in khakis and a sky blue polo shirt, for Pete's sake; it's not like he showed up in an Armani tux. Oh man, she hoped he hadn't actually brought a tuxedo with him in his expensive leather garment bag. It would make things even more awkward, if he brought a tux to wear to the wedding.

Mick glanced down at his clothes and shrugged. "So, I'll change."

Heather was proud of his calm tone of voice in the face of such antagonism from his father and Danny.

She popped the trunk of the car with the key fob. "We'll get our stuff, and then we can both change and pitch in to help."

Mick's mother's eyes widened in panic as his father shouted, "What do you mean *get your stuff*? Aren't y'all staying down at the Dew Drop?"

Mick raised his eyebrows and grinned. "Must be your lucky day, Dad, because we're staying right here with you."

Billy and Dave hustled over to help with the luggage, and Carol pointedly avoided her husband's angry stare. She tucked her hand in Heather's arm, and Heather gave it an encouraging squeeze.

"Heather, we have a sleeper sofa in the basement family room for you."

"But you can keep your stuff in my room," Susan offered with a shy smile, as she took a tentative step toward her mother, who rewarded her act of support with a grateful smile.

"And you can bunk in with me, Mick," Billy offered with a nervous glance at his father, who stood by with his fists clenched and teeth grinding.

Heather cocked her head as she observed him. It was funny. For all their differences, Mick did the exact same thing with his jaw when he was tense. Somehow, she didn't think either man would be thrilled with her observation.

Chapter 9

Heather paused on her way back to the kitchen, after changing into jeans in Susan's bedroom. Photos of the Evans kids in various stages of development lined the walls of the narrow hallway. She smiled at one image of little Mick in his Peewee football uniform.

"We're in the kitchen, Heather," Carol Evans called.

She followed the sound of her voice and found Susan and Carol in an outdated, but homey and spotlessly clean, kitchen. They were cutting vegetables and slicing cheese, and arranging them on trays for the rehearsal dinner.

She peeked out through the red and white gingham curtains at the window, to the backyard. She expected to see the men hard at work, getting things ready for the party; instead she saw the yard empty of people, but full of tables and folded up chairs.

"Where are the guys?"

"They had to run out to do some errands. They needed something at the hardware store, and to get the wine and beer."

"Mick went too?" Heather couldn't keep the surprise from her voice.

Mrs. Evans glanced up as she sliced a red bell pepper. "Billy insisted on going to the hardware store in Lola, and Dave wanted to ride in her too. Phil and

Danny took the pickup to get the keg and the wine."

That made more sense to Heather. She couldn't imagine Mr. Evans, Danny, and Mick going out for a jaunt together, unless it was to the Thunderdome. Three men enter, one man leaves. Seriously, the tension between them was out of bounds, but the younger Evans brothers didn't seem to hold any grudge against Mick. In fact, they seemed to admire him—probably wondering if they'd be able to escape the mine and the oppressive atmosphere of this house like he had.

"Billy seemed really interested in Lola. Is he a car guy?"

Susan rolled her eyes. "He's a car *nut*! That hunk of rust on blocks in the yard is his; he swears he'll get it running someday."

"He will," Mrs. Evans said staunchly. "He's an excellent mechanic."

"Does he work at a garage?" Heather asked.

Mrs. Evans cheeks turned red, and she focused intently on her pepper, maybe to avoid looking at Heather. "No. He works at the mine with his dad and brother."

"Oh." Heather didn't know how to respond.

Susan grimaced. "Billy would love to work full-time as a mechanic, but Dad's a Nazi about all the boys working at the mine with him. Thank God, I'm a girl. Mick's the only one who's gotten away." She paused, and then added meaningfully, "So far."

"It's important to him they carry on the family tradition," Mrs. Evans half-heartedly defended her husband.

Susan's knife thumped as she drove it through the cheddar with more force than was necessary. "Let

Danny carry on the tradition. He wants to do it, but let Billy and Dave choose what they want to do with their lives."

An uneasy silence settled over the kitchen. Man, Mick was going to owe her for this weekend. Talk about tensionpalooza! Although, the messed up family dynamic did give her some insight into what made Mick tick.

She spotted an old radio on a shelf over the sink. "Do you mind if I put on some music while we work, Mrs. Evans? It'll make it more festive."

Mrs. Evans cast her a grateful smile. "Sounds good, dear, but please call me Carol."

Heather flicked a switch, and an upbeat country song filled the room. "Okay, what can I do to help?"

"You could grab the celery and slice it. There's a bowl with a cream cheese and pineapple mixture in the fridge; cut the celery into little boats and fill them with it."

"Sounds yummy." Heather grabbed the celery and rinsed it in the sink. She began to sing along with the song on the radio, and Susan joined in as she worked.

Carol smiled shyly at Heather, before softly singing along with the girls.

****

The rest of the family was at the church for the rehearsal, but Mick and Heather stayed behind to finish setting up for the party.

Mick smiled as Heather danced out of the kitchen door, a tray of cheese and crackers in her hands. He'd hooked up the stereo to speakers they'd brought outside, so music filled the warm, spring air. It was a party song about drinking beer, and girls dancing on the beds of pick-up trucks, so of course his girl Heather knew all the words. Hold on, Evans—what was he thinking? Heather wasn't his girl. She was just helping him out this weekend.

But she sure was great with his family. She maintained her sunny disposition, even with his ill-tempered father, and she really helped to lighten up the atmosphere. She'd proved herself to be a good friend to him—maybe the best one he'd ever had.

She stopped at the long table, which was set up for the buffet, and leaned over to fuss with the arrangement of the platter. His attention was riveted to her fabulous ass, as she swayed her hips along to the music. He'd rather take a bite out of it than any of the appetizers on the tray. *Friend, dumbass, she's your best friend.*

"Were you staring at my ass? Did I get something on my skirt?" Heather turned around, but she swiped at her behind and craned her neck to try to get a look at it.

He grinned ruefully. "I *was* staring at your ass, but not because there's anything on it. You just look really good in that denim skirt."

She rolled her eyes, but flushed with pleasure, so Mick didn't think he was in too much trouble for ogling her.

"You've been a real trooper today. I owe you big-time. To pay you back, I was thinking next weekend we can go up to Frederick, and I'll treat you to dinner at that celebrity chef's restaurant there. I've heard it's really good."

She crossed her arms under her breasts, which only served to draw his attention from her ass up to them. They were lovely breasts, not too big or too small. They were just right.

"Are you looking at my boobs now? First you stare at my ass; then my boobs, and now you want to take me on a dinner date to a fancy restaurant? What's going on here?"

"Damned if I know," Mick admitted.

A slow song came on, and he held out his hand. "Dance with me."

She swatted at it. "What? No! Everyone will be back in a few minutes, and we don't have all the food out yet."

Shot down.

Huh.

It didn't happen to him too often, but he could always count on Heather to surprise him.

He followed her into the kitchen. "Tomorrow then, at the wedding, we dance."

She glanced over her shoulder, and he saw confusion and pleasure at war in her expression.

"Okay, you've got my I.O.U. for a dance at the reception tomorrow." She shoved a bowl of onion dip at him. "Now bring this out and put it on the table with the chips."

****

Heather tossed and turned on the thin mattress of the torture device that was the Evans' sleeper sofa.

She tossed back the blanket. You'd think it would be cooler in the basement family room, but with no windows to open, it felt still and warm.

She heaved an exasperated sigh. Maybe it was just thoughts of Mick that had her feeling toasty. He'd stuck by her side all night; oh-so-casually touching her while they talked to people, putting his big hand on the small of her back when they walked somewhere.

And who knew the small of your back was such an erogenous zone? It had never done anything for Heather before. Maybe because it had never been Mick's big, warm hand doing the touching.

What was with him tonight? They were supposed to be friends, right? Well, Bethanne and she were friends, but she'd never seen Bethanne ogle her ass before. Magda and she were friends, but Magda had never looked at her with bedroom eyes and commanded her to 'dance with me.'

As if her thoughts had summoned him, she heard the basement door open, and saw Mick silhouetted in the dim glow of the kitchen nightlight at the top of the stairs.

He clumped down them and whispered, "Heather? Are you awake?"

She giggled. "Who could sleep through the ruckus of you thumping down those stairs? I thought Bigfoot was coming to get me."

He chuckled and perched on the edge of her bed. "Don't be silly. Bigfoot? In West Virginia it's far more likely to be Mothman."

She laughed, but it was a little breathless as she took in the wonder that was Mick Evans without a shirt. His chest wasn't ripped like it had been in his playing days, but it was still broad and muscular, with a light smattering of brown hair. The athletic shorts were slung low on his hips, and her eyes followed that brown hair down its happy trail. She licked her lips.

"Heather," his voice was rough. "We're in my parents' basement, for the love of God. Stop looking at me like that."

As his hungry eyes raked over her, Heather became

very aware of her tiny sleep shorts and thin cami top, which she was sure revealed all too clearly, her breasts' traitorous reaction to his presence in her bed.

Why hadn't she packed a flannel nightgown, or better yet—a suit of armor? Yeah, *that* might have provided some protection from the desire on Mick's face as he looked at her and groaned softly.

"Maybe I shouldn't have come down here, but I couldn't sleep. I swear the cot is ninety years old and stuffed with rocks."

He bounced twice on her bed. "This isn't any better, sorry."

"It's fine." Heather knew she had to change the subject from their respective beds, or else she was going to drag him down to test the springs on hers. "I wonder if Susan's getting any sleep, or if she's too nervous?"

"Her room was quiet, when I walked by on my way here."

"They're a good team, Martin and Susan. I think they'll be happy together."

"He seems like a good guy." He paused and grinned at her. "Almost good enough for my baby sister."

"She must've been just a little kid when you left home."

"She was the cutest little thing. The only girl, we all spoiled her something rotten."

She smiled at him. "It's nice how you've managed to stay so close to her."

He nodded. "I have, and with my mom, Billy, and Dave too. Everyone except my dad and Danny."

That killed the simmering sexual tension between

them as effectively as a bucket of ice water.

"I'm sorry it's been so strained. Your father's a hard man."

"And Danny's his clone. They're both still angry with me for taking the football scholarship and going to college."

Heather plumped up her pillow behind her and leaned back. She crossed her legs at her ankles. "It's so different from when Jeff went to college. Mom was over the moon when he got his full ride to Alabama. It would've been a real struggle for her to put him through school without some help, and it was obvious raising horses wasn't his thing the way it is Jason's."

Of course, her own college scholarship was also the source of her lone serious disagreement with her mother, but tonight wasn't the time to get into her sad story.

Mick stuck the other pillow next to hers and reclined against it. When he stretched his long legs out on the bed, she saw the wicked-looking scar on his knee—the result of the surgery following his terrible injury. She fought back the urge to crawl over and press her lips to it. *Yeah, right, they were friends...no sexual feelings here, no sirree.*

"It was my ticket out. Without football—without my scholarship—going to any college would never have been an option for me, let alone going to Stanford. I don't just mean the money. My father was furious I wanted to learn something, to *be* something. He took it as a personal insult. Evans men have lived in this town and worked in the mine for generations," he imitated his father's gruff voice. "If it was good enough for all those men who came before you, why isn't it good enough for you, boy? You sayin' you're better than us?"

Heather's jaw dropped. "He actually said that to you?"

He grasped the sheet in his fist and crumpled it. "He did. I don't have anything against his choices, or Danny's either, but they weren't mine. And I don't think they're Billy or Dave's either."

"No, you're right, they're not. Billy would love to be a mechanic; he's even gotten his certification. Dave confided in me he was offered a baseball scholarship to West Virginia University. I told him my nephew Craig is going there too. I invited him down to visit, so they could meet up before they go. It's always nice to have a built-in friend at a new place, right?"

He nodded in agreement, but one side of his mouth quirked up. "You've certainly won over the Evans men."

"Some of them, your dad acts like he doesn't know what to make of me, and I think Danny just sees a pair of boobs on legs when he looks at me."

"A luscious pair of boobs, on a world-class set of legs. Danny can be a huge jerk, but on this matter I can't entirely blame the man."

"Oh you sweet talker!" Heather felt her cheeks heat up and leaned forward to pull the sheet up over her body.

Mick leaned too, to still her hand. "Don't cover up on my account. I'm sorry I teased you. I think you're really beautiful."

Heather's heart pounded at his words, and at the heat and sincerity in his tone. His hand still covered hers on the blanket, and it burned into her skin.

"Mick," she whispered, "friends don't talk to each other that way, and they most certainly don't *look* at each other the way you're looking at me right now."

He ran the back of his hand up her bare arm, and responded in a low voice that sent shivers up her spine. "Then maybe, just for the weekend, we can pretend we're not friends."

His hand reached her shoulder and continued on, skimming over the sensitive skin on her neck until he cupped her face in his big hand. She shut her eyes and leaned into his touch. "Do you think that's a good idea?"

He brushed a feather light kiss to her temple. "Right about now, I think it's an idea that has definite merit."

She tilted her face up to his, and he closed the small distance between them to kiss her. Once.

Twice.

Three times, very lightly on her lips.

His lips were firm and warm, but Heather wanted more. Hell, she needed more. She turned to press her body against his and was very aware the thin cotton of her cami was all separating them from being skin to skin. Her breasts peaked against his broad chest, and when he groaned low in his throat, she knew he felt it too—this irresistible, electric pull between them.

He pulled her on top of him and deepened their kiss. He kept one hand buried in her hair, while the other roamed freely across her body.

She put her hands on his shoulders, and then slid them down to his chest. His skin felt like silk, but silk stretched taut over the iron of his muscles.

Her hands decided to take a southerly tour of the

wonderland of his body.

Upstairs a toilet flushed and the water whooshed through the pipes to the basement. The sudden sound made them both freeze in place, as they came to their combined senses and remembered where they were.

"Someone else is awake, you'd better get back upstairs," she whispered.

His eyes widened in disbelief. "What! Why?"

"Because they might realize you're down here with me in my bed, and I don't want your family to think I'm a hussy."

"A hussy?" He grinned, and kissed her teasingly. "Honey, we traveled to West Virginia, not back in time."

She tried to suppress her smile; it was best not to encourage him. "Hussy. Ho. Call it whatever you want, but get yourself upstairs and into your own bed. Now."

She rolled off him, and pulled the covers up to her chin.

He heaved a sigh and rose from the bed. "You're a hard-hearted woman, Heather Braden."

She grinned at his back as he walked up the stairs.

He whispered over his shoulder, "Don't forget you promised me a slow dance tomorrow."

"I promised you a dance. I didn't say anything about a *slow* dance."

He chuckled before he shut the door behind him, leaving her alone and even more hot and bothered than she'd been before his little visit.

She threw the covers off and flopped down on the bed.

It would be all right. I mean how much trouble could they get into during one, little, tiny, slow dance?

Chapter 10

Heather breathed a sigh of relief when the song ended. Dave had led her around the dance floor with much more enthusiasm than grace. Between a workout to rival a Zumba class and the unusually warm spring weather she was about to sweat through her turquoise silk wrap dress.

"I'm going to get a Dr. Pepper. Can I get you anything from the bar?" Dave offered like an eager puppy.

As the next song started, she saw Mick spin by with the radiant bride beaming up at him like he'd hung the moon.

"No thanks, Dave. I'm going to head outside to cool off a bit." She fanned her face, which she feared was as red as a tomato.

She'd been to a million weddings like this one back in Rivers Bend. The ceremony had been at a sweet, little white church, and the reception was here at the local VFW Hall.

She stepped out of the building and squinted into the afternoon sun, which seemed especially bright after being in the windowless hall.

The acrid smell of cigarette smoke stung her sinuses, and she scrunched up her nose and looked to the left, where Danny was leaning against the building, having a smoke.

"Hey, Heather. Finally wise up and decide to run away from my brother?"

"Nope, I just came out for a breath of fresh air." She stared pointedly at his cigarette as she said it.

He took one last drag, and flicked the butt onto the gravel parking lot with his thumb and forefinger.

"Thank you."

"No problem, but no need to sound so surprised. I don't know how Mick treats you, but I always respect a lady's wishes."

She knew he was trying to get under her skin, but she still bristled at the criticism of Mick. "Don't you ever get tired of picking on Mick?"

"No, ma'am."

"That's too bad, because I'm tired of hearing it."

"I don't reckon we'll see each other again after tomorrow, so you won't have to suffer through it much longer."

"I don't know about that, I think now the ice is broken, you'll be seeing more of Mick."

"Mebbe. But will *you* be with him?"

"I might be. We're good friends." Her chin jutted out, and she hated she'd fallen into Danny's trap, and knew she sounded every bit as defensive as she felt.

He pursed his lips, braced one foot on the concrete wall behind him, and looked out to the road. "I saw him coming up from your bedroom last night; I'd say you two are a lot more than *good friends*. But the truth of the matter is you're just a farm girl from Virginia."

She put her hands on her hips. "And what's wrong with that? You don't think I'm good enough for your brother?"

"You've got the wrong end of the stick, Heather. I

like you just fine. What I think is my brother isn't good enough to polish those pretty high-heeled shoes you got on."

She wrinkled her nose and looked down at her shoes; then back up at him. "Thank you…I think. If you feel that way about me, what's with the farm girl crack?"

"Think about it. If Mick thinks he's too good for his West Virginia mining family, is he likely to settle down with a good ole girl from a horse farm south of the Mason-Dixon line? I don't think so."

"First of all, Mick does *not* think he's too good for you."

Danny snorted. "That's your opinion. I don't happen to agree with it."

She continued on as if he hadn't spoken. "And he most certainly doesn't think he's better than me."

"Oh yeah? He ever take you out in public? Or does he just say you're his 'friend.' " He made air quotes around the last word. "And then sneak into your bed when he thinks no one is watching?"

"He brought me here to a family wedding. I think that proves he's not ashamed of me."

"So what? He brought you to see the family; he doesn't want anywhere near his shiny, new life. Face it, we're both cockroaches to his high and mightiness."

"That's just not true."

"Has he ever taken you to one of those fancy charity shindigs he goes to?"

"Well…no…but…"

"The way I see it," he interrupted her stammering response, "And I'm just being honest here, so excuse my language, you're good enough for him to fuck, but not good enough for the snooty image he puts out there. I bet he's got some fancy woman he takes out in public, while he keeps you in bed, or with his lower-than-dirt family."

She thought about Gloria Peterson, and his lunches at the Nosh Pit with the socialite. He never took her anywhere. But he did take her here to his sister's wedding. Mick trusted her to help him navigate the stormy seas of this family visit, but why didn't he ever take her out in Rivers Bend? Even just out for a pizza as friends? Could Danny possibly be right? Her heart raced at the unpleasant thought that rude and boorish as he might be, there was a chance Danny was on to something here.

Before she could pull herself together and formulate a response, Danny looked over her shoulder and smiled sardonically. "Were your ears burning, Mick? We were just talking about you."

"My ears are just fine, thank you for your concern. I was looking for Heather, and Dave told me she was out here."

"Here I am," she chirped, and tried to push Danny's ugly insinuations out of her head as she smiled at Mick.

He returned her smile with a hint of heat in his eyes. "Heather owes me a dance, and I wanted to claim it."

"She's all yours." Danny pushed off the wall and swaggered past them into the building. "She's a damn fine woman, I hope you appreciate what you've got."

Mick frowned after him. "Was he bothering you?"

Heather saw no point in telling Mick what Danny had said to her. It would only get him all fired up, and she didn't want to be the cause of a brawl between brothers that would ruin Susan's wedding. She shrugged. "He was out here for a smoke, and I came out to cool off some. It's really hot in there."

His eyes raked over her body, and she felt the look like it was a physical touch.

"You still look hot to me."

She chose to ignore his double-entendre. "I'm much cooler now, so I'm ready for our dance."

"Are you okay? You seem a little off. I know he's not my biggest fan, but it's no excuse for Danny being rude to you."

"He wasn't rude, not about *me* anyway. He said he liked me; he thinks I'm too good for you."

He laughed shortly and without humor. "He isn't wrong."

She held her hand up to her heart. "What? You and Danny agreeing on something? Is the world ending? Because I'm fairly certain it's one of the signs of impending apocalypse."

He smiled at her joke, and crooked his arm at her. "Shall we have our dance now?"

She tucked her hand in his elbow. "Let's dance."

They entered the hall, just as the DJ queued up a slow, romantic song. The groom swept the bride onto the dance floor, and Mick followed suit with Heather.

She caught a glimpse of Danny, slumped on a barstool. He lifted his beer to her in a silent toast; a mocking smile twisted his lips.

Mick pulled her tight against his body, and slid his hands down her silk dress to rest on her lower back, with his fingertips just barely brushing the top of her butt.

He had to lean down just a bit, and rested his cheek against hers. "I love how tall you are. Most girls make me feel like a giant when we dance," he whispered.

"I know what you mean. It's nice to dance with someone taller than me. Once I put on heels, I tower over most guys."

She wrapped her arms around him, as they swayed in time to the music. Mick had taken off his suit jacket, and he wore a white dress shirt, with his tie loosened at the neck. She felt his body heat warm her fingers through the crisp, cotton shirt. The strong muscles of his back bunched as he danced, and Heather felt as though they were the only two people in the room.

She didn't think she'd ever wanted a man this much in her life, and based on the hard-all-over body pressed against her, the feeling was mutual.

"...darling, you look wonderful tonight," he sang softly along with the song, as he nudged a strong thigh between her legs.

Heather ran her hands across his back, and moved one up to the nape of his neck, which was smooth, and just a little bit sweaty in the hot room.

A click and a bright flash jolted them out of their reverie.

"What the hell?" Mick growled.

"Got it!" The wedding photographer announced cheerfully. "The bride specifically asked for a shot of y'all together. She's going to love this one! Keep me in mind for your wedding. Susan can give you my contact info."

"Thanks, but we're not even dating, let alone engaged," Heather said.

"Riiight..." The photographer winked and moved

away to capture the groom's parents, as they boogied to the disco song that started after the slow song ended.

Mick put his hand on the small of her back, and guided her off the crowded dance floor. "What made him think we were engaged?"

She shrugged. "Danny thinks we're sleeping together. He saw you coming upstairs last night from my room, and jumped to the obvious conclusion."

"Crap! I'm sorry, Heather."

"It's none of his business; I didn't even bother trying to set him straight. I just brought it up to say— first Danny, and now the photographer. We seem to be sending some kind of sexual, couple vibe out to the universe."

The muscles in Mick's jaw clenched, and his voice was terse. "Then tonight, I'll stay in my own room all night. I don't want to give Danny any more ammunition."

"If you want to talk to me, you can come down, but if you think it will cause weirdness, then don't. Your family, your call."

They stood in silence for a moment, and then a hopeful gleam lit his eyes. "Are you sure I don't need to kick Danny's ass?"

"No, and certainly not at your only sister's wedding."

"Fine. Be all reasonable, you killjoy."

"You're not fooling me. You don't really want to kick your brother's ass."

He raised one eyebrow. "I don't?" He playfully kicked out one of his feet. "Then you better tell my ass-kickin' foot, because it's ready to go."

She smothered a laugh and swatted his arm. "Stop

it!"

Mrs. Evans bustled over, looking pretty, and a little less weary than usual, in her beige mother-of-the-bride suit. She grabbed Heather's hand. "C'mon, Heather, Susan's getting ready to toss the bouquet!"

Heather dug in her heels. "Oh, no!"

"Oh, yes," Mrs. Evens replied and dragged her front and center, before abandoning her to the pack of rowdy, single women jostling for position on the dance floor.

Heather cast an imploring look Mick's way, but the big lug just grinned and shrugged.

As Susan wound up and threw the lovely bouquet of pink and white roses, Heather kept her arms glued to her sides, as the rest of the woman jostled each other and waved their arms in the air.

The bouquet flew toward Heather like it had a homing device implanted in the satin ribbon, but she didn't move her arms, and it landed with a muffled thump at her feet.

She heard Mick's loud burst of laughter, as Susan cried out.

"Heather! You didn't even try to catch it! But the bouquet picked you anyway."

The bride walked over, picked up the flowers, and pressed them against Heather's chest. She had no choice but to reach up to hold the fragrant burden.

"Face it, Heather, the flowers have spoken. You are definitely going to be the next one to be married, and I couldn't be happier. I've always wanted a sister!" Susan enthused.

Mick's laughter stopped as suddenly as it had started.

Chapter 11

Post-wedding letdown made Sunday breakfast at the Evans house a gloomy affair. Everyone missed Susan's cheerful presence. Mrs. Evans snuffled as she fried the bacon; Dave and Billy tried to lighten the mood with some good-natured brotherly teasing, but their efforts fell flat. While Danny and Mr. Evans glowered at Mick, who gave back glower just as good as he was getting.

Heather sat between the warring factions and frowned at the centerpiece. The bouquet pressed upon her after the toss sat in a vase in the middle of the kitchen table. True to his word, Mick stayed out of her bedroom last night, but it didn't seem to matter. His whole family had them married off anyway.

She couldn't stand just sitting here in the middle of this angry staring contest. "Are you sure I can't do anything to help, Carol? I make a mean piece of toast."

Carol smiled over her shoulder. "You're such a sweet, helpful girl, but no thanks. I've got cooking breakfast for my boys down to a science."

"You're a good kid," Mr. Evans observed, as he continued to glare at Mick. "I bet you never did anything to go against your parents' wishes, or to break your mama's heart."

"Don't go to Vegas with that bet, Mr. Evans, you'd lose the house."

Everyone gaped at her in shock, including Mick.

"I don't believe it for a minute—you're a doll!" Carol exclaimed.

Heather smiled at her. "Thanks, but it's the truth. My dad passed away when I was just a kid, so he and I never fought. But there was a time, right after high school, when my mom and I had such a big argument about me going against her wishes we didn't speak to each other for a good long while."

She looked at Mick and saw it in his eyes as he realized it was during the time they'd known each other.

"I never knew about this," Mick said. "That would've been when you were living in Portland."

She blinked and looked down at her hands, which were busy shredding the paper napkin at her place setting. Telling Mick about this time in front of his whole family was not what she wanted. Why had she brought it up?

Oh yeah. It was in a misguided attempt to divert Mr. Evans from his angry sniping at Mick. Damn her protective instinct! Mick was a big boy, he could take care of himself, but she hated seeing the hurt in his eyes, even as he stared down his father across the breakfast table.

She cleared her throat and finally spoke. "Me living in Portland was at the root of our argument."

"She didn't want you living so far from home? I can understand, it would tear me up if Susan moved across the whole country. I miss her like anything already and she's just moving across town," Carol said as she added more bacon to the frying pan.

"It wasn't the distance, so much as *what* I was

doing there."

Mick furrowed his brow. "You were helping your brother care for his baby daughter after his wife died. I can't believe Joyce objected to what you were doing!"

"Oh, how sad," Carol said.

There were a lot of circumstances around her late sister-in-law's death Heather had no intention of sharing with the Evans family. Mick was there, and he knew the truth, but no one else here needed to know, so she didn't reply directly to Carol's statement. It *was* a sad situation, but not for the reasons Carol meant.

"My sister-in-law died in a car accident when my niece, Samantha, was just a baby. Jeff was in his first season with the Pintos, and all alone in Portland with Sam. They needed someone to help them. My mom had the farm to run, and my older sister was married with kids of her own, so I went." Heather shrugged as if it were no big deal.

"Still not seeing why this caused such a huge rift between Joyce and you," Mick said. "Jeff couldn't leave Portland, and you'd just graduated from high school, so you were the obvious choice to help."

"That's how I felt," Heather said with a small, sad smile. "But in order to go to Portland, I put off going to college."

"But you took classes at the community college—I remember."

"It wasn't the same to my mom. To me either, really, but Jeff and Sam needed me. You see, I had a full scholarship to M.I.T. I turned it down to go to Portland to take care of Sam."

Mick's eyes bugged out of his head. "M.I.T.? *The* M.I.T.? The Massachusetts Institute of Technology?"

Heather stared at the remnants of her napkin. "Yep. Do you know another one?"

"No. Wow. That's just…wow."

Heather felt the corners of her lips tilt up at the sight of Mick's dropped jaw. "Your blatant shock at the news I could get into M.I.T. is kind of insulting, Mick."

"I'm sure he doesn't mean anything by it," Carol said in a soothing tone.

"Your brother shoulda moved back to Virginia with his baby girl," Mr. Evans grumbled.

"And pass up playing in the NFL?" Billy asked with a snort.

"Yes!" Mr. Evans slammed his fist on the table, so hard the silverware rattled. "It's just a damn game! Family should always come first."

"Just a game that pays a whole, heck of a lot of money if you're good at it, and Jeff was the best. That game allowed him to provide for his daughter in a way he never could have if he'd stayed in Rivers Bend. Our mom didn't expect him to move home, she just didn't want me to give up my scholarship to go to Portland. She wanted Jeff to hire a full-time nanny to watch Sam, or to send Sam back to Rivers Bend and my mom would take care of her, but he couldn't stand to be separated from his little girl. So I went, but my mom didn't like it one little bit, and she was angry at both Jeff and me for a long time."

"She was right," Mick said. "You shouldn't have had to sacrifice your future for Jeff."

"Heather understands how important family is— get off her ass!" Danny snapped.

"Language," Carol warned.

Danny hung his head and muttered, "Sorry, Ma."

"Sam was just a little baby, Mick, you were there, you remember, and she'd lost her mother." *For whatever her mother was worth*, Heather added silently before continuing, "A nanny would've been okay, if there was no choice, but I *wanted* to be there for her, to surround her with love. Sure, I gave something up, but I got *so* much more in return. And when I see what a great kid Sam's turned into, I don't have any regrets."

"Because you honored your family obligations, unlike my no-good son," Mr. Evans said.

Okay, this plan had backfired, and enabled Mr. Evans to turn it back around to ragging on Mick. She shut her eyes and took a deep breath. "You sure I can't make some toast, Carol?"

****

Mick lifted his index finger off the steering wheel to point at the sign for Braden Farm. "I bet you want to make a quick stop there to thank your family for not being insane."

She rolled her eyes. "Your family is *not* insane."

"After spending the weekend up close and personal with the Evans Clan, how can you say so with a straight face?"

"Because they're not. Your dad and Danny are difficult…"

He cut her off with a derisive snort. "That's putting it mildly."

She went on as if he hadn't interrupted, "But everyone else is great. Your mom and Susan are sweethearts, and Dave and Billy are a lot of fun. No family is perfect."

He glanced at her, then turned back to watch the road. "Not even yours? Because from where I stand, y'all look pretty damned Norman Rockwell-ish."

"Is that an insult?"

"No way. I have total Braden envy."

"I did get pretty lucky in the family lottery, but we all have our quirks and flaws. And while your father might be a serious crick in the ass," she paused and snuffled. "At least you still have him. And while you do, there's always a chance for you two to reconnect; I don't think you should take it for granted."

He reached across the console to take her hand. "I'm sorry, Heather, I wasn't thinking about the fact you've lost your father. I was being insensitive."

"It's okay. Can I just give you a piece of free advice?"

He signaled and turned Lola onto Main Street, which was deserted on a Sunday evening. "Sure."

"Don't lose touch with your family again. Grit your teeth and bear it when you're with your dad and Danny, and enjoy your time with everyone else. You never know when any of them will be gone. And once they are, you can't get the time back."

He eased into a spot in front of the Nosh Pit, which was closed all day on Sunday.

She turned in her seat to face him. "I'm sorry. I didn't mean to get all preachy on you, it's just family is important to me. When my dad died, it brought all of us closer together. I've read death can drive some families apart, but it didn't work that way with us. We all pulled together to look out for each other. It's a great support system; we all know we'll never be alone. And I want the same thing for you too."

He cleared his throat, and when he spoke, his voice was thick. "But I am *always* alone. The original lone wolf, that's me. I'm used to it."

She squeezed his hand. "If you're happy living your life alone, it's all good. But if you're not, don't turn away people who care about you. You've got family and friends; you don't have to be alone."

He looked deep into her eyes, and she felt it burn all the way down to her toes. She shivered, even though the night was warm. She felt feverish, hot and cold at the same time.

Desire sparked in his whiskey colored eyes. His voice was deep as he asked, "How about tonight? Do I have to be alone tonight?"

Chapter 12

"No," she whispered.

He cupped her cheek with one big hand; she leaned into the touch ever so slightly.

"Are you sure?"

"Yes."

He smiled. "No and yes, is that all you're going to say?"

"Maybe." She tried to keep her face serious, but couldn't hold back a small smile.

He chuckled. "For the record, 'yes' works for me, but if your answer is 'no,' or even 'maybe,' I'll respect those too. I can just take your bags upstairs and then be on my way."

"No."

His face dropped as he released her face, and reached for the door handle. "Okay, I understand."

She reached across the center console to still his hand. "That's not what I meant. I'd like you to come up, I only meant I can carry my own bags." She blushed and continued. "If you're going to stay over, you'll need your bags too, and there's no need to load you up like a pack mule. I don't want you to get worn out before we even get to my apartment."

He let out the breath he hadn't even realized he was holding. After a weekend of tension with his family, and essentially foreplay with Heather, he had not been looking forward to spending the night on his own in his cabin, with its big, cold, lonely bed.

He grinned at her. "So, you don't want me worn out—got big plans for me, huh?"

She grinned back as she unbuckled her seat belt. "You better believe it!"

****

Mick followed Heather up the stairs to her apartment over the Nosh Pit. He was already a big man, but lugging all of their bags up this narrow stairwell, he was worried he'd get wedged in, and they'd have to call the Rivers Bend Volunteer Fire Department to pry him out. It would be a real mood killer.

He heard the jangle of Heather's keys as she unlocked the door and threw it open with a flourish.

"Ta da! Be it ever so humble…"

Mick followed her into the apartment. "Where do you want the bags?"

"Just dump them anywhere; we can worry about them later."

Was she as anxious—okay, forget anxious and call it what it really was—was she as *hot* for him as he was for her? Her loud stomach rumble put that question out of his head.

"I'm sorry I didn't stop for lunch, I was just enjoying driving Lola on the open road so much," he said with a frown.

The fresh air from having the top down, and the loud music Heather had cranked up on the amazing sound system, had done a good job of blasting away memories of his father and Danny's disdain for him; however, he hadn't thought Heather might want food. He felt like a selfish jerk.

"No problem. I was having fun too; I didn't think about it until my tummy reminded me just now."

"But it's Rivers Bend on a Sunday night, where are we going to get food? The mini-mart at the gas station is the only place open. How about a hot dog and a slushie? Tell you what, since I clearly know how to treat a lady, I'll go wild and even get you the nachos, with the scary mystery cheese matter on them."

Heather held up her index finger and spoke as she walked into her little kitchen. "Hold on, we might not have to resort to mystery cheese. If I know my sister, Deidre…" She opened the fridge door, peered inside it, and crowed triumphantly. "And I do! We've got leftovers from the Nosh Pit!"

Mick squeezed between the old school shiny aluminum and red kitchen table to peek over her shoulder at containers and wrapped up sandwiches.

"She knew I'd be getting in too late to get food, and she knows me well enough to know I don't have anything to cook here. She gave me some coleslaw, potato salad, and sandwiches left over from Saturday service at the Nosh Pit."

"Bless her," Mick's response was heartfelt, as talking about food made him realize he was hungry for more than just Heather.

She held up a sandwich in each hand and read the writing on the paper wrapped around them. "We've got Virginia ham and cheddar, and turkey with Havarti. Do you want to split them so we each get some of both?"

His stomach grumbled this time, and Heather laughed. "I'll take that as a yes." She gestured with her head. "Plates are in that cupboard. Would you please grab a couple for us?"

"Sure." He grabbed two dishes and set them on the table with a clatter.

"What do you want to drink? I've got beer, wine." She pointed through the pass-through between the kitchen and the living room with the hand holding a tub of potato salad. "Or if you want, I'm quite the mixologist, I can whip up a cocktail. Right now, I'm trying to perfect a frozen mint julep for my mom's annual Kentucky Derby party. Want to be my guinea pig?"

"Maybe later. Did I see diet cola in your fridge?"

"You did. I'll get it for us, and you divide up the sammies."

He peered into the living room through the pass-through, and saw a vintage tiki-style bamboo bar. "I love the way you've decorated this place."

She looked over her shoulder as she opened the freezer door to get ice for their sodas, which she plunked into their glasses. "Are you being sarcastic?"

"No, why would you think I was?" Mick took a sip of the cola she handed him and looked at her over the top of the glass.

"Because everything in here came from yard sales and my mom's attic, and you strike me as more of a professional interior decorator kind of guy."

He shrugged. "I used a decorator for my place in Portland, because I had no idea how to do it, but I like what you've done here. It's funky and eclectic; it's you."

She bit her lower lip, and peered at him, as if still trying to decide whether or not he was picking on her. "Thanks."

They sat next to each other at the table and dug into

their impromptu dinner.

Mick closed his eyes his bliss as he took his first bite. "Mmm...this was so thoughtful of your sister. Still want to tell me your family isn't perfect?"

She rolled her eyes as she chewed, and swallowed hastily. "They're great—I give you that—and since we became adults we all get along really well, but we're not perfect. Jeez Louise, didn't you listen to a word I said in the car?"

He put his sandwich back on the plate, and took her free hand. "I did, Heather, I'm sorry if you thought I didn't listen. You shared something real and personal, and I get it. I do. You inspired me, and I'm going to try to get along better with my dad and Danny."

"Good." She smiled at him and turned her hand in his, so their fingers intertwined. "I'm glad. It won't be easy, but this way even if they don't come around, at least you'll know *you* did everything you could."

He rubbed his thumb against her palm and felt her shiver at the touch. He lifted their joined hands and pressed a kiss to the spot his thumb caressed.

She licked her lips, and suddenly he was hungry for something other than the sandwich. He leaned toward her and kissed her lips; he felt her grip tighten on his, as she returned his kiss with fervor.

He whispered against her soft lips, "Want to finish dinner later?"

She nodded and peeked at him through her lashes, with uncharacteristic shyness, which made him worry she'd changed her mind.

"Are you sure, Heather? If you don't want to, I'll understand. There are clearly issues. I'm still your boss, we've got a complicated history together..."

She cut him off with a kiss. "Can't we worry about all that stuff later?"

A slow smile curled up the corners of his mouth. "Sounds good to me." He ran his knuckles along her cheek. "I've wanted this, wanted *you*, since the first time I saw you eleven years ago."

She rubbed her face against his hand, and then surprised him when her pink tongue darted out to lick his finger. "Me too, and I'm not a patient woman. I've never waited for anything this long in my life. We can figure all the other stuff out tomorrow."

She stood and tugged him up with her.

He scooped her up into his arms and carried her out of the kitchen. She kissed him at the sensitive juncture where his neck met his shoulder. Had she remembered how it made him wild after all these years? "Okay, I've never been in your apartment before. Which way do I go?"

She laughed and twined her arms around his neck. "I love how you're strong enough to carry me around like I was a petite, little thing like Magda."

He smiled. "Glad my brute strength and size is finally good for something besides football. Now…bedroom?"

"Last room on the right."

He strode down the hall with purpose to Heather's bedroom, and when they entered it, he wasn't surprised to see how messy it was. Working with Heather had taught him she was super-efficient, but her office always looked like a tornado had just swept through it. Her bedroom was much the same.

He placed her carefully on the unmade bed and bent down to kiss her. She reached up and pulled him down on top of her. They both laughed as the bed bounced, and creaked ominously. Mick looked at it for the first time. It was clearly old enough to qualify as an antique, but not fancy. Someone had painted it white, with purple flowers painted on the headboard. Mick didn't know diddily about flowers—were they heather, like her name? He wondered if Heather had painted it herself.

"This bed wasn't made for a man my size; I hope I don't break it."

"I've had this bed forever. It's sturdier than it looks." She blushed. "Let me rephrase that, because it made me sound a little slutty."

He chuckled. "I don't think you're slutty." He punctuated his next words with kisses to her forehead, nose, and finally her lips. "I think you're amazing, smart, funny, and sexy as hell."

As he stretched out next to her, the bedsprings complained...loudly. Heather giggled.

"Are you sure this thing is going to hold up?"

"Only one way to find out." She kissed his neck, and pulled his shirttails out of his pants.

After eleven years of unfulfilled desire for each other, neither was in the mood to go slow. They undressed in a frenzy. Clothes flew all over the room, and they never stopped kissing each other, touching each other.

When she reached down to take his hard length in his hand, he groaned as a most unwelcome thought popped into his head.

She pulled back to look at him, she loosened her grip on him. "That didn't sound like a groan of pleasure. Did I hurt you?"

"No! Trust me, baby, hurt is the last thing I'm feeling. It's just I had no expectations about this weekend. I really meant it when I said we'd just be going together as friends, so I don't have any protection."

"Oh! No worries. I've got it covered."

Heather jumped out of bed, and Mick admired the view of her body as she hurried across the hall to her bathroom. She had the long, lithe build of an athlete, combined with the curves that made her all woman. She came back, waving a box of condoms. "Here you go; thanks for thinking of it, I was too far gone."

Mick effortlessly caught the box she tossed to him, and pulled out a foil packet. He hadn't lived like a monk for the last eleven years, but he didn't want to think about another man leaving condoms here. He knew it wasn't fair, or even rational, but he felt jealous and possessive of Heather. Tonight wasn't the time to think about those feelings, or what they might mean.

Heather hopped back into bed with him and the bed creaked. "So, where were we?"

Mick pulled her against him, and shuddered at the sensation of her silky skin pressed against his hard body. "Right about here. I want you so much, Heather, I'm not sure if I'll be able to show much finesse this first time."

She ran her hands down his arms and slipped the foil packet out of his fingers, smiling at him as she tore it open. "Fast works for me this time too, but next time…"

He grinned. "Next time, I'll show you some of my better moves."

"Ooo, the man's got moves," she teased as she

rolled the condom onto him.

As he slid into her welcoming heat, they both moaned. Mick had never felt anything like the way they moved together. He realized this was the first time he'd made love to a woman. Raw, wild sex, yeah, he'd had plenty of that, but this was different. Heather was different. He felt like something had clicked into place and he suddenly understood what all those sappy love songs meant. It was a thought he expected to terrify him, but as he continued to stroke inside her, he felt nothing but a bone-deep calm, a sense of belonging...of rightness.

Heather's eyes fluttered shut, and her body gripped him in waves. No sound had ever sounded sweeter than his name on her lips, as her release washed over them both. It brought his own climax on, and he roared his release.

****

Heather woke up early, and felt satiated, content, and—cold? She pulled the covers tighter around her, and wondered where Mick was. The man was like a blast furnace. He put off so much heat while he slept; she thought the chill when he was gone must be what had awoken her.

She smiled as she snuggled into bed. Mick had not lied when he said he had moves. The first time they'd made love was the best she'd ever experienced...until the second time, which managed to be even better. And when he woke her up in the middle of the night with his talented fingers and mouth—hoo boy—round three was the best yet, and it blew her away.

Rustling noises and a muffled curse made her open her eyes. Mick stood in the middle of the room in all his naked glory, and was his body ever Greek god glorious! He bent to rub his big toe as if he'd stubbed it.

"Mick? What are you doing?"

"Shit! Sorry I woke you. I was looking for my clothes."

He didn't want to wake her? And he was looking for his clothes?

What the hell?

She sat up and pulled the covers over her breasts, suddenly feeling shy and vulnerable in front of this man, who had explored every inch of her naked body the night before. "You were going to get dressed and sneak out while I was sleeping?"

He pulled on his boxer briefs and shook his head. "No! What kind of man do you think I am? I was going to wake you up to say goodbye."

"Goodbye?" She managed to croak the word out around the lump in her throat. "Is that what this is?"

He found his shirt, and clutched it in one hand as he sat on the bed next to her. The mattress dipped and squeaked, causing Mick to chuckle. "You were right about this bed being sturdier than it sounds. If we didn't break it last night, nothing ever will."

He pried one of her hands off the covers she clutched against herself, like a shield, and held it in his big, warm hand.

Heather bit her bottom lip. She was so confused. Last night had been unbelievably special to her, and she thought she'd seen the same wonder she was feeling reflected in Mick's eyes. But here he was, getting ready to bolt out of her apartment before dawn.

"What's going on, Mick?"

"Nothing. I know you like to get to the office early

on Monday morning, and I was trying to find my clothes so I could go home and grab a shower before I headed into work too. Your unorthodox approach to clothing storage made it hard to find my clothes. I've heard good things about dressers and closets; you might want to give them a try sometime."

Heather looked around the room, which did seem to have a good portion of her wardrobe strewn about everywhere but the closet or dresser. There were jeans on the floor, her work polos crumpled on a chair, and one bra was even artistically draped over the mirror above her dressing table. She was pretty sure it was the bra she had on last night.

She lifted one bare shoulder. "If you're looking for Suzy Homemaker…"

"I'm not," he interrupted firmly. "I was teasing you, Heather."

"Okay, then on to your second point—my apartment may not be the penthouse of the Ritz, but I *do* have indoor plumbing. You could shower here; you don't need to sneak out while I'm sleeping to go home to shower."

"I wasn't sneaking! I was going to wake you. I just didn't like the odds of us actually making it into the office today at all, if we were both naked when I did it."

"You have a problem with showering here?"

"Your brother is my boss, and he's one of my oldest friends."

"I'm not seeing the connection to my shower."

"It's not your shower, per se, but I'm seriously breaking the guy code by sleeping with a buddy's sister, and I don't want him to find out about us by the two of us waltzing into the office together, with a just-laid glow about us."

"There's a glow?" She grinned, in spite of her misgivings.

"*You* glow," his answer was serious. "It's one of the best things about you. Wherever you go, you bring the sun with you."

She blushed, and looked down, feeling pleased and a little bit like a jerk all at once. She'd allowed Danny's snarky comments from the wedding to worm their way into her head. When she woke up and thought Mick was sneaking out, she'd heard Danny's voice in her mind. *You're good enough to sleep with, but not good enough to be seen in public together.*

She mentally stuck her tongue out at Danny. After spending the whole weekend telling Mick to ignore his brother's jibes, it turned out she was the one who let Danny get to her.

Chapter 13

Heather drummed her fingers on her desk, as she booted up her computer. Never a real girly-girl, she was showered, dressed, and at work in no time. She'd even beaten Mick into the office. She wondered if she could be happy with a man who took longer than she did to get ready, but decided if it came with nights of unbelievable sex like last night, she could make the sacrifice.

What she wasn't so sure about was if she could be with someone who was so uncomfortable in his own skin. She furrowed her brow. Maybe Mick's prep time took so long, *because* he wasn't comfortable with himself. And he needed the time to make his appearance perfect before he went out in the world.

When Mick was alone with her, he was a very different person from the one he chose to present to everyone else. She hoped her Mick was the real one, but she didn't know for sure if he was. Danny's words still flitted around her consciousness—was she just a dirty, little secret for Mick?

Seeing him over the weekend with his family, in his native West Virginia, had been a real eye-opener for her. His father and Danny were so awful to him, but was the custom-tailored, handmade Italian leather shoe wearing man, more a response to them, or was it based in snobbery and a rejection of his coal-mining roots?

She sincerely hoped it was the former, because avoiding their nastiness was something she could understand. If it was shame about his family history driving him, it would be a deal-breaker for her. Heather might have her flaws, but she was a woman who was comfortable in her own skin, and she had never been ashamed of her family's farming lifestyle.

Only time would tell which Mick was the real Mick, and she needed to seriously consider how hurt she would be if the snob turned out to be the real person. He broke her heart the first time around, and she suspected this time, with grown-up feelings at play, it would be even worse. What they had together—when they were in private, Danny's snide voice in her head reminded her—was real, and true, and it deserved the chance to develop. It meant leaving herself open to the kind of heartache she'd spent her whole adult life avoiding.

She realized her computer had started up while she was sitting here lost in thought. She shook her head, as if the movement would clear away the confused thoughts like cobwebs, and clicked on the keyboard as she got to work. First things first, it was Monday, which meant she had to get the week's calendar ready for Jeff, Cisco, and Mick.

"Damn," she cursed as she opened her calendar, and saw a reminder for the gala to benefit Jeff's organization to help inner-city kids. With everything else going on she'd totally forgotten it was taking place this weekend. And given developments with Mick it had also slipped her mind she was going to the benefit with Chase Harper. A bass player with an up and coming alt-country band, Chase was on the road most of the time, but he was playing in the Mid-Atlantic region this week, and had agreed to meet her in Baltimore for her brother's charity event.

Chase and she weren't serious. He had too much of a gypsy soul to give up the road and settle down in one place, and Heather's roots ran deep in Rivers Bend, but she didn't feel right about going on a date with him in light of her budding relationship, or whatever it was, with Mick.

She glanced at the time on her computer screen— seven o'clock. It was too early to call Chase. The only time he had ever seen this hour of the morning was if he still hadn't gone to bed from the night before. She tapped on her keyboard to set a reminder to call him this afternoon when he'd be awake and explain about things with Mick. They flirted with each other some, but Chase was her friend, and she knew he would understand. She knew Jeff was looking forward to seeing him, so she wanted to let him know he was still welcome to come to the benefit, but she wanted to make it clear to him if he went, it wouldn't be as her date.

A little later, Heather heard her brother's voice in the hall. She felt butterflies in her stomach when she heard him talking to Mick.

They paused at her door, and she made a concerted effort not to gaze past Jeff to look at Mick like a smitten schoolgirl. *Get a grip, Braden!*

"Hey, Heather, do you mind if we interrupt you for a minute? I want to go over this week's schedule."

She spun her desk chair to face them. "Sure. I emailed it to both of you."

Jeff waved his smart phone. "Got it right here!"

As her brother began to discuss the groups booked at the Retreat for the upcoming week, Heather risked a glance at Mick and received a slow, sexy wink. Her heart pounded, and she felt her face flush. Man she was so far gone for this guy!

"Okay, that's it for Retreat business. One more thing though, this Saturday is the benefit." He tapped on his phone to call up a document stored there. "Mick, I have you down with one guest."

Heather's head shot up from the schedule in her hand so fast she was amazed she didn't give herself whiplash.

The muscles in Mick's jaw worked, so she knew he was tense, but his answer was like a direct hit to her solar plexus.

"That's right. I'm taking Gloria Peterson."

What did he mean? He still intended to go with Gloria after what happened between them last night? Heather felt her stomach lurch, but fortunately, Jeff was staring aghast at Mick, so her brother didn't notice her discomfort.

"Dude, I thought I warned you about that woman! She's poison"—he shrugged—"but you're a big boy, so I guess it's your funeral."

Mick didn't answer. Probably because his jaw was clenched so tightly it locked up on him.

"Heather, I have you down with Chase. I'm looking forward to seeing him again; glad he's in the area this weekend."

Mick's gaze burned into her, and she thought she saw an actual wisp of steam come out of his ears.

Heather had no idea what was going on in his head, but in hers, she heard Danny's voice on an endless loop.

Good enough to sleep with, but not to be seen in public together. Was Mick's brother right? Danny even specifically asked about charity events like this one, so maybe he was on to something. He didn't seem to know much about Mick, beyond his preconceived ideas about him, but even a blind squirrel finds a nut sometimes.

Well, she knew one thing for sure, if Mick was going with Gloria, she wasn't about to cancel her plans with Chase. She didn't trust her voice not to wobble, so she swallowed hard and nodded mutely in response.

Jeff was too preoccupied with the file on his phone to notice. His head bobbed as he tapped on the small screen. "Good. Thank you both for your support on this. It means a lot to me."

He wandered out of the office and left her alone with Mick. The tension between them was as thick as the fog had been on the Potomac this morning.

"Who's Chase? Were those his condoms at your place?" Mick ground out between clenched teeth.

"What? Where did *that* come from?"

"I was wondering whose condoms they were last night. So…are they his? Chase's?" He spat out the name.

Heather could still hear Danny's voice pounding in her head like a tribal drum—*good enough to sleep with*—but anger was starting to mix in with her shock. "So what if they do belong to Chase? Have you been celibate? What about Gloria?"

"I haven't slept with Gloria," he said through gritted teeth.

She shrugged with feigned indifference, but his answer was worse than if he was sleeping with Gloria. Danny's words played on a loop in her mind—*good enough to sleep with.* "Maybe not, but you think she's worthy to be seen in public with you. It's why you're going to the benefit with her and not me."

His eyes widened, and his jaw finally unclenched enough to drop. "What the hell do you mean? I asked Gloria to the benefit before things started between us, and I don't want to cancel on her so close to the event. It would be rude."

"And God forbid you be rude to a lady like your precious Gloria."

"What are you talking about? And who are you to be so angry about me going with Gloria? You're going with someone else too—remember, your date with *Chase*?"

She pounded on her keyboard to open up her calendar and poked her finger at the reminder scheduled on her screen. "I was going to call Chase this afternoon to tell him about us, but now I guess there's no point—there is no us."

He frowned and stepped up behind her to look at the screen. "We both made dates before, but it's no reason to say there is no us."

She felt small as he towered over, and she didn't like the feeling so she stood. Even standing, she needed to tilt her head a little to look at his face, which given she was 5'9" was an unusual experience for her, but she felt less vulnerable this way.

She tried to turn off the sound of Danny's voice in her head, but it just echoed the fears she started to suspect were reality. "But you don't plan on canceling your date with Gloria."

He glanced away from her steady gaze. "No."

She raised her voice, in part to drown out Danny's

voice, but the words she spoke were the same. "So *I'm* good enough to sleep with, but Gloria's more acceptable to be seen with at a social function like Jeff's benefit."

Mick's eyes bulged at her words, and he raised his voice too, "You're more than just someone to sleep with…"

"Since I'm her honorary big brother, I'm pleased to hear it," Cisco's Brazilian accented voice interrupted him from the doorway to her office. "But I'm not sure her blood brother would feel the same."

"Cisco," Mick began, but was cut off by his friend.

"Don't explain it to me—save it for Jeff, and be glad his office door is shut, or he would've heard this whole thing."

He tossed a set of keys to Mick. "There's a golf cart out by the barn. Since you two seem determined to yell at each other about your personal business, take it and go somewhere private to finish this argument."

****

Mick glanced at Heather as she drove the golf cart on a trail bordering the river. The silence between them was as strained as the tight expression on Heather's normally sunny face. God, was it happening already? Was he sucking the joy and vitality from her the way his old man had done with his mother?

She veered off the path, and he grinned in spite of the situation. She drove the golf cart as wildly as she drove a car, and with as much abandon as she lived her life. His smile faded. She had been happy, until one night with him, and now there were lines of tension bracketing her beautiful lips.

She turned off the cart's motor and hopped out; she

walked to the riverbank, and wrapped her arms around herself in a defensive gesture. It was like a kick in the gut that Heather felt the need to protect herself against him.

She stared down the incline to the river and asked, "Think this is far enough for privacy?"

"Depends on how mad you are at me, and how loud you think you might yell."

"The drive calmed me down some; I don't think the hollering will be too loud."

Mick stepped up to her side, and looked out at the constantly rolling river. He wanted to draw her into his arms, to reassure her everything would be all right, but he couldn't. He didn't know if it would be, and the way Heather still held herself protectively away from him made him think it might not be.

"Want to tell me what you meant back at the office about how I view you and Gloria, because I sure as hell didn't understand."

She shrugged and he thought he saw a glimmer of tears in her eyes. Great. He was a helluva guy. Now he made her cry. He ground his molars together—he would *not* be his father.

"Okay. I won't press you on it, so how about this one, who's this Chase guy, and what is he to you?"

"He's mostly a friend, but we've gone out sometimes too. Nothing serious, or exclusive."

The man must be a fool. If Mick was ever lucky enough to go out with Heather, he couldn't imagine ever looking at another woman. But he couldn't afford to think that way, because if there was one thing this morning was proving to him, it was Mick Evans was not the best man for Heather Braden. Still he couldn't stop himself from asking, "Why not?"

"He's a musician. He's on the road a lot, and he's a real free spirit."

"Just like you. I mean the free spirit part is like you, not being a musician."

She darted a glance at him and then looked out at the river for what felt like hours, but was just a few moments. When she spoke, her voice was small and hurt. "You don't know me at all, do you?

"I think I do."

She shook her head. "But you don't. You always say things about me being wild, a party girl, a free spirit, and that's not me. Yeah, I'm generally a happy person, but I'm not a flake. I work hard; I love my friends and family. I'm smart. I was valedictorian of my high school, bet you didn't know that about me."

"No, I didn't. How could I know it, if you never told me? Like the M.I.T. thing, I didn't know about it either, even though you turned down the scholarship right before we met. You'd think it might have come up in conversation."

"All the fighting with my mom about my decision was too raw back then; I didn't want to talk about it." She squinted as she thought, and then said, "Maybe it's my fault you see me the way you do."

"What do you mean?"

She took a deep breath. "When we met I was ready to reinvent myself. You didn't see me as 'good girl' Heather." She made air quotes, then wrapped her arms around herself as though she were cold, even though the warm spell they were having made the day a comfortable temperature. "You didn't see the nerdy girl, the captain of the girls' lacrosse team, the senior class president."

"You did all those things?"

Her mouth curled as she looked at him. "Thanks for the shocked tone of voice. It's very flattering."

His grin was sheepish. "Sorry. I just had no idea."

"No, you didn't, and so you treated me like a regular girl, a *fun* girl. I liked it, but a little part of me always hoped you'd see the real me. No, not the *real* me, because fun Heather *is* a part of me too, but I wanted you to see the *whole* me. And you never did."

Mick exhaled with a whoosh. "Is that what you meant about me asking Gloria to the benefit? You think I see you as some sort of wild-girl-fuck-buddy I enjoy in private, but Gloria is the lady I take out in public?"

"Well, Danny said…"

He held up his hand like a traffic cop telling her to stop. "Wait. *Danny* said? My brother Danny? The one with the ax as big as Paul Bunyan's to grind with me? Please, enlighten me, what did *Danny* say to you?"

She blushed and avoided his intent gaze. "He said you would never be okay with dating me, because I grew up on a farm in Virginia."

He raised his eyebrows. "On account of my lofty childhood as a coal miner's son in West Virginia?"

She cleared her throat. "Danny seemed to think you felt like I was good enough to…y'know…"

At first he didn't understand where her stammering response was headed, but when realization dawned, he was so furious he was afraid he was going to pop a blood vessel. Damn Danny to hell for his big mouth and his little mind.

"To what, Heather? To fuck? Is that what last night felt like to you, because it sure as hell didn't feel like that to me. It felt like more...a lot more."

"No." She shook her head and repeated more emphatically. "No. It didn't feel like that's all it was to me either."

"So what changed between last night and this morning? The benefit thing of Jeff's this weekend?"

She sighed and nodded. "Danny specifically mentioned you wouldn't want to be seen with me at a fancy charity event. When you said you weren't going to cancel your date with Gloria, I felt like maybe Danny was right after all; you'd sleep with me, but you'd take a socialite like Gloria out in public."

He mentally calculated how long it would take him to get to West Virginia to kick Danny's interfering ass. He ran his hand over his jaw, and decided to be completely honest with Heather, since honesty seemed like the only way he might salvage the situation. "I've always been ashamed of the way I broke things off with you in Portland. Yeah, I was young and stupid, but I should've known better than to drop you with no explanation. It was a chickenshit thing to do."

"True. But it happened a long time ago. You've apologized to me, and I'm over it; I think it's all right if you stop beating yourself up about it now. Besides, what does it have to do with our current situation?"

"As it happens, quite a bit. After I was such a jerk to you, I promised myself I would never treat another woman the same way again. And *that's* why I don't want to cancel on Gloria. Last week she was going on about a new dress and shoes; I didn't want to dump her with no explanation, and until I talk to your brother, I didn't want to tell a gossip like Gloria about you and me."

He stood in front of her to clasp her shoulders and ducked his head to look straight into her eyes. "It was most definitely *not* because I think Gloria is better than you. I'd be proud to be seen with you there, to be seen with you anywhere! Hell, if I got invited to Buckingham Palace, I would be honored to have you on my arm."

Heather smiled a little. "Are you expecting an invitation to the palace anytime soon? Because I'd need plenty of advance notice about it, serious shopping would have to be done."

He brushed the lock of hair that had fallen over his eye back, and winked at her. "I don't have any immediate plans with the Queen, or even William and Kate."

Heather bent her neck and lowered her eyelids to avoid his gaze. He put his finger under her chin and gently raised her head. "What's going on in that M.I.T. worthy brain?"

She frowned and narrowed her eyes, and Mick was pretty certain he'd managed to say the wrong thing again, but didn't know what it was.

"Talk about ancient history…what does my acceptance to M.I.T. have to do with anything? I didn't go there, and I never even think about it anymore, so why are you?"

"I just think it's cool you're so smart M.I. freakin' T. offered you a scholarship."

"*Eleven years ago!*"

"But still, it's impressive."

She gestured between them. "Is my old scholarship offer what this is about? Maybe Danny wasn't totally off base."

Mick's jaw dropped. "Of course he was off base! What do you mean?"

Her body language had relaxed some as they talked, but now she crossed her arms defensively across her chest again. "I mean, you didn't sleep with me, or say you'd be proud to be seen with me at an event like Jeff's this weekend, until you heard about M.I.T. It's like you suddenly think I'm worthy of you, and that idea plain old makes me furious!"

Mick thought she wasn't just angry, he saw hurt in her eyes too. He had a fast car, and he could seriously be in West Virginia by the time his brother's shift in the mine ended. And he would kill Danny. There would be plenty of time on the drive to calculate the slowest and most painful method possible.

"One major flaw in your argument—I've wanted you for eleven years."

"Physically, yeah, and you enjoyed spending time with me alone. Even back then it was always alone; you didn't take me out in public."

"Heather, you agreed at the time we should wait before we told Jeff about what was happening between us. As I recall, it was *your* idea to keep him in the dark, which is why we never went out in public. I was *never* ashamed of you. Never."

Something in his tone seemed to make her straighten up and peer into his eyes. She furrowed her brow over her clear, gray eyes, and he was afraid she could see straight to his dark soul.

"I believe you, Mick."

"Thank God!" He heaved a sigh of relief. Maybe things were going to be okay after all, until her next words stopped him cold.

"You aren't ashamed of *me*. You're ashamed of *you*!"

Chapter 14

"I'm very proud of what I've done with my life," Mick replied in measured tones.

Damn. There were a lot of dumb women in the world—women who didn't look below the surface. Hell, he'd dated more than his fair share of them, so why did Heather, the one woman he really cared about, have to be so insightful? Because it was *why* he cared what she thought of him. She was whip-smart; it was one of the things that attracted him to her. In spite of his opinions on her fun-loving character, long before he knew about the M.I.T. scholarship offer, Heather's quick-witted sassiness is what drew him to her like a food network host to a barbecue competition.

She put her hands on her hips and screwed up her mouth as she stared at him. "You've come really far and you *should* be proud, but it's not what I meant and you know it. You're ashamed of where you come from, so you need a date like Gloria to give you social cred."

"I'm not ashamed of where I'm from, but people form a lot of mistaken opinions about you when they learn you're from the mountains of West Virginia. I don't want to behave like a stereotype and give them more fuel for their fire."

"Who do you think is judging you based on your hometown here in Rivers Bend? The only person I can think of who might do it is Gloria, and you're *choosing* to spend time with her."

"In an attempt to keep my mind off of you," he snapped. "And look how well *that* worked out for me. I still ended up making love to you, and now you're angry with me."

"I'm not angry."

He raised an eyebrow.

"Okay, I'm not angry *anymore*. I'm confused, and I'm trying to figure out what's going on in here." She stood on tiptoe and tapped his forehead with one finger. "What happened to you to make you this guarded?"

"You mean aside from my father's raging disapproval of me?"

"Yes. I don't think it's the only reason you're the way you are."

Now it was his turn to cross his arms across his chest in a defensive posture, which he did, but remained silent.

She rolled her eyes. "Fine. Shut me out."

He stared at her a moment longer and then blurted out, "I've gotten hillbilly jokes everywhere I've gone since I left home: college, the other guys on the Pintos…"

"Not Jeff and Cisco?" Heather interrupted.

"No. Never them, but all the other guys, on the team and in the front office."

Light dawned in her eyes and her full lips formed an 'O'. "The guys who were ribbing you about me the day you dropped me like a hot potato."

He nodded once. "Yep. About how only a hillbilly like me would be going after an underage girl. You know the kind of thing: *you can take the boy out of the hills…*"

"That's just dumb! I wasn't ten, for God's sake! I was almost eighteen and only a few years younger than you." She narrowed her eyes. "Not to mention quite of few of them had made a play for me too; I just wasn't interested in any of them. The only one I wanted was the boy from West Virginia who they decided to pick on about me. Coincidence? I think not."

"Those miserable sons of bitches!"

She shrugged. "Seems to me like they were trying to eliminate competition and you fell right into their trap. So, who else?"

"People in business have made wisecracks. I have to be better than everyone else in the room all the time."

She smacked him on the bicep, and she packed quite a wallop. He rubbed the spot as she hollered at him, "You *are* better than everyone else in the room all of the time. How do you not know it?"

"At a certain level in business, you're running with the old-boys network, and not the good-ole boys network, so I can't let Mickey Evans, Phil and Carol's little boy, slip out in front of those people. They'd eat him alive. You heard that jerk I was on the phone with my first day; you know what I'm up against."

She shook her head, and her hair swung over her shoulders. "You've got it backward. People like the bozo you were talking to inherited their money, power, and position. Mickey Evans worked, struggled, and fought for everything he has. When push comes to shove, my money's on Mickey to win out over those entitled yahoos."

"Thank you, but it's not the way the real world works, Heather."

"Yeah, it is! Or it can be, if you're not trying to

keep up with the trust fund baby set."

"Those are the people I deal with at work, and I can't let my guard down around them. In a perfect world, it wouldn't be the case, but this is not a perfect world. Far from it."

She threw her hands up in the air. "I can't make you see in yourself all the great things I see in you. The things that make you the best man in *every* room you walk into, you've got to see it for yourself. And until you do, I think we need to cool it."

"What? You're dumping me?"

She ran her hands through her hair and exhaled hard. "I guess I am. I don't want to be with someone who doesn't value the same things I do, which is ironic, because you have all the traits I admire—brains, initiative, you're a hard worker, a self-made man, but *you* don't admire those things. If we keep going with what we started lasted night, I'm just going to get hurt by you again, and that is not going to happen. I'm not going to let it."

****

Heather had never been so glad to go to an oil change appointment before in her life. At least it gave her a chance to leave the office for a little while. After their intense conversation, Mick retreated to his office, and she'd helped check-in a group of guests. Clearly, avoiding each other was not a viable long-term plan at work, but they both needed time to cool off and think. *This* is why you shouldn't get involved with someone from work, especially your boss. Although, she wondered if their long, complicated history together made last night inevitable.

She pulled up to the empty service bay at Miller's

Garage. Ed Miller had been running the business for as long as Heather could remember. One of her earliest memories was riding shotgun with her father when he'd bring the pickup truck here for service. Her dad always bought her candy out of the ancient vending machine as a treat, and they'd split a cola from the red cooler out front. The garage smelled like oil, and the scent always made her long for a peanut butter cup and a Coke, and it made her miss her dad like crazy. He had been a larger-than-life character—full of life, fun, and good humor. A huge hole opened in her soul when he died of a heart attack when she was still a kid. Deidre and Jeff got to spend more time with him than Jason and she had, and she used to be so jealous of them because of it.

The grizzled mechanic waved as he walked out of the garage and up to her car. He pulled a cloth out of the pocket of his greasy coveralls and wiped his hands before opening her car door.

"Hey, Heather! Who've you got in there with you?"

"Petunia. She's Magda's dog, I'm going to bring her by the library to visit with Magda while I wait for my car."

He ran his hand over his bristly crew cut. "Might be a bit of a wait. I have some emergencies today, and no one to help me. I sure wish I had someone to work with me here, someone who could learn the business and take over when I retire." He winked. "Don't know a good, young mechanic by any chance, do you?"

Heather slung her purse over her shoulder, scooped Petunia up from the passenger seat, and got out of the car. "Actually, I might know someone. I met a guy over the weekend who would love to work as a mechanic.

143

Are you serious?"

"I'm as serious as a heart attack. I'd love to meet this fellow; see if he's got what it takes."

"I'll feel him out for you and let you know what he says."

"Thanks, Heather! The day is looking up for me."

Glad it was for somebody. Heather's day started out great, but it went gone downhill fast. She was in dire need of a little girl time. "I'll be at the library or the Nosh Pit if you need me. Otherwise, I'll be back to pick up my car later. No rush, since you're running behind, I'll use it as an excuse to stay in town for lunch."

Heather clipped the leash onto Petunia's collar and stooped to put the dog on the pavement. She straightened and with a cheery wave to Ed, she started down Main Street toward the library. Everyone she passed knew her, and it took a while for her to make her way down the road, as she had to stop every few feet and chat.

She waved to her sister through the plate glass window of the Nosh Pit, and then walked by it to go next door and entered the red brick library building.

Magda sat at the circulation desk, and Petunia gave a quick yip of pleasure at the sight of her beloved mistress. A rescue dog, Petunia suffered unknown torment before Maggie took her in and filled her little doggie life with love. Kind of like her brother Jeff, when Heather stopped to think about it. He was sad and lonely until Maggie blew into town and swept her big, strong brother off his feet. Now Jeff was the happiest he'd ever been.

Magda slid off the tall stool and came around the counter to squat down to scratch Petunia's ears. "She's here!" Magda yelled over her shoulder.

"Finally!" Bethanne's voice hollered back from the office.

"Jeez! Didn't they teach you two the importance of using your inside voice in library school? I never dreamed *I'd* be the one shushing the librarians."

Bethanne laughed as she came through the door marked 'Librarian.' She propped her hip against the end of the circulation desk, and loosely crossed her arms. "Cool your jets, Heather; we're the only ones here."

"Two for the price of one, I didn't expect both of you to be here."

"It's the changing of the guard. I worked the morning shift and Bethanne's here for the afternoon."

"And when I heard you'd be here around lunchtime, I came in early. I was dying to hear how your weekend with the oh-so-yummy Mick Evans was." Bethanne waggled her eyebrows.

Heather frowned, as she tried to think about how much she could tell her friends. Mick's issues were private, and were his to share with others or not as he saw fit. She didn't want to betray his confidence, but she was sad, and really needed the support of her best friends right about now.

"The weekend was mostly good. Last night was amazing. Today totally sucks."

"Ookaay…" Bethanne drew out the word. "Then I vote we start with last night. I like the sound of 'amazing.' "

Magda straightened up and tried to put her arm around Heather's shoulders, but their height difference made it a tricky maneuver, even with Heather in sneakers and Magda in high heels. "Come on into the conference room. We were hoping you'd stay and have lunch with us, so we got a Margherita pizza and salad from Mancini's. Let's pig out, it might make today suck a little less."

They followed Bethanne into the library's meeting room, and the tantalizing aroma of the hot pizza, in its box on the round conference table, made her stomach grumble. She grinned ruefully. "Sorry. With all the drama this morning, and a group checking in at the Retreat, I didn't get a chance to eat breakfast."

As they ate, Heather gave them an edited version of the weekend's events, one which gave them the flavor of what happened, without giving away Mick's secrets. But leave it to insightful and empathetic Magda to see beyond what Heather said.

"Wow." Magda took a sip of her soda through the straw. "I pegged him as the kind of guy I went to prep school with; I never would've guessed he came from a family of coal miners. His dad sounds like a pill. Kind of like my grandmother, so insistent their way of life is the only way."

"Like your grandmother, but without the phenomenal wealth and power." Bethanne crumpled her napkin and tossed it on the table.

"How are things going with Grandmommy Dearest?" Heather asked.

Magda smiled. "We've made a little progress. She still doesn't like my choices, but at least we're speaking again. I think her personal secretary, Ned, has something to do with it, which is nice of him. He actually seems to *like* my grandmother."

"I'm sorry, Maggie, but she hurt Sam, and I have trouble getting past it with your grandmother. I'm not sure I'll ever like her." Heather grimaced.

"Trust me, if she wasn't the only blood relative I have left, I wouldn't have anything to do with her, but sometimes family is tough, especially when you want to follow your own path. I can relate to Mick; it's hard to straddle two worlds."

Okay…Heather had definitely not told them anything about Mick's issues with that, it was too personal, so when she spoke her voice was a little sharper than she intended, "What do you mean?"

"You know how my dad was just a regular guy, and my mom was…"

"Heir to one of the biggest fortunes in the U.S.; with a pit viper for a mother?" Bethanne suggested.

Magda threw her napkin at her oldest friend. "Yeah. That. I was always trying to fit into one of those worlds, but I didn't belong anywhere, at least not until I came to Rivers Bend. And Mick ran with the big dogs of industry when he worked for the Pintos, but comes from much humbler beginnings. Maybe I'm just projecting my own emotions onto him, but I imagine he feels the same way I did. It's no fun, and it's lonely. You know him better than I do, Heather, do you think that's how Mick feels?"

Heather hesitated and Maggie held up her hands. "I don't want you to betray his confidence, so don't answer me if you can't."

Bethanne grinned. "Let's get off all this serious stuff and get back to last night. *Amazing*—that was your word for it, right? Spill."

Magda held up her hand as if she were stopping traffic. "Hold on, I want to get to the bottom of what went wrong, and fix it. I think Mick and Heather would be good together."

Bethanne leaned back in her chair and crossed her arms. "I can tell you what went wrong. I've known Heather since the first day of kindergarten, and this is her typical pattern."

Heather choked on her sip of soda and sputtered, "My typical pattern? What the hell are you talking about?"

"Puh-leeze! You know what I mean."

Heather raised her eyebrows and tossed up her hands in frustration. "No, I don't have the least little clue what you mean."

"When things start to get too close for comfort with a man, you find some fault and get out before you think the guy can."

"I don't do that."

Magda sat between them, and looked back and forth like she was at a tennis match.

Bethanne shook her head. "Sorry, but you do. Or you pick guys who won't commit, so you can keep things from getting too deep."

"Okay, that is so not true."

"Really? Who were you going with to the benefit this weekend? Before things happened with Mick."

"Chase Harper, and by the way, I'm still going with him. Mick is going with Gloria Peterson."

"Yuck." Magda screwed up her face in distaste.

Heather nodded and slapped her hand on the table. "I know, right? She's the worst!"

"Who's Chase Harper, and how does he prove Bethanne's point?" Magda asked.

"He's just an old friend of mine. We go out sometimes."

"When he's around, which isn't often," Bethanne interjected. "He's a musician, and he's on the road ten months out of the year. And the other two months he lives in Richmond, which is still a little far to be reasonable dating distance. He's Heather's perfect man."

"I'm starting to take offense at this conversation," Heather bristled.

Bethanne leaned forward to reach across the table to grasp Heather's hand. "I'm sorry, sweetie, I don't mean to hurt you, but it's true. Not to be an armchair psychologist or anything, but I think it's because of your dad dying when you were so young. You don't let men get close, so you won't be hurt when they leave. But what you don't realize, is they don't all leave, so you're missing out on the happiness you could have if you let someone in to share your life."

Heather blinked against the sudden, hot rush of tears stinging her eyes. "The last time I did that was eleven years ago, and look how well it turned out."

Magda scooted her chair closer to rub Heather's back in support. "Let me guess, it was Mick?"

Heather swiped at a tear that escaped and rolled down her cheek. "Yeah, it was Mick. So forgive me for not wanting to run blindly down that road again."

Bethanne nodded in understanding. "He was a jerk to you back then, believe me, I remember. I was the one you called, crying, every day for weeks after it happened, but it was a long time ago; I'm sure he's grown up since then; maybe you should give him another chance."

"There's stuff going on with him you don't know about, and I think it will end with me getting hurt again, and guess what? You'd *still* be the one listening to me cry on the phone, Bethanne, is that really what you want?"

"Of course not. I love you, and I want you to be happy. I think you have a shot at happiness with Mick, if you don't blow it."

Heather took a sip of her soda and thought about her friend's words. Bethanne didn't know about Mick's issues with his family and background, and Heather hadn't shared his brother Danny's thoughts on Mick and her relationship. So Bethanne and Magda didn't know it was inevitable Mick would leave her to have someone more polished and elegant on his arm. In time, he'd want the type of woman who would reinforce the image he'd worked so hard to build…a woman like Gloria. Until he came to terms with who he was, and where he came from, she wouldn't—*couldn't*—let him into her heart, or her bed, again. It had nothing to do with any lingering abandonment issues she might have after her father's sudden death. Did it?

Chapter 15

Mick entered the ballroom of the Inner Harbor hotel, with Gloria firmly attached to his arm. She was beautiful, and had made it perfectly clear on the drive to Baltimore she was willing, but Mick felt no attraction to her. Instead, his attention was drawn to Heather across the crowded room, as if he was a laser-guided missile, and she was his target.

He strode through the crowd, dragging Gloria along for the ride. He would not be deterred from his mission, even when several members of the Ravens organization he knew from his NFL days, and who were active in Jeff's community centers, called out greetings. He lifted a hand in response, and continued to plow through the mass of elegantly dressed people to get to the only one whom he cared about tonight.

"Hello Heather."

He felt Gloria's nails dig into the fine wool of his tuxedo, as she clutched him possessively when they reached his destination.

"Mick, Gloria."

He could be wrong, but he thought Heather's greeting actually caused icicles to form on the crystal chandelier hanging over their heads.

"Where's Chase?" Mick asked with what he hoped was a smile on his face, although he suspected it looked more like a scowling death mask.

"Here I am. Who's asking?"

A man appeared at Heather's side, carrying two glasses of champagne, one of which he pressed into Heather's hand. Mick would describe him as being one of those terminally hip poseurs, if not for one small thing, this guy was the real deal. Chase was the man who every middle-aged guy with a piercing and a soul patch wished he could be. He was thin and lithe, in that way musicians always seemed to be; he wore one of those ultra-trendy new tuxedos with the skinny pants and close-fitting jacket.

Standing next to him, Mick suddenly felt like Bruce Banner after someone pissed him off—like a huge, hulking beast. Seeing this guy with Heather even made him want to smash like the Hulk too. He snuck a glance down at his hand to make sure it hadn't grown green and ham-sized.

"Chase Harper, this is Gloria Peterson and Mick Evans."

"So pleased to meet you," Gloria trilled.

"Mick's my new boss at the Retreat," Heather added to musician boy.

"Cool. Nice to meet you both."

Chase bobbed his head, with its longish, messy brown hair, and his smile reached his crystal blue eyes. Clearly, this was the first time Chase had heard about him. Heather hadn't thought enough of him to mention him. And her *new boss*? Is that all he was to her? It seemed like a helluva lot more when they were rolling around on her squeaky, old bed a few days ago, and she was screaming his name.

He started when a hand clapped him on the back, he was so lost in his thoughts of Heather he'd totally lost track of his surroundings, and that wouldn't do at a work function. He knew Jeff and Cisco were counting on him to network, and hopefully drum up some new business with the high rollers here tonight. He needed to get his head out of his ass and focus.

"Mick, Gloria, thanks so much for coming tonight. I appreciate the support."

Jeff's lazy grin caused a lot of people to take him at face value, and think he was a laid-back, dumb jock, good ole boy, but Mick knew better; he knew Jeff was as sharp as a tack, with excellent business instincts. Jeff's good opinion meant a lot to Mick, and he certainly wasn't going to earn it by mooning over the man's baby sister while she was on a date with someone else.

"Mind if I steal Mick for a little while? There are some folks here I want him to meet."

****

As her brother led Mick away, Heather heard a young woman's excited voice. "Oh my God! It's Chase Harper! We saw you play last night at Ram's Head."

Chase was pulled into a conversation with his fans, while they snapped photos with their phones. Heather was left alone with Gloria Peterson.

Oh joy.

"Don't you look sweet," Gloria's voice was syrupy and insincere.

Heather smoothed the skirt of her flirty lavender cocktail dress. She had felt like she looked fun and chic, until Gloria had appeared on Mick's arm, in a slinky black number Heather was sure was fresh off a Paris runway.

"Thank you, Gloria. You look lovely."

In Virginia, good manners were deeply ingrained, and Heather was a Virginia girl through and through. Even if she wanted to toss her drink in Gloria's face and rip the woman's extensions out of her head, like a Real Housewife of Rivers Bend, she couldn't help herself from observing the social niceties drummed into her for as long as she could remember.

"It's very nice of you to come all the way to Baltimore to support Jeff's cause."

Gloria waved one hand in a graceful gesture, the kind Heather was never able to pull off. "Oh, it's nothing. I pop into Baltimore now and again. My sister lives here."

"Really? I had no idea." If pressed, Heather would never guess Gloria had a sister or parents. She always assumed Gloria had been cloned in a trophy wife laboratory.

"Lily's the baby of the family, from my father's third marriage. She's a teacher here in Baltimore."

Gloria spoke with such disdain, you'd think she was confessing her sister was a stripper on Baltimore's infamous Block, instead of a teacher.

"An admirable profession," Heather observed.

"Hmm," Gloria's reply was skeptical. Her unusual purple eyes narrowed, reminding Heather of Scarlett O'Hara. "I'm hoping she can join Mick and me for breakfast tomorrow morning."

Heather felt like Gloria had punched her in the stomach, and she was seriously reconsidering the whole toss-her-champagne-into-Glo's-smug-face-pull-out-her-fake-hair option.

Mick was going to sleep with this horrid little woman—less than a week after he'd made love to her.

The champagne tossed around in her stomach like a tiny sailboat in a hurricane.

"What about you and that darling man you're here with, are you two staying in town tonight?"

"Yes, we are." Heather's smile was tight. She was not an easy liar, given her honest nature, but this was more of a half-truth than an out-and-out lie. Chase and she *were* both staying in Baltimore tonight, just not together. Heather was sharing a room in this hotel with her mother, and Chase was staying somewhere else with his bandmates.

She felt Chase's hand on her lower back as he rejoined them, and it left her cold. When Mick had put his hand in the same spot last weekend, she'd felt like a family of excited chipmunks were dancing her tummy. Now...nothing. Huh.

"Sorry about the interruption, ladies."

"Please don't worry, it's the price of celebrity." Gloria flapped her false eyelashes at Chase. Good golly! Didn't the woman have *any* original parts on her body?

"It looks like they're starting to serve dinner, Heath, what do you say we find our seats and slap on the food bag?"

She responded to Chase's slow grin with what she hoped was a bright smile of her own, but the night was wearing her down. At least Chase was getting her away from Gloria. "Sounds good, Chase. Gloria, enjoy your evening."

Gloria's smug smile at her words, as she looked in Mick's direction made Heather's blood boil. "Oh, I intend to, Heather, with a charming escort like Michael, how could I not?"

As Gloria walked toward Mick, Chase looked down at where Heather's nails dug into his arm with a wry smile. "Why do I get the feeling there's more going on here tonight than I know about? Like one of those foreign films from the seventies, where everyone's swapped partners, and no one is saying what they really mean?"

****

Mick didn't know if it was a blessing or a curse Heather and her date were seated at another table. This way he didn't have to listen to them flirt with each other but they were only one table away, so he could still hear Heather's warm laughter, and he couldn't stop himself from looking at her, any more than he could stop himself from breathing.

He still didn't really understand why she'd broken things off with him, some bullshit about him learning to love himself, but she'd been dodging him at work all week, so he knew she was deadly serious about it. She wasn't playing some coy game the way Gloria would. There might be a kernel of truth to her excuses, but he honestly didn't believe they were the only reason Heather was on the run. However, he was damned if he knew what was going on in her head. All he knew was he didn't want things to be over between them, and it was killing him to watch her with another man. And not just with any other man, but one who appeared to be the polar opposite of him. Chase seemed genial and carefree, where Mick was intense, lean where he was muscled, and Chase managed to hold on to Heather when he couldn't.

He watched with a clenched jaw as the band started up some old-school Sinatra tune and Chase pulled out

Heather's chair and led her to the dance floor. Chase twirled her with a roguish grin on his face, and Heather's pretty purply dress floated around her until she looked like the center of a pretty spring flower. *His* pretty spring flower, the voice in his head roared.

Gloria followed his gaze. "They make a darling little couple, don't they?"

He made a noise low in his throat, and sincerely hoped he hadn't just growled, but he was afraid he had. He'd never felt so jealous in his life.

"They're staying here in Baltimore tonight," Gloria added.

Correction, *now* was the most jealous he'd ever been. How could Heather sleep with this guy so soon after they'd been together? He made the same sound again, and darned if it wasn't a growl after all.

Gloria tiptoed her scarlet fingernails up his arm, and said in a wheedling tone, "I'm sure we can still get a room here. Isn't there any way I can change your mind about staying with me tonight?"

"No, Gloria, I told you I'm heading back to Rivers Bend tonight. If you want to stay here, I'd be happy to arrange transportation home for you tomorrow."

No way was he going to stay here and risk seeing Heather and Chase in the morning; he wasn't altogether sure he would be able to hold back from punching the other man. And it didn't even take into account his amazingly colossal lack of attraction to Gloria, in spite of her beauty and blatant availability.

"It won't be necessary, if you're not staying there's no point in me staying." Gloria leaned back in her chair and sighed. "This night is not at all what I was hoping it would be, Michael."

"I'm sorry, Gloria."

And he was. Knowing how he felt about Heather, he should never have brought another woman to this event.

She leaned forward and pressed her breasts against his arm. "Then make it up to me. Stay with me tonight."

He should want to. Gloria was everything he thought he wanted, but he was as cold as the Bering Sea in January at her touch. On the other hand, why the hell not? If Heather was going to spend the night with her musician friend with benefits, why shouldn't he take advantage of what Gloria was so freely offering?

He watched Chase gather Heather into his arms, as the band segued into a slow, romantic song, and he knew he could never be with another woman when his feelings for Heather were so strong.

Damn it all to hell! Was Gloria's tongue in his ear? What was it going to take to convince this woman 'no' means 'no'?

****

"Did she just shove her tongue in his ear?"

Chase turned them on the dance floor, so he could see who she was watching, with what Heather feared were sparks shooting out of her eyes.

"Yep. Looks like."

"How horribly tacky!"

Chase's brows drew together. "You seem mighty interested in your boss's sex life."

She flushed and looked down at her feet. "Mick isn't just my boss."

"I didn't think so. During dinner he was looking at me like wanted to turn me upside down and mop the floor with my head. Look, Heather, you and I have never been exclusive, so if he makes you happy, it's all right with me. I'm just wondering why you two aren't here together tonight?"

"Mick and I are not seeing each other."

"But you said he's not just your boss," Chase frowned in confusion.

"No. Yes. I don't know. It's complicated."

"Sounds like," Chase drawled.

"I'm sorry, Chase, I never should have brought you here, when I'm so confused."

"No worries, darlin', we're friends before anything else, right?"

"Right." She smiled at him in gratitude for his understanding.

He pulled her a little closer and ran his hand up her arm. "Doesn't mean I'm gonna stop trying, though."

****

Heather rapped on the hotel room door with her knuckles to give her mother a little warning before she inserted her key card. The lock gave two little beeps and she pushed open the door.

Her mother stood in front of the mirror on the dresser; she was still in her dove gray silk evening gown, which had a strap over one shoulder and draped her mother's still trim figure beautifully. Heather sent a silent thank you out to the good gene pool gods, as her mother looked more like a Grecian goddess than a sixty-something grandmother.

Joyce smiled at her in the mirror. "Hi, honey. I wasn't sure when you'd get in, knowing Chase, I figured y'all would be going to some party at one of those after-hours club he always seems to know about."

Heather shut the door behind her, and slipped out

of her strappy silver sandals. "There was something like that happening, but I wasn't up for it. Jason went with Chase." She grinned at her mom. "I doubt he'll be much help at the farm tomorrow."

Her mother laughed and turned to face Heather. She leaned her backside against the dresser. "We didn't schedule any riding lessons tomorrow, for just that reason. Hank and I can take care of the animals without Jason for one day, but my charming son is in heavy demand as a riding teacher, and oddly all his students are single, young women."

Heather tried to beat her blues to smile at her mother's joke, which was funny, but she knew there was a great deal of truth to it. Girls all over the county wanted to be the one to tame wild Jason Braden, but as his sister, she sincerely doubted anyone ever would.

Joyce cocked her head as she regarded Heather with her lips turned down. "You know I try to mind my own business, but I've got to ask. When, precisely, did your life turn into a soap opera?"

Heather could see her own reflection in the mirror behind her mother, so she knew she resembled a fish on the dock, mouth open, eyes wide. She turned her back on that unlovely image, and tossed her evening clutch on the turned-down bed. She reached for the chocolate on the pillow and unwrapped it. "I love when they leave candy for you. I wish someone would slip into my apartment and do it for me every night."

Her mother crossed her arms, and narrowed her eyes. "Turn-down service is nice, but you should know me well enough to know I'm not so easily distracted. What's going on with you and Mick? And Mick and Gloria? And you and Chase?"

When she put it that way, it did make it seem like the plot of a telenovela. She popped the candy into her mouth to stall for time. She closed her eyes briefly in bliss as she relished the chocolaty-minty goodness.

"After four kids and three grandkids, I'm onto that trick too. As soon as your mouth isn't full, I'm just going to ask again, and we're out of chocolates, so you'll have to answer me then."

Heather swallowed with a gulp. "What do you mean?"

Her mother sighed. "You're really going to make me do this the hard way, huh? Okay, will do, the gossip all over town was Mick had thrown over Gloria to bring you to meet his family, but then Chase was your date tonight, and Mick was with G.G. again."

"G.G.?"

"Ghastly Gloria."

Heather giggled.

Her mother's features softened from her hard-ass inquisitor mode. "And you both may have been here with other people, but Mick spent all night glowering at Chase, and I've never know you to pass up a party, yet, here you are, in a hotel room with your mother, while your little brother is out partying with your date."

"It's been a long week. Work was crazy, and I'm getting ready for finals. I'm beat." She worried at her bottom lip with her teeth and peeked at her mother through her bangs. "So…Mick was glowering?"

"Yes. You would have noticed it yourself if you hadn't been so studiously avoiding looking at him all night."

As Heather protested, her mother held up her hands. "Stop. Don't even try to tell me I'm wrong, I know my kids like the back of my hand. Plus, Mick and G.G. sat at my table, so I got a first-hand look at Mick's reaction to you and Chase. That boy gives good glower, and G.G. did not look at all pleased to have her date staring at you all evening."

Heather rolled her neck to relieve some of the stress that had taken up residence there over the last few days. "Well, G.G. is getting all of his attention now. She made it crystal clear to me they were spending the night together in Baltimore tonight, and then they're meeting her sister tomorrow morning for breakfast. A fancy hotel room followed by a meet-the-family meal sounds pretty darned serious to me."

Her mother frowned. "Nothing like that came up at dinner."

"I don't think Mick would bring up his sexcapades with G.G. at a charity dinner," Heather snapped.

"No, he wouldn't. You're right, he's a real gentleman, and a gentleman doesn't talk like that in front of people, but I really thought something was starting between you two, and I was happy about it! What happened?"

Her mother's gentle concern brought a lump to Heather's throat. She blinked at the sting of tears behind her eyes, as she bent over her suitcase to dig out her nightshirt.

"And that Snoopy nightshirt tells me you never planned on a romantic evening with Chase…"

"Mother, please! I do not want to discuss romantic evenings with you."

"Then let's leave Chase for the moment and get back to Mick."

"You're not going to drop this, are you?"

"No."

"Mick has some personal issues he needs to work through."

"Don't we all?"

Heather shrugged. "Sure, but he needs to come to terms with where he comes from, and to learn to love himself before he's ready to love someone else."

"That sounds reasonable."

"You have 'but' written all over your face."

Her mother flashed a brief grin. "*But*, I worry you're just making an excuse to get out before you can get hurt."

"Why is everyone saying that to me?"

"Because it's what you do."

"I do not!" Heather scrunched up her nose. "Do I?"

Her mother wrapped an arm around her waist and pulled her into her side. Her warmth and her familiar powdery scent enveloped Heather, and she remembered feeling this comfort from her mom her whole life— from little hurts, like skinning her knees, to big ones, like losing her dad.

As if she read her mind, her mother said, "I know how hard it was for you to lose your dad. You were always a real Daddy's girl."

"It was hardest for you."

"Maybe, maybe not. You were so young; I had his love for a long time, and I wouldn't trade those years with him for anything. I want you to experience the same sort of love one day."

"I will. Maybe Mick's just not the right man for me."

"Maybe, maybe not."

Heather smiled. "Is that your phrase of the day?"

They laughed and spoke together, "Maybe, maybe not."

"Just don't close yourself off from possibilities in a misguided effort to guard your heart. Not everyone leaves, and some things, *some people*, are worth the risk. Maybe Mick is one of them."

"Maybe, maybe not." Heather tried to keep her face solemn, but couldn't hold back a smile.

"Cheeky girl!" Her mom swatted at Heather's arm. "Why do I even bother?"

Heather hugged her. "Because you're the best mom ever."

****

Gloria squirmed a little in her seat, and whined, "This is not the type of car I imagined you driving."

Mick gripped the steering wheel and focused on the stretch of highway in front of him, which glowed orange in the streetlights. He fought back a yawn. It probably would have been better to spend the night in Baltimore, but he knew he would've spent what remained of the night fighting off Gloria's unsubtle advances.

"No? What did you think I'd drive?"

"Something more luxurious and elegant seems like it would be more your speed. Not some sort of high-powered muscle car."

The engine roared as he pressed down on the gas pedal, and he bit back a smile as Gloria fell against the seat back at the sudden acceleration. "Funny you mentioned speed; it's one of the things I like best about Lola."

"Lola? You named your car?"

"Heather did, after the showgirl."

"Showgirl?"

"You know…from that old song?"

Gloria lifted one shoulder, and sighed as she examined her manicure. "Must be before my time."

"Heather's younger than you and she knew the song."

He realized he was poking the lioness, but Mick thought it might be the way to finally disenchant Gloria. She had him in her scopes, and she wasn't giving up, no matter how many 'thanks, but no thanks' signals he sent her way. Maybe out and out rudeness would succeed in getting her to back the hell off; he regretted not heeding Jeff's advice and keeping his distance from this woman in the first place.

She made a moue of displeasure. "Heather and I are around the same age."

He glanced at her, before turning back to focus on the traffic whizzing by. Rivers Bend had already turned him back into a real country boy, and this city traffic was unnerving him a bit. "Really? Then you must've been young when you had your daughter."

Gloria took a deep breath and turned her head to look out the passenger side window, but not fast enough he didn't see her thoroughly pissed off scowl. "I'm a little bored with the topic of Heather Braden, and I'm still angry with you over last weekend. The whole town has been buzzing about how you chose the little farm girl over me."

"Little? Heather is 5'9", and you're what—five foot nothing?"

"Don't try to chance the subject, you made me a laughingstock!"

"I'm sorry, Gloria, it wasn't my intention." His

words were sincere. He never meant for Gloria to get dragged into the middle of his current mess of a life. He didn't want to be with her, but it didn't mean he wanted her hurt by his actions.

She nestled into the seat, and looked like a fancy, pampered cat at his apology. "That's all right. I feel better about it now."

"Now?"

"Sure, seeing her with that musician tonight cleared things up for me. He's not really my type, but he has a certain sex appeal. And they're clearly a couple, which means you're available again."

"A couple? You think they're together?"

She narrowed her eyes and smiled. "We've been over this, Michael, they *are* staying together in Baltimore tonight. What do you think?"

Mick wasn't sure what was going to crack under the pressure first—the steering wheel, which he clutched in a death grip, or his teeth, where he ground them together. He still couldn't believe Heather was sleeping with another man less than a week after he'd made love to her, because if he was going to be honest with himself, he knew making love was what he'd done for the first time in his life. Being with Heather had been more than getting off and getting gone, and now she was spending the night in another man's bed. He didn't believe it about Heather. She was the female version of a stand-up guy, and he couldn't see her jumping into bed with Chase so soon after what they'd shared. Maybe Gloria was lying.

"Heather told you that herself?"

Gloria glanced at him out the corner of her slanted eyes, and the reflection of the orange streetlights on her raven-colored hair, made her look demonic. He wasn't sure he would believe this woman if she told him the grass was green, but it seemed like she was telling the truth about Heather and Chase.

"Yes, although anyone with eyes could see they were going to end up horizontal. Did you see the way they moved together on the dance floor? It's always a good indication of what a couple is like between the sheets, but, to answer your question, yes, your precious Heather told me they were spending the night together."

Mick couldn't loosen his jaw enough to respond. Luckily, Gloria didn't seem to mind the silence and they made the rest of the drive in almost complete silence. It was a far cry from his laugh-filled road trip with Heather last weekend.

After what felt like a three-month trek, rather than an hour and a half drive, Gloria pointed to a driveway, guarded by a massive wrought-iron gate. "There's the turn into my drive."

He stopped at the box. "What's the code?"

Gloria rattled off four numbers, and when he entered them into the keypad, the gate swung open with a loud creak. Thank God they were almost to her house. The news about Heather and Chase had him ready to explode, and he didn't want Gloria to see how much her words had affected him.

Just when he thought the long, tree-lined driveway would never end, they reached her huge Georgian style mansion. He pulled around the circular drive to the front door, and killed the engine. Much as he would like just to slow down and shove Gloria out, his inner southern gentleman forced him to see her to the door. He caught a glimmer of triumph in her eyes, as he got out to open her car door.

She held out one limp-wristed hand, and he reached down to help her out of the low-slung car. The slit in her black dress exposed a lot of Pilates-toned leg as she arose, but all Mick could think of was Heather with Chase, and her mile-long legs wrapped around the other man.

Gloria stood between the car and him and was pressed way too close for comfort. She fluttered her eyelashes at him, and Mick wondered if they were fake. They seemed improbable, almost like big, black moths perched on her eyelids. He thought of Heather and her natural beauty, and held back a wince.

"I was hoping I could persuade you to come in for…" she paused and licked her lips before continuing, "…a nightcap."

Mick cleared his throat and took a step back. "Sorry, Gloria, it's late."

She slid one hand up his arm and squeezed his bicep, and for one moment he thought she actually purred. "So what? You'll turn into a pumpkin? Come in."

Mick didn't think she only meant for him to come into her house, the glint in her eyes told him she really wanted him in her bed and in her body. "I'll have to take a rain check."

He tried to back up one step, but Gloria tightened her grip on his arm, and she was a freakishly strong little thing.

Before he realized what was happening, and could take measures to stop it, Gloria wound her hand around his neck and yanked his head down to lay a kiss on him.

Not too long ago, Mick might've gone for it, but

now it left him cold. Running in his mind like a movie, were his memories of Heather's kisses, and how Chase was the no doubt overjoyed recipient of them at this very minute.

He held himself very still, and didn't respond at all. Finally, Gloria pulled back, and her eyes were stormy, but her voice was deadly calm, "Guess you weren't kidding about the turning into a pumpkin thing. I would've gotten more response from a gourd." She smoothed her hair, before pulling her house key out of her evening bag. "Thanks for a lovely evening, Michael."

Funny how Gloria was the only person in the whole town who called him by his full name, the name he preferred, but it managed to get on his last nerve. He was Mick to the rest of the population of Rivers Bend, and he wondered why it was starting to feel so right to him.

God damn it! It shouldn't feel right to him. Gloria was the type of woman he needed. She was adept in social situations, and made it as clear as the crystal from which she sipped her champagne she would be a firecracker in bed. Maybe most important of all, he was pretty sure she was hard enough under her pretty veneer he'd never be able to break her, the way his father broke his mother's spirit.

Maybe the best way to protect Heather, and ensure she led the happy life she deserved, was for him to move on with someone less likely to be hurt by him. Someone he didn't care as much about, who didn't care as much about him. Someone like Gloria.

He ran a hand through his hair as he forced himself to say, "I'm sorry tonight wasn't what you were hoping for. How about dinner tomorrow night to make up for it?"

Chapter 16

Mick was uncomfortable in the formal country club dining room, where Gloria had chosen to have dinner, the way he always was in this type of environment. He shot his sleeve under the tailor made suit he wore like armor, or like camouflage, to blend into the rarified atmosphere.

He lifted his chin and looked around; it was like every other snooty club he'd ever set foot in, plush carpet under his Italian leather shoes, white tablecloths, the tinkle of fine china and silver, and a muted version of an old standard being played on a grand piano.

He froze in his surveillance of the room, as his eyes landed on the last person he expected to see—Heather. She was with a man, a man who was *not* Chase. What the hell? How many guys was she seeing?

This man was attractive, with brown hair and an easy smile, but Mick was happy to note he was a lot more ordinary looking than Chase.

He dragged his eyes away when he realized Gloria had begun her procession to their table. As he trailed in her wake, it felt as though she knew everyone here, and they stopped at each table so she could introduce him to her friends.

He was saying all the right things, but a good portion of his attention was still on Heather and her mystery date.

****

Heather squirmed a little on the plush cushioned seat.

Ty grinned at her across the table. "You hate it here." It wasn't a question.

"I'm not super-comfortable here, no. When you said you'd take me out to dinner as a study break, I thought you meant a pizza from Mancini's. If you'd told me you wanted to go to the country club, I wouldn't have said yes."

"I know, why do you think I didn't tell you until I picked you up? And I wouldn't have even told you then if you weren't wearing sweats. I had to 'fess up since I needed to tell you to change clothes." He paled under the blaze of Heather's ferocious scowl. "Look, it's not my favorite place either, but I have a membership here for professional reasons, and I appreciate you coming to help me make an appearance, and to use up my food and beverage minimum for this month."

Heather smiled at her best friend's brother, who over the years had become a good friend to her also. Especially since Bethanne and Cisco got married, Ty and she spent even more time together. "You sweet talker, you! Way to make a girl feel special."

"Making girls feel special is not my forté." He winked at her.

A woman's tinkling laughter broke the buzz of muted conversation around them, and Ty and Heather both turned their heads to locate the source.

"Oh joy. Gloria Peterson and her latest victim, who is unbelievably hot, by the way. Wonder who he is, and if there's any chance he actually bats for my team."

"He's Mick Evans"—Heather ground out through

clenched teeth—"and I hate to disappoint you, but he plays for my team."

Ty widened his eyes. "*Your* team—interesting."

She blushed and picked up her water goblet with a shaky hand. The condensation from it dripped on the crisp tablecloth; Heather swiped at it before taking a sip. "Not *my* team, my team...I mean, not me personally...I just mean..."

"He's straight. I get it. I wasn't trying to suggest you and he played one-on-one for your team." He leaned back and took a sip of his beer. "At least not until your lame, stammering response. After that, I've got some questions."

Heather traded her water goblet for her wine glass, because she knew Ty rarely pulled his punches, and she knew she would need the alcohol for this conversation. "Okay, let me have it. What do you want to know?"

Ty glanced at Mick and then back at Heather. "I recognize him now from the christening party. I was distracted that day, otherwise I would've noticed his incredible hotness, and your barely disguised attraction to him, and been on your case about it sooner. If you and the hunka-hunka burnin' CEO are an item, then why is he here with Gloria Peterson? And why are you here with me? And why did you go out with Chase last night? Do you have some sort of diabolical plan to keep all the smokin' hot guys in the South to yourself?"

Heather grinned and shook her head. She played up her southern accent. "Ya got me. I'm fixin' to be a redneck femme fatale. Watch out, Daisy Duke! Gay, straight—no man is safe!"

Ty leaned forward to clasp her hand, where it rested on top of the table. "Seriously, Heath, it's a lot more drama than you usually have in your life. Bradens are the most loyal people in the universe, and *you* are the most loyal of the Bradens. You've always been there for me, so if you need me now, I'm here for you."

Before she could swallow the lump in her throat to answer, Gloria's royal procession through the dining room stopped at their table.

"Ty, Heather, I never expected to see you two at the club," Gloria enthused with false cheer.

"I don't know why not. I've been a member here since I finished law school and moved back to the Bend." Ty kept his voice light and the grip on Heather's hand tight.

She glanced up at Mick, and realized her mother was right. If glowering were an Olympic event, Mick Evans would take home the Gold medal.

Gloria followed his stormy gaze to Ty and Heather's joined hands. And the brief narrowing of her gaze expressed her displeasure their handholding seemed to bother Mick. Gloria slid her arm through Mick's, and pressed her breasts to his side. She flashed a bright, triumphant smile at Heather, and it became clear why Ghastly Gloria had stopped at their table. The country club dining room might be fancier than the cafeteria at Rivers Bend High, but it certainly felt like high school all over again. And the prom queen was here to show off her handsome, football player date to the nerdy girl. Except now Heather wasn't sixteen anymore and she didn't feel intimidated by Gloria. Furious at Mick, yes. Intimidated by Gloria, no. She sat a little higher in her chair, and held on to Ty's hand, mainly because it seemed to bug Mick, and his being bugged really seemed to bug Ghastly Glo. It was a win-

win.

"I think it was more a dig at me, Ty, rather than you. Isn't that right, Gloria?"

****

Mick admired the way Heather called Gloria out on her bitchiness. And speaking of Gloria, when had she attached herself to him like a limpet? Mick had been so focused on the lawyer's heartfelt words to Heather when Gloria and he had come up to the table, their easy camaraderie, and their still-clasped hands he hadn't noticed Gloria going to full-body contact mode with him. He tried to disengage, but she just held on tighter. Her grip was like one of those toy Chinese finger traps; the harder you try to escape, the tighter they get.

"Since Heather is your employee, I don't need to introduce you two, but I don't think you've met her escort. Michael Evans—Ty Harris."

Gloria made a point of stressing Heather was his employee, but right now, seeing her look so fresh and natural in her silky blue top, with her hair tousled—all Mick could think of was Heather, and not at all in an employer-employee kind of way. He remembered her on top of him in her messy bedroom just a week before. And now...his eyes flickered to her hand in another man's and wondered how everything had gone so wrong so fast. Maybe Danny was right about him, and he was a colossal fuck-up who didn't deserve a woman like Heather.

This lawyer seemed like a nice guy. He could see Heather settling down with someone like him. He started as he realized the guy had finally let go of Heather's hand to stand and extend it to Mick in greeting.

Donna Simonetta

"Nice to finally meet you, Mick. My brother-in-law has talked about you a lot."

"Your brother-in-law?"

"Cisco."

"You're Bethanne's brother?"

He'd never heard Bethanne's brother dated Heather, but there was clearly a deep connection between them. With Rivers Bend gossip being what it was, it was a miracle this morsel had escaped him. And what about Chase? How did the musician fit into this scenario? A feeling gnawed at his gut he was missing a key piece of the puzzle.

A furrow had formed on Gloria's brow, and Mick sensed this meeting had not gone according to her plan, whatever her twisted plan had been.

She tugged on his arm. "Our table is ready, Michael."

Heather leaned back in her chair and crossed her long legs. "Don't let us hold you up, Gloria."

Gloria frowned in response to Heather's easy smile, and Mick realized Gloria had intended to intimidate Heather, but fallen short of her goal. Way short, in fact, she couldn't even see the goal line from where she stood.

"Nice to meet you, Ty. Heather, I'll see you in the morning."

"Actually, no you won't, boss. I'm on vacation this week. Don't you look at the schedules I painstakingly prepare for you?"

Gloria beamed. "So, Ty and you are kicking off your vacation with dinner out together. How sweet, we won't intrude any longer." She tugged Mick away from the table.

176

****

Ty ran his hands through his reddish-brown hair and scratched his head. "If I'm not wrong, and I so rarely am"—he grinned—"that man has no clue I'm gay, and he was jealous of us."

Heather frowned and glanced over her shoulder to see Mick pulling out Gloria's chair for her, while G.G. seated herself like a queen on her throne. She looked back at Ty. "You think?"

"I do. Didn't you notice the way he glared at us holding hands? He did not like it, and this is not a boss reaction. It's a boyfriend reaction; what the hell is going on with you two?"

"Nothing"—she flushed under his unblinking stare and fiddled with the cloth napkin on her lap—"now."

"But something did happen?"

"Yes, but seriously, Ty, could we please talk about something else? *Anything* else, even mind-numbingly dull legal talk would be fine with me."

He screwed up his mouth as he searched her eyes. "Sure. Fine. But if you ever need to talk…"

"You're there for me. I know, and I appreciate it."

He paused a beat and then said, "So, graduation coming up, that's big stuff. How many tickets do you get?"

"They limit it to four, since there are so many of us graduating, but I don't know if I'm going to walk."

Ty's jaw dropped. "What? After all the years and hard work you've put in to get this degree? You've *got* to go to graduation."

She held her glass of Pinot Grigio up to the glow from the candle in the center of their table, and stared at the light reflected in the pale liquid. She shrugged.

"What? Is this topic off limits too?" Ty slapped the table in exasperation and the heavy silverware rattled. The voices around them hushed at the clatter. Ty leaned in to whisper, "That was a little harder than I intended, but I've got to tell you the other off-limit topic is staring at us, and he is *not* happy."

Heather fought the urge to look for herself, and decided to stick with the safer topic at hand. "I guess I'll go to graduation. It's just I'm not a kid; sometimes I feel like a senior citizen around the other people in my classes. And Saturdays are busy days at the farm and the Retreat. I hate to ask anyone to take the time off to go."

"Trust me, you won't have to ask; we'll all be fighting each other to get one of the four tickets to be there to cheer our girl on."

"It would make for some fine entertainment at Mom's Derby party this Saturday."

Ty deepened his voice to sound like the ring announcer at a pro wrestling event. "Be there or be square for the Graduation Ticket Death Match, this Saturday, live at the Braden Farm!"

****

Gloria's eyes glittered in the flickering candlelight and Mick didn't think it was from passion. In spite of her syrupy tones, he knew a pissed off woman when he saw one, and he was looking at one across the table right now.

"I am *not* a woman who is happily disposed to playing second fiddle, Michael, just so you know."

"I never thought you were."

She arched her eyebrows. "Then you should have known better than to put on your little caveman display over Heather Braden when you are with me this evening."

"I *never* behave like a caveman."

Her words stung. Caveman was one step below redneck.

"Oh good gracious, Michael! If you'd had a club hidden in your lovely suit of clothes you would have conked her over the head and dragged her off to your cave. Such a display." She tsked her tongue.

"I don't think it was that bad, and I…"

The end of his sentence was cut off by Gloria's sharp interruption. "At *my* club; in front of *my* friends…oh yes, Michael, it was *that* bad."

Mick picked up where he'd been cut off, as if she hadn't interrupted him. "…never intended any disrespect to you."

The waiter provided a much needed cooling off period for them both when he came to the table to take their order.

From Mick's point of view, the whole purpose of this dinner was to help him pull away from Heather, and yet here he was with his stomach in knots, because Heather was here with yet another man. And right now, Gloria was a whole lot less appealing to him than Heather.

Gloria gave new meaning to the phrase 'high maintenance,' but she was only interested in superficial, and a woman with a shell as hard as Gloria's would never break under his darker moods. He needed to remember why he was here with Gloria, and forget about Heather and her date. Heather deserved a nice guy like Ty, and not someone who was a clone of his mean-spirited father.

He forced a smile to his lips. "Since we're at a country club, I'll use a golf analogy: may I have a mulligan, and we'll start this evening over?"

Her feline smile made Mick wonder why she just hadn't ordered a bowl of cream for dinner and been done with it. "If you can focus on *me* while we're in front of my friends, and pretend Heather Braden is back in the barn where she belongs, I think a mulligan can be arranged."

Mick bit back the harsh defense of Heather her snarky words inspired in him. Heather was not his to defend. That was Ty's job, or Chase's, he wasn't precisely sure whose job it was, he only knew it wasn't his. Remembering the way Heather held her own against his father and Danny, Mick realized she didn't need any man to defend her. He felt such pride burn in his heart as he thought about her spunkiness, he wondered anew what he was doing on a date with Gloria.

He rolled his neck, and smiled at some long story Gloria told him about people he didn't know, and frankly could give two shits about, and wondered when his social life had gotten this complicated. He just knew he had to hang tough for Heather's sake. She was better off without him.

Chapter 17

Bedlam reigned in the normally serene lobby of the Retreat. Voices were raised as one group tried to check in, and Mick hung up the phone after a frantic call from the leader of the second group due to arrive this morning, who was stuck at the airport with his entire staff, because the minibus hired to transport them had yet to arrive.

He needed to get on the horn to hunt down the van, but first he had to listen to this woman's interminable discussion about the importance of her special diet, in which she apparently wouldn't eat anything that had been cooked. Who the hell had come up with this one?

"I'll personally notify our chef about your dietary considerations, ma'am."

Pacified, the woman thanked him and moved away, and he heard Jeff's amused drawl at his ear. "Our *chef*? Mrs. Wilson is going to be thrilled with her promotion."

One side of Mick's mouth quirked up. "Mrs. W. will be less thrilled when she hears this woman doesn't want to eat anything that's been cooked above a certain temperature. What's that about anyway? And do you have any idea who I can contact about the M.I.A. minibus?"

"And now you know why I consider my sister indispensible. It's not about nepotism. She keeps this place running like a top. Did you ever see a clusterfuck like this check-in when she's here?"

"No. I've been blissfully unaware of what the check-in process required."

"That's because Heather has it as organized and coordinated as the D-Day invasion. Only with freshly-baked cookies."

Mick slapped his forehead. "Cookies! I forgot to get the goddamned cookies from the Nosh Pit! Is it really only Monday? Because it feels like later in the week—Wednesday at least, if not Thursday. Friday would just be wishful thinking."

"It's not just Monday. It's Monday *morning*, my friend. The whole Heather-less week stretches before us. And this is precisely why I wanted my sister and you to work out your differences. We can't afford to lose her."

"You won't." Mick would leave before he let Heather lose her job on account of him.

As the last guest left the lobby, peace was restored.

"I think the number for the airport transportation service is in Heather's office, c'mon," Jeff said as he walked toward the door from the lobby to their office area.

If Mick hoped the change of venue would get him off the hook conversationally, he was about to be doomed to disappointment.

Jeff flicked the light switch by the door, and the fluorescent light came on with a low hum. He lifted a Rolodex off of her desk and flicked through the cards.

"Old school," Mick observed.

Jeff snorted. "I know, right? Heather keeps all this info on her phone too, but she calls the Rolodex our insurance, in case she's ever hit by a bus. She knows

Cisco and I could never find anything on her computer."

"Hit by a bus, huh? Do we even have buses in Rivers Bend?"

"Nah, but she likes to be prepared for anything and everything. Here it is!" He yanked a card out, but held it between his thumb and forefinger like a magician getting ready to do a card trick. "I'd like to talk to you about something before I let you take this card."

Mick's stomach clenched. He didn't like where he suspected this talk was going.

"You took my sister home to meet your family weekend before last."

"I thought that was old news."

"I've been busy with my daughter and Maggie, and getting ready for the benefit so I'm a little behind the times. I just heard about you and Heather on Saturday night."

"There is no 'me and Heather.' "

Jeff raised his eyebrows, and waited in silence for Mick to continue.

"Okay, maybe for a very brief time I thought there might be a Heather and me."

Jeff continued to stare. "When was that 'brief while'?"

"I want to be completely straight with you. So, in an effort for full disclosure, the first time was eleven years ago in Portland."

"Son of a bitch!" Jeff's voice was not its usual lazy drawl. He'd never seen his old friend angry before, and it was not a pleasant thing. Jeff's face was red as a summer tomato as he shouted, "She was just a baby then!"

"I thought she was older than she was. As soon as I found out she was under eighteen I ended it."

"Aren't you just a fucking saint? If that was the first time, when was the second?"

"Since I've been in Rivers Bend. We got close again, but it didn't work out."

Jeff dropped his head back and screwed his eye shut. "Man, I really don't want to do this."

"Do what?" Mick asked warily.

"This." Jeff drew back his right arm and punched Mick in the face.

****

Heather sat on her little back porch, a textbook open on her lap. She could hear the bustle of the breakfast rush below her at the Nosh Pit, and wondered how things were going at work with two groups due to arrive at the Retreat today. She shrugged before trying to focus on her studies again. She had her first exam tonight, and with all the Mick drama lately, she'd fallen a little behind with her schoolwork.

She needed to stop thinking about him, or about work, and just concentrate on getting through her exams and her graduation. Between her brother, Cisco, and Mick, she was sure they had things under control at the Retreat.

Her cell phone rang, and she picked it up off the small wrought iron table next to her chair. She peered at the screen to see who was calling, and smiled when she saw the name.

"Billy! I'm so glad to hear from you. I guess you got my message."

"I did! I'm totally psyched, Heather. You're the best! Do you think this guy is serious about needing a mechanic?"

"He is. Are you interested?"

"Am I ever!" Billy's voice enthused through the phone.

"Ed asked me to give you his number, and if you're interested, he wants you to call him. After we get off, I'll text his number to you." She paused and frowned before continuing, "Have you thought this through? Working with Ed Miller, eventually maybe taking over his garage, would mean you'd move here to Rivers Bend. It won't be a popular choice in the Evans homestead."

There was a brief silence, and when he spoke, Billy's voice sounded older than the excited boy he'd sounded like initially. "I know. And it means a lot of angry bullshit here, but I *can't* work in that mine for the rest of my life like my dad has. I just can't! This might be my ticket out, and I'd be an idiot not to take it."

"But it's going to be rough, especially with your dad and Danny."

"I know, but Mick did it; I can too."

"It hasn't been easy for Mick though…"

"And this might make it worse for him. I don't want to make things uglier between Mick and my dad, but what if this is the only chance I get? I don't want to let it slip away."

"At least you can talk to Ed Miller about the job. Maybe after you do, you won't even be interested in it."

"I really doubt it; working on cars all day sounds great!"

"Remember you'll be away from home for the first time. I was more homesick than I expected to be when I moved to Portland," Heather warned.

"I'll have you and Mick there." Billy's voice sounded happy and confident once again.

After chatting a few more minutes, they hung up, and Heather gulped. What had she put in motion here? When she heard about the mechanic's job, she'd thought of Billy right away, but didn't consider the long-term repercussions until later. Mick's father was going to be furious, both with Billy and with Mick. And Mick would more than likely be furious with her.

She took a deep breath and picked her textbook back up. If she survived finals with all the craziness going on right now in her normally placid life, it would be a freaking miracle.

****

Mick rubbed his sore jaw. "I guess I deserved that."

"You deserved more than just one punch, you sorry son of a bitch, but you're my friend so I don't have it in me to give you a full-on beat down." Jeff rubbed his knuckles. "We're talking about my kid sister; I had to do something! I mean, seriously man, of all the women in the world, why did you have to mess around with one of my sisters?"

"It's not like that, Jeff, I wasn't just messing around with Heather. I really care about her."

Jeff shook his head and continued as if Mick hadn't spoken, "I know I followed the same M.O., before I met Maggie. You keep things light, make sure the girl knows the score, and nobody gets hurt. But I never—never—messed with a buddy's sister!"

Mick felt his own fists clench, and he fought against the urge to pop Jeff in the face for thinking the worst of him. "I told you, it wasn't like that with

Heather. I really like her."

"Then why are you dating Gloria fucking Peterson?" Jeff growled.

"Because Heather dumped me!" Mick shouted in frustration. "Heather broke up with me, and I know she deserves someone better than me, so I thought I'd make things easier for her and go out with Gloria fucking Peterson. Happy now?"

Jeff raked his hands through his already messy hair, making it stick up even more. "Shit, man, of course it doesn't make me happy. I'm sorry."

Mick raised an eyebrow. "You're sorry she dumped my ass? You socked me in the jaw for dating her, and *now* you're sorry she broke things off with me?"

"Hell yeah, I'm sorry! If you really care about her, that's a whole different thing. You'd be one of the few guys on the planet who is just barely good enough for my sister. I don't know what this bullshit is you're spouting about her deserving someone better." Jeff narrowed his eyes. "Is it Chase? Is he why she broke up with you? Because, I like him, but I don't think he'll ever settle down. She's just gonna end up hurt by him. You're definitely a better alternative than Chase."

Mick opened his mouth to stretch it out, and flinched when he rubbed the tender flesh where he suspected he was going to have a helluva bruise later. "Then I'd hate to be Chase when you catch up to him, if this is what you do to the guy you think is better for your sister."

"So it *is* because of Chase?"

Mick shrugged. "I don't think so. She talked a lot about *my* shortcomings, so I think she broke up with me on account of me—not Chase, or even Ty."

"Ty?" Jeff's jaw dropped to the floor. "What the hell does Ty have to do with anything?"

"She's dating him too. I saw them out to dinner with each other last night, and she's going to spend this vacation with him. Not with Chase, and most definitely not with me."

"You think she's on vacation with Ty? Tyler Harris? About 5'11', reddish-brown hair?"

"Yeah, that's him. Bethanne's brother."

Jeff's slow grin was firmly back in place on his face. "I know who Ty Harris is. He's one of my closest friends."

Mick scowled. "Your best friend, Heather's best friend's brother, how fucking cozy and perfect for all of you if Heather and Ty end up together."

"Put the green-eyed monster back in his cage, buddy. Ty is all of those things, and a great guy to boot, but there's no way he's dating Heather."

"I saw it with my own eyes. You're not the best judge; let's face it, you didn't think she was dating me either, and she was."

Jeff laughed a deep, hearty rumble that shook his broad shoulders. When he got enough breath to speak, he wheezed out, "Ty is gonna love this when I tell him."

"Tell him what?"

"That big, tough, icy Mick Evans got his panties in a wad with jealousy over Ty's affair with Heather!" A fresh bout of laughter overcame Jeff at the words, and he had to bend over at the waist to catch his breath.

"Want to let the man you just punched in the face in on the joke?"

"Ty and Heather are friends—good ones—but they'll never be anything more, because Ty is as gay as the day is long. He's much more likely to be interested in dating you than he is in Heather."

Chapter 18

Heather drove up the gravel drive winding through the woods; her emotions were confused. On the one hand, she was excited beyond belief to have just taken her last final exam. Barring unforeseen flunkage, she'd be graduating from college at long last. On the other hand, her stomach clenched as she considered what it might mean for her—should she stay at the Retreat? Or even in Rivers Bend? This was her home, and the idea of leaving its comforting arms made her feel queasy. She consoled herself by thinking she didn't have to make any big decisions immediately.

The light got brighter as she pulled into the clearing in front of the cabin Mick was temporarily calling home. Magda had stayed here before she'd moved into Bethanne and Cisco's little cottage, when they moved into their new home, musical houses, Rivers Bend style. The rustic cabin she approached was shaded by tall trees, and through her open car windows she could hear the river rushing by just beyond the cabin.

Boy she was dreading this conversation with Mick. She'd put it off long enough, maybe she'd waited too long, but she'd set the wheels in motion for Billy, and she needed to smooth the way for him as much as possible. She wondered if the brothers had spoken yet. They hadn't as of her last conversation with Billy, but he might've called Mick today.

She took a deep breath and pushed her oversized, round sunglasses up on her head as she got out the car. In the distance she heard the muted sounds of music and laughter from the cocktail party one of the Retreat groups had scheduled for tonight by the pool, which was located just through the woods from Mick's cabin.

"Heather. This is an unexpected surprise."

Mick's deep voice rumbled from the shadows on his porch, and she jumped at the sound. She hadn't seen him in the shadows.

"Sorry, I didn't mean to scare you. I thought you knew I was here." Mick unfolded his long body from the Adirondack chair where he had been sprawled; he walked to the top step and leaned against the post.

Heather's mouth went dry, and other parts of her body got wet, at the sight of him. Mick must have taken a shower right after work, his normally immaculate hair was still wet and unstyled; he wore a pair of loose, low-slung athletic shorts. That was it…just shorts. His feet were bare and so was his muscled chest, still damp from his shower on this humid, late spring evening.

He took a sip of the bottle of beer he held loosely in one hand. She tried to swallow, but her throat was the Sahara. She knew she had to speak, was all too aware she was just standing here like some mute geekazoid, but the sight of a half-naked Mick, combined with the post-finals muzziness of her brain, left her completely unable to think of a blessed thing to say.

"Can I get you one of these?" Mick tilted the green bottle in her direction.

Grateful for some conversational guidance,

Heather smiled. "No, thank you. I'm on my way out to dinner with the girls to celebrate taking my last final today."

"The girls?"

"Bethanne, Deidre, Maggie and my nieces, Sam and Caitlin."

"Sounds like fun."

"Yes, I'm really looking forward to it."

After a brief silence, when she didn't say anything else, he said, "Not to be rude or anything, but why are you here, Heather?"

Not to jump your very fine bones, no sirree, bub! Okay…some thoughts were best left unsaid. "I needed to talk to you about something."

Mick flopped back into his chair and stretched his long legs out in front of him. Heather walked up the three steps, and sat on the top one, with her back resting against the post.

"That's interesting, because there's something I wanted to talk to you about too."

His icy voice took her by surprise. It was at odds with his relaxed body language. True, they hadn't spoken since she'd told him they needed to cool it between them, if you didn't count the awkward meeting at the country club, and Heather didn't. But she wasn't expecting the deep freeze from him.

Curious about what had crawled up his butt and died, Heather said, "Okay, you first."

He took a swig, his eyes smoldering as he looked at her over the bottle as he drank. "Fine. I'll go first. Why the hell didn't you tell me Ty Harris was gay?"

Heather blinked. She'd been braced for him to tear into her about interfering with his family, by getting

Billy the interview with Ed Miller at the garage. She was not expecting a discussion of her friend's sexuality.

"It never occurred to me to tell you?" Her confusion at the sharp left turn into Weirdsville their conversation had taken, turned her statement into a question.

"It was easier to let me think you were on a date with him last Sunday? And that you were going on vacation with him this week?"

She wrinkled her nose and frowned. "I never told you either of those things."

"No, but you certainly didn't tell me they weren't true."

"I never told you the Earth wasn't flat either, because I thought you were intelligent enough to figure it out on your own. Clearly, I was wrong about you."

"But Gloria said—"

"Gloria?" Her voice sounded shrill, even to her own ears, and she tried to modulate it. "Gloria is the one who made you think Ty and I had a thing going on?"

"She said some of it right in front of you; you didn't correct her."

"Because I didn't hear her! I try to tune Gloria out as much as possible when she talks. It's kind of like when Petunia is after a squirrel—she yaps and yaps, but after a while it just becomes white noise to me."

"Oh."

"Why does it matter to you whether or not Ty is gay? I didn't have you pegged as a homophobe."

"I'm not. Ty seems like a good guy, and he could be sleeping with the whole starting line-up of the Pintos for all I care, but I thought you were on a date with him, going away with him on vacation…"

Heather held up her hand to cut him off. "And it would matter to you *why*? Those are ideas you got from *your* date. From the woman you were still with from the night before…"

"No, I wasn't," he interrupted.

At his quiet denial, relief flooded through her, relief she had no business feeling, since she had been the one to break up with Mick. He was free to see whomever he chose, even if it was Ghastly Gloria. Still. It felt good to know he hadn't spent Saturday night with Glo.

"You weren't?"

"No. I hadn't seen her since I dropped her off at home after the benefit Saturday night."

The feeling of relief grew. "I thought you were spending the night in Baltimore, and having breakfast with her sister Sunday morning."

"We weren't, and we never planned to. Why would you think that?"

"Gloria told me."

One side of his mouth turned up in a way that turned her insides to jelly. "Gloria. The same one you told me you never listen to? The one whose voice is just background noise to you? She told you these things, and you simply believed her?" He stopped and stared past her, and then shook his head slowly. "But I have to admit you weren't the only one who took something she said at face value. Did you and Chase spend the night together at the hotel in Baltimore on Saturday?"

She blushed and turned her face away from him. "No, but I might've let Gloria think we did after she told me you were spending the night with her. I shared a room with my mom at the hotel. Chase stayed somewhere else."

He put the beer bottle on the table next to him, and wiped the condensation on his hands from it on his shorts. "Looks like we both had some mistaken ideas about how quickly we'd each moved on."

"Looks like."

They sat in silence for a few moments. The music from the party drifted through the woods to them, old Motown.

Heather was irritated she had fallen for Gloria's lies hook, line, and sinker. She should've known it wasn't true, and the other woman would try to stir up trouble between Mick and her.

"How did your exams go?" he asked with genuine interest.

Heather had two brothers, so she wasn't too surprised from his point of view that the moment was over and the discussion was closed. Two women would've talked it to death. She smiled at the thought. She always had been enough of a tomboy to like the men's way better.

"Pretty well, I think." She sat in the sun, and he was shadowed by the overhang of the porch, so she just noticed the bruise on his strong jaw line. "What happened to your face?"

"I walked into something."

"Into what?"

He grinned ruefully. "Your brother's fist."

Her head fell back and thumped against the post. "Jeff did that to you? Why? What the hell is going on at work? I *knew* I shouldn't have taken this week off."

"It wasn't a work-related disagreement. It was

more of a…well…*you*-related dispute."

She gasped and covered her mouth with her hand. "Oh God, Mick, I'm so sorry!"

"It's a big brother's prerogative. I knew going into it with you that getting socked in the face by Jeff was inevitable." A slow grin spread across his face. "It was worth it."

"You two have been fighting all week?"

"No. This happened on Monday, and we're guys. I dated his sister. He punched me in the face. Problem resolved. Back to work."

She shook her head in disbelief. "Men are such simple creatures."

"Yep." He nodded agreement. "What did you need to talk to me about?"

She bit her bottom lip. Here it was, the topic she was dreading discussing with him. "Have you talked to Billy this week?"

"My brother? No. Why? Is everything all right at home?"

"Yes! Nothing's wrong." Her words came out in a breathless rush to reassure him. She paused before adding, "Not wrong, precisely. In fact, it might turn out to be good news."

Mick pulled his legs up and straightened his posture in his chair. "Now you're making me nervous."

"I got my oil changed last week at Miller's Garage. Have you met Ed Miller yet?"

Mick's forehead wrinkled. "You have totally lost me. How did we get from something going on with my family to your oil change at Miller's Garage?"

"Ed is getting older; he's starting to think about retirement, and he has no one to pass the garage on to.

He asked if I knew a young mechanic who might be interested in working with him and eventually taking over the business. Right away, I thought of—"

"Billy." He finished her sentence and clipped the name so short, his jaw snapped shut, and his teeth clicked together.

"Yes." The word caught and she cleared her throat before repeating it with more force, "Yes. I called Billy to tell him about the opportunity." She peered up at him through her choppy bangs. "He didn't call you?"

"I had a voicemail from him, but it's been so crazy at work without you this week, by the way, on Monday I need to talk to you about a raise, you totally deserve one. I haven't had the chance to call him back. I was going to give him a buzz tonight. Why do you ask? Is there something more you need to tell me?"

"He spoke to Ed, and they hit it off over the phone. Billy's coming to Rivers Bend next week to interview with him in person."

Mick ran his hand over his jaw without thinking, and winced when he got to the bruise. This woman was causing all kinds of pain and turmoil in his life. Again. "What you're telling me is Billy is going to quit the mine to move to Rivers Bend and become a mechanic."

"He's coming to see if he'd like it; he might not want to do it after the visit."

Mick raised his eyebrows. "Are you kidding me? *Of course* he's going to want this job. It's what he's wanted to do since the first time he touched a car engine, and I have to admit it would be nice to have him here, but the old man is gonna be pissed."

"With both of you?"

Mick inclined his head and lifted the bottle off the

table. Before he drank from it, he looked at her over the lip of the bottle. "With *all* of us. Don't think not being an Evans will help you escape my old man's wrath, Miss Braden."

She swallowed hard. "I can handle his wrath, but how about yours? Any wrath on your part?"

He thought for a long time, and the sounds of the party in the distance made Heather want to run to it to escape from this uncomfortable conversation. He was taking too long to think about his answer. She had overstepped her bounds and he was angry. She licked her dry lips and looked longingly to the sound of the boppy hits of the eighties now playing at the party. It sounded happy, and more important, it sounded far away from the dressing down she feared she was about to get from Mick.

Finally he shrugged. "I'm not sure how I feel about you interfering with my family. It's like you're my girlfriend, but without any of the benefits of being in a romantic relationship. A small part of me is pissed you meddled, but the rest of me knows you did it with good intentions, and maybe it's the push Billy needed to get out." He took another drink from the bottle and shook his head. "I don't know what I'm feeling about you right now, Heather. I really don't."

The tightness in Heather's chest loosened a little. At least he wasn't furious with her, but she didn't think he only meant he didn't know how he felt about her with relation to her interference. He could just join the confusion club, because she was right there with him. Their relationship had gotten so complicated, it felt like the plot of a nineteenth-century Russian novel, transplanted to modern, small-town Virginia.

She rose and brushed off the seat of her pants. "I'll have to wait for another time for you to figure things out. I've got to pick up Sam and meet everyone for dinner."

As she walked to the car, she heard his footsteps on the porch, and then his deep voice rumbled, "Congratulations on finishing your last exam. You should be really proud of yourself. I know I am."

She raised a hand in acknowledgment and got into her car. As she turned her car around to pull out, she couldn't resist another peek at Mick. He stood on the top step of the porch, one shoulder leaning against the post. And my-oh-my that was one fine glower on his face. She never thought she was the kind of girl to fall for some kind of brooding, Gothic romance novel hero, but she had to admit to herself Mick's Heathcliff routine really did it for her like nothing else did.

She blasted the air conditioning to cool off a little before she had to face her friends and family, with their all-seeing, all-knowing eyes. This thing with Mick couldn't go anywhere, and she wasn't in the mood for the Spanish Inquisition, Rivers Bend style, so she didn't want her flushed cheeks and bright eyes to give anything away over dinner.

****

"Something is *so* going on with you," Bethanne observed sagely out of nowhere. The talk had all been about her graduation and the Derby party tomorrow.

She brushed her bangs off her forehead and said too quickly, "There's nothing going on with me. Why would you say that?"

"Don't kid a kidder, Heather. We all know you well enough to know something's up, I'm the only one brave enough to say it."

"Brave or brazen?" Heather challenged with a jut of her chin.

Bethanne narrowed her eyes. "Why were you late getting to the restaurant tonight?"

"I had to stop to talk to a friend before I picked up Sam."

"Mm hm. What friend?"

"A friend. Sheesh, Bethanne, what's with the third degree? I was only five minutes late."

"And you're being so defensive—makes a girl wonder where you were."

"I told you—with a friend!"

Her sister Deidre looked around the table, before saying with emphasis, "All your friends are here, darlin', so I've got to wonder who you were with too."

Bethanne leaned back in her seat, before turning her head to look at Sam so fast her hair spun out around her. "When your Aunt Heather picked you up tonight, what direction did she come from? Was it the main drive to the Retreat?"

Sam squirmed in her seat. "No. She came from the road leading to the guest cabins."

Bethanne shot up in her seat, and yelled as if she were a lawyer interrogating a witness, "Ah ha! The road to the guest cabins…interesting. Would those be the same guest cabins where a certain Mick Evans is currently residing?"

Heather felt her face heat up, as she picked up her Dark and Stormy and slugged some back. "Really, Bethanne, you need to get out more and stop watching reruns on TV. This isn't an old crime drama, and you're not a lawyer. This was *supposed* to be a dinner to celebrate me taking my last exam today."

"Don't knock Perry Mason, everyone cracked under his cross-examination. So...were you or were you not late because you were with Mick Evans?"

Sam excused herself to go to the ladies room, and Heather's mom leveled a look at Bethanne. "When my granddaughter gets back, will you please leave her out of your interrogation? Better yet, drop the whole thing altogether."

"Thanks, Mom!"

Joyce swung her head to look at Heather. "Don't be too fast with your thanks, missy, I just don't want Sam to be put in an awkward position, but I *do* want to know what you were doing coming from Mick's place tonight."

Heather's eyes drew round. "Why is everyone so interested in this? I stopped by Mick's to tell him Ed Miller is interviewing his little brother about a possible job opening at Miller's Garage, on my recommendation. That's all, end of story."

Caitlin leaned forward and asked eagerly, "Mick has a little brother? How old is he? Is he as hot as Mick?"

"Down girl," said Deirdre. "My boy-crazy daughter, ladies."

"I'm not boy crazy, but you can't deny if Mick's brother is as good looking as he is, it's worth knowing about him before every other girl in town."

Deidre rolled her eyes and looked at Heather. "So are you back with Mick? He didn't bring Gloria into the Nosh Pit all week."

"That's because he didn't take a lunch break all week," Bethanne said. "Cisco told me without Heather there, the Retreat was a zoo, and Mick was a real trouper about pitching in with everything. He was running himself ragged trying to do his job and Heather's."

"Here comes Sam, so I don't want to be talking about her friend's mother when she gets back to the table, but just so you will all stop match-making, I'll just say, I saw Mick Sunday night, when he was out to dinner at the country club with Gloria. Seeing them together didn't feel good, I'll tell you that! So, please, stop trying to push us together. It's not happening."

Chapter 19

The whir of the blender outdoors on a sunny May Saturday meant only one thing to Heather: her mother's annual Kentucky Derby party. For as long as she could remember, it was one of her favorite days of the year; it ranked right up there with her birthday and Christmas.

She lifted the lid off the blender and an icy mist formed over the frozen green slush. She sniffed it before she poured it into the cocktail glasses. *Yum!* The minty-bourbony aroma of the cocktail she made for the party was tantalizing on a warm day.

The guests were due any minute; right now, only the Braden family was gathered to sample the first round of her frozen mint juleps.

She loved the traditions of this party. It was always outdoors, weather permitting, family and close friends only, and everyone was dressed up in their Derby finery. Much like at Churchill Downs, hats were de rigueur, and Heather was especially pleased with her hat this year. She wore a pink and tangerine swingy mini dress and had decorated her hat with color-coordinated silk flowers and feathers.

Her sister Deidre had opted for a sparkly fascinator this year, and Heather knew they were trendier, but she just loved getting to wear the big hat. It made the day feel even more special.

Magda jumped into the spirit of the day, and her

crazy, corkscrew blonde curls were topped with a hat that would do the royal family proud, in a pretty turquoise color to match her dress.

Jeff wrapped an arm around Magda's shoulders and hoisted his glass with the other. "To Derby Day!"

"Derby Day!" They all toasted in unison as they clinked their glasses and then sipped.

Jason took a heartier swig than everyone else. "Whoa!" He yelled as he pressed the heel of his hand to the bridge of his nose. "Brain freeze, but holy frozen bourbon, Batgirl! This is your best Derby cocktail yet!"

Heather held out the edges of her dress and curtsied. "Thank you, thank you very much."

With all the craziness of the visit to Mick's prickly family, taking her finals, interpersonal drama with Mick, Chase, and Gloria, she was so happy to be here with her family and their closest friends—enjoying the day together.

The long driveway to the family farm wound its way through green fields with their round hay bales, and lined with white fences. A car came into view as it drove down the way.

Jeff squinted into the sun to better see who the new arrivals were. "Looks like Cisco, Bethanne, and the rugrat are here."

As more cars followed, Heather took a hasty gulp of her drink. "I'd better get another blender of juleps going."

Magda stepped up beside her behind the makeshift bar. "How can I help?"

"I think I'm good, but a little company is always nice." Heather frowned as a familiar Mercedes pulled up in front of her mother's house. "I guess Mick invited

Gloria."

"No, Sam invited Hadley; I bet Gloria is just dropping her off."

Hadley got out of the car without a backward glance at her mother and ran to greet Sam. But instead of the car turning around and pulling right back out, the way Heather was mentally willing it to do, Gloria turned off the engine and emerged from the black vehicle like a butterfly from a cocoon. Her fitted dress and enormous hat were the same shade of lavender as her eyes.

Heather mashed the mint with a little too much vigor. "Hope you didn't bet too much, because it looks like Gloria is here to stay, and I can't imagine my mother invited her, so that leaves Mick."

Magda adjusted her giant hat. "I still don't believe he'd invite her. She had her sights set on Jeff when I moved here, so I've seen her in action before; I wouldn't be surprised if she's using her daughter to crash the party. The woman is shameless!" Magda hesitated and looked from the glass pitcher to Heather's face; the hint of a smile played at her lips. "I think the mint is dead."

Heather's hand stilled, and she looked down at the fragrant, green pulverized mess. She reached for the squat bottle of Maker's Mark, and she looked at the driveway, where Mick was arriving in Lola. "Looks like we're about to find out if he asked her or not."

Mick put the top up on Lola and got out. As he straightened the jacket of his well-fitted suit, Heather saw his gaze flicker to the Mercedes and his previously happy expression darkened.

Magda nudged her with her shoulder. "Doesn't

look like he's too happy to see the Glo-mobile. I'm going to join Jeff, if Gloria bombs out with Mick, Jeff might need my protection from her."

Heather watched as Gloria moved toward Mick as fast as her five-inch heels allowed. She was a little ashamed by how happy his world-renowned glower made her feel when it was directed at Gloria and not at her, but the power of the glower held no sway over Gloria, who clasped his arm and chattered happily to him as she tottered along on the grass at his side.

Jeff widened his eyes and raised his hands in the classic palms-up gesture meaning 'wtf,' and Mick responded with a grimace and a slight shrug.

Heather kept making the pitcher of frozen mint juleps like a robot, without even looking at what she was doing, because her attention was focused on Mick and Gloria, as they greeted Heather's mom. After a few moments of social niceties, Gloria dragged Mick off to the barn.

Heather's gut clenched. It was none of her business what they did in the barn, but she knew what her brothers used to do with their girls in the barn in high school, and the jealousy washed over her like a tsunami, taking her breath away.

Mick was her friend—yes, he was a friend whom she'd seen in all his glorious nakedness, but he was just a friend now. If he wanted to play farmer's daughter and the traveling salesman in the barn with Ghastly Gloria, it was not her concern. Right?

"Hey, Aunt Heather!"

She jumped as her niece chirped a cheery greeting. She'd been so lost in her own tortured thoughts about what Mick and Gloria were doing in the barn she hadn't noticed Sam and Gloria's daughter approach.

"Hi Sam, Hadley. You both look lovely."

And they did, although Sam looked sweeter in her floral sundress and the straw hat Heather had helped her niece decorate with silk flowers. Hadley's dress and hat looked too old and sophisticated for her, but then having Gloria for a mother had turned the child into a little thirty year old.

"Thanks, so do you. Do you have anything for us to drink?"

Heather smiled as she squatted behind the long folding table, and lifted the white tablecloth to reveal a small fridge underneath running off power supplied by an extension cord run from the house. "It just so happens I whipped up a non-alcoholic version of our drink just for you."

She pulled out a pitcher filled with the slushy, mint-green concoction. She stood and pulled two empty glasses to her and poured. As she did so, the two girls chattered away together.

"Did Mr. Evans invite your mom? Because I don't think my grandma did."

Excellent question, young Sam. I was wondering the same thing.

Hadley rolled her eyes and heaved a deep sigh. "No. She just tagged along with me. I don't think he wants to go out with her anymore, but she told me she wanted to give him one more shot at glory, before she agrees to marry that old ambassador geezer she's been dating."

Heather snuck a glance at her niece to see how much of that world-weary speech Sam understood. These kids were eleven, for Pete's sake! How was

Ghastly Glo raising poor Hadley? Talking with the girl about having sex with one man when she was about to marry another. She let out a small whoosh of relief when she saw the wrinkles of confusion on Sam's brow. At least her niece didn't seem to understand what Hadley meant.

As she handed the girls their drinks, she mulled over what Hadley had just said. Gloria was going to marry some ambassador? Did Mick know about it? Heather didn't think so. He didn't seem too into Gloria, she even suspected it was just a rebound thing from her that drove him to continue going out with Gloria, but Heather wasn't sure, and if she was wrong, Gloria had the power to really hurt Mick.

****

Jesus H. Christ! Gloria was like an octopus in a fancy hat. She'd taken him to the barn to show him the horse she boarded with the Bradens, but as soon as they left the bright sunlight outside for the dim confines of the barn, she'd been all over him like a cheap suit. He struggled to get her off him, in a way that wouldn't hurt the much smaller woman, and finally was able to pull her tentacles—um, hands—off his body.

She stamped one of her little feet in those ridiculous shoes, and he was surprised the pencil-thin heel didn't snap under the pressure.

"Damn it, Mick! It's not like I'm asking for a lifelong commitment."

He frowned. "You're not?"

"Hell no, I just want to have a little fun with you. I never dreamed you'd be such a killjoy."

Mick's brows drew together. "Word around town is you want to get married again, so I thought…"

As realization dawned in her purple eyes, Gloria threw her head back and laughed. She reached up to adjust her hat, and humor still bubbled in her voice. "And you thought I wanted to marry *you*? Oh, Michael, you silly boy, I don't want to marry you."

"You don't?"

"No. Do you want to marry me?" She asked with an amused smile.

"No."

"Then we're on the same page." She licked her lips. "So, since we're in a barn, how about a roll in the hay?"

Mick blinked. "You just want to have sex with me?"

"You *did* think I wanted to marry you! I'm so sorry, Michael, I'm about to accept a proposal of marriage from a real gentleman, a diplomat."

"Then what are you doing here with me?"

She lifted one shoulder. "He's quite a bit older than me, and I wanted a fling with a big, hot stud like you before I take the plunge."

Mick rubbed the back of his neck as he processed her words. "Do you mind if I ask, *why* you don't want to marry me?"

She trilled in laughter again. "My, my, you sound like a Victorian miss. Fine, I'll tell you the truth, you're sexy and successful enough, but you'll always be a coal-miner's son from West Virginia, and I deserve more in a husband."

He felt his jaw drop and she arched an eyebrow before continuing. "Did you think I didn't know about your humble beginnings? I do, and it's not for me. I want the finer things in life, and my gentleman friend can give them to me. I'm going to be an ambassador's wife, but he's elderly, and you're beautiful, like the statue of David, and I want you to fuck me. Is that what they'd say in the hills? Can I make myself any more clear, Michael?"

He staggered back a step. He didn't give two shits about Gloria, so he was surprised by how shocked and hurt he felt in light of her disdain. "You're being crystal clear, Gloria, so I'll do you the courtesy of being just as honest with you. I don't want to sleep with you. I didn't before, and I sure as hell don't want to now."

Gloria narrowed her eyes and little lines formed around her mouth. "Because of Heather Braden?"

"None of your business."

"Then what's the problem?" She whined.

"You're not really my type, but more important, I might not have been born with a silver spoon in my mouth, but *I'm* too good for *you*. I've achieved a lot in my life; I'm not some gigolo." A horse nickered in his stall, and brought another analogy to mind. "Or some stallion you can buy for a stud fee. Jesus, Gloria, how could you think so little of me? Of yourself?"

Gloria's eyes widened and she stepped back, her spine stiff. "A simple 'no' would have sufficed. Good bye, Michael."

She turned on her heel and rushed out of the barn.

A horse whinnied softly, and Michael walked over to the stall to stroke the animal's glossy, chestnut nose. "Can you believe what just happened?"

The horse bumped his hand gently.

"I guess my bloodlines aren't good enough for her, and considering she's the kind of woman who would tell a man, who's not her fiancé, she wanted him to fuck her in a barn, it's really saying something about how low she thinks I am."

****

Jason dragged Heather out from behind the bar and took over her mixologist duties. Heather took advantage of the free time to chat with her sister and her friends, but kept an eye on the barn. Gloria rushed out, looking fit to be tied, Heather caught a glimpse of an angry scowl marring Gloria's pretty face, before the woman ducked her head and rushed to her car. Good. It looked like Mick had sent the shrew packing.

But where was he? Gloria didn't speak to anyone before she peeled out, kicking up gravel, at least five minutes ago, and Mick still hadn't come out of the barn and rejoined the party.

Totally distracted, and a little worried about Mick, she made an excuse to Deidre and her friends, and made her way to the barn.

The lighting inside was low, and she was momentarily blinded when she left the glare of the day for the dimly lit barn. She heard the soft nicker of her brother Jason's horse, and called out in the direction of his stall, "Hiya, Buddy."

"Hi Heather."

She jumped, and then laughed as her eyes adjusted and she saw Mick leaning against the stall door. "I was talking to the horse." She pointed to the sign above the stall. "His name is Buddy."

Mick smiled, but it didn't reach his eyes. "I've been wrong about a lot of stuff today."

She patted Buddy's neck. "I saw Gloria running out of here. Are you okay?"

He stroked the horse's neck on the other side, and

she realized if she stretched her fingers out just the littlest bit she'd be touching Mick, but friends didn't stroke each other's hands, while they imagined stroking other body parts, so she resisted the impulse.

"Why wouldn't I be okay?"

To hell with these friend rules. She stretched her hand across the warm muscles of Buddy's neck and touched Mick's hand. "I heard Sam and Hadley talking. I know Gloria is going to marry someone else, and I'm sorry."

He scowled. "And you think that's what's bothering me? Gloria marrying another man?"

She raised her eyebrows and looked around. "Well you are spending the best party of the year in a dark barn with Buddy."

A slow smile replaced the scowl, and he waggled his eyebrows. "I'm more interested in being in a dark barn with *you*." He scratched the horse's neck. "No offense, Buddy."

Heather felt her face heat up, and she snatched her hand back. "I'm not much into being second choice."

"Trust me, you're not. Going out with Gloria was a total rebound thing for me. That woman is a piece of work. But you, Heather, sometimes..." His voice was serious and ardent.

"Sometimes, what?" She prompted in a whisper.

His voice went low, husky, and his sexy southern accent made an appearance. "Sometimes I want you more than I want my next breath."

She inhaled sharply. That was *not* what she was expecting to hear. The gears in her mind turned so loudly while she tried to figure out what was going on she was amazed it wasn't spooking the horses.

He shoved both hands in his pockets and slouched out of the barn. He muttered as he brushed by her, "Forget I said anything."

A rectangle of bright light appeared when he opened the door, and she was again plunged into darkness when it slammed behind him.

Heather's jaw dropped, and she looked into Buddy's huge brown eyes. "Forget what he said? Not freakin' likely."

****

Mick blinked in the glare of bright sunlight. He wondered if he could just get to his car without anyone seeing him—he wasn't feeling up to an afternoon of dodging Heather after his colossal fuck-up of telling her how much he wanted her. He'd been reeling by Gloria's rejection, and he said things he shouldn't have. Nothing he did would ever be good enough for the people who mocked him for his background, so why the hell did he even try? He never dreamed Gloria was just looking for a roll in the hay. He really thought she wanted to make him her next husband.

Lost in his thoughts, he jumped at the gentle throat-clearing to his left.

"Hi, Mick. Sorry, I didn't mean to startle you, but I saw you come out of the barn, and I wanted to make sure you were okay."

"Hi, Magda. I'm fine, but thanks for your concern." He pasted a smile on his face as he answered.

Magda raised her eyebrows, and put her hands on her hips. "Really? Because you don't look fine. You look all agitated, and kind of like you were figuring out how to make a break for it."

He chuckled. "Okay, you got me. I had a little run-in with Gloria, and then Heather, and I thought maybe I could head home before anyone saw me."

Magda tucked her hand in the crook of his arm, and led him to a bench in the shade a little away from the entrance to the barn. She sat, and pulled him down with her.

"Tell me all about it."

He grimaced. "There's nothing to tell. Gloria is marrying someone else. Which doesn't bother me, because I sure as hell didn't want to marry her…"

"But it's still a slap in the face."

"Yeah. You sound like you really understand."

"I think I do. I was engaged to someone else before I met Jeff. I didn't love the other man, our relationship was a huge mistake, but still, when he cheated on me, I was shocked and hurt."

"But it was for the best, because now you've got Jeff."

She nodded and smiled, deep dimples peeking out as she did. "Absolutely! But Pierce thought so little of me solely because of who my father was."

"Who was your father?"

"To Pierce, my Dad was a nobody, just a regular, blue-collar guy. Totally beneath his notice, but my maternal grandmother is the queen bee of their social circle, so he deigned to become engaged to me. In his heart, he would never have been able to get past it, and would've spent his whole life looking down on me. Who needs that kind of disrespect?"

"Not me," Mick agreed.

They watched Heather come out of the barn, and rejoin the party without noticing them on the bench.

"No, you deserve much more out of life, out of

love. You deserve a woman who loves you for you, the way Jeff loves me for me."

Mick knew Magda wanted that woman to be Heather, but he knew the truth. He was in no way good enough for Heather.

"Yeah, well, I'm gonna go it alone for the time being."

They sat in silence for a few moments, before Magda said, "I know what it's like to straddle two worlds, and not to feel like you belong in either one. It's how my life used to be, and it sucked, but it doesn't have to be that way."

Mick rested his forearms on his thighs and turned his head to look at her. "What did you do to change it? Was it hard for you to get past?"

She bestowed a beaming smile on him. "It was the easiest thing I ever did."

"Really? Is it something I could do?"

"You've already done it, Mick. I moved to Rivers Bend, and found my love here, found my *home* here. It's the round hole for my round peg, and I think it might be yours too, if you let it be."

Chapter 20

Stretched out in one of the porch chairs, the river burbling by next to him, the sunlight dappled through the green leaves, a cool soda, and the Sunday *Washington Post* to peruse…in Mick's opinion you couldn't ask for a better Sunday afternoon. Unless a certain sassy member of the Braden family was in the other chair, and he didn't mean Jason.

He thought about what Magda said to him yesterday. He was glad moving to Rivers Bend had led her to Jeff and changed her life, but it wasn't that simple for him. He had to be brutally honest with himself, and admit there was more of his old man in him than he liked. He could be moody, and had a dark side he didn't want to inflict on Heather, so he didn't see the same happily-ever-after happening for him that had happened for Magda.

But he could make a nice life here for himself, nonetheless, and it was what he was going to try to do. Seeing Heather at work every day would be rough, and he didn't want to think about how hard it would be to watch when she started dating someone else, but it was a sacrifice he was willing to make for her.

Certain he was doing the right thing, he took a sip of his coffee, picked up the magazine section to flip to 'Date Lab,' the blind date story was a guilty pleasure for him, although he didn't know why he enjoyed it.

The people could really irritate him. Sure, sometimes the paper screwed up and put together people who were clearly wrong for each other. But a lot of the time, like today's couple, the people were perfect for each, but too blind to see it. He tried to ignore any similarities to his own life.

He heard the rumble of a powerful engine and threw the magazine on top of the rest of the newspaper strewn at his feet. Sounded like his brother Billy had arrived!

He grinned as the ancient red truck rattled into view. He whistled low between his teeth, wait a minute, rattled was unfair. The chrome gleamed, the fresh paint job shone, and the engine purred like a contented lion. His brother restored the old wreck into a glistening gem. Looked like this mechanic thing might be the perfect gig for his little brother after all.

He grinned, amazed to feel so much happiness at the sight of one of his family members pulling up to his cabin.

Billy sat in the cab of his truck and gestured to Mick with his index finger he'd be a minute longer. It looked like he was on his phone; he must've called Mom to let her know he'd arrived safely.

Finally his brother tossed the phone on the seat next to him and got out of the truck. A wide smile split Billy's face.

In some ways, looking at Billy was like looking at himself ten years ago. The family resemblance was strong between them, they had the same brown hair and eyes, the same tall athletic build, high cheekbones, but Billy had a natural, good-natured easiness about him Mick had never possessed.

"Hey bro, this place is freaking awesome!"

Mick went down the stairs and they did the one-armed guy hug and back pat thing.

"Thanks, I like it here. Jeff and Cisco have made a really nice place."

His brother's face beamed with pride. "And they brought you in to make it even better."

Mick felt a little embarrassed by the brotherly pride; it was a new thing, and he didn't quite know how to feel about it. "That's the plan. Hopefully I won't fuck it up too bad."

"You won't," Billy replied with confidence. He joined his hands and lifted his arms over his head to stretch, and looked around while he did. His eyes lit up when they hit the river. "Is that the Potomac down there?"

"Yep."

"Sweet."

Billy opened the passenger door of the truck and pulled out a duffel bag. He grabbed the phone and tucked it in the front pocket of his jeans, before slamming the door shut.

"Nice ride, I didn't see it when we were there for the wedding. You do all this work yourself?"

"It was at a buddy's garage when you were in town. He let me do the paint job there." Billy's chest puffed out with pride. "And yes, I did all the work myself."

Mick shook his head once. "Drive this truck to the interview, and Ed Miller would be a fool not to hire you."

Billy blushed and scuffed his sneaker in the dirt. "Thanks. It's sort of what I was hoping when I drove it here."

"I bet the old man is not happy about this trip."

One side of Billy's mouth turned up. "You could say that. His face turned so red, I was afraid he might pop a blood vessel. Everyone else is being supportive, although Mom isn't thrilled about me moving away, but she took me aside and told me I should follow my dreams."

Mick cocked his head. "*Everyone* else is cool? Really?"

Billy shrugged. "Not Danny, but I can't be worried about what he thinks. He hates everything."

"Healthy attitude." Mick wished he had felt the same way when he left home.

Billy slung the duffel bag over his shoulder and loped up the steps to the porch.

"You can either sleep here, on the sleeper sofa, or take a room up at the Retreat, where you'd have an actual bed and some privacy."

Mick hoped his brother would stay with him, but he didn't want to force the issue, if Bill would rather have some distance between them. He'd been a strictly long-distance brother for a good chunk of Billy's life, so if his brother didn't want to get too close now, he would respect his decision.

"I'd rather stay with you, if that's cool."

Mick felt tension he wasn't even aware he'd been holding, release from his shoulders. He opened the screen door and stepped aside to usher his brother inside. "Of course it's cool with me. I kinda wanted the chance to hang out with you."

Billy tossed his duffel down on the wide plank pine floor, and looked around the rustic cabin with interest.

"Me too, but I thought staying here might cramp Heather and your style."

His eyes caught on the two framed football jerseys on either side of the stone fireplace and his face lit up with boyish glee. "Are those Jeff and Cisco's jerseys?"

"Sure are."

"They should put up yours too."

"Nah, I only played one season before I got hurt, no one would want to see my old jersey. And about Heather and me, well, there is no Heather and me, so there's no style cramping happening with you staying here."

"Oh man." Billy's face crumpled before his eyes narrowed with suspicion. "What did you do to mess it up with her?"

"Nothing!"

"Hmph," Billy expressed some brotherly skepticism, and then his eyes searched Mick's face. "I hope this won't be weird then, but Heather invited us to dinner at her mom's house, and I kinda already accepted for both of us. She said to come over anytime, and told me you knew how to get there. I'm sorry, Mick, I thought you were a couple."

"It's okay. Heather and I aren't going out, but we *are* friends. Dinner with the Bradens will be fun." He looked down at his bare feet, grubby shorts, and ripped T-shirt. "Guess I'd better change though, huh?"

****

"That's all of us, don't worry, we won't expect you to remember all of our names straight off." Joyce Braden smiled, after she completed the lengthy introductions to her big family.

His brother was looking a little dazed by the warm,

loving Braden family, which was so very different from their own.

"Not quite like the Evans homestead, huh?" Mick spoke quietly to his brother, as the babble of conversation and laughter resumed around them.

Billy grinned and shook his head. "Nothing like it, but I have to say, I *like* it!"

Across the room, Deidre and Hank's daughter, Caitlin, flushed a pretty pink and smiled shyly at Billy before quickly looking back at the baseball game on television.

A feeling of déjà vu spread through Mick. Before he could warn his brother Caitlin was just a kid, Heather appeared with two beers. She handed the bottles to them. "Welcome to Rivers Bend, Billy! How do you like it here so far?"

Caitlin peeked at them out of the corner of her eyes, and a wide grin spread across Billy's face. "I like it just fine."

Heather followed his gaze to her niece. "Why don't you head over to watch the game?"

"Thanks, I think I will."

As his brother planted himself on the sofa right next to Caitlin, Mick frowned. "You shouldn't encourage that situation."

Her brow furrowed. "Why not? He's new in town, and I thought he'd like to get to know some young people. Plus your brother Dave and Caitlin's brother Craig are both going to WVU next year, I thought Billy would like to meet him."

Before Mick could answer, Jeff came up and slapped him on the back. "Hey man, good to see you here." He smiled at his sister. "Ty tells me we have to have some sort of death-match thingy to get tickets to see you graduate."

She rolled her eyes. "Not true. I only get four tickets, which is just enough for Mom, Jason, Deidre, and you. The death-match thing was just some warped flight of Ty's imagination."

"Sounds good. Next Saturday then—you walk."

She smiled at her brother. "At long last!"

Jeff's expression grew somber. "I'm sorry my issues delayed all this for you."

She punched her brother's arm. "Never say that! Helping with Sam, watching her grow into such an amazing person, has made it all worthwhile. I wouldn't change a thing." Jeff wrapped one arm around her neck and pulled her to his side for a combination of brotherly hug and stranglehold. "I'm proud of you, sis. You've worked your ass off to get here. And Sam and I never would have made it without you."

"Dinner's ready!" Joyce Braden called from the dining room, which set off a stampede of Bradens to the table.

****

Having the top down on Lola for the drive home made conversation with his little brother difficult, as the wind whipped around their heads, but he felt they needed to have this talk, and sooner rather than later.

"You spent a lot of time with Caitlin today."

Billy stuck his arm on the window and smiled. "Yeah, she's a great girl."

Mick's chest tightened. "She's just a kid."

Billy shrugged. "She's three and a half years younger than me."

Mick gripped the steering wheel and said through

gritted teeth, "She's still in high school—"

"For another month."

"She's only seventeen!"

"She's turning eighteen soon."

"But—"

"Chill, bro! I'm just yanking your chain. I spent just as much time with Craig today, but you didn't notice it, because you were so busy glaring at me if Caitlin so much as laughed at one of my jokes. I was actually thinking Dave would like her a lot. What did you think I was going to do, run away with her?"

"I may be over thirty, but I know flirting when I see it, and she was flirting with you."

"She's a teenage girl; of course she was flirting with me. It's what they do, but she didn't mean anything by it. Man! When did you turn into such an old fart?"

"I'm not, but for one thing, she's younger than you. And for another, there's not much point in starting something when she's going to college in the fall."

"She told me she's going to UVA. I told you once there was nothing going on between us, but even if there was, Charlottesville's not that far away."

UVA—Caitlin was just as smart as her aunt! But his brother had gone a completely different route; Billy started working in the mine right after high school. "Maybe not geographically…"

His brother's casual position tensed. His fists clenched, and he narrowed his eyes as he turned his head to look at Mick. "What exactly are you trying to say?"

"College is a whole different world. Caitlin will be surrounded by boys her age, who share the same interests…"

Billy held up his hands. "Whoa! Are you trying to say you think she's too good for me?"

Mick's mouth went dry. He was so not good at this big brother thing. "I would *never* say that."

"But you're thinking it, implying it. Jesus, Mick, I can't lie, it stings like a bastard you think I'm such a piece of shit."

"Piece of shit? Who the hell said anything about a piece of shit? I think you're a great guy; I just didn't want you to get hurt."

Billy shook his head and stared straight ahead. "You're worried she's too young, I get it, respect it even. It's why I told you I think Dave and Caitlin would hit it off, so you'd stop worrying about it. But if you think I shouldn't go for it because you think she is out of my league, on account of who I am and where we come from, well I'm sorry, but that's just fucked up. What about Dave? Is he good enough for her on account of his going to college, or is he always doomed to be a piece of shit in your eyes because of where we're from?" He gave a short, humorless snort of laughter. "Where *you're* from, may I remind you."

Mick felt as if the truth of Billy's words punched him in the gut. He had been thinking all of those things, in part because of his own past with Heather, but mostly because of all the old insecurities stirred up by Gloria's derisive words about him yesterday.

He didn't want Gloria, and he never did, not really, but what she said made him realize his background would always keep him separate from folks like Gloria, or a lot of the people he met in the upper echelon of business in which he worked.

He could wear the right clothes, speak with the right accent, mix with the right people, but to them he'd always be Mickey Evans from East Bumfuck West Virginia. Did any of it still matter to him? At this point, he really didn't know. Magda made a lot of sense yesterday, but he wasn't sure Rivers Bend would fix his problems, the way it had fixed hers. He still felt like an outsider, and was afraid the darkness he inherited from his father would always keep him one.

"You okay, Mick? You've gotten really pale. Look, I'm sorry; I shouldn't have said all of that shit to you."

Jesus, Billy's rapid-fire, nervous apology made Mick realize the kid was afraid he was going to blow up like their old man would. He rolled his neck, and realized he wasn't going to erupt like their dad. He was confused, frustrated, and angry, but all with his own damn self, not with Billy. He wouldn't take it out on his brother. He couldn't.

He loosened his fingers on the wheel, and forced a smile to his lips, to set Billy at ease, to make him see he wasn't a hotheaded loose cannon like their father. "No, you were right to say it to me, and I think maybe what you said is true; that's why it threw me for such a loop. I'm sorry if you thought I was mad at you. I'm not. I'm mad at myself."

They'd pulled up in front of his cabin, so he cut the engine and clasped his brother on the shoulder. "And one more thing needs to be cleared up right now. No one is too good for you, Bill, I mean it. You may have decided to pass on college, but you're a helluva lot smarter than me about a lot of stuff. I'm sorry I made you feel like I thought you weren't good enough for

225

Caitlin. I guess sometimes I can be as small-minded as our old man."

Billy threw the car door open and furrowed his brow. "Were there drugs at the Bradens that I missed?"

"What?"

"Because you must be high if you think you're as small-minded as the old man." He got out of the car and slammed the door behind him.

Mick cut the engine and followed slowly, as he pondered Billy's words. Hope flickered in his chest; maybe, just maybe, he wasn't as bad as his father after all.

Billy knocked on the porch rail to get his attention. "Are you gonna unlock the door, or just stand gaping in the driveway all night? I've got to get some rest before my interview tomorrow."

A grin spread across Mick's face. "God knows you *do* need your beauty rest, if you ever hope to be as pretty as me."

"Oh please! You're going to be crying yourself to sleep tonight, because you've noticed I'm way prettier than you ever were."

Mick punched his brother in the arm as he passed by to unlock the cabin door. He liked this brotherly thing they had going on. He'd missed it, spending all these years on the other side of the country.

Billy rubbed his arm. "You're still pretty strong for an old dude."

"Old! Who you callin' old, Junior?"

Billy brushed past him to get inside. "The mental faculties are going already? I'm sorry!"

He shot his older brother a sly smile, as he went straight to the fridge and pulled out a soda. He popped the top on the red can, and took a slug. "You want one?"

"You're offering me my own soda? How generous of you, thanks, I will take one."

Billy took another can out of the fridge and gave it to Mick, as he opened the front door again. "It's a nice night, I'm gonna sit on the porch for a while. Coming?"

"Sounds good. I'll be right there." Mick stood for a moment and stared at the door with a goofy grin on his face. Yeah. He had missed being with his brothers, and it felt damn good having Billy here with him. Stuff with Heather might still be all fucked up, but this felt good… right.

"C'mon, Gramps! What's taking you so long? The joints not what they used to be? Must be hard. Or not. I hear that goes too when you get old."

"Oh don't even go there, you young whippersnapper!" With a grin, Mick threw open the rattly screen door.

"Nothing to worry about, they got pills for that now, old man."

"I'll give you pills, you sorry young son of a bitch!"

Billy laughed in response, as Mick plopped in the seat next to him and they stared out at the glow of the moon reflected in the river as it rushed by the cabin.

"It's good to have you here, Bill."

Chapter 21

Mick knew he was stalling, as he stopped in Jeff's kitchen to pour a cup of coffee before he went into the office, where he knew he'd see Heather. His morning meeting outside of D.C. had been successful. The sales manager of a large corporation had signed up for multiple team-building sessions at the Retreat for her staff, but now he was back and it was time to face the music. He knew from the schedule she'd emailed him Heather would be hard at work at her desk right about now, and there was no choice left, but to see her.

Aside from their conversation about Billy and the awkward conversation in the barn at her mother's Derby Day party, they hadn't spoken to each other alone since their trip to West Virginia. There had been no opportunity to talk to Heather with her whole family around last night, and he was afraid if they didn't clear the air soon, things would always be awkward and stilted between them, and that would be like a punch to his gut. Heather was one of the only people he ever knew with whom he felt comfortable enough to be himself and loosen his tight control. He couldn't hold back a smile as he remembered how he'd even relinquished control to Heather in the bedroom for a while, and it had been amazing!

With the clusterfuck his personal life had become, he knew those times with Heather were history. He could still see the hurt, but also remarkably pissed off, expression on her face when she saw him at dinner with Gloria that night at the country club. Sure, she'd extended an olive branch at her mom's Derby party, but he knew it would be a cold day before Heather would trust him again. He couldn't really blame her—he didn't trust himself not to hurt her again. In fact, given his gene pool, it was inevitable.

Mick Evans was no coward; he had to face Heather sooner or later, and he'd always been of the mind if something scared you, it was best to face it head on, so he squared his shoulders, took a fortifying sip of his hot coffee, and opened the door to the Retreat offices.

He heard Heather squeal, and frowned as he turned the corner and saw Heather being lifted off the ground in the hearty embrace of some guy in a suit.

Jesus, Mary, and Joseph—*another* guy? How many of them was Heather seeing? Okay, that wasn't fair, he knew now Ty was gay, so that only left Chase and him, but who was this mystery man? He was too big and burly to be Chase.

As the man lowered Heather, his face was revealed, and it was none other than his brother Billy. Mick left at the crack of dawn to beat the D.C. traffic to get to his appointment on time, so he hadn't seen his brother all dressed up in his suit for his interview. He couldn't believe he hadn't recognized him.

"Mick, I'm so glad you're back! I was just telling Heather Mr. Miller offered me the job at the garage! Isn't it awesome?"

His brother's excitement was contagious, and Mick grinned and high-fived him. "Hell yeah, it's awesome! But I had no doubt you'd get the job."

"Me either," Heather agreed staunchly.

"You two were more confident than me, I was a nervous wreck! I know I'm a good mechanic, but I don't have a lot of experience working in a garage."

"I knew as soon as he saw the amazing job you did on your own truck, he'd offer you the job on the spot."

Billy's face grew ruddy. "Thanks, Mick. And thank *you* Heather, for recommending me."

Heather patted his back. "I was happy to do it. Heck, it's good for both you and Ed Miller. When do you start?"

"As soon as possible. I need to head home, and give my notice at the mine. I don't have much stuff, so packing will be easy, and then I'll come back here."

"I know it's pretty tight quarters, but you're welcome to stay with me in the cabin," Mick offered.

"Thanks, bro, but there's an apartment over the garage Mr. Miller says I can have, if I'm on call at night in case there's an emergency. It's even furnished. Nothing fancy, but it's got everything I need."

He pulled his phone out of his pocket and looked at the time. "I'd better get a move on; I need to get on the road. I have to be at work in the morning, and I want to give my notice as soon as possible, so I can get back here and get started at the garage."

Mick looked intently into Billy's eyes. "Do you want me to go with you? Help you deal with the old man?"

Billy shook his head. "No offense, man, but you being there would just make things worse. I can handle it."

"It's not going to be pretty," Mick warned, as he remembered the ugly scene when he announced his scholarship to Stanford.

Billy grimaced. "Trust me, I know, but it'll be worth it in the end. Hell, I'll get to do what I love for a living, how many people can say that? I'll just remind myself of all the good stuff to come, while I take his guff."

Heather beamed and gave Billy another quick squeeze. "I'm so happy for you! It's going to be great having you here in the Bend."

"Thanks for everything, Heather." He squeezed her back, and then gave Mick the one-armed man hug. "I'll text you when I get home, Mick, and thanks for letting me crash at your place."

Billy hastened away to pack up and head home.

Heather pursed her lips and furrowed her brow. "How much notice do you think he'll give, two weeks?"

Mick shrugged. "I don't know, probably. Two weeks is pretty standard. Why do you ask?"

"I was just trying to figure out how much time we had."

"Time for what?"

"To get his apartment ready for him."

"What do you mean? Billy said it was furnished."

Heather flashed him a cheeky grin. "It has been a long time since you lived in a small town, hasn't it? You've forgotten how things work. I'm sure the apartment's a dusty wreck with the bare minimum of stuff in it. I've got to mobilize everyone to get things clean and nice for Billy by the time he gets back to town."

Mick watched Heather bustle back into her office to start working the phones to organize the population of Rivers Bend to make his brother's transition to the town as smooth as possible.

Huh. Things with Heather didn't seem awkward at all. He walked into his own office and set his coffee mug down on a coaster. He leaned back in his chair, as he mulled over what it meant. He knew he should just be happy Heather seemed cool with him, but he couldn't help but feel she was *too* cool, and damned if that fact didn't sting.

He rubbed his jawline. Heather *had* seemed friendly and normal at her mom's house yesterday, as had he, but he knew it had taken some effort for him to act as though everything was okay between them in front of her family, and he'd assumed Heather was doing the same thing, but today she seemed like it was taking no effort at all.

"Hey, Mick?"

Heather's cheery voice at the door tore him out of his reverie; what was he doing mooning at his desk thinking about feelings, anyway? They'd make him turn in his man card if he kept it up, but Heather always could turn him inside out.

He forced a smile to his lips, if she could be chill with him, then he could be chiller. "What's up, Heather?"

"I wondered if it would be all right with you if I skipped out for a bit? I just spoke to Ed Miller, and he said he could let me into the apartment over the garage now, so I can scope out what needs to be done, and what Billy might need to get started. You know like sheets, dishes, that kind of stuff."

"That's real nice of you to do Heather. You go on ahead, and take your time."

He heard the southern accent he'd worked so hard to lose creep out, when he spoke to Heather.

She offered him a mock salute. "Thanks, boss! Everything is quiet here, but I'll be back as soon as possible, and you can always text me if something comes up."

Boss? Is that all he was to her now? That was a little *too* chill for Mick's liking.

He gave himself a mental smack upside the head. He *was* her boss, and if it was the only way she saw him now, then it would be the best all around. For him, for their work together at the Retreat, and most of all it was best for Heather to put some distance between them.

****

"Okay, Mrs. Wilson, I'll be sure to check and see what's needed in the kitchen," Heather called out with a cheery wave at the Retreat's motherly housekeeper, as she tossed her purse onto the passenger seat of her car.

She watched Mrs. W. walk back inside, and then slid behind the wheel of the car. The smile faded as she exhaled with a whoosh.

Her cheeks felt sore from all the phony smiling she'd been doing lately. It hadn't been easy for her, but she couldn't keep going with this back-and-forth, hot-and-cold stuff Mick and she were doing.

That being the case, the only thing she could see to do was to plant herself firmly in the friendly employee role. Okay, considering she'd seen her boss in all his naked glory it was a bit of a stretch, but treating him like a close, family friend was doable. She could fake it until she started to believe it was all she shared with Mick. Even if it killed her, and as memories of glorious, naked Mick now filled her thoughts and knowing she'd never be able to go there again, she feared it just might.

****

Heather returned to the Retreat a couple of hours later, in significantly better spirits. She had been right. The apartment had the bare minimum of furnishings and fixings, and it was in dire need of a thorough scouring. Undertaking a project like this would keep her hands busy and her mind off Mick, both the real-life boss Mick, as well as the naked lover Mick who still danced around her brain.

Great.

Now imaginary, naked Mick was dancing like a Chippendale.

She took a deep breath, and opened the back door to Jeff's kitchen. She needed one of Mrs. Wilson's homemade cookies to fortify her, and to drive sexy Mick out of her mind, to be replaced by boss-man Mick. However, she'd been beaten to this afternoon's batch of cookies.

"Hiya, Aunt Heather."

Her niece Sam sat at the kitchen table with her best friend, Hadley. The girls had two tall glasses of milk and were munching peanut butter cookies. Neither girl looked as cheerful as they normally did, and Sam's greeting was decidedly glum.

The table was tucked in the corner of the sunny kitchen, surrounded by windows on two sides. Sam sat on the window seat, and Hadley sat across from her, slumped in a chair. Heather pulled out the ladderback chair at the head of the table, and grabbed a cookie from the platter.

"Hi ladies, what's got you both looking so blue?

Hoping for the cherry-chocolate chip cookies today instead of the peanut butter?"

Sam mustered a weak smile at her little joke, but it quavered a bit at the edges. "The cookies are fine; it's personal stuff."

Heather took a bite of her cookie, and decided this conversation might call for a glass of milk too. She stood and pulled a glass out of the cupboard, which she filled with milk from the carton in the refrigerator door. "This sounds serious, can I help?"

She took her glass and sat back down at the table.

Hadley slumped down farther in her chair and shook her head. "Thanks, Miss Heather, but you can't help."

Sam didn't seem to agree; she bounced in her seat and her smile was now wide. "Maybe she *can* help you, Had."

Hadley took a bite of her cookie and shrugged as she chewed and swallowed. "I don't see how."

Heather thought back to when she was twelve, as she tried to figure out what the girls problem might be, and decided it probably had something to do with boys. "You never know, I might be able to help. What's up?"

"You're a responsible adult, right?" Sam asked eagerly.

"Some people might argue I'm not, but on a good day, I'd have to say, yes, I am a responsible adult. Why do you ask?"

Heather was clueless, but Hadley seemed to realize what Sam was getting at, and sat a little taller in her chair. "It won't work. Will it?"

Heather looked between the two girls through narrowed eyes; this whole thing was starting to sound

Donna Simonetta

less and less like boy trouble. "Do you two want to let me in on the secret?"

Some silent communication went on between the two girls, and finally Sam blurted out, "Could Hadley come and live with you, Aunt Heather?"

Heather thought about the palatial mansion where Hadley lived, and then her own tiny place. She laughed, "In my one-bedroom, one-bathroom apartment over the Nosh Pit? Why on Earth would Hadley want to live there with me?"

Hadley gulped, and her eyes were like saucers. "*One bathroom?*"

"Yep," Heather replied and took a swig of her milk.

Sam held out her hands in a placating gesture. "Okay, okay, Had. It's not the greatest apartment."

"Hey!" Heather interrupted in indignation around a mouthful of cookie.

"Sorry, Aunt Heather." Sam slanted a glance at her aunt, and then turned her attention back to her friend, "But at least it's in Rivers Bend, Hadley."

"This conversation is getting more and more cryptic and I'm starting to get worried. Would you one of you please tell me what's going on?"

"My mother is getting married to some rich old fuddy-duddy."

"Hadley, that's not a nice thing to call someone," Heather corrected gently. Knowing Hadley's mother, it was probably accurate, but still not nice.

"Sorry," Hadley managed to say without actually sounding the least, little bit sorry.

"The fuddy-duddy, sorry Aunt Heather, Hadley's mom's fiancé, is an ambassador to some tiny county in

236

Asia. A former Soviet republic, or something like that, we don't know precisely what it means, but we know it's far away, and Hadley is going to have to move there…"

"Or my mom's favorite option—I could go to boarding school in Switzerland," Hadley said with a heart-rending sigh.

"And I take it you don't want to do either of those things."

"Nope."

"What about living with your father? I know it would still mean moving away from Rivers Bend, but at least it would be in Virginia."

Hadley's eyes filled with tears, and she stuffed a whole cookie in her mouth.

"Her dad said she can't live in Richmond with him," Sam whispered.

"What? Why not?" Heather was flabbergasted. What kind of man would send his daughter to live in some remote Asian outpost or to a boarding school thousands of miles away where she didn't know a soul?

Hadley swallowed the cookie hard, as if it were made of concrete. "He said with the baby there's no room for me."

Heather had never met Hadley's father, but she knew he was a wealthy man, and it was just an excuse, as he lived in a huge home in Richmond with his new family. Her heart broke for Hadley. She wasn't always the easiest child, and with Ghastly Gloria as a mother it seemed inevitable, but deep down she was a good kid with a big heart.

"I'm sorry, Hadley, it sounds like you're in an awful bind, but I don't have room in my apartment."

Realizing it sounded a lot like Hadley's father's excuse, she added rapidly, "Seriously, my place is tiny!"

"It is," Sam conceded with a sigh.

Hadley's mouth twisted into a smile, "No offense, Miss Heather, but this plan lost me at one bathroom."

"No offense taken, sweetie." Heather patted Hadley's hand. "Is there any other family you can go to who would be closer than Asia or Europe?"

"My Aunt Lily lives in Baltimore. She's a teacher there; I texted her, but she was at work and couldn't talk, so she texted back and said she'd call me when she got home."

"Maybe she can help," Heather said with encouragement. If the woman was a teacher, she couldn't possibly be as shallow and materialistic as Gloria, right? And she must like kids. "Baltimore isn't too far away. I could bring Sam to visit on weekends sometimes."

Hadley screwed up her mouth, and her tears threatened to make a comeback. "But it won't be the same as being in the same school every day, and pretty soon it'll be too much of a pain to keep in touch, and you'll make new friends, and everyone will forget me. It's what always happens."

"It won't happen with me," Sam said in a way that reminded Heather very much of Jeff. Like father, like daughter, both were loyal to the core.

"Let's wait and see what your aunt has to say, Hadley, maybe she'll have some good ideas."

"Aunt Heather's right, Had. When Dad and I needed her, Aunt Heather moved across the whole country to help us; I'm sure your Aunt Lily will help too."

At Hadley's dejected, hopeless expression, Heather sent up a silent prayer Aunt Lily was a better person than her sister, Gloria, and she'd come through for her niece, and give her a place to live.

The girls put their milk glasses in the dishwasher, and ran upstairs to Sam's room, calling out their thanks as they went.

Jeff appeared in the doorway to the Retreat offices, his hands shoved into the pockets of his worn jeans. "They tell you about Glo's plans?"

She nodded, and asked her brother with gravitas, "Do you ever think about how lucky we were to be born into the Braden family?"

He walked over and snagged a cookie from the platter. "I sure do. Every time I bring Hadley home to her mom's house. We may not have been rich like Gloria, but we always knew Mom and Dad loved us, and we always had each other's back."

He raked his hand through his perpetually messy hair, a tell of anxiety for him. "And you know I've still got yours, right, kiddo? I shouldn't have forced Mick on you here at work, but he's one of my best buddies, and I didn't know..."

"Jeff, chill. It's all good." She forced her phony smile back into place. "I'm a big girl. I can work with Mick. No worries about me."

He smiled back at her. "Always so tough."

"Nah! Not me."

He slumped in the seat Sam had just vacated.

"You're not looking so tough right now, Jeff. What's up?"

"I just wish I could offer to take Hadley here with us, and I know Sam is a little p.o.'ed with me I'm not."

"Sam floated living with me out there as an option, but Hadley was put off by the idea of having to share a bathroom with me," she smiled, as her brother chuckled. "But I can't say I wasn't relieved. Taking care of someone else's child like that is a big responsibility."

"It's not the responsibility so much for me. Hell, I figure not many people could do a worse job raising a child than Gloria, but I'm hoping there are going to be some big changes in our household soon, and they'll impact this decision."

"That's more cryptic than you usually are, Jeff."

He smiled his lazy smile and asked, "Can you keep a secret?"

"You know I can."

"I do." He leaned forward and lowered his voice. "I'm going to ask Maggie to marry me."

Heather squealed, "I'm so happy for you! About damn time!"

"Hey! It hasn't been that long."

"I guess not, it just seems like you two have been together forever. She's fit in so well with our family, I can't even remember a time she wasn't here. You were made for each other."

"Thanks, sis, but mum's the word! I haven't asked her yet. I have to go to D.C. on Thursday for a board meeting for my Foundation. Maggie's coming with me, and we're going to stay at the Hay Adams. I'm going to ask her then."

"Very posh! I approve. Do you have a ring?"

"I do. It's probably not as big as the one Pierce gave her…"

"But on the plus side, you would never try to

kidnap her at gunpoint the way Pierce did." Heather pointed at him with a cookie.

"There is that. One point in my favor anyway."

"I have a feeling you could give Maggie a ring out of a gumball machine, and she would wear it with love and pride because it came from you." Heather flashed him a grin. "No accounting for taste."

He laughed. "Thanks for keeping my head from getting too big. Anyway, it's why I can't offer to take Hadley in. I don't want to commit Maggie to something that big without discussing it first."

"Maybe this aunt in Baltimore will come through for the poor kid, and you won't need to worry."

Chapter 22

"I swear, Maggie, I'm walking over to the apartment as we speak." Heather held her cell phone to her ear, as she looked both ways before trotting across Main Street to Miller's Garage. "I'll be there in two seconds to sign for your delivery, so stop worrying and go have fun with my brother. Okay, I'm here and I'm hanging up now. Bye!"

Ed Miller straightened up from under the hood of a car. "Hey, Heather! What can I do for you?"

"Hi, Ed. I was wondering if you could let me into the apartment? Maggie and Jeff ordered some of that assemble-it-yourself furniture, and since they're in D.C. tonight they asked me to come over to sign for the delivery. Maggie's ready to pop a gasket about it. "

Ed scratched his head. "Huh, popping a gasket? That doesn't sound like Maggie; she's usually pretty calm." He reached into his pocket and pulled out a key. "Anyhow, here you go."

She flashed him a smile as she took the key from his outstretched hand. "Thanks. I'll bring it back when I'm done."

"I'm heading out for the night soon as I finish with this car, so if I'm not here when you leave, you can just hold on to it."

"Thanks! I've been in and out of here so much that would probably help. I wouldn't have to bug you every time I need to get into the apartment."

"Having a little visit with you never bugs me, Heather. You're a good girl, and it's mighty kind of you to make things so nice for Billy." He ducked back down under the hood, so his last words were muffled, "Have a good night now."

"You too!" She called over her shoulder, as she climbed the staircase on the side of the garage that led to the apartment above it.

She let herself in, and a few minutes later she heard someone clomping up the steps—must be the deliveryman. She rushed to the door and threw it open for him. Her jaw dropped when instead of a man in brown shorts, she saw Mick with his hand raised as if she'd caught him just as he was about to knock.

"You're not the deliveryman!"

He looked down at his jeans and navy Retreat T-shirt and shrugged. "No. I'm not. I saw Ed downstairs, he told me you were here and you'd let me inside. Sorry to disappoint you."

"Oh no," she hastened to reassure him, with her deeply ingrained good manners. "I'm not disappointed...well, maybe a little..."

He raised an eyebrow, and she felt her cheeks heat up—sheesh!—she was never this awkward with people. Normally she could chat and charm with the best of them, but Mick turned her into a babbling goofball in no time flat.

She took a deep breath. "I was expecting them to deliver a bed and dresser; Maggie asked me to come over and sign for it. She seemed to think it would arrive any minute, and I was frantically trying to beat the deliveryman here, but I'm starting to worry I missed him."

Mick wrinkled his brow. "That's funny, Jeff asked me to come over after work to assemble a bed and dresser. Why wouldn't he just ask me to sign for it? Why drag you over here too?"

Heather pursed her lips. "I think we've been set up by Jeff and Maggie."

"You think?"

"I do. They arranged for both of us to be here at the same time on a flimsy excuse."

"I don't know about flimsy. Furniture is coming and it does need to be put together. Maybe Jeff thought I wouldn't get here in time to sign for the delivery. Also, I haven't been over to see the place yet, and Jeff knows I want to help get it set up for my brother. Maybe it's just a coincidence."

"Hmm." Heather frowned and narrowed her eyes with suspicion.

"Now that I'm here, may I come in?"

Heather stepped aside quickly, and bumped into the old-fashioned avocado-green laminate kitchen counter behind her. "Of course. I'm sorry. It's your brother's apartment; of course you want to see it. Come on in."

Great, she winced inwardly. Babbling Heather was back in control.

The ghost of a smile showed in his eyes and on his lips as he entered the kitchen. "Thanks. The place looks real nice. You've done a good job here; I really appreciate it."

Mick was a big man, and he really filled the little kitchen. Suddenly it felt too small for the two of them. Heather stepped into the living room, now furnished with odds and ends donated by their fellow Rivers Benders.

"Thank you, but I can't take all the credit, everyone's chipped in, donating stuff for the apartment, as well as their time to help get it cleaned up for Billy."

"Still, *you're* the driving force, and I know Billy's going to be over the moon when he sees his new place."

He put his hands on his narrow hips, and looked around the apartment; he jerked his head to the tiny ancient television set on the steamer trunk across from the plaid sofa. "Maybe I can upgrade the TV to a new flat screen for him."

"I bet he'd like that! Mrs. Warren donated that one, but it is pretty old. Maybe he can use hers in the bedroom, so her feelings won't be hurt."

"You're one of the kindest people I've ever known, Heather Braden."

His voice was husky, and she felt breathless as their eyes locked.

A loud thump from the outside stairwell broke the moment with a jolt. Heather jumped at the noise. "Must be the furniture delivery!"

Mick reluctantly dragged his eyes from hers, and cleared his throat. "I'll get it. He could probably use some help getting the stuff up those stairs. I bet those boxes weigh a ton."

****

Two hours later, they sat on the parquet floor of the bedroom. They were hot and sweaty, and not for any fun reason. Surrounded by pre-cut pieces of wood, and plastic bags, Mick directed his laser focus at the dresser drawer he was attempting to assemble.

Heather tossed a piece of paper to the floor beside

her, and wiped some sweat from her forehead, where it beaded behind her choppy bangs. "Who knew the Swedes hated us so much?"

Mick sat on the floor with a tiny hex wrench gripped in his large hand. He frowned at the ancient air conditioner rattling in the window. It was making a lot of noise, but doing little to cool off the room. "You're just hot and cranky."

"No, I'm not!" She grabbed the piece of paper in her right hand and slapped it with her left. "Seriously! Look at the assembly illustrations. What the heck is this supposed to mean?"

He squinted at the black and white drawing. He grinned at her and waggled his eyebrows. "It's simple. It means 'insert Tab B into Slot A.' "

She yanked the instruction sheet back and scowled at it. "Where do you see that on here?"

He shrugged. "I don't, but it's what those things always seem to say." A slow grin spread across his face. "We've got this, babe, because *no one* is better at inserting Tab B into Slot A, than you and me."

She rolled her eyes, but her face flushed in a way Mick suspected had nothing to do with the under-functioning air conditioner.

Mick rolled his head on his neck until it cracked. "Your brother is so going to pay for this. He orders all this build-it-yourself crap, and then beats feet out of town, and leaves me to assemble it."

"*Us* to assemble it, you mean. I still think Maggie set this whole thing up to throw us together. Since she met my brother, she's turned into a hopeless romantic."

Mick picked up two pieces of wood, and screwed them together. "I shouldn't complain anyway. It was generous of Jeff to buy this stuff for Billy. Putting it together is the least I can do."

Heather bit her lip as she studied the sheet, and then dug through the wood on the floor to hand him a piece of wood. "I think this is the one you need next."

"Thanks. We make a good team."

Heather furrowed her brow, and he wondered if she was going to ask him what kind of team they made—a question he was not prepared to answer, but she eventually chuckled and went for a joke response. "You look like you should be in one of their ads. A hunky male model assembling a bedroom set, now *that* would get the ladies into the store!"

He grinned as he held up the finished dresser drawer. "One down, three to go."

"Ugh! But now we've done the first one the rest should go easier, right?"

"Right," he replied with a confidence he wasn't quite feeling.

For a few minutes they worked in a companionable silence, until Mick asked, "Is that what you like about me?"

"Your mad ability to assemble furniture designed by some sadistic Swede? You betcha!"

He didn't smile at her joke. "No, I meant my looks. Are they why you like me?"

"You *are* pretty," Heather teased, but her smile faded.

He kept his attention focused on putting together drawer number two, as if her answer didn't matter to him at all, but Mick was pretty sure he wasn't fooling Heather. He could never fool Heather.

"I can't lie. I noticed how handsome you were

when I first met you, before I knew anything about you. Your looks might have been what drew me to you, but they're not what kept me around."

"No?" he asked with skepticism.

"No. And I'm a little insulted you think I'm so shallow." She ticked off his positive attributes on her fingers, "You're smart, loyal, good to your brothers and sister…"

He interrupted with a snort, "Sure I am."

"You are! Why else would you be sitting in this hotbox of an apartment, after working a long day, assembling furniture so your brother will be happy in his first place?"

"If I really wanted to help Billy, I should've gone home with him to face the music."

"How did it go when he told your father about moving to Rivers Bend?"

"About as well as you'd expect. The old man went ballistic, Mom tried to calm things down, and he turned on her. Dave tried to defend Billy and Mom, and Danny turned on him. Danny spilled the beans about Dave going to WVU next year, and the old man got so steamed Billy said he almost blew through the roof of the house like a busted hot water heater. I should have been there."

"Yeah, I can see how you'd hate to miss such a fun time."

"You know that's not what I meant. I should have been there to help them out."

"Help them? Mick if you had been there, you might as well have put on a match costume, lit your hair on fire, and jumped into a big old pool of gasoline."

The comment tugged a reluctant smile to Mick's

lips. "Vivid imagery there, Heath."

"But it's not an exaggeration. I know you want to help, but you being there would have seriously inflamed an already heated situation."

He bobbed his head once. "Yeah. You're right. I'm too much like the old man; if I'd been there we would've gone at it…"

Heather's jaw dropped, and she interrupted him, "Is *that* what you think? You're just like your father?"

"Yeah."

She shook her head. "You're not like Phil."

"Don't kid yourself, Heather, I am. The same dark moods and bad temper…"

"Listen to me carefully here, Mick. You are nothing like your father. Sure, you can be a little brooding and serious, but you don't have his short fuse, or bad temper. If you did, you would've tossed these evil furniture pieces out the window, and said the ratty old bed in here was good enough for Billy. Instead, you've been patiently working on it for two hours, and with a minimum of cursing. I've got two brothers, a brother-in-law, and a nephew, I *know* how much cussing and tossing of tools goes on during this kind of project. If your supposed bad temper was ever going to surface, this would have been the time, and it didn't. Trust me, you've been a saint."

He rolled his eyes. "Saint Friggin' Mick, that's me."

She screwed up her mouth and stared at the noisy air conditioner, as if she expected it to wheeze out the right thing to say. "I don't know how to convince you, Mick. I'm not sure I can. This is another thing you need to come to on your own, but I know, without a shadow of a doubt, you're a good man. If you have a little of your father in you, you have a whole lot more of your mother's kindness and patience."

As he took a breath to respond, she held up her hand. "Whatever you're going to say, stop it. You're not going to convince me otherwise, so don't waste your time."

"You are one stubborn woman."

"I've been called worse."

Mick glowered at the air conditioner, as it turned off with an especially loud rattle. "Tomorrow after work, I'm going to drive down to Leesburg to get a new A/C unit and a bigger television for the living room. Do you want to come?"

"Do you think it's a good idea, us spending more time together, doing couple-y things?"

He smiled slowly, and Heather shivered in response to his intense stare.

He crawled through the furniture parts strewn on the floor, like a panther to a gazelle.

"As a matter of fact, I think it's a bad idea of epic proportions, but I can't seem to stop myself where you're concerned."

Jesus, what was he doing? He'd promised himself he'd stay away from her for her own good, but hearing her defense of him created a flicker of hope in his chest. Maybe she was right, maybe he wasn't like the old man after all, and that thought flicked all his switches to 'full steam ahead'! He had to have his mouth on her, his hands on her.

He paused for a moment when he reached her, and looked deeply, searchingly, into her gray eyes. If he saw any hesitation or fear there, he'd force himself to pull back…somehow.

His heart pounded, as all he saw in her eyes was a mirror reflection of his own desire.

"Heather," he managed to rasp out with longing, before he leaned in to kiss her.

He meant to keep it gentle and caressing, but as soon as their lips touched it was like a rocket went off and flared between them. Mick tried to tell himself, before he abandoned rational thought altogether, it was just mutual lust, but he knew in his gut it was a whole more than lust on his part.

He tried to pull her closer, but Heather was already there, and trying to climb him like a tree. He molded her soft curves to his hard body, which was growing harder by the second, and moved his lips to the soft skin just below her ear. Her head lolled back on her neck, and her breath came in soft, sexy pants ratcheting his desire up even higher.

They raised up on their knees, by some unspoken accord to press themselves together as tightly as possible.

"Ow!" Heather exclaimed.

She pulled a drawer front out from under her knee and tossed it aside with a clatter.

Mick felt his old knee injury complain about his current position, kneeling on pieces of wood.

He looked around the room for a more comfortable spot, and his gaze landed on the new mattress still wrapped in plastic and propped against the wall.

He jerked his head toward it. "What do you say we christen that? It'll be a lot less painful."

"What? We can't use your brother's new mattress! He hasn't even slept in it yet; it just wouldn't be right."

Donna Simonetta

"How about we re-locate to the sofa then, do you have any moral objections to it?"

"No. It came from Jason's place, so I'm sure it's been christened plenty." She shuddered gently. "But I *really* don't want to think about my little brother just now."

"Me either." Mick grinned, before he stood up, and then leaned down to gather her in his arms and pick her up off the floor. He lowered his mouth to her throat, where he nipped her lightly and then soothed the spot with his tongue. "What can I possibly do to distract you?"

Heather moaned softly. "That was a good start."

She wrapped her arms around his neck as he carried her to the living room, and sank onto the sofa with her in his lap. She tugged his T-shirt up and he released her from his arms long enough for her to lift it over his head. Her eyes devoured his bare chest, and he was glad he hadn't let his body go to hell when he'd stopped playing football.

His head fell back against the sofa as her fingers explored his torso, and when one soft hand dropped a little lower, he was afraid he was going to go off like a teenager. Only Heather had ever held this kind of power over him. He wasn't a man who gave away control easily, but he happily ceded it to Heather as she stroked him through his jeans. However, when her other hand went to work on his fly, he stilled it with a firm grasp.

"My turn," he said with a cocky grin as he flipped their position and secured Heather beneath him on the sofa.

She squirmed under him, and he about lost his mind.

252

"But I wasn't done yet," she complained.

"Oh, we're not done yet, babe," Mick promised as he held both her hands above his head with one of his own. His other hand was busy molding one of her breasts, which this position thrust up to him so enticingly. "We're not even close to done, but we are wearing way too many clothes."

"Mmm...good point," Heather murmured, as Mick set about putting that error to rights.

"I get lucky now and then."

Like right freaking now. Mick looked at Heather lying on the sofa, naked, with a half-smile playing at the corner of her luscious lips. He reached down to get his pants off the floor, pulled out a condom from the pocket.

Heather snatched it from his hand, with a cheeky grin. The wrapper crinkled as she opened it. "Allow me."

When she slid it onto him, Mick feared he would lose it; her hands on him felt so good. He leaned down to press a kiss to her lips, and stroked into her as he did. They moaned against each other's lips. Mick maintained eye contact with Heather as he slowly moved inside her. Sex had never felt this way to him before. Not even the other night at Heather's apartment. Sure, it had been off-the-charts amazing, but there was a playfulness then he wasn't feeling now.

Heather arched her back slightly, and as he slid even farther inside her it felt like the contact with her body touched his soul. Heather's release rippled around him, and he felt it down to his toes. He came with her name on his lips.

****

At first Mick's weight pressing her into the sofa was a welcome pressure, but as Heather felt his harsh breathing start to slow as his big body relaxed, her mind began to race and his weight started to feel like an anchor dragging her down.

What had just happened here was more than sex, way more. It started out teasing, but by the time they got to the big finish, things had taken an intense turn, and it had felt like a vow.

Heather struggled to catch her breath, as Mick stroked her arms lovingly.

Lovingly? What the hell did love have to do with it? It couldn't have anything to do with this situation, that was for damn sure!

This so shouldn't have happened again. She shouldn't have allowed it to happen. She snorted to herself at the thought. *Allowed* it to happen? Hell, she practically *willed* it to happen.

She should have left after the furniture delivery came, but no, she had to stay to help Mick assemble it, and look where that epically bad decision had gotten her.

Okay. It had gotten her underneath Mick following the most mind-blowing orgasm of her life. At one point she was afraid she was going to blackout from pleasure, but that wasn't the point, she reminded herself. This was all too much…too much feeling, too much fear about the future, and too damn much pressure.

She looked at her contribution to the living room furnishings, a black and white cat clock on the opposite wall. As its eyes shifted and its tail swished away the seconds, her panic grew. She needed to get out of here to regroup.

"Look at the time," she said breathlessly.

Her voice seemed to rouse Mick out of his blissful stupor, and he shifted his weight off of her. "I was crushing you; I'm sorry."

If only it were the source of her discomfort, then her problems would be so much simpler and easier to solve. But the fact she still couldn't catch her breath, even without his body pressing into her, told another story.

"It's okay. Really it is. But, look at the time. I've got to go...somewhere..."

He furrowed his brow, and said with quizzical amusement, "Thanks for being so specific."

She wriggled out from under him, and reached for her clothes. She dressed in record time, while Mick reclined deliciously, mouth-wateringly nude on the plaid sofa, like he was some great pasha in his harem. He seemed loose, easy, happy, everything Heather was not feeling following their lovemaking. *Sex*, she corrected herself angrily, it was just sex. Not lovemaking.

"This rush to get out of here, was it something I said?"

"Huh? No." Heather fastened her jeans and grabbed her purse off the coffee table. "It's just the time. And I've got to be..." Her explanation trailed off without any actual, you know, explanation. She knew she was being lame, but she still couldn't catch her breath, and the pressure on her chest was increasing to the point where she felt like she was moments away from a full-blown panic attack. Her mind refused to cooperate, and think of something reasonable to say.

"Somewhere?" he suggested with a smile.

She didn't see what he could possibly be so amused about here, but she'd take the lifeline. "Right. Somewhere. So, I'll see you tomorrow at work?"

She ran off so fast she created more of a breeze than the rattly old air conditioner had managed to do all evening.

****

Mick shook his head as the door slammed, and wondered where Heather had gotten all her nervous energy. He felt like an overcooked noodle, an extremely satisfied overcooked noodle.

He smiled as he looked at the old-fashioned cat clock he knew had to have come from Heather. Its cool mid-century, kitschy vibe was just her style.

He shook his head. Better not think about Heather's touch right now, or he'd never get moving again, and he needed to get moving. Somehow, their incredible bout of lovemaking had scared his furniture assembly assistant away, and now he was on his own to finish it.

He sat up and reached for his pants. As he pulled them on, he wondered what could have sent Heather running into the night like he was the big, bad wolf. From his point of view it had been the best freaking sex of his life, and he was hoping for another taste.

He refused to even consider it hadn't been great for her too; he *knew* it had, her reactions couldn't have been faked. Heather had been right there with him. So what scared her?

He stood and pulled on his T-shirt.

Heather might have the right idea; maybe he should be frightened of the intensity of what just happened between them too.

He rubbed his jawline as he walked into the bedroom to resume his furniture assembly. Maybe the blood was having a hard time working its way back up to his brain, but he couldn't figure it out right now.

He'd give Heather the space she seemed to need tonight, and he'd see her at work tomorrow.

Chapter 23

By the time Heather got down Main Street to the Nosh Pit the feeling she was in imminent danger of hyperventilating passed, but anxiety still made her heart race and her ears buzz.

"Hiya, Heather! Are you just getting home from work? It's a little late, do I need to get Mom to talk to Jeff about being a slave driver?"

She jumped and clutched her heart at the sound of her sister Deidre's voice calling to her from the alley.

"Jeez! Way to give a girl a heart attack, Dee, pop out of an alley at night!"

"Sorry." Deidre grinned without even a hint of apology in her voice or expression. "Where have you been?"

"I went over to the Billy's apartment after work to do some stuff. No need to sic Mom on Jeff. What are *you* doing working so late?"

"I had some paperwork to do." Deidre peered at her in the orange light of the lamppost. "Are you okay? You look like you've seen a ghost. Oh my God! *Have* you seen a ghost? Is Miller's garage haunted? Maybe we could get one of those TV paranormal investigation teams here! Although that little apartment would be small potatoes for them; they probably wouldn't come down here just to investigate it. The main building at the Retreat is over a hundred years old, right? Have you ever seen anything ghostly there?"

Irritation and amusement at her sister's fascination with paranormal television programs helped to tamp down her anxiety about what had transpired with Mick. "Cool your jets, Hermione, I've never seen anything supernatural at either place. You're going to have to find some other way to lure ghost hunters here. You know with all the Civil War activity in this area, Rivers Bend should be crawling with ghosts. Maybe you can get the show that investigated an entire town for supernatural activity to come here."

Deidre bounced in place. "I was just saying the same thing to Hank the other night! The Bend would be a perfect location for them to investigate…and I just realized you're busting my chops. Not nice, little sister, not nice at all."

Heather smiled weakly. "I'm sorry. I couldn't resist."

"You look a little better now, but you're still awfully pale. Did you eat dinner?"

"No, I totally forgot."

"C'mon into the Nosh Pit, I can give you soup and a sandwich."

Heather followed her sister into the alley to the back door, which led into the café's kitchen.

The metal stool grated against the tile floor, as Deidre pulled it over to the island in the center of the small restaurant kitchen on her way to the industrial refrigerator. "Have a seat while I pull something together for you."

"Thanks, Dee, you're such a mom at heart."

"It's what I do; I'm not sure what I'll do with myself when the twins go to college next year. Brace yourself for meddling, I'm going to have a lot of time on my hands."

As Deidre popped some soup into the microwave to warm up, and put sandwich fixings on the counter, Heather said, "If it means you fix dinner for me every night, I could learn to love your empty-nest syndrome."

Deidre smiled and rolled her eyes as the microwave beeped. She pulled out the steaming container and dumped its fragrant contents into a bowl, which she placed in front of Heather. "Chicken noodle, eat. I'm worried your blood sugar is low; you're still not looking so great. Kind of pale and pasty."

Heather blew on a spoonful of soup before eating. As she swallowed the comforting, delicious broth, she closed her eyes and groaned with pleasure. "Oh gosh, thanks for the compliment. If this soup wasn't so darned good, I might take offense."

Deidre cut the turkey sandwich in half and shoved the plate across the island to Heather. She leaned back against the counter and crossed her arms against her chest. "If it wasn't a ghost that spooked you, what's wrong?"

"Nothing," she lied around a mouthful of sandwich.

"Don't try to fool your older sister, I know you too well for it to work. Spill."

She swallowed hard and lowered her gaze to the bowl of soup, as if the little cubes of carrots were the most fascinating sight in the world. Maybe the alphabet noodles would miraculously spell out the answers to all of her problems. She swirled the soup with her spoon. "I wasn't exactly alone at the apartment over the garage just now."

"No? Who else was there?"

"Mick."

"Ah."

Heather glanced up at her sister, before looking back into her soup bowl. "What is that all-knowing sound supposed to mean?"

Deidre shrugged. "Knowing you were with Mick explains a lot to me. Did y'all kiss?"

Heather's face flushed, and it wasn't because of the hot soup. "Kissed and then some."

"Oh yeah." A slow smile spread across Deidre's face. "How was it? Mick looks like a man who knows his way around a woman's body."

Heather stared at her sister in a pointed manner, with her eyebrows raised, and let her silence speak for her.

"What? I'm married, not dead. I love Hank, but a woman notices these things. And don't dodge the question."

Heather knew when her sister set her jaw and crossed her arms any resistance would be futile. She sighed and said, "It was un-freakin'-believable."

"Ah."

"Again with the 'ah'! Tell me, great guru, what my answer revealed to you?"

"It tells me you *were* spooked by a ghost, but not one the television show can help us hunt."

"Oh good, now you're moving on to riddles."

"No riddle. I just meant Dad's ghost caused your flip."

Heather choked on a spoonful of soup. "I did *not* see Dad's ghost! Do you think *you've* seen Dad's ghost?"

Donna Simonetta

"No. I meant his figurative ghost, not his literal ghost."

"I'm still not getting what you mean."

Deidre pulled two juice glasses out of a cupboard, retrieved a bottle of white wine from the fridge, and filled them.

"Do you have a liquor license?" Heather took one of the glasses and clinked her juice glass with her sister's.

"Wise ass. You know I don't. This bottle is for personal consumption only, and this is a conversation screaming for a little Pinot Grigio."

Heather took a sip. "I'm not sure I want to know the answer to this question, but how does Dad's ghost, soup and a sandwich, and a glass of wine have anything to do with sex with Mick?"

"Not just sex with Mick," Deidre corrected as she pointed her glass at Heather. "I believe the direct quote from you is 'un-freakin'-believable sex' with Mick. I think things with him got a little too real for your comfort zone tonight, and it sent you into a full-blown anxiety attack. It's been a pattern for you, although never quite this bad before. Mick must be something special."

Heather tilted her little diner juice glass to slug back a healthy amount of wine. "Bethanne said something similar to me recently."

Deidre topped off Heather's glass with more wine. "I'm not surprised. Bethanne knows you almost as well as I do, and we've both been worried about you for years."

"You have? Why?"

"I guess because we both found great partners, and

we'd like the same thing to happen to you. Life isn't always easy, but if you have someone to share the burdens with, someone who'll support you when you're down, and vice versa, the load's a little lighter. And we worried it won't happen for you, because you've created a catch-22 situation. If you really like a guy, he doesn't stand a chance with you, because once you see he's a keeper, you get flipped and run."

"I don't run. I never run from anything." Heather jutted out her chin.

"Oh sweetheart, I love you to pieces, but you run from relationships with men like a rabbit from a greyhound."

Heather took a bite of her sandwich, and chewed it contemplatively. She wanted to be offended by her sister's words, but she had to admit they rang true.

"And you think Dad's figurative ghost has something to do with my 'pattern'?"

"Because I love you, and I know this is hard for you, I'm choosing to ignore the sarcastic air quotes and just answer your question. Yes, I do. I don't think it's a conscious thing, but I believe you're afraid any man you let yourself love is going to leave you like Dad did."

"Dad didn't leave—he died."

"I know, and up here." Deidre leaned across the counter and tapped Heather's temple. "In your big, intelligent brain, you know it too, but in your heart it's a different story. It thinks Dad left you, and it sucked big-time, so now you're always going to leave before you get left."

Heather blinked. Picked up her sandwich, and put it down again without taking a bite. She blinked again.

"You think?"

"I do. But here's the important thing to remember, not all men leave. Dad loved life, and all of us, so much. He wouldn't have died when he did if he had any choice in the matter. And my Hank doesn't leave."

"I don't understand why you don't feel the same way; have the same fear as me? I mean you lost Dad too, and you've been happily married to Hank for forever."

"True, but I'm ten years older than you. It makes less of a difference now we're both grown, but when Dad died I was already an adult, and you were still a kid. It was horrible for me, and I still lost him too young, but my head was in a different place developmentally than yours was. Plus, since I *have* been with Hank forever, Dad knew him, and approved of him. He always thought Hank was a good horse man."

"From Dad there was no higher praise." Heather smiled wistfully.

Deidre's eyes looked a little brighter, as if there might be a tear or two wanting to leak out, but didn't. "Knowing Daddy liked Hank, and wanted us to be together meant the world to me."

Heather nodded. "It would. It's weird to think whoever I marry will be someone Dad didn't know."

She went back to eating her dinner, while Deidre sipped her wine, and looked through to the empty restaurant. The two sisters didn't talk about their father like this often. They frequently shared fun, fond memories of him, but this kind of deep talk was something they avoided by mutual, unspoken agreement.

Heather swallowed her last bite of sandwich, pushed the plate away, and said, "Granted, I don't have a ton of experience with men, since I might date a good bit, but as everyone but me apparently knows, I don't ever let things become serious with a man, I've never felt like this before. You were right earlier when you said I was close to a full-blown panic attack. Why now? And why Mick?"

Deidre shrugged. "You have to figure those things out for yourself, but I'd guess it's because he means more to you than the other guys did. And when you love someone…"

"Hold on! No one said love! Did I say love?" Heather shook her head furiously as she interrupted.

Deidre rolled her eyes. "Fine. You didn't say love specifically, so we'll say when you *care for someone*, is that better?"

Heather nodded, and gestured for Deidre to continue.

"When you care from someone, the sex is different, more. It can be intense; I think the depth of your emotions is what scared you tonight."

"So what do I do? Before we…you know…"

"If you're doing it, you should be able to say it Heather, *made love*."

"Had sex," Heather corrected firmly.

"Cared for each other in a physical way?" Deidre suggested with a grin.

Heather wadded up a napkin and tossed it at her sister, who just laughed.

"I'm sorry, Heather, I couldn't resist. So what happened before you…you knowed?"

"Mick asked me to go to Leesburg with him

tomorrow night to buy some stuff for his brother's apartment. Should I still go?"

"I don't see why not. How did you leave things with him after you...you knowed?"

Heather felt her cheeks grow hot, and mumbled, "I kind of just threw on my clothes and bolted. I moved so fast, I'm surprised my clothes aren't inside out." She reached up and felt for the tag on her collar, and heaved a sigh of relief when she found it where it should be.

Deidre laughed. "The bolting might make a dignified recovery a little trickier, but I think you should go into work like usual, and go shopping with him tomorrow night just like you planned."

Heather felt her pulse start to race again, and stammered, "And if we get serious? Because I think maybe we'll end up getting serious?"

"Sugar, you already *are* serious. Your brain just needs a little time to catch up with your heart on the subject."

Heather gulped. "How do you do it with Hank? It hurt so much when Dad died; don't you worry about Hank dying all the time?"

"I confess I do spend a fair amount of time at the grocery store reading labels to make healthy choices for him, when he'd be happy existing on pork rinds and beer. And the thought of him passing makes my heart hurt, but the thought of not being with him now, in order to save myself the pain of losing him later, is just not an option. I wouldn't trade any of my time with him; it's too precious. You can't live your whole life worrying about how it's going to end. You live. You love. You let yourself be loved. And sometimes, yeah, you'll hurt, but it's all worth it."

****

Friday at the Retreat was crazy busy with Jeff still away with Maggie, so Heather didn't have to face Mick without a crowd around them. At the end of the day, it seemed her luck had run out.

He stood in the doorway to her office and twirled his car keys around his index finger. "Are you about ready to head out for our shopping trip?"

Huh. His voice was so casual if Heather hadn't been there last night she never would've imagined they had amazing sex, following which she'd panicked and run out on him.

"Um...yeah...sure. Just let me log off and I'm good to go."

She tapped at her keyboard, and as the screen went black, she pulled her purse out of the bottom drawer of her desk.

"Mind if we take Lola?"

She smiled, in spite of her jangled nerves about being alone with Mick. "You never need to ask me. I'm always willing to go for a spin in Lola, especially if I'm driving."

They walked out through the empty kitchen. Normally at this hour, Mrs. Wilson would be whipping up dinner while Sam did her homework at the table, but with Jeff out of town, Sam was staying at her grandmother's house, and Mrs. Wilson got the night off work.

Mick's laughter at her attempt to drive the Mustang broke the uncharacteristic silence. It was a deep, hearty chuckle Heather felt all the way to her core.

"Nice try, but I'll be driving tonight. I'm more in the mood for a leisurely drive, not your Speed Racer driving style."

He held the kitchen door open for her as he spoke, and they stepped outside. Heather swatted his arm in a playful reprimand as she passed by, which only earned her an unrepentant grin from Mick.

When they reached his car, Mick opened the passenger door and bowed while gesturing with a flourish for her to be seated. He waited until she was settled, shut the door, and skimmed around the hood of the car to get in on the driver's side.

"What do you want to do first, shop or eat?" He asked as the hit the road.

Heather chewed on her bottom lip. The evening was shaping up to be more of a couple activity than it was two friends out to pick up some things for an apartment they were working on together. Of course, it was significantly less of a couple activity than the screaming sex they'd shared the night before, so she was probably just being silly and letting her relationship phobia take the wheel.

Mick glanced at her and said with a wry grin, "I didn't think it was that hard a question, Heather."

She exhaled and released a breathy laugh at the same time. "You're right. Sometimes I think I make things harder than they need to be."

"I don't know; it's been my experience you make things just hard enough." He winked at her.

She rolled her eyes, but her cheeks heated at his words, and she chose to ignore them. "I say we shop first, and then eat."

He pulled on to Route 15 South, and grinned over at her, which made her heart race. He had such a devastating smile. "Sounds good to me. Then would you mind directing me to a store where we can get a TV and an air conditioner? I'm not a big shopper, so I'd like to get it over with in one stop. That'll leave us plenty of time for more interesting activities."

She'd given a lot of thought to her conversation with Deidre. As a matter of fact, Heather was pretty sure she'd done more tossing and turning than she did sleeping last night, but she hadn't come to any conclusions about what she should do. And until she did, she didn't think Mick and she should leap into any activities more interesting than shopping and a burger.

"Okay, but I have my graduation tomorrow, so I'm going to have to be home early."

"Right. Your graduation tomorrow. Sorry to drag you out tonight. You must have to get up early in the morning."

Oh sure, now Mick was going to be all thoughtful and considerate. It made her feel even more like a panic-stricken jerk.

"It's okay, but I do have to be up with the birds tomorrow. I'll have to go home right after we're done. Alone." She added after a pause, in case he thought she meant something else.

She noticed the muscles flex in his jaw, a sure sign he was grinding his teeth.

"I've got it, Heather. I don't like it, but I've got it loud and clear. You don't want a repeat performance of last night."

Seriously was it five hundred degrees in this car? She fiddled with one of the vents to point the air conditioner right at her, like it would really help. Embarrassment was her problem, not the ambient temperature.

"Not tonight, no, but I don't want to rule it out forever."

One side of Mick's mouth tilted up, "Good to know, because the thought you were nixing it forever had me seriously bummed."

Heather decided moderate honesty was the best policy, so Mick's feelings wouldn't be hurt, and she wouldn't rush into anything she wasn't sure she was ready for yet. "I just have so much going on right now, and I'm so confused about us, and how I feel about it. I need a little time to figure things out."

"What things?"

"Things."

"That clears it up for me, thanks."

She heaved a deep sigh. "Things like what happened last night."

"Do you mean the best sex of my life?" He interrupted.

She felt pleasure suffuse her that she wasn't alone in feeling that way about last night. She smiled and peeked at him. "Yeah, that. It makes it hard for me to think when it's happening…"

"Then we're definitely doing it right," Mick interrupted again with a cocky grin.

"Too right, maybe. That's why I need a little time without us getting physical to help me figure everything out."

Mick gave a sharp nod. "Sure. I can't say I'm not disappointed, because I am, but I understand. Would it help to talk about it?"

The last part came with the universal male lack of enthusiasm for talking about feelings.

It made Heather smile. "Noble offer, but no. I just

need some time to think and work things out for myself."

Chapter 24

The next morning, Mick stood in front of the newly installed air conditioner window unit, and let the cool air blow over him. The new machine hummed quietly. It was much better than the shake, rattle, and roll of the old one on the floor at his feet, which was soon to be relegated to the dumpster.

Last night hadn't turned out quite the way he'd wanted it to, which would have been Heather and him, naked and sweaty in tangled sheets, but it had been good nonetheless. They'd talked and laughed, and really enjoyed each other's company. He didn't remember ever being so comfortable out with a woman before. Usually he was so careful not to let the suave façade slip, but with Heather he could just be himself, and it was liberating.

He looked at his wristwatch. It was later than he thought, he better get a move on, so he could shower and change before Heather's surprise graduation party at the Retreat. He smiled as he gathered his tools, and broke up the air conditioner box for recycling. He could tell last night Heather was clueless about the party her family and friends had been working so hard to put together for her.

It wasn't easy keeping a secret in gossipy little Rivers Bend, but somehow they'd beaten the odds and done it. Heather really thought she was going to have a quiet lunch with her family after her graduation ceremony.

As if.

She busted her ass working full-time and going to school at night, and everyone was so proud of her. A bash to end all bashes was in the works to celebrate her accomplishment this afternoon at the Retreat.

He heard what sounded like a herd of elephants clomping up the exterior steps, and thought someone else must be coming by to help get the apartment ready for his kid brother. Mick was truly touched by the hard work and generosity of the people of Rivers Bend in welcoming Billy to the town.

A key grated in the lock, and he heard the unmistakable grumble of his father's voice.

"This is what you're leaving home for, huh? Some dump over a garage, so the owner can use you for round-the-clock labor while he sits on his ass? Hope it's worth breaking your mama's heart."

Shit. This was so not how he wanted to spend his Saturday morning. He didn't think Billy was due to arrive until tomorrow, and he certainly hadn't expected the old man to come along.

His eyes bugged out of his head as his mother's gentle voice reprimanded his father, "Billy is not breaking my heart, Phil. I'm proud he's following his dream."

"His dream? More like a nightmare if you ask me." His brother Danny snorted in derision.

Hail, hail, the gang's all here.

Mick picked up his toolbox and stepped into the living room. "I don't recall anyone did ask you, Danny."

"Mick! What a nice surprise!" His mother beamed.

He enveloped his tiny mom in a bear hug. "For me too, Ma, I wasn't expecting Billy until tomorrow."

Billy dropped a box on the floor with a thump, and they did the one-armed man hug as Billy said, "Mrs. Braden called to invite us to Heather's surprise party, so we came today instead."

Their brother Dave stood with his hands on his hips as he surveyed the room. "Bro, this place is sweet!"

His father and Danny snorted derisively in response, but Billy didn't seem to hear them, as he looked around and nodded. "It looks way better than when Mr. Miller showed it to me. Where'd all this stuff come from?"

Mick smiled, and felt his heart swell with pride for Heather and the other citizens of his newly adopted hometown. "Heather got the whole town to pitch in. People have been donating stuff and their time to fix it up for you. What do you think?"

Billy stood in front of the television set Mick bought last night and mounted on the wall this morning.

"Sweet flatscreen! Who would give away something this nice?"

Mick shifted on his feet. "Uh…it's from me."

"No way, man! It's too much!"

"Think of it as a housewarming present."

"Wow. Thanks, Mick!"

Mick nodded in reply. He hadn't intended to admit the TV was a present from him in front of the whole family. If the old man and Danny had lasers in their eyeballs, he'd be a burnt-up little pile of ashes on the floor with the way they were glaring at him.

Time for a subject change, "Where's Susie Q?

Didn't she come with you?"

His mom smiled. "She did. Martin and she ran down the street to get coffee at a little place we passed on the way through town."

"The Nosh Pit? Heather's sister owns it, but she's at Heather's graduation this morning, so she won't be there now."

"How come you're not at the big graduation ceremony? Since you and Heather are such *good friends* and all."

The oily insinuation in Danny's voice made Mick bristle, but he tamped down his anger. Danny was just trying to get his goat, and he refused to take the bait.

"She only could get four tickets, so her mom, sister, and two brothers are going."

"Her mother sounded like a lovely person on the phone. It was so nice of her to invite us to the party today," his mother said with a gentle smile.

"The Bradens are a nice family," Mick replied.

"What's that supposed to mean?" His father's chest puffed out like a bantam cock ready for a fight.

"Just what I said. They're a nice family. They've made me feel really welcome here in Rivers Bend."

"I'm looking forward to meeting Craig Braden at the party," Dave piped up, "He's Heather's nephew, right? He's going to WVU next year too! Billy hooked us up and we've texted a couple of times this week. It'll be nice to know someone there when I start school."

"If you came to work in the mine, like the Evans men have always done, you'd know everyone, and you wouldn't have to worry about meeting new folks."

Mick didn't like the direction his father was trying to take the conversation in so he changed the subject again. "I've just got to put some stuff in the dumpster and recycling bin outside, then I'm going to run home to clean up for the party."

"I'll help you bring the trash out," Billy volunteered eagerly. "It's the least I can do, with all the work you and everyone else has done on the apartment."

The tension still shimmered in the air when Susan burst into the apartment with her new husband in tow, both holding Nosh Pit coffee cups. Susan's trademark positive energy was in full force, and blew away the tension like cobwebs in a breeze. "What a cute little town! And this is a great place, Billy! I thought Mom and I would be so busy cleaning it for you we'd miss the party like a couple of Cinderellas, but it's spic and span, which is great! We won't get all messed up before the party."

Mick wiped his dirty hands on his jeans. "Speaking of getting messed up, I'd better head out now, because I certainly did get dirty this morning. Billy, can you find your way back to the Retreat, or should I come back here to show y'all the way?"

"I'm good." Billy winked. "It's not that a big a town; I can find the way. See you at the party."

****

Heather and her family were all in her sister's super-sized SUV, coming back from her graduation ceremony. She couldn't believe it was over. It took her so many years, and gobbled up so much of her time outside of work she felt at loose ends now, and a little uncertain about her future.

Adding to those anxious feelings was the fact Jeff hadn't said anything about his proposal to Magda.

She'd expected news of their engagement to be the first thing out of Jeff's mouth this morning, but he'd said nary a word. Had Maggie said no?

Jeff's voice broke into her fretful thoughts. "Hey, Deidre, can you swing by the Retreat so we can pick up Sam and bring her to lunch with us?"

His voice was casual, but his question increased Heather's uneasiness. She'd assume Sam was with Maggie, and they'd both be joining the family for lunch, but Jeff only mentioned his daughter.

Her heart tightened at the thought Maggie might have rejected her brother, but also, because she'd grown to love Maggie too, and worried her friend might leave Rivers Bend if her romance with Jeff ended.

Heather thought they were blissfully, disgustingly happy together, but you never really know what went on in other people's relationships. Maybe Maggie wasn't happy living in such a small town.

They pulled up to the front entrance to the Retreat, and Heather peered out of her window, but didn't see any sign of Maggie's Mini Cooper. She might be parked in the back, though. A lot of people chose to bypass the front door and use the back door, which went straight into the kitchen of Jeff's private living quarters.

She didn't want to ask him in front of the rest of the family, because as far as she knew, Jeff hadn't told anyone else he planned to pop the question to Maggie in Washington.

"Um, Heather..." Jeff's voice sounded hesitant and a little nervous, which made Heather's heart sink. Her über-confident, alpha male of a brother *never* sounded nervous. "I need something from your office. Sorry to bother you on your big day, but would you mind coming in with me?"

Oh God! Maggie *had* turned him down, and Jeff wanted to tell her in private. It was the only reason Heather could think of to have Jeff nervously trying to get her alone.

"I need to use the powder room," her mother said.

Deidre chimed in, "Me too."

"Looks like we're all going inside," Jason said with a resigned sigh.

So much for getting Jeff alone to ask him what the heck happened with the proposal. The stop at the Retreat was turning into a field trip for their entire family.

Heather trailed up the front steps after them, distracted by her worried thoughts. She was the last one through the front door into the lobby.

"Surprise!"

Heather jumped out of her skin at the roar of what appeared to be the entire town of Rivers Bend assembled in the Retreat's ballroom and spilling into the lobby.

"What are y'all doing here? What's going on?" She clutched her hand to her chest.

Jason's lazy smile creased his face. "You don't think we'd let a big occasion like you *finally* graduating from college go unnoticed, do you?"

Tears formed in her eyes, and she blinked rapidly as she looked around at everyone. There was a huge banner reading 'Congratulations Graduate!' stretched across the lobby, and balloons and flowers were everywhere.

"How did you pull all this off without me knowing

about it? I was working here all day yesterday."

"I know! We thought Mick and you were never going to get out of here so we could start decorating." Bethanne laughed.

"And cooking," Mrs. Wilson added.

"I'm surprised I have any air left in my lungs after blowing up so many balloons in such a short time."

The last came from Magda, who stood next to Jeff's daughter, Sam. Heather tried to discreetly look at Maggie's left ring finger, and in spite of her happiness at the surprise party for her, she felt a pang of disappointment when she didn't see the sparkle of a diamond there.

She saw Mick standing in the doorway to the dining room and asked him, "Did you ask me to go shopping last night to get me out of here?"

He grinned, in the flirtatious way he reserved for only her, which never failed to rev her engine. "No. I asked you to come with me because I hate shopping and wanted your help. Did I know there was a barn full of people anxiously awaiting our departure, so they could get into the house and get all this ready for you? Yes. Yes, I did."

Heather beamed and looked around the room filled with all the people she loved best in the world. "Oh my gosh...this is just...oh my gosh..."

Jeff hooked her around the neck with one of his brawny arms, in a move part noogie and part brotherly hug. "This truly is a day for the record books; we've made my chatterbox sister speechless."

He raised his voice over the answering laughter. "Thanks to all of you for coming today to celebrate Heather's graduation. There's plenty of food and drink in the ballroom, and we've set some tables up out back, if anyone wants to sit outside. Maggie and Bethanne even tried their hand at creating a special cocktail to honor the woman of the day, the way she's done for all our special occasions since she turned twenty-one. Much like the real person, the 'Heather' cocktail packs quite a wallop! Cisco and I have been taste-testers, and can vouch for their potency, so if anyone needs a designated driver, my niece and nephew will be happy to oblige."

"The *Heather*?" She arched one eyebrow at her two best friends, who'd come up with her namesake drink.

"Yep." Bethanne nodded with satisfaction as she handed a cocktail glass filled with a frosty, purple beverage.

"We used a berry puree to get the color. See, it's purple, Heather, like the flower you're named after, get it?" Maggie bounced on the balls of her feet in excitement.

Heather took a sip and her eyes popped. "Holy moly! Jeff wasn't kidding about the wallop! Folks, be sure to take advantage of Caitlin and Craig's offer of rides home, y'all are gonna need it! What's in here besides berry puree?"

"What isn't in it?" Cisco winked as he leaned down to kiss her cheek. "Congratulations, Heather, I'm proud of you, *meu amiga.*"

Mick joined them, and placed his hand on the small of her back and leaned down to kiss her cheek also. As the subtle, spicy scent of his expensive cologne teased her nose, she marveled at how Cisco's kiss had been brotherly, and left her unstirred, but Mick's almost

280

identical smooch, had her hormones all churned up, like butter at a pilgrim's house.

"Me too, Heather. Working here, and let's face it you keep this place running, so it's not a low-pressure job, and going to school took a lot of hard work and dedication. Good job."

"What he said," drawled a deep voice with a strong southern accent behind her.

She whirled around. "Chase! What are you doing here?"

Chase hugged her, and she caught a brief glimpse of fire in Mick's whisky-colored eyes.

"I wouldn't miss it for the world, are you kidding? I have to leave early to get to our Saturday night gig in D.C., but I had to be here for you, darlin'."

Heather heard a low rumble from Mick that sounded suspiciously like a growl. She shook her head once. It must've been her imagination. However, the devilish glint in Chase's eyes as he looked over her shoulder at Mick, made her think maybe it wasn't her imagination after all.

Chase slipped her drink out of her hand and said, "The Heather, huh? I've gotta take me a taste of that."

He held her gaze over the rim of the glass as he sipped, and now there was no mistaking the tension radiating from Mick's big body at her back.

Heather was usually adept in social situations, but she had no clue how to handle this one. She didn't want to hurt either man's feelings by siding with the other, although she was fairly certain Chase was playing an impish game, while Mick was deadly serious.

"Hello, gentleman."

The sound of too vigorous backslapping pulled her

out of her thoughts with a jolt. Her little brother Jason, well *little* only in the sense of age, as genetics and working the farm had made him big and strong. Currently, he had one muscular arm around the shoulders of each of the two men vying for her attention.

Jason's smile looked easy, but Heather felt a flicker of unease. Maybe it was the way Chase tried to use a sinuous twist to get away before he winced and stayed in place, but Heather just knew Jason had a death grip on Chase and Mick.

Her brother jerked his head toward the dining room. "Why don't you go on in and greet your other guests. We're just going to hang back here for a minute. Have a little guy talk."

Easy Virginia charm rolled off Jason in waves, but Chase and Mick both regarded him with wariness.

Over the years, having two overprotective brothers taught Heather putting the fear of God in potential dates wasn't necessarily a bad thing. Jeff did this handshake thing where he'd greet Heather's date at the door—and back when they lived together, he *always* greeted her dates at the door—he'd look all friendly and harmless, kind of how Jason looked right now, but shake their hands with some sort of Vulcan death grip designed to weed out the weak and the ill-intentioned. If Heather thought a guy was a keeper, she always thought she'd warn him, but she'd never really felt any of her dates were keepers.

Heather could handle herself, and had become pretty good at weeding out the losers by herself over the years, but decided this was her party and she wanted to enjoy it, and not get caught up in this little drama, so she shrugged and flashed Jason a grateful smile.

"You're absolutely right, Jason, I'm forgetting my manners. There's a room full of people in there for me; I've got to go talk to them. See y'all later."

****

She waggled her fingers at them, and darted into the dining room.

The traitor.

Mick frowned at Jason's hand, where it appeared to rest on his shoulder. Actually, resting was a dramatic understatement of what Jason was doing. His grip was so tight, Mick feared he'd have a bruise in the shape of Jason's fingers there tomorrow. He stood still as a statue though, and refused to let Jason see his discomfort.

Musician boy made one more futile attempt to escape Jason's clutches, but gave up with a put-upon sigh and said, "I thought we were friends, man."

Jason turned his head so he could beam at both of them. "We are friends. I'm friends with both of you; that's why I'm helping you out here. I'm sure Jeff's got a measuring tape around here somewhere. Why don't we find it, and you two can just whip 'em out and see whose is bigger? It would be quicker than whatever the hell you were both just doing, which would have been much funnier to me if it wasn't over my goddam sister! Us being friends, is the only reason I'm not taking both of you out back and spraying you down with the freakin' hose. Listen up, Heather worked her ass off to finish her degree, and we're all going to act like big boys and focus on her achievement today, got it? There will be no more making *my sister*." He glared at them each in turn as he said the last two words,

283

"uncomfortable with your competitive dick-swinging bullshit."

He slapped both of them on their backs, while he grinned jovially.

Chase actually staggered forward a step at the force of it, Mick noticed with satisfaction as he stood his ground in the face of what had been a really hard shove in the back, all under the guise of a friendly back pat.

"We clear here, gentleman?" Jason nodded in approval at their silence. "Good. Good. Now let's go get us some beers and enjoy the party."

Chapter 25

Heather noticed Jeff slip through the door to his living quarters behind the check-in desk, and saw her opportunity to finally get him alone and find out what happened with his proposal to Maggie.

She smiled at Mick's mother and made a polite excuse, so she could follow Jeff. She hadn't been able to pin him down all afternoon, and was pretty convinced he was avoiding her.

By the time she got to his half of the house, Jeff was nowhere to be seen, but Maggie's little Shih Tzu padded down the hall from the kitchen to greet her.

"Hi Petunia. Who's a good girl?" She gave the wriggling dog a quick scratch behind the ears. "Where's Jeff at, girl? Can you make like Lassie and show me where he went?"

Heather was only joking, but the freakishly smart dog turned and trotted up the stairs. She glanced over her shoulder at Heather with her one good eye, as if to be sure the dopey human was following her.

Heather grinned and shrugged as she followed the dog upstairs. Now Petunia was on the hunt there was no stopping her determined progress. Maybe Mrs. Warren, who was Master of the local hunt club, should look into using a pack of Shih Tzus instead of hounds.

Petunia made a beeline for the open door into Jeff's bedroom at the end of the hall, Heather followed, and called out as she entered the room, "Jeff, are you in here?"

"Sure am, Sis, what's up?" Jeff sat at the edge of his bed, and looked up from smart phone as he spoke.

"I've been trying to get you alone all day!" Heather sighed in exasperation. "I finally had to chase you in here to talk to you in private. What happened in D.C.? I noticed Maggie isn't wearing the ring. I'm so sorry, Jeff! Why on earth did she say no? Doesn't she realize what a catch my big brother is?"

She heard the door to the master bathroom click open behind her, as Magda answered for Jeff, "I most certainly do realize what a catch Jeff is. That's why I didn't throw him back—I said yes!"

Heather whirled around to see Maggie's beaming face. "You did?"

"I did!" Magda's smile lit up the room, and the two women squealed as they hugged.

"That was way more girly-girl than I've ever seen the two of you act before," Jeff's amused drawl interrupted them.

"If there's ever a time for girlish squealing, it's when you give me another sister! And I really love her too! I couldn't ask for a better second sister."

Magda's blue eyes grew round as she squealed again, "A sister! I've got a sister!"

"Two actually, and a brother," Heather said with an affectionate grin.

"I get the man I love *and* his big, wonderful family! I'm just on cloud nine." Maggie practically floated over to Jeff, who pulled her to sit on his lap.

"You and me both, Maggie darlin'," he said as he pressed a kiss to her temple.

Heather flapped her hands. "I don't get it! If you're engaged, why haven't you told everyone? And where's your ring?"

Maggie leaned back to pull open the nightstand drawer, from which she pulled out a little blue box. "Here it is, wanna see?"

"Hell yeah! I want to see it! I want to see it on your finger! Why aren't you wearing it?"

"Today's your day, Heather, we didn't want to steal your thunder," Jeff said.

Heather looked up from Maggie's left hand, where she'd been admiring the lovely diamond solitaire set in platinum. "Screw that noise! We've got everyone gathered in one place. Let's go downstairs and tell them all your good news!"

****

Mick wasn't sure how it happened, but at some point in the afternoon, Heather's graduation party had turned into Jeff and Magda's engagement party. Lunch had turned into supper, and supper had turned into dancing. He was currently leading Heather's sister Deidre around the tiny dance floor in the ballroom.

Her cheeks were flushed, and her eyes shined as she smiled up at him. "Thanks for dancing with an old married lady, Mick. Hank is the best husband and father in the world, but I cannot get him to dance to save my soul."

Mick looked over at Deidre's husband and smiled. Hank sat at a table that had been pushed aside to create a makeshift dance floor in the dining room. He held a beer bottle loosely in his fingers, and his long legs were stretched out in front of him. Hank always reminded Mick of an old West gunslinger, and he wasn't surprised to learn the stoic horseman wasn't a big fan of dancing.

"Happy to oblige." Mick smiled down at Deidre, who wasn't as tall as her sister Heather.

"You're a nice man," Deidre observed. "I hope you can be patient and stick with Heather. I know she can be like a skittish colt with men, but she's a great girl, and well worth the effort."

"I agree. Heather deserves the best there is; I'm just not sure that's me."

Deidre swatted his upper arm. "Oh pshaw! Anyone with two eyes can see y'all are meant for one another, Heather just needs to realize you're going to stick, and you need to realize you deserve happiness."

Much struck by her words, Mick's feet had stopped moving.

"Why did you stop dancing? Did what I just said come as some sort of surprise to you?" Light dawned in her eyes. "Oh my stars, you're just as clueless as my sister, aren't you?"

****

Mick leaned on the railing in the shadows of the back porch, and watched as the party continued into the night in the backyard. It was a fun party, but Mick needed a little time alone to process his conversation with Deidre. Could happiness with Heather be as simple to achieve as her sister had made it seem?

The slam of the screen door told him his alone time was about to end. He glanced to his right, expecting to see Jeff or Jason approach, but raised an eyebrow when he saw it was none other than his rival for Heather's affection.

"Chase. What do you want?"

"I was looking for Heather."

Mick ground his teeth together. Of course the son of a bitch was looking for Heather.

"I've got to get going if I have any hope of making my gig on time, so I wanted to say goodbye to the guest of honor."

Mick jerked his head to one of the tables set up in the yard, for the dinner Mrs. Wilson and the ladies of Rivers Bend had hurriedly prepared from luncheon leftovers, when it became clear the party wasn't going to stop anytime soon.

"There she is, holding Cisco and Bethanne's baby, so they have a chance to hit the dance floor."

"Is that your mom and sister with her?"

"Yup." Mick hoped if he kept his responses brief Chase would be on his way all the faster.

"Nice folks, but your dad..." Chase shook his head. "He's a tough old bird. You're nothing like him."

"Maybe not on the surface, but I'm just like the old man."

Chase chuckled. "Nah. You're about as much like him, as I'm like my father, and I used to think Gypsies left me on my parents' doorstep, that's how different he and I are."

Mick smiled in spite of his dislike of Chase. He had a similar fantasy when he was a kid, convinced he couldn't possibly be his father's biological child.

"Your father is a hard man, brusque, rude, and judgmental. No offense."

"None taken. He's all of those things."

"And I don't see any of those traits in you. I kinda wish I did, so I could warn Heather off of you and clear the way for me, but in all good conscience I can't do it.

You seem like a good guy, and Heather wouldn't be as into you as she is if you were a douche."

"She might just not see it in me yet. And I'm not sure she *is* all that into me."

Chase scowled. "She is. It pains me to say so, but she never looked at me the way she looks at you."

"How's that?"

"All soft and gooey, like she might finally be getting ready to let down some of those walls she's put up to protect herself." He narrowed his eyes and crossed his arms across his chest. "And if she does open up to you and you hurt her, you're going to answer to me."

One side of Mick's mouth turned up, "If I hurt her, I think you'll have to get in line behind her brothers."

****

"If it isn't my three favorite ladies all together, what a pretty sight."

Mick's voice warmed Heather like a sip of good bourbon. She smiled and bounced baby Cisco on her knee.

"Oh you sweet talker!" His mom flapped her hands at him dismissively, but pleasure shone in her eyes.

Heather was so happy to see Mick reconnecting with most of his family.

He held out his arms. "Why don't you give the little guy to me and give your arms a rest?"

Heather handed over the happy, burbling baby. "Thanks, Mick, for a tiny person, he was starting to feel like he weighed a ton."

Mick made a funny face at the baby boy and was rewarded with a gummy smile. He smiled back as he eased into a seat at their round table.

"I don't know I've ever seen such a happy baby before. It gives a girl ideas," his sister said.

"I'd like to be a grandma someday, Susan, but you and Martin should enjoy a little time alone first. Y'all need to get used to each other before you introduce a little one to the mix."

"Plus, there's no guarantee you'll get a happy little guy like Cisco here." Mick smiled at his mom. "Remember how fussy Susie was when she was this age?"

"I was?"

Their mother nodded. "Colic. You couldn't help it, but it did make you fuss. And Mick was a happy baby, but he had his days and nights mixed up, so I'd just catch forty winks when I could. Children bring a lot of joy into your life, but they're not always easy."

"Sam was such a good baby; I think she spoiled me for any potential future children." Heather smiled as her mind went back to those happy times with her niece. She adored the time she spent with her sweet baby niece, and never understood Sam's mother's lack of interest in her daughter.

"You were good with her, a real natural," Mick said.

"You helped a lot. Your big brother experience certainly came in handy."

Susan stood and winked. "All this talk about enjoying our time together as a couple has me wanting to dance with my husband. I'm going to find Martin."

"Have fun," Mrs. Evans said as Susan walked away. "It's nice Martin will dance with her; I could never get your father onto the dance floor."

"I think Susie's wedding was the first time I ever

saw him dance," Mick observed with a frown.

After a brief silence, Heather said, "Where are y'all staying tonight? I have a tiny apartment, so I don't really have room to put anyone up, but I can try to squeeze someone in on the sofa."

"Thank you, dear, it's so sweet of you to offer, but your brother Jeff offered us rooms here at the Retreat. He hadn't taken any groups for this weekend on account of your party, so there's plenty of room at the Inn. You have such a kind, welcoming family, Heather."

"I like them," Heather replied with a cheeky grin.

Mrs. Evans peered into the kitchen window, lit up like a yellow square against the night. "Looks like your mom and Mrs. Wilson are hard at work in there. I think I'll go on in and see if I can help."

She stood up and beamed at Mick, Heather, and the baby. "The two of you sitting together with that darling child, now that's what I call a pretty picture."

Mick rolled his eyes as his mother walked away. "My ma has a lot of really good traits, subtlety is not one of them. Sorry about that."

Heather stretched out her legs and took a sip of her purple, namesake cocktail. "It's okay. Maybe it's just the *Heather*s talking here, but I think the sight of you dandling a baby on your knee is a pretty picture too. Women are such suckers for a big, strong man who's good with children."

Mick's sexy grin made her shiver in spite of the warm night. "Why Ms. Braden, you're gonna make me blush. Are you saying you're a sucker for my big, strong self?"

"You wish!" She snorted.

"Yeah. I do."

Whoa! She'd thought Mick was just playing around, but his response was dead serious. She bit her bottom lip, and decided to go out on a limb. "Maybe I am. Just a little bit."

Mick peered at her intently in the dim light of the candle on the table. "How many of those purple drinks have you had?"

"Enough to make me admit I'm a little bit of a sucker for you, but not so many I don't know what I'm saying."

"That's what I was hoping." Mick's teeth showed white in the dark. "When this shindig is over, may I take the guest of honor home?"

Heather leaned back in the white resin chair, and stretched her legs out until they almost reached Mick. She took a deep breath and searched his face, for what she wasn't sure. A reassurance it would be the right thing to do? A guarantee he wouldn't vanish from her life? She didn't see the answers to either of those questions in his handsome face, but what she did see there was desire for her, and tenderness for his friend's baby, whom he held safe in his strong arms. And maybe that was enough for now.

"Sure," she said so softly she feared he wouldn't hear her.

His smile widened as he bounced baby Cisco on his knee. "Really? Good." His smile turned devilish, "Do you think the party will be over soon? Like *really* soon?"

She laughed and slouched down in her seat, to give her legs the extra room they needed to reach him and kicked him in the shin. "No. And I am the guest of honor, so we're here to the bitter end."

The screen door squeaked open, and the light from the kitchen silhouetted Jeff and Magda.

"Here she is!" Maggie said with a bright smile.

The couple clomped down the stairs and sat at the table with them. Magda reached her hand to the candle in the center of the table, and twisted it in the light to admire the sparkle of her engagement ring.

Jeff scooted his chair a little closer to hers so he could rest his arm on the back of it.

"Pretty rock," Mick said with a warm smile. "Best wishes, not that you need them. If ever a couple was made for each other, it's you crazy kids."

Jeff grinned. "Thanks, Mick. I'm a lucky man. Want me to take my godson for a bit?"

"Nah, I've got him."

The baby burbled happily as Mick bounced him. "We've got a good rhythm going here, and he's happy and quiet."

"Bethanne and Cisco are saying their goodbyes now. It's past his bedtime, so they'll be out to get him soon," Maggie said.

"Speaking of home, there's something I wanted to talk to you about, Mick," said Jeff.

"Yeah?" Mick eyed his friend a little warily.

"Maggie's going to be moving up to the big house now that we're engaged, and we were thinking you might want to move into her cottage when she moves out. The cabin's got to be getting a little claustrophobic."

Relief relaxed the line of Mick's jaw. "I thought you were about to kick me out."

"Hell no! Why would I do that?"

Heather cocked her head as she looked at Mick. His cranky father had done a serious number on him. Mick really believed one of his oldest friends would toss him out on his ear without warning.

"I don't know," Mick said.

"So do you want the cottage?" Jeff asked.

"Sure, if you're positive about it. The cabin is great, you can't beat the view of the river, but we're losing potential revenue with me keeping paying guests out of it. Plus, I miss having a real kitchen. It's hard to cook an actual meal in the kitchenette."

"You can cook?" Magda raised her eyebrows.

"You don't have to look quite so surprised. I'm 33 years old, and I don't want to eat takeout every night. It was either learn how to cook or survive on cold cereal and bologna sandwiches." Mick shrugged. "I learned how to cook."

"You'll love the kitchen at the cottage then," Magda said eagerly. "Bethanne and Cisco renovated it before they moved in. It's got all top-of-the-line appliances, and a laundry room."

Mick nodded his approval. "No more lugging my laundry to the Suds and Go on Main Street? Sounds like a plan to me. On one condition, you let me pay you a fair rent for the place."

Jeff absently massaged Magda's shoulder as he said, "I wasn't planning on charging you rent."

Mick frowned and shook his head. "Paying rent's a deal breaker for me. I'm no sponge. I've been feeling bad enough about staying in the cabin; there's no way I'm moving into the cottage and not paying you for it."

"Fine," Jeff conceded. "You can pay rent. Let me talk it over with Cisco, and we'll settle on an amount next week."

Magda's sunny smile brought the dimples out in her cheeks, "It's settled then. It looks like Rivers Bend is getting under your skin, just like it did mine! I started out in Cabin 5 with no intention of living here permanently, moved to the cottage, and now I'm putting down roots and staying for good."

She was staying because Maggie was marrying a Braden. Was she implying Mick was going to follow in her footsteps about that too? And was Mick bouncing Baby Cisco a little more vigorously with nervous energy at the thought? Heather certainly felt the early signs of another panic attack at the idea. Her throat tightened and her heart pounded. *Marriage?* Give her a break, she'd been barely able to commit to going home with Mick *tonight*, let alone *every* night for as long as he stuck here in Rivers Bend. His deep rumble of a voice intruded on her thoughts.

"If you're moving up to the big house, are you two going to have a short engagement and get hitched soon?"

"I'd like to get married as soon as we can, but Maggie here wants a wedding with all the trimmings, so it might take a while to pull it all together."

Mick lowered his voice, and Heather noticed the baby's eyes drooping as he fought a losing battle with sleep. "I wouldn't have thought a big wedding would be your thing, Maggie."

She shrugged. "Not big. I don't care if it's just us and our close friends and family, but I want the big, white dress, and loads of flowers. And I want to get married in that sweet little church where Cisco's christening was held. But mostly, I want everyone we love in one room, to share the moment with us."

Jeff squeezed her shoulder, and Maggie peeked up at him through her crazy corkscrew curls. "Being part of a big happy family is new to me, and I want the wedding to go with it. How about you, Heather, when you get married don't you want the whole nine yards?"

Heather shook her head so vehemently her bangs flopped into her eyes. She brushed them aside as she said, "I can't imagine getting married, but if I did, I think I would want to elope. Maybe to Vegas, and we could go to one of those tacky wedding chapels and have an Elvis impersonator perform the ceremony."

"Way to embrace the sanctity of marriage, Heath." Jeff snorted.

Mick's gaze burned into her, as he stared at her over the sleeping baby's downy head. "No, I see Heather's point. It would be just the two of you, committing to your life together."

"Just you and Fat Elvis," Jeff said with skepticism.

Maggie wrinkled her cute little nose. "It always *is* Fat Elvis they impersonate. I wonder why? I would rather see young hot Elvis."

Jeff laughed, "But there are helluva lot more guys who look like Fat Elvis, than like young, hot Elvis."

Magda squinted at Mick. "With a little tweaking of your hair, you could pull off Hot Elvis, Mick."

Jeff started to guffaw, but quickly smothered his laugh, as it caused the baby to stir, and threatened to wake him. "Hey, we just got Mick here, and he's bringing in a lot of new business. Don't tempt him away with thoughts of a glitzy career as a Hot Elvis impersonator."

Heather leaned forward to peer at him. "I don't see

Hot Elvis."

"Thanks." Mick grinned. "Way to build up a guy's ego, Heather, tell him he's more Fat Elvis than Hot Elvis."

"I didn't mean that! I'm just not sure I see Elvis at all."

"Squint," Maggie suggested.

Jeff fought another burst of loud laughter and wheezed, "Stop, Maggie, I'm trying not to wake the baby, but you're killing me here…*if you squint, Mick will be hot, I swear*. Priceless!"

The screen door slammed, and they all turned to see who was coming.

"I wonder what tore Jason away from his harem? When last I saw him he was on the dance floor surrounded by a bevy of his groupies, dancing in a circle around him," Heather said.

"And this girl he's with is not at all his usual type," Jeff added.

Jason's taste did run to long-legged, curvy blondes and girls with a bra size bigger than their IQ. This woman at his side was an average height brunette. Her hair was cut in a cute layered pixie style, and she wore funky dark-rimmed eyeglasses. In her jeans and flowy top, she was much more casually dressed than most of the party-goers, and she looked definitely brainy.

"Hey y'all," Jason called out as they approached, and Heather held her fingers to her lips and pointed at the sleeping baby.

"Sorry," Jason said in a much softer voice, "I didn't see the little squirt. Have any of you seen Peanut and her posse?"

"Sam and her friends? They're up in her bedroom.

Why?" Jeff replied.

"This is Hadley's aunt from Baltimore. She's here to pick her up, and they weren't in the dining room, so I offered to help her hunt them down."

Jeff rose and shook her hand, "I'm Sam's dad, Jefferson Braden, but please, call me Jeff. It's nice to meet you." Maggie stood up and moved to his side, so he slung his arm around her shoulders and said, "And this is my fiancée, Magda Horvath. Over there is my sister, Heather Braden, and our friend, Mick Evans."

Mick started to stand up, like a good Southern gentleman, but the woman gestured for him to stay put. "Please don't get up, in my experience it's best to let sleeping babies lie. Hi everyone! I'm Lily Davis, and it's great to meet all of you."

"Not Diemer or Peterson?" Maggie asked, mentioning the last names of Hadley and her mother.

Lily shook her head, and Heather noticed her hazel eyes twinkle behind her big glasses. "Gloria was a Davis a few husbands ago. It's our father's name."

"Let me run up to Sam's room to get the girls," Jeff said.

"I'm a little early, but when I got here from Baltimore, Gloria said she had a party to attend down in D.C., and took off right away. I rattled around in her house for a while, so I decided to come now, but I hate to cut Hadley's time with her friends short. I can wait in my car, or just come back later."

Her response was more direct and lengthier than Heather would've expected, and Lily's accent sounded a lot like Maggie's. "Please join us, Lily. Can I get you a drink or something to eat?"

Lily smiled and sat in an empty seat. "No thanks.

Gloria's chef prepared something for me. I would've been happy with a PB&J, but he whipped up a gourmet meal for me, which I ate in solitary splendor in the dining room."

Heather smiled. "A chef? That must be nice."

"You'd think so, wouldn't you?" Lily wrinkled her nose and frowned.

Heather decided to change the subject, "You live in Baltimore, but that doesn't sound like a Bawlmer accent to me. Where are you from originally?"

Lily grinned, and imitated a Baltimore accent, "I can speak Bawlmerese with the best of 'em, Hon, but I'm from Connecticut originally."

Maggie beamed at her. "Me too! Whereabouts?"

"I'm from Westport, and I have to confess Gloria already told me you're from Greenwich."

Maggie frowned. "Stratford, actually. My grandmother has a home in Greenwich, but I grew up in Stratford with my dad."

Lily rolled her eyes. "That's Gloria for you. Why mention where you're *really* from, when she can name-drop Elizabeth Mallory and Greenwich?"

There was a brief silence, as no one felt comfortable acknowledging that harsh truth about Gloria to her sister.

Jeff cleared his throat and said, "It was nice of you to come out here so fast to see Hadley. The poor kid's been in a spin about moving."

Lily's friendly eyes grew flinty. "I know, and I feel awful Gloria put her in that position. I'm pretty irritated with my half-sister right about now, and that's probably why I just made you guys so uncomfortable with my witchy comment about her. Sorry."

"It's been rough on Hadley. She boards her horse out at our farm, so I see quite a bit of her, and she's been nervous about her future. Are you going to take her back to Baltimore?" Jason asked.

Lily craned her neck to look up at him. "No. I have a small place in a so-so neighborhood there. It's all I can afford on my teacher's salary and it's okay for me, but I wouldn't want to move Hadley in there. I'm going to move here, so she can stay in her own house and at the same school with all her friends. I'm interviewing for a job in the middle school on Monday."

"That is so nice of you," Maggie said warmly.

"Yeah. Leaving a small apartment in a bad neighborhood to live in Gloria's mansion out on River Road, what a sacrifice," Jason said with uncharacteristic rudeness.

"Jason Braden!" Heather gasped. "It's a wonderful thing Lily is doing! It's a good thing Mama is in the house, so she didn't hear you! Where are your manners? Apologize to Lily this instant!"

"Sorry, *Mom*," Jason scowled, but said stiffly to Lily, "My sister is right. I forgot my manners. I'm sorry for my rudeness."

"It's okay," Lily smirked at him. "I tore you away from all your admirers inside; you're bound to be a little cranky."

Heather looked from her younger brother to Lily, amazed a woman called him on his bull. Usually women fell under his spell, and let him get away with anything. Of course, he was not being his usual, charming self with Lily for some reason. Given the amount of time Lily's niece spent in various Braden homes, Heather sincerely hoped the two would get over their animosity toward each other. Even if they couldn't be friends, she hoped they would be able to be civil to one another.

The screen door flew open with a bang, and a herd of twelve-year-old girls thundered down the stairs. Baby Cisco awoke with a start and howled.

"Aunt Lily! You're here! I can't believe it!" Hadley shrieked, as she threw herself into her aunt's waiting arms.

Lily hugged the girl tightly and said, "I'm here to stay, kiddo, so get used to me."

Chapter 26

Heather sat on the red couch in Mick's cabin and stretched out her long legs. Mick leaned against the counter in the kitchenette. He rolled up the sleeves of his white dress shirt. "This is some warm spell we're having. It's the middle of the night and still so hot. Can I get you something to drink? Water?"

Heather kicked off her shoes, and turned to rest her back against the arm of the sofa so she could see Mick behind her in the kitchen. "It takes a while to adjust to the weather when you first move here from Portland. Luckily Jeff, Sam, and I moved back in the winter after football season, so it was cooler. But that first summer...phew!"

Mick took a sip of his own glass of water. "So, you're saying you don't want a drink? Y'know, since you're so warm-weather tough and I'm such a wuss?"

"That's not what I meant, and you know it! And I'd love a glass of water. People have been pouring those *Heather* cocktails down my throat since we got to the party. I could use a little hydration."

"One glass of water coming up!"

Mick reached to take down another glass from the cupboard, and Heather admired the flex of his muscles in his broad shoulders, under his well-fitted shirt. His buns in his dress slacks, on display since he'd shed his sport coat as soon as they got to the cabin, were a fine

303

sight too.

She wriggled her toes. This was nice, coming home together from a party. It felt cozy and comfortable, but with the promise of hot and steamy still to come. Maybe this was how married couples felt. The thought made her stomach lurch, or maybe it was just the *Heathers* she'd consumed. Could she be making progress in her fear of commitment? Normally the thought of the 'M' word would have her running out the door in a blind panic, but in spite of a little queasiness, at the same time it also felt right being here with Mick like this, and she didn't feel the need to flee. Baby steps.

Mick handed her a glass, which was already coated with condensation. He lifted her legs, as he sat down on the opposite end of the sofa, and placed her feet in his lap.

"It's nice Sam's friend won't have to move. Gloria really is a piece of work, so ready to stick her own kid in a foreign boarding school, just so she can play at being an ambassador's wife. Her sister seems a lot more human, and down to earth," Mick said.

"That's not hard to do, the Kardashians are more down to earth than Gloria, but Lily *does* seem nice. It will be fun having a woman in this town who is impervious to my brother Jason's charms. He's gotten spoiled by all the female attention he gets." Her sentence ended on a moan as Mick rubbed the arch of her foot with his strong hands. "Mmm, that feels so good."

He smiled at her and it held the promise of more fun to come from those big hands. "Lily and Jason really didn't seem to like each other much. I wonder why?"

Her eyes had fluttered shut with pleasure, but she opened them as thought about it. "I don't know. I've never seen Jason be so rude to anyone before. Maybe it's because she's the only woman who didn't automatically succumb to his charm."

"Maybe he's attracted to her. She's kinda cute if you like that whole Bohemian thing she's got going on."

She laughed. "I don't think so. She's not Jason's type. Most of his girlfriends aren't the brightest bulbs, and Lily seems really smart. Plus, and perhaps more important, we are not twelve anymore! He's not going to pick on a girl because he thinks she's cute."

She purred like a kitten as he continued to work his magic on her tired feet.

Mick chuckled at her reaction. "And yet, some might say it's exactly what we were doing when I first came to Rivers Bend. You seemed like you were ready to give me a pair of concrete shoes and dump me in the Potomac, but look at us now."

"Yeah, but we have a history together. I had a very good reason for being ticked off at you."

Uh oh. Maybe bringing up the past wasn't very smart. Mick's foot lovin' stopped abruptly.

"You did have a good reason, eleven years ago. Not now."

"Nooo." She knew her hesitant answer wasn't at all convincing, but she couldn't help the hesitation in her voice.

Mick frowned. "Are you still mad about what happened back then? I thought we were past it."

She rubbed his thigh with her foot. "We are. I am.

305

What happened in Portland is behind us, I swear."

It wasn't his fault her brother clearly thought more of Mick professionally than he did of her. She busted her ass for Jeff at the Retreat, but Mick was the one Jeff had working toward a partnership, not her. It stung. She knew she shouldn't hold it against Mick, but sometimes unwanted thoughts popped into her head.

He caught her foot and recommenced the rubbing. "Glad to hear it. You scared me for a minute there."

Determined to not make Mick pay for things that weren't his fault, she said, "I'm just tired. It's been a long day."

Heat warmed his eyes, and when he spoke his voice was deep and rough. "Then maybe I better get you to bed."

She made a show of arching her back and stretching. "Bed sounds like a plan."

Mick waggled his eyebrows and tugged on her ankle. She squealed as he pulled her onto his lap. He stood, with her cradled in his arms, and she marveled at the strength it took.

"C'mon, lady, let's get you tucked into bed."

She saw the world go upside down as he hoisted her over his shoulder into a fireman's carry.

"Mick!" Her breath came in gasps, as the blood rushed to her head. "What are you doing?"

She giggled as he swatted her bottom, which was currently positioned right next to his face.

"Sweeping you off your feet. Isn't this what people mean by that? Did I get it wrong?"

She heard the laugh in his voice and turned her head, which made her realize she was in the perfect position to reciprocate, so she gave his tight buns a slap.

"I had a lot of *Heathers* tonight; you won't be laughing if I yip all over these expensive slacks."

She felt his hands shift their grip on her, and then the world spun again until she was right side up, as he turned her and gently tossed her onto his bed. She bounced once, and then Mick was on top of her. He pressed butterfly kisses to the spot below her ear that made her heart stop; his hands ran down her body from the outside curve of her breasts to her hips. Her breath caught audibly, and she felt his lips curve into a smile against her throat.

"I take it you like this kind of sweeping-off-your-feet better?"

She shrugged with feigned indifference. "It's not bad."

He raised his head and grinned at her wolfishly. "Not bad? Not *bad*? I'll give you not bad!"

His hands slid up her waist, and she tensed in anticipation of what he would do to improve on his earlier stroking to stoke her fires. Instead, she jumped as he launched a tickle offensive. She writhed on the bed and gasped, even as she laughed. "Stop it! You know how ticklish I am! Fine. I admit it—I'm swept off my feet!"

His hands stilled. "Was that so hard?"

She used her legs, and the element of surprise to flip him, so he was on his back on the bed, and she was on top of him. The hint of a smile played around his lips, and he raised his eyebrows.

She answered his unspoken question. "Raised by brothers, remember? I learned a few tricks. And you forgot, Michael Evans, I know where you're ticklish too."

As she spoke she wriggled her way down his body and ran her hands up his pant legs to tickle behind his knees.

He squirmed and laughed. "Uncle! Uncle!"

She stroked her hand back down his calf, and grinned up the length of his body at him. "We seem to be at a stalemate."

She knew with his superior size and strength he could turn the tables with no problem, but he didn't. Instead, Mick wove his fingers together and put his hands behind his head, and said with a grin, "You win, have your wicked way with me, woman."

She licked her lips. "I don't know where to start."

"Are you taking suggestions?" he asked helpfully. "Because if you are, I have a few."

She smiled at him, trying to school her features into a wide-eyed, innocent expression, in spite of feeling full of playful devilishness. "Nope. Thanks for the offer, but I think I've got it."

His groan, as she straddled him and undid his belt buckle, was her only answer.

****

Mick stood at the bathroom mirror, and knew he had to stop grinning like a well-satisfied fool if he had any hope of shaving, but he couldn't seem to wipe the smile off his face. Last night with Heather had been amazing. And she hadn't run away this morning. Well, sort of, but she wasn't running scared this time. She'd just borrowed Lola to run to her place to change her clothes.

There was a big brunch at her mom's house this morning, and she couldn't very well show up in the same dress she'd worn to the party last night. Although, given Rivers Bend's propensity for gossip, he was sure it would be all over town that she'd driven his car to her place bright and early, while still wearing said wrinkled dress.

Grinning, he shook his head, looked at his reflection in the mirror, and tightened the fluffy white towel knotted low on his waist. This was actually his second shower of the morning. The first was with Heather, and he'd concentrated on washing her sexy, sudsy body, after which no one was much interested in getting clean.

He practically couldn't recognize the man in the mirror, and he definitely couldn't remember the last time he'd felt this happy. He knew for a fact that he'd never had so much fun with a woman in bed before. Oh, he was no monk, and he'd enjoyed some steaming hot sex in the past, but it was never been as light-hearted, fun, and playful as it had been last night with Heather. He felt like he could relax with her and just be himself. And, man, did it ever feel like a gift. One he wasn't sure he deserved, but he was no fool, and he had no intention of turning it down.

A buzz filled the steamy bathroom as he turned on his electric shaver and ran it over his face. As he did so, he wondered how long before Heather got back in Lola. He shook his head in wonder; he still couldn't believe he let her borrow Lola. There wasn't another woman on Earth he'd trust with his precious car, although even his amazing sex-addled brain had to admit loaning it to a crazy lead-foot like Heather might not have been the wisest thing to do.

The grin crept back across his face as he shut off the razor and slapped on some aftershave. He knew

Heather was a speed demon behind the wheel, but she was always in control. He didn't want her back because he was worried about Lola. He wanted her back because he missed her. After half a freaking hour, he missed her. Christ, he was a sap about this woman.

He heard the door creak open, and her shoes clack on the hard wood floors. Heather was back, and a sense of calm and happiness washed over him.

He saw her reflection appear in the mirror behind him as she came through the open bathroom door. Jesus, she looked beautiful! Dressed in a red V-necked top, white skinny jeans, rolled up at the ankles, and a pair of flat sandals on her feet, she looked casual and comfortable, but she did it for him more than any woman in an expensive, designer outfit ever had.

She rolled her eyes, "Man, Evans, you're higher maintenance than me. I've driven back to my place, gotten ready, driven back here, and you're still in your towel?"

She looked him up down in an appreciative perusal. "Not that I don't appreciate the view, because I do…"

Her slow, sexy smile had his body preening at the attention, and his towel tented in the front. She chuckled and tossed him the car keys. "Mmm…it looks like the view appreciates being appreciated."

He easily caught the keys one handed, and she snapped her fingers. "Damn. I was hoping that would make you drop the towel."

One side of his mouth quirked up, "I've got good hands. Didn't you read my press releases when I played for the Pintos?"

"I don't need to read your old publicity to know

you've got good hands. I've got personal knowledge of their many talents. It's why I wanted the towel to drop!"

"Later, baby, I promise you'll get a demonstration, but I'm gonna want to take my time peeling you out of those sexy, tight jeans. And time is something we don't have right now."

She sighed, and stepped out of his way at the door. "True. Although, your little speech made me care a lot less about getting there late, and people guessing what we've been doing."

He brushed past her and walked to his closet. He peeled the towel off and tossed it past her into the bathroom.

"Rawrr…"

He smiled at the noise she made, which sounded like a cross between a sex kitten and a lion, much like his Heather. "Are you checking out my nekkid ass?"

"You better believe it, Evans. But, you're right, I went to a lot of trouble to get in and out of my apartment all stealthy like a ninja, so no one would see me coming home in yesterday's clothes, or see your car at my place. I don't want to have done all that for nothing."

He pulled on a pair of black boxer briefs as she spoke, and took a pair of dark gray slacks off the hanger. "Speaking of my car, I'm hoping Lola survived the trip in one piece?"

He buttoned up a crisp white shirt as he asked her.

"Of course she did! I don't know why you're always talking smack about my driving. I'm good! Jeff and Cisco even sent me to one of those NASCAR camps for my birthday last year, and all the instructors said I was a natural."

He tucked the shirt into his slacks, and maneuvered the zipper up over a certain body part still hopeful it would be getting some more of Heather's attention before brunch. "That's why I asked. Being a natural stock car racer does not involve skills that translate well into a short drive across town."

"Your precious baby is fine, Mick. I parked her in the alley behind my place, so no one would see it out front on Sunday morning, and get the rumor mill going. No one else was parked there, so no one even breathed on her."

He chuckled as he took his wallet off the dresser and slid it into his back pocket.

"Are you finally ready, prima donna?"

"I am *not* a prima donna. I just care about my appearance and personal hygiene. Is that a crime, Ms. Braden?"

They continued to bicker playfully all the way to the car, where Mick opened the passenger door for Heather with a flourish.

She rolled her eyes as she brushed past him and settled in the car. "Message received. You'll be driving, since you're not comfortable with my so-called aggressive driving."

"So-called?" He laughed as he shut the door and skirted around the hood to get in the driver's seat.

Heather launched back into a comical defense of her driving, as Mick buckled up and started the car.

Mick just smiled and drove. He never had as much fun with anyone as he did with Heather, both in bed and out of it.

****

Bethanne and Magda cornered Heather at the first possible opportunity. She was in the kitchen when they pounced. Her back to the door as she poured a cup of coffee, she never heard them coming.

"Word on the street is Mick's car was parked outside your place this morning. Early enough to give the impression it was parked there all night. Scandalous!" Magda said.

Startled, Heather sloshed the coffee a little, before she replaced the coffee pot, and turned to face the inevitable inquisition. Well, inevitable in Rivers Bend. She should've known she couldn't keep a secret of this magnitude in a town where gossip was a lettered sport.

Bethanne peered into the bowl of fruit salad on the counter next to her, and snitched a huge red grape, which she popped into her mouth. Heather smacked her hand, and made a desperate grab for a subject change. "Don't grope the food before we put it out for brunch."

"I'm not groping the food, but thanks for the segue. Groping. Mick's car at your apartment at the ass-crack of dawn. Tell all."

Heather leaned back against the counter and held her mug with both hands as she took her much-needed first sip of coffee of the day. She'd been running around town like a nut all morning, with no caffeine, and this had the makings of a conversation requiring coffee, and lots of it.

"Who told you they saw Mick's car at my place, a Marine Recon sniper? Because it was parked in the alley, and I turned the outside lights off, so no one could've seen it without night vision goggles, and a long-range site, you big snoop sister!"

"Marine Recon has nothing on Deidre. She ran into

the Nosh Pit to grab some juice for your mom, and she saw it there. Come on, Heath, give us some deets."

Magda swatted Bethanne's arm, as she spoke to Heather. "We don't need details. We just want to know how things are going with you guys. Does this mean you're a couple now?"

Heather could feel her face heat up, and took another desperate sip. Nope. Just as she feared, there was not enough coffee in the world for this conversation.

****

Jason lifted his niece, Sam, and sat her on the white fence. Mick was so used to the climate in the Pacific Northwest; he'd forgotten how glorious this area of the country was on a spring day. He leaned on the fence, and looked out at the green grass, the brilliant blue sky, dotted with fluffy white clouds, and the beautiful horses grazing in the field.

Jason pointed to an exceptional looking chestnut horse and said, "One of his offspring is running in the Irish Derby next month."

Mick didn't know much about horse racing, but he knew enough to know that was huge in terms of the Braden's operation, and whistled low. "That's impressive. Congratulations."

"It's a big boost for the Braden Breeding Program Dad started. We're all really stoked."

Billy looked out at the big, powerful animals. "I've never been on a horse, but I sure would like to try it sometime."

"We could teach you," Sam piped up. "Uncle Jason has classes, or will do private lessons, and he's an amazing teacher."

"I'm guessing a private lesson would spare me public humiliation, but I suspect a class would be more in my price range," Billy said with a smile.

Jason waved his hand dismissively. "Don't worry about money. If you're serious about learning, I'd be happy to teach you how to care for the horses, and how to ride. If you like it, maybe you can help us out some time, we can always use an extra hand around here."

Billy's grin was almost as bright as the big yellow sun in the sky. "Thanks, man, I'd love to! Mick, do you want to learn too? Maybe Heather could teach you."

"Aunt Heather doesn't ride," Sam said as matter-of-factly as if she were saying the 'sky is blue today.'

Mick turned his head to look at the child. "She doesn't? How did she grow up on a horse farm, and not learn to ride?"

"She knows *how* to ride, she just doesn't do it," Sam said.

"Since our dad died," Jason explained. "Heather was a real Daddy's girl, and the two of them would ride, and groom the horses together. She'd chatter away at him the whole time. It was their thing to do together, and after he passed, Heather just stopped riding."

Mick felt like he'd just taken a hit to the breadbasket. Having never lost a parent, he didn't have any idea how much the loss of her dad had impacted Heather until just this moment. He knew she had some abandonment issues, but he realized he'd underestimated just how much they controlled her actions in the present.

Eleven years ago, when he stupidly dropped her without any explanation, he unintentionally fed her fears of being abandoned by a man she loved.

He exhaled deep from his abdomen, and leaned his forearms on the fence. He watched the Irish Derby runner's daddy pose in the field like he was having his portrait painted. He heard the conversation go on without him, but it was just a buzzing sound, like a hive of bees, while his mind was completely occupied with Heather, her old hurts, and how he could help heal them. Because he realized something else this morning, he loved Heather like nothing else on Earth, and he was determined to prove to her he wasn't going anywhere this time…at least not without her by his side.

Chapter 27

Mick managed to snag a seat next to Heather at the Braden's dining room table, and since their combined families made a large group, even with the younger members sitting at card tables, he was pleased to have to sit pressed tight against her. They were so close together he could feel the warmth of her body from shoulder to legs. He gave her thigh a nudge with his, and she turned to look at him he gave her a slow, sexy wink. She blushed, but favored him with a saucy grin in return.

His mom sat next to Heather's mom at the head of the table, but over the buzz of conversations, and the clatter of silverware on dishes, Mick couldn't hear what they were discussing. Whatever the topic was, the two ladies were smiling and really animated. It had been a long time since he'd seen his mom so happy and vibrant, and she looked ten years younger.

His mother raised her voice, so she could speak to his father across the table, "Phil, Joyce is going to Ireland next month to see the Irish Derby! Isn't that exciting?"

"Seems like a long way to go to see a horse race," his dad grumbled.

Joyce beamed at him, as if he had not just been surly and rude. "It is a haul, but one of our stallions sired a horse running in it, so I'm just thrilled to bits to be able to go! I'll know some horse folks when I get there, but I wish I had someone to travel with me."

His mother's eyes grew soft and dreamy. "I wish I could go with you."

As his father choked on his beer, Joyce clasped her hands together and said, "Carol, what a marvelous idea! You could come with me; we'd have so much fun!"

His mother grew pink and cast a sidelong glance at her husband's scowling face. "I couldn't possibly go. Could I?"

"No!" His father barked, which might have been a miscalculation on his part, based on his mom's reaction.

She straightened her spine, lifted her chin, and spoke with conviction, "I don't see why not. I don't have any little ones at home, Susan's wedding is over with, and Dave will be at WVU football training camp by then."

"What about Danny and me?" his father asked, and Mick almost felt sorry for the man. He looked so confused by the normally gentle woman's defiance.

His mom didn't seem to be having any such problem. She waved her hands dismissively. "You and Danny are grown men. You're both capable of taking care of yourself for a long weekend."

"I've always wanted to see Ireland," Joyce enthused. "Maybe we could take a couple of weeks and travel around the country."

"What about a passport, Ma?" Danny interjected. "You need one to go to a foreign country, and you don't have one."

His mother's face fell, and Mick felt like decking his brother for selfishly dashing his mother's hopes.

He must have tensed up enough for Heather to

notice, because she gave his knee a reassuring squeeze before saying, "Passports can be expedited. I can drive you down to the passport office in D.C., Carol. We'll have to wait in line, probably for ages, but you'll have your passport in time for the Irish Derby."

Hope brightened his mother's eyes. "Really, Heather? It might be possible? And you'd help me?"

"Of course it is, and of course I will." Heather smiled at his mom. "It will be so much fun for you two to go to Ireland. I just wish I could join you, but it's such a busy time at the Retreat."

"After we eat, I'll look online to see what Mrs. Evans needs to do, Grandma," Caitlin called over from the kids' table.

"Y'all are so kind and helpful." Carol beamed.

His father's fearsome scowl encompassed them all. "Just a regular bunch of Helpful Hannahs."

"Dad and I have to work tomorrow, Ma; we're going home right after we eat. When do you think you could go to Washington to do this passport business?" Danny set his jaw and asked, his support clearly with the old man, as usual.

"Y'all go ahead home today, and leave Mom here. She can stay in my cabin, and do what she needs to do in D.C., and then I can drive her home next weekend," Mick said, also fulfilling his family role and falling in squarely on his mom's side, and in opposition to his dad and Danny.

"But where will you stay?" his mom asked.

Mick glanced at Heather. "I'll find a place to crash, Mom; don't worry about me."

There was a general snickering around the table at his pronouncement, which caused Heather to turn red as a beet and smack him under the table.

"Carol…" His father's voice held a warning tone, thick with the promise of unpleasantness to come, and Mick ground his teeth, and half-rose from his chair, ready to defend his mother.

Carol glanced at him, and her smile, while small and tight, was determined, and he slowly lowered himself back on his seat.

"Phil, would you please help me with something in the kitchen?" his mother asked, as sweet as the tea at the Nosh Pit.

His father frowned at the transparent excuse to get him alone to talk, but rose from his chair and stomped to the kitchen.

His mother stood and smiled at everyone. "Y'all go right ahead with your meal. We'll be back in a jiffy."

Mick tensed as his mother followed the old man into Mrs. Braden's kitchen.

Heather rubbed his hand, where it was clenched into a fist on his lap. She whispered to him, "Don't worry, Mick, your mom has it under control."

Mrs. Braden smiled warmly at them all. "Eat up, everyone, before it gets cold."

The silence gave way to the clatter of silverware as everyone followed her command, for, gracious as it was, there was no doubt it *was* an order to continue with their meal, and to give his folks some privacy. Even Danny shoveled eggs into his sullen face, while he listened to Deidre chatter away about the weather.

He took a deep breath, and followed suit. It did seem like everything was under control, and there was no sense in letting this delicious food go to waste.

****

"Thanks for letting me use your cabin this week, Mick. Jeff needed all the available rooms at the Retreat, so I appreciate it. Joyce said I could stay with her, but I didn't want to impose, and I suspect you won't mind the chance to stay with your girl."

His mom hinting about his sex life, now that's not at all awkward. Mick's face flushed as he reached for the spare sheets on the closet shelf. "Jeez, Mom, can we *not* talk about Heather and me."

His mother efficiently stripped the sheets off the bed, as she spoke in a matter-of-fact manner, "I don't think we can, Mickey. I think there are things about Heather and you we need to discuss."

Mick set the clean sheets on the nightstand and gathered the old ones as his mother took them off the bed. Anything to avoid eye contact with his mother, as she seemed determined to discuss his sex life with Heather.

"What do you want to discuss, Mom?"

He heard the smile in his mother's voice, as she said, "Not what you seem to think I want to discuss. Believe me, I don't want to hear details of my kids' sex lives any more than y'all want to tell them to me."

He tossed the sheets in the wicker laundry basket housekeeping left in his cabin for used towels and sheets. "Okay. I can't even pretend that's not a relief."

She laughed as she shook out the fitted sheet. Mick stood on the opposite side of the bed, and caught one side of the sheet to help her.

"Thank you, honey; it's much easier to make a bed with two people. I appreciate the help. With Susan married and out of the house, I'm on my own with these kinds of jobs. Dave helps some, but he's been so busy with senior activities, and I don't want to be a burden to him during what should be one of the most fun times in a young person's life."

"No reason Dad and Danny can't help you."

His mom smiled gently. "Which brings me around to what I want to talk about. They can't help, because they're just not made that way. They wouldn't even think to help me with my chores. They make the money and I tend to the household jobs, is their way of thinking. They believe there are things men do, and things women do, and never the twain shall meet. You're different."

"Maybe not about gender roles, but about other things, I don't think I am, not deep down."

His mom snapped the top sheet, and he caught his end and tucked it in on his side of the bed.

"I was afraid you felt that way, and it might be what's always held you back from getting serious with a girl. I see how special Heather is to you, and I don't want this idea to come between you two." She reached across the bed and grasped his hand, and forced him to hold her gaze. "Listen to me, Mickey, you are *not* your father, and Heather isn't me."

Mick squeezed her hand, and then released it. He tossed the fluffy comforter on top of the bed. "I don't know, Mom, I think I'm just like the old man, and Heather and you share a lot of qualities. You're both loyal to your family, hard-working, kind-hearted…"

His mother smiled as she spread out the comforter. "Thank you, sweetie-pie, I appreciate the comparison, but I meant Heather is nothing like I was when I met your father. I was so young and inexperienced, and Heather has it all together and she's so self-confident."

She handed Mick a pillowcase and kept one for herself. As they both stuffed the down pillows into the white cases, she continued, "You do have some of your daddy's traits, that's true, but they're the good ones— the traits that made me fall in love with him way back when. You love your family, and are so strong. You're both good men..."

Mick snorted.

"You are. But your father is also a hard man. A judgmental man, with a very narrow view of the world, and that's where you're different."

Mick grabbed the pile of clean folded towels from the chair next to the dresser, and brought them into the bathroom. He thought about his mom's words as pulled his used towels off the rack, and put the clean ones in their place. Hope flared in his chest. Could his mom be right? Did he have his father's good points, but not the bad ones? Could he have a relationship with Heather and not end up browbeating her the same way his dad did with this mom?

"I'm going to get a cola, and sit on the porch," his mother called from the bedroom. "Do you want one too?"

"Sure, Mom, that sounds good. Thanks."

He heard the ice clinking into glasses in the kitchen as he balled up the dirty towels and put them in the laundry basket for housekeeping to deal with in the morning. There were some definite advantages to living on Retreat property, but he was looking forward to getting into his own place, even if it meant washing his own sheets and towels.

He took a deep breath. His mom knocked his whole world off its axis with one simple statement.

Could it really be that easy to have everything he wanted with Heather?

The screen door slammed, and the loud bang pulled him back to the moment. He walked out to the porch, where his mom sat in one of the Adirondack chairs with two icy glasses of cola on the table between the chairs. He sat in the other chair, picked up a glass, and took a refreshing sip.

He turned to look at his mom, who looked completely relaxed and at peace as she watched the river flow by the cabin.

"Can I ask you a personal question, Mom?"

She laughed in a happy way, and seemed much more like the mom he remembered from his childhood, than the quiet, timid woman she'd become over the years with his father. "You can ask, but I'm making no promises about answering."

His lips tilted up, "Fair enough." He paused and took a deep breath. "Why did you stay with Dad all these years?"

Her smile stayed in place, but she winced just a bit. "Boy, oh boy, you don't pull any punches do you?"

He inclined his head. "I did say it was personal."

His mom took a long drink of cola, and looked back to the river to gather her thoughts before she finally spoke. "I guess the short answer is because I love him."

Mick frowned and shook his head once. "Could you give me the long answer then, because I don't really understand the short one?"

She turned her head to smile at him, but looked back to the river as she talked, "I'd just finished high school, and we got married right after, we were so young. I was crazy about him. He was a couple of years older than me and was the strong, silent type. He seemed so romantic to me, like the hero in one of those gothic romances I love to read. We had you right away, and he was so excited to have a son."

Mick cast her a narrow-eyed, skeptical look.

"He was!" His mother defended her point of view. "He was so proud to have started our little family. He would stand next to your crib and look at you with such wonder in his eyes. Your daddy is a very old-fashioned man, and he believes raising the babies is women's work, so that's what I did. And the babies kept coming."

"So you stayed with him for us?"

His mom shrugged. "In part, yes. I never could've supported you kids. I didn't have any outside work experience. I'd been a wife and mother from the time I was eighteen." Her eyes grew soft. "And I do love your father, Mick. He's a good man, deep down."

"*Real* deep down." Mick snorted.

She frowned. "I don't like hearing you talk about your daddy that way. He's a tough man, but he worked hard in the mine all his life to support us, and he's never laid a hand on any of us in anger."

"He didn't have to; he did plenty of damage with his words."

His mother took a deep breath and nodded. "True. And being the oldest boy, I think he was hardest on you. And you always wanted such different things in life from him. You were such a smart boy, so good at sports, and you wanted to see so much more of the world than our little town, and the inside of the mine. It hurt him, and I think it scared him, so he lashed out at you even more. I'm sorry for that, and sorry I didn't do more to ease your way, but I have to be honest, I didn't want to lose you either."

His mother's sadness and raw honesty made his eyes burn. Past the lump in his throat, he said, "Oh, Ma, I'm sorry too. I didn't want to leave you, but I just couldn't spend my whole life in that damned mine."

She reached across the table and patted his hand. "I know, Mickey, there's no need for you to apologize for who you are and how you're made. God gave you brains and drive, and it would have been wrong for you to ignore those gifts. Although, I can't deny I'm thrilled to bits you've decided to move back so close to home. The whole family is."

Mick raised a brow. "The *whole* family?"

His mother's answer was firm. "Yes. Some of us just know how to show it better than others. You have to understand, Mickey, you're the first one in either of our families to go to college, so when you were born, we didn't even think of it as something our child would want to do. From the second he heard he had a son, your father dreamed of working with you, the way he'd worked with your grandpa. When you didn't want to do it, he was thrown for a loop. It hurt him. Deep."

"I guess I can see that," Mick conceded grudgingly. "But he's held onto his anger for years. Why has he never gotten over it? When I started in the NFL, people would say things like, 'your father must be so proud of you,' and I'd smile and shrug. They thought I was being modest, but I was so ashamed he wasn't proud of me; I never wanted anyone to know."

His mother's eyes glistened. "I can't make excuses for his behavior; I've done it for too many years. He held onto his hurt and anger for too long, and when Dave and Billy made noises about following your footsteps out of town, it stirred it all up again for him. Now Danny is a whole lot like your father. He never wanted to do anything but follow the family tradition and work in the mine alongside your dad. And seeing Phil so upset about your brothers and you, has made Danny a little hurt and jealous. He followed in your dad's footsteps, always did what was expected of him, and he doesn't understand why it wasn't enough. Why *he* wasn't enough for your father. That's why he's so resentful about you."

Mick stared straight ahead, and huffed out a deep breath. "I never thought about it like that. Man, no wonder Danny is always on my case."

"Jealousy is a terrible thing, and whether he meant to or not, your father fostered those feelings with Danny. My hope is someday, Danny and you will realize he's who he is, and you are who you are, and there can be some sort of peace between you boys."

"I'm seeing things in a new light after talking with you, Mom, so I'll try harder with Danny from now on, but there's a lot of years of anger and resentment between us. I can't make any promises things between us will change."

His mother held his hand on the table between them, and blinked back tears. "All you can do is try, son, and I appreciate it more than I can say. I tried my best with you kids, but I should've stood up to your father a long time ago."

Mick squeezed her hand. "You are now, with your trip to Ireland with Joyce."

She raised her head with pride. "I am, aren't I?"

"You are, and I'm proud of you."

She swiped a tear from her cheeks with her other hand. "That means a real lot to me, Mickey. I hope your daddy comes around and stops being so mad at me."

Mick wanted to assure his mother his father would get over it, and everything would be sunshine and rainbows, but in his experience the old man could hold onto a grudge like nobody's business. "What are you going to do if he doesn't, Mom? I don't like to think of you living with that kind of crap. You deserve more."

His mother jutted out her chin. "I do. It's taken me too long to realize it, but I do deserve more. So, if Phil can't get over me taking a once-in-a-lifetime trip with a new friend, then I guess I'll have to move on and out, because I do deserve more, and I'm not letting his bad moods and opinions rule my life anymore. And neither should you, Mickey. Let yourself be happy with Heather, because you deserve happiness too."

Chapter 28

Heather heaved a sigh of relief as the frantic rush of checkout ended, and the mini-bus taking the guests to the airport pulled away down the long, winding driveway through the woods. Jeff and she waved and smiled until it was out of sight, and they both let the grins fall from their faces.

Jeff rolled his shoulders to ease some tension and exchanged a knowing glance with her. "That was a tough group, very demanding. You really earned your salary and then some this week."

Her pulse picked up at his words: *And then some?* Had she misunderstood the situation? Were Jeff and Cisco going to offer both Mick *and* her a piece of the Retreat at Rivers Bend?

"Thanks, Jeff. I love what I do here."

They turned and walked into the lobby.

Jeff gestured to the door to their offices. "Want to come back to my office? I'd like to talk to you about something on that subject."

Heather's heart rate went from a mellow folk song rhythm to death-metal pace. It seemed like Jeff was going to offer her part-ownership; her dreams weren't about to be dashed!

She preceded him through the door he held open for her. "Sure. That sounds great."

Jeff frowned, and his brows formed a 'V.' "It

does?"

His surprise puzzled her. Didn't Jeff know how much a stake in the business she'd worked so hard to build would mean to her? "Well…yeah. Of course it does."

"Okaaay." Jeff drew out the word in a dubious tone, as he sat behind his desk, and she took a seat opposite him.

Jeff fiddled with a little pile of paperclips on his desk, as he stared at them with the intensity he usually reserved for Magda, his daughter, and football. Either they were the most fascinating paper clips to ever come off the assembly line, or her brother was avoiding eye contact with her. *Weird.*

"This is really hard for me," he said at last.

She smiled at him. "Don't be nervous. I think I know where you're going with this little talk, and it's what I've always wanted."

Jeff looked up, his eyes wide with surprise. "It is?"

She nodded. "Yes! Well…not *always*, but ever since we started the Retreat."

His eyebrows shot up so fast and far, she was afraid they were going to shoot off his face and through the ceiling. "It is? That long?"

"Sure," she said with a little less confidence, as she started to suspect she didn't know what was going on here.

"Okay then. Since this is clearly so important to you, I don't want you to feel obligated to stay on account of Cisco and me. We want you to follow your dreams, baby sister."

Her heart, which had been beating like a hummingbird, felt like it stopped entirely for a moment, before it plummeted to her toes. "What? Follow my dreams to where?"

Jeff shrugged, clearly perplexed by her question, and he held out his hands, palms up. "I don't know. Wherever they take you?"

She narrowed her eyes. "Hold on a minute here, Jefferson Lee Braden…"

He winced at her use of his full name. "You sounded just like Mom the time she caught Ty and I sneaking a beer in the barn when we were kids. Why am I in trouble? I don't *want* you to go…"

"You're *firing* me? That's what you wanted to talk to me about? You're freaking firing me?" Her voice sounded shrill, even to her own ears, but she couldn't seem to care. She was so furious she was about to let Jeff long for the manure-shoveling punishment he got for the beer drinking episode.

His eyes shifted, and he went back to bending the crap out of the poor paperclips. "Not *firing* you…exactly. I definitely wouldn't call it firing you."

"Oh no? Then, do tell, what would you call it?"

He hesitated, eyes squinted as he seemed to search for the right words. "I'm not sure what I'd call it…maybe releasing you?"

"Releasing me." She was pleased her voice was back to its normal, lower register, and less like a fishwife, but she was still ready to string her older brother up in the tallest tree she could find.

He responded only to her apparent calmness, seemingly unaware of the danger he was still in at her hands. Okay. She knew she wouldn't *really* kill her brother, but no jury in the land would convict her if she roughed him up just a little.

"Yes. Releasing you to your future."

"My future doing what, precisely?"

"Your future to pursue your dreams, Heather." He cocked his head. "I'm starting to feel like this conversation has lapped itself. What am I missing here?"

She snorted. "Magda has been good for you; it took you way less time than usual for you to realize you're being a complete and total dumbass."

He threw down the paperclips, and they skittered across the desk, as his nervousness as a boss in an uncomfortable conversation with an employee gave way to good old brotherly anger. "I'm a dumbass now? What the hell, Heather? I'm trying to do what's best for you—what *you* want—even though it's going to leave me and my business in complete chaos, and *I'm* a dumbass."

Her head actually snapped back on her neck at his words, as if she'd been smacked upside the head. Words failed her, and she felt like a just-caught fish, with the way her mouth kept opening and closing. She swallowed hard, and spoke, "I think I'm starting to figure out what's going on here. Cisco and you think I want to leave the Retreat now that I have my degree?"

Jeff flopped back in his big, leather desk chair, visibly relieved at the lessening of the tension in the air between them. "Exactly. Yes."

She scowled at him, and he tensed up again, and squirmed in his seat. "Then you're *both* dumbasses!"

He sat up straight, and grabbed another poor, defenseless paperclip. "Why? You worked so hard for your degree; we assumed you wanted to use it to move on to bigger and better things."

"Bigger and better things?" she parroted his words back at him. "*What* bigger and better things? Homelessness and the unemployment line? I did work hard in school, yes, but it's because I'm a hard-worker. Hey, you know what else I worked hard on for years? This stinking business! I've been in it every step of the way since it was just an idea we had in a bull session with Cisco when we all lived back in Portland."

He nodded. "You have been with us since the beginning. You oversaw the property renovation while we finished the football season in Portland. Hell, you even used to help us clean guest rooms before we could afford a chambermaid. You've been a clutch player on this team. We'd never have the success we do now if it hadn't been for all your help."

Tears, both angry ones and sad ones, burned her eyes and throat. Her voice was rough when she spoke, "I worked hard because the Retreat is my dream. I love what I do here; I helped you build this business from nothing, and now my reward is to get fired." She chuckled humorlessly. "Sorry, not fired, *released*, while you offer Mick, who is doing a great job, but has been here for like two minutes, a partnership?"

Now Jeff looked like one of the fish they'd catch when they went out on his little bass-fishing boat. "Hold on here, the Retreat is your dream? You don't want to leave us? Your goal wasn't some hotshot job in D.C. or Baltimore, but a piece of the Retreat?"

She touched her index finger to the tip of her nose. "Bing, bing, bing, bing, bing! Give the man a prize!"

He sank back into his chair again. "Well, hell, Cisco and I completely misinterpreted the situation."

"Ya think?"

He frowned at her. "Sarcasm isn't going to help us here, Ms. Snark."

"Sorry. I just can't believe you thought I wanted to leave! I love it here, and when you started talking to me about offering Mick a partnership, I couldn't believe my ears. I assumed you'd offer me some stake in the business once I had my degree. I know I don't have the capital to buy in, the way Mick does…"

Jeff interrupted her, "No, but you've got a fortune in sweat equity invested here. Money is not the issue. Cisco and I honestly thought we were sacrificing the good of the business for your happiness. We were trying to do what was best for you. Damn, girl, do you know how many times the two of us have cried into our beer, trying to figure out how in the hell we would keep this place going without you? We'd never be able to find anyone to fill your shoes"—his eyes twinkled— "and not just because your feet are so big."

She smiled, and fought against the tears of relief, which burned her eyes and threatened to spill down her cheeks. "Hey, I'm really tall! If I had little feet, I'd just topple over."

He laughed. "I need to discuss details with Cisco, but if you're serious about wanting to stay at the Retreat…"

"I am," she interrupted.

"Good. Thank you, Jesus!" he grinned. "Then we can offer both Mick and you a stake in the business. Cisco and I want to maintain a controlling interest, but we'll be able to offer you both lesser percentages. Mick's business acumen and sales contacts are helping propel us to the next stage, but you've been integral to getting us to where we are today. Your day-to-day management skills keep operations running smoothly. We'd be honored to have you as a partner too."

She blinked rapidly. "Dang! I don't want to cry."

Her big, burly brother laughed once. "You don't? That's funny, 'cause I'm about one second away from bawling here!"

****

As she hauled herself up the stairs, Heather could hear muted music wafting through her apartment door. She smiled, and felt a little bit of the pressure of the workweek, not to mention the emotional upheaval of her meeting with Jeff, melt away with each step.

Mick must be home from his business trip to Baltimore. She'd missed seeing him at work today, and was glad he was staying with her this week, so she could see him tonight. She pulled her apartment key from her pocket, and was just about to insert it in the lock, when the door flew open.

Mick filled the doorway, and in his dress slacks, with his button-down shirt open at the neck, and the cuffs rolled up over his forearms, Mick looked every bit as edible as the amazing aromas coming out of her tiny kitchen. Embarrassingly, her tummy rumbled at the tantalizing smells.

Mick grinned as he wiped his hands on a striped dishtowel, and then tossed it over his shoulder. "I thought I heard you coming up the stairs! I'm glad you're hungry. I made dinner for us."

He stepped aside to let her in, and shut the door behind her. She froze in amazement one step into her apartment. The little table, where she usually sat to eat her yogurt in the morning and her takeout at night, was set with her mismatched dishware, and the fat relaxation candle she used when she took a long soak in her tub with a good book. On the funky tiki bar she'd bought at a yard sale when she first moved in to her own place, sat a bottle of wine from a local winery and two glasses.

Mick stepped up behind her and wrapped his arms around her. She leaned back against his strength and warmth, and thought even though she'd been lucky enough to be raised with love, in a big, loud, happy family, she'd never felt as treasured as she did at this precise moment. She finally got what her mother meant, when she told her even though she'd lost her husband—Heather's father—too soon, she wouldn't have done anything differently, because the time spent together was worth it. She rubbed her head against Mick's cheek, and wondered how to let him know she was willing to face her fears of losing him, like she'd lost her father, and take the big leap into life with him.

Her stomach rumbled again, this time she thought it was in protest of the delay in eating the delicious-smelling food. "I can't believe you did all this for me."

"I knew the group we had in at the Retreat this week was a bunch of demanding jerks, so I figured you'd be exhausted and hungry tonight. Before I left for Baltimore this morning, I threw the fixings for pot roast into the crock pot."

"Wow. *Cooking* in the crock pot, what a concept! I just bought it because it looked kitschy and retro, I thought it went with my apartment."

She felt his body shake as he laughed. "Surprise! It cooks food too."

She moaned, and felt his arms tighten around her in response to the sound. "On top of all your other mad-skills, you can make pot roast too? You really are the perfect man, aren't you?"

He pressed a quick kiss to the top of her head, to add to his perfection for her, he was the only man she'd ever dated who was tall enough to do it, and released her to walk over to the tiki bar.

He poured them each a balloon glass of red wine, as he spoke, "I didn't want to eat out every night, so I learned how to cook. But I have to admit, since I usually just cook for myself, I only know how to make guy food like pot roast, and I started thinking while I was waiting for you to get home, you might not like pot roast."

She took a deep breath of the intoxicating fragrance of roasted meat and aromatic vegetables, and said in a deeply heartfelt manner, "I *love* pot roast! Thank you! And do I smell biscuits baking?"

He handed her a glass of wine and clinked his glass to hers. They both took a sip, and then he ducked his head sheepishly as he answered, "You do, but they're just from a can. I didn't have time to make them from scratch today."

She savored the taste of the hearty, peppery red wine on her tongue, and shook her head. "I can't believe you're apologizing for not having homemade biscuits for me. When I'm cooking, I consider the canned ones to be homemade. And truthfully, I *do* eat takeout most nights. If I'm doing the 'cooking.' " She made air quotes around the last word, "I'm microwaving a frozen dinner."

His phone chimed in his pocket. He pulled it out and tapped the screen to stop the sound, before calling over his shoulder as he rushed to the kitchen, "That timer means the biscuits are done. But I want you to have a chance to relax a bit before we eat. Why don't you sit down and enjoy your wine while I pull the biscuits out of the oven."

She sighed with happiness as she sank into her comfy sofa. "You don't have to ask me twice. It *has* been a long week. I feel like a queen, Mick, thank you again."

She heard the clatter of the cookie sheet from the kitchen, and his voice from the pass-through opening cut into the wall between the kitchen and living room. "I should be the one thanking you for taking my mom to Washington, and helping her jump through all the hoops she needed to, in order to get her passport expedited."

She slipped out of her shoes as he talked, stretched her legs out, and wriggled her tired toes. "No need to thank me, I'm good at organizing stuff, and we had a nice day together. My mom is so excited to have her as a traveling companion, I was happy to do it for both of them."

He came back in the room and sat next to her; his long legs stretched out next to hers. "Still, I know what a hassle that kind of thing can be, and I appreciate it. My mom hasn't always had a lot of help, and it means a lot to me you went out of your way to rearrange your schedule during a busy week to help her."

She bumped his leg with hers. "Anytime."

He snaked his left arm around her shoulders, and took a sip of his wine with his right. She nestled in against his broad shoulder. *Heaven.*

They sat like that for a few moments before he spoke again, and listened to the classical music playing from his iPod on the docking station in the kitchen. She usually listened to country music, but this was nice. The piece he'd chosen to play was peaceful and soothed her jangled nerves.

He cleared his throat, and when he spoke, his voice sounded just the littlest bit unsure, which was not like Mick, "While I was in Baltimore today, I arranged for an outing for tomorrow, and I'd really like for you to come."

She inhaled the fresh piney scent of his aftershave, as she nuzzled his neck, near where her head rested. "We don't have any guests at the Retreat tomorrow, so I think I can get away. What's up?"

"I met with a guy I know from back in the day, who's with the Orioles front office now. And by the way, I think we'll be doing a retreat for their staff in the off-season. But, anyway, he arranged for a bunch of us to go to tomorrow's game at Camden Yards. I thought it would be fun for Mom to go to the city. We could walk around the Inner Harbor, and then take in the game."

His voice still sounded nervous, which confused her since his offer was freaking awesome! She jolted up in her seat and bounced in place. "Are you kidding me? I *love* the O's! Count me in!"

He smiled, and she thought he looked relieved at her answer. She was a rabid Orioles fan. Did he really think she'd say no? Maybe it was because he usually dated more sophisticated girly-girls like Gloria. But a good-old girl like her couldn't think of a better way to spend an early summer day than at the ballpark

"Good," satisfaction was evident in his voice, and he repeated a little louder, and more firmly, "Good.

That's good."

She swatted his arm. "Was there any doubt in your mind? Beer, crab cakes, and my favorite team, how could I say no?"

"I thought you might like the Nationals."

She shook her head with vigor. "No. A lot of people in Virginia do now, but I was an O's fan before the Nats came to Washington, and I'm an O's fan still. I bleed orange, baby! Oh! And I just remembered they're playing the Yankees tomorrow! It should be a great game."

A slow smile spread across his face, and the glimmer in his brown eyes made her feel like she was missing a good joke. "I'm really hoping it will be a memorable one."

Chapter 29

As they took their seats at Camden Yard, in the first row right behind the home dugout, Heather couldn't contain her excitement. She squeezed Mick's hand. *"Oh my God!* These are the best seats I've ever had! How did you get them to give us these seats on one day's notice?"

Her brother Jeff slapped Mick on the back, as he edged by them, with Magda in tow, to take their seats. "You wouldn't believe it if he told you, Heath."

She exchanged a glance with Magda, who looked like she didn't have a clue what they were talking about either. Her friend shrugged and said, "I don't know, and I don't care, I'm just going to enjoy it! And if it means Mick gave up his first-born child, well then, so be it."

Bethanne came up behind them, decked out in as much Oriole orange as Heather was. "Me too!" She slapped Cisco on his butt. "This is my first baby-free outing in like forever! It was nice of Deidre to offer to watch him today. Now, fetch me a beer and a hot dog, Husband."

"Ooo!" Magda exclaimed. "Me too, Jeff, please. Except I want a crab cake, since we're in Baltimore. I think it's a law or something."

Cisco swept his arm like a courtier as he bowed at the waist. "Your wishes are our commands, my ladies."

Their two mothers took their seats, and Mick

asked, "How about you three? What can I get for y'all?"

The 'y'all' made Heather's heart hopeful that maybe Mick was happy living in a small town in Virginia now, and might be content to settle here with her.

Before any of them could answer, Ty took a seat next to Heather, and answered, "Beer and a pit beef sammie, man, thanks."

Mick reached over Heather and knocked Ty's O's cap off his head. "Not you. You're coming with me. I'll need your help carrying stuff back."

By the time everyone settled in a seat, it was time for the national anthem. It always seemed especially moving to sing it here in Baltimore, where it was written, and Heather joined in loudly and belted out the extended 'Oooooo' traditional at Baltimore sporting events.

When the Anthem was over, Bethanne leaned over to call out to Mick, "If you think that was bad, you're going to want to pretend you don't know Heather during the 7th inning stretch song."

Mick tugged gently on Heather's ponytail, where it stuck out of the back of her O's cap, with the cartoony-looking bird on the front. "I'm actually looking forward to it."

Heather bestowed a beaming smile on Mick, before turning to stick her tongue out at Bethanne. "See, Freshy Fresherton, some people appreciate my musical skills."

Ty snorted in the middle of a sip of beer. "Yeah. I'm sure that's the skill of yours he most appreciates."

"Children…be nice," her mother said in a warning

tone.

Heather bounced in her seat. "The game's about to start, people; unless you're cheering on the O's or booing the Yankees, I don't want to hear a peep out of you!"

****

As the game went on, Heather noticed Mick getting progressively more restless. He'd stopped cheering for the Orioles, and had a death grip on his beer. By the time the seventh inning stretch was starting, Heather was afraid he was going to pop a blood vessel, and she had no clue what was up with him.

She cheered loudly for the O's as they made their way back to the bench, and one of the players winked up at her. He said loudly enough for them to hear, "See, I told you football players can't control their women."

"I don't even pretend I can, and y'know the truth is, I don't want to. Just be glad they're cheering for y'all, because you don't want to hear their trash talk," Jeff drawled as the players laughed.

Heather poked Mick's arm, and pointed to the costumed mascot on top of the dugout. "Here comes the Bird! He usually pulls someone from this section up to dance, maybe he'll ask one of us!"

Mick just gulped, as if he were trying to swallow a baseball. She looked away as an announcement came on the P.A. system that the Bird would be joined this afternoon by a special guest, who wanted to send a message to one of the O's most loyal fans.

Heather turned back toward Mick, as the first chords of the familiar song started to play, and was shocked he wasn't in his seat.

As a familiar deep voice started singing, Bethanne

and Magda shrieked and pointed. Heather looked where they were pointing, and was stunned to see Mick next to the Bird on top of the home dugout.

And he was singing.

To her.

The Orioles seventh inning stretch song: "Thank God I'm a Country Boy."

He held her gaze steadily, as he sang, as if she were the only other person in the ballpark filled with thousands.

The Bird grabbed her hand and pulled her on top of the dugout. He danced a couple of do-si-do steps with her, before he twirled her and passed her off to Mick, who danced with her as he sang the lyrics about being grateful to have a simple, country life.

Left without a partner, the Bird grabbed Bethanne and pulled her up to finish the dance with him.

As Mick sang the last note, Heather squealed and threw her arms around his neck. "I can't believe you just did that!"

He smiled at her, and held her close. "Neither can I, but I figured go big or go home. I knew it would take a grand gesture for you to realize I'm not going anywhere. Rivers Bend is my home. *You* are my home."

Now wasn't the time to tell him, but she'd already realized it in a much quieter, more personal way, last night when he'd cooked her dinner. Instead, this was the time to show appreciation for his bravery for serenading her in front of a stadium full of people, with a song designed to celebrate his humble, southern roots. "That's the nicest thing anyone's ever said to me."

"I love you, Heather, so much."

In answer, and oblivious to the fact they were still

being shown on the big screen in the stadium, Heather planted a major kiss on her man. The catcalls of both the crowd, and the Orioles players, who stepped out of their dugout to watch the show, reminded her they were on display. She felt her cheeks flush, but threw back her head and laughed with pure joy. "I love you too, my crazy, country boy!"

He scooched down, so he could look straight into her eyes, and said with gravitas, "That's good, because I'm not going anywhere. You get that, right?"

"I think the whole city of Baltimore gets it, Mick!" Ty called from his seat.

"Oh, right." Mick hopped off the dugout, and put his hands on her waist to lift Heather down too.

"I get it, Mick," Heather replied with equal seriousness.

He nodded once in satisfaction. "Good, because you and me, we're a team from here on out. I mean, no one gets out of this life alive, but I'll be with you for the whole wild ride we're given, if you'll have me."

Heather seriously hated crying, but it was really hard not to at the moment. She struggled to speak around the lump in her throat, but finally gave up, and nodded mutely in response. She felt someone bump her from behind, and looked up to see the Bird, who'd shoved her toward Mick, and now mimed hugging himself.

She gave a watery laugh, and followed orders, by hugging Mick. "If the rest of our life is going to continue the way it's starting, it's going to be one wild ride."

"With you, I'd expect nothing less," Mick said with a grin, before dipping her and taking her lips in a passionate kiss, as their family, friends, the Orioles Bird, and a ballpark full of strangers cheered.

A word from the author...

My career has been a winding road. I worked in the business world for years, got my MLS and worked in a school library, and am now living my dream as an author. I love to read and write contemporary and fantasy romance.

I live in Maryland, with my husband, who is my real-life romance hero. We both enjoy traveling to visit our far-flung family and friends and spending time on the beach with an umbrella drink and a good book.

Thank you for purchasing
this publication of The Wild Rose Press, Inc.

If you enjoyed the story, we would appreciate your
letting others know by leaving a review.

For other wonderful stories,
please visit our on-line bookstore at
www.thewildrosepress.com.

For questions or more information
contact us at
info@thewildrosepress.com.

The Wild Rose Press, Inc.
www.thewildrosepress.com

Stay current with The Wild Rose Press, Inc.

Like us on Facebook

https://www.facebook.com/TheWildRosePress

And Follow us on Twitter
https://twitter.com/WildRosePress